Dee Williams was born and brought up in Rotherhithe in East London where her father was a stevedore in Surrey Docks. As a child Dee was evacuated during the war, although she kept returning to London because she was so homesick, and in 1940 she witnessed the night of the Blitz. Dee left school at fourteen, met her husband at sixteen and was married at twenty; she now has two daughters and two granddaughters. In 1974 she and her husband opened the first of several ladies' boutiques in Hampshire but eight years later they both moved to Crete and later to Spain, where Dee first started writing. She and her husband now live near Portsmouth. *Polly of Penn's Place* is Dee's second novel, and she is currently working on her third, also set in Rotherhithe.

D0533311

Also by Dee Williams

Carrie of Culver Road
Annie of Albert Mews
Hannah of Hope Street
Sally of Sefton Grove
Ellie of Elmleigh Square
Maggie's Market

Polly of
Penn's Place

Dee Williams

headline

Copyright © 1992 Dee Williams

The right of Dee Williams to be identified as the Author of
the Work has been asserted by her in accordance with the
Copyright, Designs and Patents Act 1988.

First published in 1992
by HEADLINE BOOK PUBLISHING PLC

9

All rights reserved. No part of this publication may be
reproduced, stored in a retrieval system, or transmitted,
in any form or by any means without the prior written
permission of the publisher, nor be otherwise circulated
in any form of binding or cover other than that in which
it is published and without a similar condition being
imposed on the subsequent purchaser.

All characters in this publication are fictitious
and any resemblance to real persons, living or dead,
is purely coincidental.

ISBN 0 7472 3845 6

Printed and bound in Great Britain by
Clays Ltd, St Ives plc

HEADLINE BOOK PUBLISHING PLC
A division of Hodder Headline PLC
338 Euston Road
London NW1 3BH

For my husband Les and my two
daughters, Julie and Carol

Chapter 1

Polly Perkins, elbows on the kitchen table, cupped her face in her hands and watched her mother hack at the loaf of bread.

Behind Mrs Perkins sat Polly's grandfather, in his old, straight-backed wooden armchair, reading his newspaper. His holey-slippered feet rested on the large ornate brass fender. At each end was a box: one held a few pieces of coal, the other junk. It was only the fender's sheer size that stopped Mrs Perkins from taking it to the pawnbroker's. The chair's faded floral cushions, tied to the back and seat were, like the old man's grey cardigan, dotted with tiny burn holes. Often a lighted piece of tobacco fell from the end of his hand-rolled cigarette, which he would bang out with much arm waving and hollering.

'Dad. You gonner sit up at this 'ere table?' her mother's harsh voice made the old man jump.

'What is it? What's the matter?' He must have been dozing behind his newspaper. It slipped to the floor, and lay in a crumpled heap at his feet.

Sid and Billy began to laugh.

'And you two can shut yer faces.' Mrs Perkins waved the bread-knife menacingly at her sons before turning on her father-in-law. 'And pick up that paper, it makes the place look untidy. It's a pity we don't 'ave a bit more respect and a few more manners in this 'ere 'ouse. And you can take yer elbows off the table, young lady.'

Polly quickly hid her hands under the table when the bread-

1

knife was pointed in her direction.

'If my mother' – Mrs Perkins raised her eyes to the ceiling – 'God rest her soul, could see what I've finished up with, she'd turn over in 'er grave.' She continued attacking the loaf as if it was to blame for her troubles.

'We gonner 'ave all that again, Doris. Dunno why yer always 'as ter bring yer mother into it, she's been dead fer Gawd knows 'ow long.' The old man stood up, smoothed down his sparse grey hair and limped to the table, scraping his chair on the lino as he tried to get in close. ''Sides, she was only too glad ter git rid of yer. Fought yer found yerself a nice cushy little number when yer latched on and married my Tom.'

Polly looked down at her hands nestling in her lap. She didn't like them talking about her dad; the memory of his death still hurt.

Grandad put his arm on the table and leaning forward added, 'And yer got yerself a 'ouse full of furniture inter the bargain – wot's left of it. You ain't done ser bad.'

'Humh.' Doris Perkins tossed her head and pushed back a loose strand of her short dark hair which was now sprinkled with grey. She tucked it into the tortoiseshell slide she wore just above her left ear. 'And I got you wiv it.'

Polly glanced at her beloved grandad and grinned. At eleven years old she wasn't always too sure what he was talking about.

She looked across at her brother Sid, stuffing great thick doorsteps of bread and jam into his mouth. He was only two and a half years older than her, but acted like boys twice his age. He called Polly names, and was always pushing and hitting her. When she fought back and told him she didn't like him, he laughed in her face to make her angry, and he enjoyed getting into scraps and fights at school. She knew he was their mother's favourite, but that was only because he brought home vegetables he said he found round the back of the barrows at the market – Polly had her doubts about the truth of that. Miss Harris at school said it was wrong to steal, it said so in the Bible.

Billy, the youngest of Doris Perkins' three children, was sitting next to Polly licking the jam off his fingers. He was nearly eight. A frown wrinkled Polly's brow. Her dad used to say he came with the Wembley Exhibition; that was in 1924 when she was only four. She remembered being carried around on her dad's broad shoulders that day. Her mum was happy then, always laughing and smiling. She'd hung on to Dad's arm with one hand, and held Siddy's hand with the other – but Billy wasn't there.

Polly loved Billy and secretly hoped he wouldn't grow up to be like their big brother, who she knew stole things. Once she saw him take some sweets from the corner shop, but when she told her mother about it she was told to stop tittle-tattling, and to mind her own business. Siddy threatened to punch her face in if she dared breathe a word of it to anyone.

Her mother pushed a slice of bread and jam towards her. ''Ere are.' She plonked one in front of the old man. 'When I think of all the sacrifices I made when I got married, it makes me sick.'

'Don't let's go through all that again, Doris. Yer knows I'd work if I could. What 'appened in the past is over, and yer can't bring Tom back. What's upset yer this time? They been giving yer a 'ard time at work?' Grandad winked at Polly.

Her mother cast her eyes up to a riding whip that was curled up and hung on the wall above the fireplace.

The old man followed her gaze and fidgeted in his chair. He began nervously tapping the table. He was agitated, and as he narrowed his blue eyes, said with a tremble, 'Don't start on that again. It's no good you looking up there. You ain't pawning it and that's that.'

'Oh yes, we could all starve ter death and yer'd still leave it stuck up there. Just a bloody dust harbourer that needs cleaning – that's all it is.'

'I don't ask you ter clean it,' he snapped.

'I should fink not.' Doris Perkins threw the bread-knife on to the table. 'But I still have you and the kids ter feed, and find the rent and coal money.' She wagged her long thin finger at

3

the old man. Slowly and deliberately the words came from her taut lips. 'I'll 'ave it one day, just mark my words.'

'It'll be after I'm carried out in me box and not before.'

She tossed her head and mumbled something that sounded like, 'That could be arranged.'

Polly looked from one to the other. They all knew the story about the whip that had pride of place on the wall above the mantelpiece. The handle was made of silver with leaves and garlands of flowers skilfully worked and woven on to it. When Grandad ceremoniously took it down to clean, she was allowed to hold it. To Polly it was like holding something sacred; she loved running her fingers tenderly over the handle, feeling the bumps and dips. The leather whip was fine, almost like string. Grandad knew the trick of making it crack very loud, but only when her mother was out. It spent most of its life curled up high on the wall.

Polly also knew why it hadn't been pawned along with all the other ornaments and knick-knacks they used to have around the house before her dad died. It was the only possession Grandad had of his father's, who for many years had been a cab-driver to a wealthy family, and it was given to him on the day ill-health forced him to retire. Grandad had told them many times about his parents, who on the following week had taken a day trip down the Thames on the pleasure-steamer 'Princess Alice'. They were going from London Bridge to Sheerness, and Grandad, who was six years old at the time, was spending the day with his Aunt Molly.

Polly would often clamber on his knee when her mother was out and ask him to tell her the story about his mum and dad. The old man had told her that, according to the newspapers, on their way home, when the ship came up the river and rounded Woolwich bend, another ship, the 'Bywell Castle', came from the opposite direction and sliced the paddle-steamer in two. Almost everybody on board was drowned, including his mother and father. He was lucky that Aunt Molly, a spinster lady, was willing to bring him up, otherwise he would have gone into a home.

4

Polly looked lovingly across at him as he pushed his chair away from the kitchen table and slumped in the armchair. Poor Grandad. He'd had so much unhappiness in his life. A great sadness welled up inside Polly. She could feel some of his hurt through her own grief when her father died. That was another blow to him – he was Grandad's only child. She never knew her grandmother, he didn't talk a lot about her – only that she died soon after the war in the great 'flu epidemic. Her picture stood on his chest of drawers. She had a lovely smile and kind eyes, and a very tiny waist. Polly knew he loved her dearly.

'Margaret, Margaret. Stop daydreaming and git on and clear the table.' Her mother's voice broke into her thoughts.

It was only her mother and the teachers at school who called her by her real name. When she asked her dad why he always called her Polly, he would gather her up in his strong arms, sit her on his lap and sing the song about 'Pretty little Polly Perkins of Paddington Green'.

'We don't live in Paddington,' she used to say. 'We live in Rovverhive.'

'I know, but you're my "Pretty little Polly Perkins".'

She remembered being cradled in his arms as he softly sang to her, gently rocking her back and forth as he stroked her blonde hair.

Her arm was being shaken. 'I'll 'elp yer Pol,' said Billy, scrambling off his chair.

'You take the bread out, then.' She followed him into the scullery carrying the plates which she plonked on the wooden draining-board.

'I'll wipe up for yer if yer like.' Billy looked up at her.

She filled the enamel bowl with cold water and, tossing in a handful of soda which she took from the stone jar standing on the window sill, swished it round and round. Polly was gangling and skinny, and a good head and shoulders taller than him. 'Naw, s'all right, you go out and play. I'll manage. 'Sides there ain't much on Thursdays.'

'Don't want to.'

'Why not? 'Ere, 'ave some of the kids been knocking yer about?'

'Naw, course not.'

'You sure?'

'Honest. Cross me 'eart and 'ope ter die.' He crossed himself. His two front teeth were missing and the gap made her laugh. 'What yer laughing at?' His face crinkled and his large blue eyes almost disappeared. Polly always thought he looked like the angels in the pictures they had in church – with his big round eyes set in his round, rosy-cheeked face, and a mop of tousled fair hair sprouting out in all directions. She could see him with wings, and flying around playing a harp.

Laughing at the thought of that she said, 'Yer looks funny wiv yer teef missing.'

A sadness came over him. 'I bet you looked funny when yer lorst yours.'

She gave him a playful shove. He laughed, and buried his head in the multi-coloured stripes of the threadbare towel hanging on a nail behind the door that led out into the back yard.

'Right, what's going on out 'ere?' Sid parked himself in the doorway. He leaned against the door frame and folded his arms. 'Mum said 'urry up and finish clearing the table.'

'Couldn't you 'ave brought sumfink out?' Polly pushed past him and collected the remaining plates, cups, and the sticky jar of plum jam with the knife still standing upright in it.

The following day on their way home from school, Polly and Billy were playing 'he'.

'You're it,' shouted Polly, touching Billy's arm as they raced round the corner into Penn's Place, where they both stopped dead in their tracks. There seemed to be hordes of kids charging about, and some men and women were unloading furniture off a hand-cart and all going into Number 13, next door to their house.

'That's been empty fer years,' said Polly as they got nearer. 'I don't ever remember anyone living in there. Grandad said

6

he's seen rats as big as cats running about in the back yard.'
Polly counted five kids: one of the girls looked about the same age as her.

''Allo,' said the girl as Billy pushed their gate open. She was plumpish and very untidy. The front of her pinny was grubby, and her long dark hair hung round her face, straggly and dishevelled. She brushed her hair away from her face and tucked a stray lock that had hung over her large brown eyes behind her ear.

''Allo,' said Polly. 'Yer gonner live 'ere then?'

She nodded. 'D'yer live in there?' She pointed to Number 15.

'What's yer name?' asked Polly.

'Shirley, what's yours?'

'I'm called Polly, and 'e's Billy.'

Billy climbed on to the black iron gate that was rusting through lack of paint. Polly began pushing him backwards and forwards. It squeaked loudly, its worn hinges calling out for oil. ''E's me little brother.' She gave him another push before going up to the front door and pulling the key through the letter box. Opening the door and disappearing inside the house, she giggled and raced along the passage ahead of Billy, shouting, 'Grandad, grandad. Quick, quick, come and look out the frontroom window.' She pushed open the kitchen door. 'There's new people moving in next door, and they've got loads o' kids.'

The old man roused himself from his chair and shuffled along the passage to the front room. 'I wondered what that racket was. All afternoon we've 'ad kids yelling and shouting all over the place.' He pulled the lace curtain to one side. 'Humh, that's not gonner please yer mother, 'aving that lot living next door. Billy, stop jumping on that sofa.'

Billy slid off the hard, shiny, brown leather sofa that stood in the middle of the room. There used to be a beautiful embroidered firescreen in front of the empty fireplace, but that too had been pawned, along with the long-legged wooden aspidistra stand, which had once held a dark-leafed plant, filling and overflowing a large green pot, and which had graced the front

7

of the window. This room now smelt damp and musty; it had never been used since Tom Perkins' funeral.

Doris Perkins would have sold the three-piece suite long ago if she'd had her way, but it belonged to the old man, and was the only furniture left in the room. Grandad knew it was only a matter of time before it went.

Excitedly Polly said, 'There's a girl living there like me, 'er name's Shirley.'

Grandad turned to look at her. 'Oh Polly, fer Gawd's sake wipe yer nose. Can't yer feel those candles running down, yer dirty little toe-rag?'

'I've lorst me bit a rag.'

'Well use the bottom of yer pinny then.'

She wiped her nose. 'I'd better lay the table 'fore Mum gits in.'

The old man shivered. 'This is a bloody bare cold old room. Come on, love, let's git in the kitchen, it's nice and warm in there.'

Doris Perkins came home from work an hour later and, even before removing her hat and coat, sank wearily on to the hard wooden upright chair opposite her father-in-law. 'Margaret, take this inter the scullery.' She handed her a shopping bag.

Polly returned to the kitchen and pushed the knives and forks into the middle of the table which was covered with a piece of faded oilcloth. The centre of the cloth's painted flowery pattern had been scrubbed away years ago, leaving a bright coloured border of red roses climbing up a brown trellis, hanging over the edge.

'Got yer a nice piece of 'addick fer yer tea, Dad.'

Polly smiled to herself, and thought, We always 'ave 'addick on Fridays, just as we always 'ave bread and jam on Thursdays when the money's run out.

She glanced at her mother and suddenly realized how painfully thin she was. She wasn't round like Miss Harris and the other teachers at school, whose bosoms stuck out and their

8

beads rested on them. Polly sheepishly cast her eyes down to the two small buds she knew were hidden under her liberty bodice. She was pleased at being able to put a cardigan over her jumper to hide them, even if it was like her mother's – well-darned at the elbows. She knew Sid would take the mickey as soon as he found out she was growing up at last.

Although it was cold, her mother still wore the same thin, washed-out cotton skirts in both summer and winter. She had cut down her thick ones for Polly who, she said, never seemed to stop shooting up.

Her mother stretched her legs out in front of the fire. Even under her thick, darned lisle stockings, the lumpy knotted veins, and mottling – brought on through sitting too near the fire – showed through. Her ankles were red and swollen with chilblains; she bent down to scratch them with equally red and swollen hands. 'Friday's the best day of the week. Tom always used ter say it's the only day's work yer gits paid for.'

Polly's brow furrowed, and again she looked across at her mother. She didn't often talk about her dad.

Grandad carefully folded his newspaper. 'You all right, Doris?'

'A bit tired, that's all. Must be me age.' She pointed to his newspaper. 'I'll git Sid ter git yer a new one.'

'Best wait till Sunday, they're the fickest. Then it takes me all week ter read it, and they're best fer putting over yer feet at night. Paper 'elps ter keep yer warm.'

Polly wondered what was wrong with her mother. Why was she so quiet? Polly was aware she worked hard, but she never said too much about her jobs. They knew she left the house very early in the morning, long before anyone was up. She worked over the other side of the water, cleaning a factory in the East End. Her mother always walked to work winter or summer as she couldn't afford the bus fare. In the afternoon she did for a lady in the pub round the corner. Polly sighed. Things were so different when her dad was alive.

Something banging against the wall startled them.

'What the bloody 'ell's that?' Doris Perkins sat up straight. 'What's that noise?'

The kitchen door flew open and Billy burst in. 'Yer seen that lot next door, Mum?'

'What?' Once more Doris Perkins' looks and voice were back to normal.

'Looks like a family's moved in there. Didn't yer see 'em when yer come in?' asked Grandad.

'No, it was all dark. Who'd wanner rent that damp place? Must stink ter 'igh 'eaven in there.'

'Dunno,' said Grandad. 'They look a right old bunch ter me.'

'How many in there?' She nodded her head towards the wall.

'Dunno. This street's gone ter the dogs these past few years. When me and Annie first moved 'ere it was all respectable like. Now look at it, there's all sorts of 'obbity 'oys down 'ere now.'

Mrs Perkins gave a hollow laugh but didn't make any comment as she took a penny from her purse. 'Billy, git the pudding basin and go round and git a pen'orth of liquor.'

Billy went into the scullery.

Mrs Perkins shouted after him. 'Don't fergit the plate.'

He returned carrying a china basin and an enamel plate. He ran through the kitchen with the basin on his head.

'Mind that basin, it's the only one I've got,' she called as he disappeared from the room. She turned to Polly. 'Margaret, where's Sid?'

'Dunno, I ain't seen 'im. 'E ain't come 'ome from school yet.'

'Well 'e's got ter go round the coal yard and git a bag of coal when 'e gits in.'

At that moment the front door slammed and Sid ambled into the kitchen. His socks were as usual, like Billy's, wrinkled round his ankles and halfway into his boots. Boots that were two sizes too big for him and had come from one of the market's many second-hand stalls. Trousers that once belonged to his

10

father had been cut off to just below his knees to give him room to grow into them – they were held up with a length of string tied round his waist. He pushed his brown hair – which was combed forward and cut straight across his forehead into a fringe – out of his eyes. Brown eyes that were narrow and, Polly always thought, sly-looking. He cuffed his nose with his coat sleeve. 'Seen that lot next door?'

'Not yet,' said his mother.

'Six kids she's got. Four boys and two girls.' He put his elbow to his waist and hitched up his trousers.

'You seem ter know all about 'em,' said Polly.

'Been in there, ain' I?' He nodded his head in a cocky manner towards the wall.

'What's she like – the mother?' asked Doris Perkins.

'Fat,' came back the answer. 'The old man's got a barra down the market. Fruit and veg.'

Doris Perkins picked up her other shopping bag and made her way into the scullery without voicing her opinion.

Billy returned from the pie-and-eel shop clutching the basin covered with the chipped enamel plate. He kicked the door shut behind him, and deposited the basin on the table.

'Nice bit of fish this Doris,' said Grandad, dipping his bread in the parsley sauce.

Friday's treat was the thick, delicious, creamy-white liquor, with green thick bits of parsley. As Polly dipped her bread in it she couldn't understand how they would argue and row nearly every Thursday, yet the next day, pay-day, they'd be as nice as pie to each other.

Sid began choking and spluttering. 'I've got a bone stuck,' he croaked.

His mother jumped up and began pounding him on his back. His eyes bulged as he gasped for breath.

'All right, all right. It's gone.' He shoved his mother's hand away.

''Ere, 'ave a drop of tea ter wash it down,' she said, returning to her chair and pushing a chipped cup with no handle towards him.

Polly and Billy started laughing.

'It ain't funny,' said Sid, swallowing hard and holding his throat.

That made them laugh even louder.

'You two, that's quite enough of it,' said their mother.

'I'll git you,' croaked Sid furiously and flicked a fish bone across the table.

'Oh, that 'urts.' Polly rubbed her face where the sharp point of the bone pricked her.

Sid laughed and screwed up his eyes; they almost disappeared into two small slits. 'I'll teach yer ter laugh at me,' he said spitefully. Balancing a bone on the prongs of his fork, he carefully took aim and flicked it at Polly.

She yelled in pain, quickly covering her face. 'Me eye. Me eye,' she spluttered, her voice muffled behind her hands.

Once again her mother rushed out of her chair. She pulled Polly's hands away from her face. 'Oh my Gawd,' she said softly.

Polly was screaming. 'Mum, Mum, I can't see . . .'

Chapter 2

On Monday afternoon Polly walked along the road clutching her mother's hand. She held her head on one side, as the left eye was covered with a large wad of cotton wool and heavily bandaged, obscuring her vision.

They turned into what the kids always called the posh end of Penn's Place. That was only because the first house along the row always looked clean and nicely painted, and it was the only one with a window-box in the front. They passed the long row of identically placed windows, all looking alike save for different curtains – like one long continuous building.

It was winter, and the far end of the road was shrouded in yellow smoke from the chimneys of the large red-brick factory that dominated the view at the bottom of the road. In summer, if the sun was bright enough, it would filter through the smoke and warm the houses, and the people who lived at that end of Penn's Place.

As they walked along, Polly looked at the front doorsteps. Some had been freshly whitened, while others were grey and neglected. The houses had black iron gates fronting their area: some still stood, neat and upright, some were hanging on only one hinge at drunken angles, while others had been ripped off and slung in any dark corner. Although she had lived here all her life, she was beginning now to look at things differently.

Kids were running about shouting and playing. A couple of boys were kicking and fighting over a newspaper that had been rolled into a ball: their noise bounced off the walls. Some of them had boots and coats, others didn't; most of the boys had holes in their trousers.

In 1932, London, like a great many other places in Britain, had high unemployment, and this was a poor neighbourhood. When the Means Test man came riding around on his bike, the kids yelled and chased after him. They knew he was calling on homes and making his decision on how much money people would finally get after they had pawned almost all of their home and belongings.

''Allo Polly,' shouted Shirley. She was turning a long piece of rope tied at the other end to a lamp-post and a young skinny girl, who had grown out of her coat, was skipping in the middle of it. 'Cor, yer looks like a wounded soldier. Does it 'urt?'

Not wanting to stop and talk, Polly nodded, and quickly disappeared into her own house.

''Allo love.' Grandad struggled out of his chair and held her close, the comforting smell of tobacco all about him. 'We ain't 'alf missed yer this weekend. Did they look after yer in that there 'ospital?'

She nodded as the silent tears ran from her deep blue eye and on to his chest.

'What did the doctor say?' He addressed his question to her mother.

'Shh.' She inclined her head towards Polly.

Freeing herself from Grandad, Polly ran out of the room and up the stairs to the bedroom she had shared with her mother since her father died. Throwing herself on the bed, she cried. The more she cried the more it hurt. She knew what her mother was telling him; she had overheard the doctor saying they couldn't save the sight of her left eye.

After the safety of the hospital she felt alone and vulnerable. Would her mum make a fuss of her now? If only her dad was here. But she knew Grandad and Billy would be kind, and what she wanted more than anything else at this moment was to be loved. Yet somehow she just couldn't face them right now.

Gradually the tears subsided. She turned over on to her back

14

and gazed up at the ceiling. Her mind was blank. How different everything looked with only one eye. She studied the grey flaking distemper curling at the edges, defying gravity. The brown rings, made from the rain-water that used to drip, drip, into enamel bowls with monotonous regularity before the landlord put new tiles on the roof, had left stains that had spread and interwoven, making pictures and pretty patterns.

'What will I look like when the bandages come off?' she whispered. A sob rose from deep within her. 'Oh Dad,' she said out loud. 'I'll never be your "Pretty Little Polly Perkins" ever again.' She turned over and buried her face in the pillow.

There was a gentle tapping sound at the door. 'What d'yer want?' she shouted.

The door opened slightly and Billy poked his head round. 'You all right, Pol?'

'Humm.' Sitting up she wiped her nose on her sleeve, trying to pull herself together.

'Mum said ter tell yer tea's ready.' Billy's eyes were fixed firmly on the floor and with his hands deep in his pockets he kicked his boots one against the other.

He was about to go when she asked, 'Is Sid downstairs?'

'Naw, 'e ain't come 'ome from school yet. I s'pect 'e's in next door. 'E's 'oping ter 'elp the old man wiv 'is barra down the market.' He lifted his cherub face. Polly wanted to hold him and cuddle him – but she knew he'd push her away thinking she'd gone daft or something. 'Anyfink else yer want, Pol?'

'No, I'll be down in a minute.'

Billy closed the door and Polly slid off the bed. She walked slowly towards the triple mirror on the dressing-table, and examined her reflection from all angles. It didn't shock her quite so much now; in hospital she had looked at herself in any mirror or surface that reflected her image. But would the sight of her face shock her when the bandages came off? Quickly she turned away and went downstairs.

In her usual seat at the table, Polly kept her head bent very low. Sid came in and sat down without a word. Nobody spoke during the meal, and when they finished she began clearing the table as normal.

'Leave that. I'll see ter that,' said her mother.

Polly was taken by surprise. 'But I always do it.' Then she glanced up and gasped. 'Where is it? Where's it gorn?'

They all followed her gaze to the empty space above the mantelpiece.

'Where's the whip gorn?' she asked again.

'I've pawned it,' said her mother.

'Oh Mum, yer didn't?' She looked at Grandad, horrified.

He tried to smile. 'It's all right, love, I said she could.'

'But why? Why?'

'We needed the money, that's why,' answered her mother curtly.

'But we've needed money before, and Grandad always said . . .'

'It was different then,' interrupted the old man.

'They 'ad ter pay fer yer 'ospital,' piped up Billy.

She sat down and gripped the edge of the table. 'Yer did that fer me?'

'Yes love. I wanted yer ter 'ave the best.'

Leaping up she rushed over and threw her arms round his neck. 'Oh Grandad, Grandad.'

'Steady on there gel,' he said, trying to control his voice.

Nobody noticed Sid quietly slip away.

For the rest of the week Polly never left the house other than to go to the cottage hospital to have the dressing changed and drops put in her eye. She had always been shy even with two noisy brothers, and since her dad died she had become more withdrawn than ever. The thought of going to school wearing the bandage terrified her: she knew the kids would laugh and take the mickey out of her when the bandages came off, so she pleaded with her mother to let her stay at home, at least till then.

Polly was quite happy to be with Grandad. Over the years he had taught her to draw, and she had become very good. The only time she came face to face with Sid was at meal times. Even then he would not look her full in the face, sensing the terrible hate that burned within Polly.

On Friday afternoon she was sitting at the table drawing when Sid walked in. Hate filled her mind. She pressed the pencil hard on the paper, and the lead broke with a sharp snap. She vowed to herself that one day she would get even with him.

Grandad looked up. 'You all right, Pol?'

'Yes. I pressed too 'ard and broke me pencil,' she said quietly.

'Give it 'ere, I'll go and sharpen it for yer.' The old man began to struggle out of the chair.

'I'll do it,' said Sid, quickly snatching the pencil from Polly's clenched fist, so avoiding her threatening look.

It was the first Monday in November, and a week after Polly had come out of hospital. Today they were going to take the bandages off. Polly was very nervous. All week she had been hiding behind them, now today all the world would see her sightless eye. Her mother's hand was shaking almost as much as her own when they walked into the doctor's room.

'Sit down Margaret. Nurse, draw the curtains.' Carefully the doctor unwound the bandages and, with a flourish, removed the great pad of cotton wool. He took his torch and peered into her eye. 'There young lady, I bet that feels better.' He pulled at her eyelid.

Polly blinked rapidly. 'I still can't see out of it.'

'No, my dear, and I'm afraid you never will.'

She knew that already, but thought she'd tell him just the same. 'What does it look like?' she whispered.

'Not too bad, a bit cloudy that's all. Here, see for yourself. Nurse, open the curtains and give Margaret a mirror.'

She blinked at the light and cautiously took the hand mirror the nurse offered. The dead eye was criss-crossed with tiny broken veins. The dull, hazy, blue-grey iris stared back at her.

17

The pupil had disappeared, and the eye seemed to dominate the mirror.

'The veins will heal in time, and it won't look so bad then,' said the doctor.

Knowing she would be looking at it for the rest of her life, she handed the mirror back without another word.

That night, sleep wouldn't come. Polly lay in the big bed next to her mother, listening to her steady breathing. Normally she would have been asleep long before this, but tonight her mind was racing and her thoughts jumbled. The familiar night sounds that filled the air seemed loud and intrusive. The shouts and scuffles from drunks as they left the pub; the cats fighting and calling for their mates, making the dogs bark; the noise from trains shunting and banging against the buffers, filtering down from the top of the high arches that ran along the bottom of the road. Now and again, in the far distance, the deep mournful tone of a ship's hooter joined in as a ship made its way along the River Thames.

She lay flat on her back with her matchstick legs stuck straight out. Her feet were cold, even though she was wearing Grandad's socks, and despite the extra weight of the coats her mother had thrown over the threadbare blankets. Her arms were rigid at her sides; the only movement she could make was to clench and unclench her hands which, because she was nervous, were sweaty. She wanted to wipe them, and desperately longed to bring her knees up, but knew all these movements would disturb her mother. Her thoughts drifted on.

Next week it's me birfday, she thought. I'll be twelve. I wish Dad was still alive, I had nice birfdays then, and nice presents. I don't get any now.

Her mind was filled with that awful day when the men from the docks came and told them a stack of wood had fallen from a high crane and on to her dad. He was still alive when her mum rushed to the hospital – when she came home they knew he was dead. At first her mother cried all the time; then she had to go out to work and was bad-tempered and miserable; then she

18

started shouting at everyone. Poor old Grandad: it wasn't his fault he couldn't work. He was in the war and his leg was injured, and he got gassed.

Tears ran from the corner of Polly's eyes and filled her ears. It surprised her that she could still cry out of her blind eye. Slowly and very carefully she brought her hand up to brush away her tears gently. She lightly fingered the lid of her blind eye. In the darkness it didn't seem any different from the other one.

Putting her hand over her good eye, she strained through the blackness, trying to see the yellow glow from the street's gas-lamp which always shone through the thin, faded curtains. There was nothing. Hastily she pulled her hand away. The sudden movement disturbed her mother.

She turned over, letting her arm fall across Polly, drawing her close. 'Tom,' the whisper came in her sleep.

Polly held her breath and squeezed her eyes tighter to stem the tears that were ready to flow. 'She misses 'im like I do,' she said to herself in wonderment. Happy at that, she relaxed and, nestling comfortably in her mother's arms, soon drifted into a sound, untroubled sleep.

''Ere are,' said Shirley. 'Billy said it was yer birfday terday, so me mum got yer this.'

Hastily Polly undid the brown paper parcel. 'It's Ludo,' she shouted. 'Cor, fanks.'

And for the first time the lady who worked in the office at the factory where her mother cleaned gave her a present. She was so proud of the royal-blue dress with its lacy Peter Pan collar that she preened and pirouetted all round the room. The lady in the pub where her mum worked gave her a box of chocolates.

'It's 'cause they feel sorry for yer,' said her mother.

Polly didn't know whether to be happy or sad at that.

On Saturday Shirley asked her and Billy in to tea. 'Wear yer new frock. Mum said cause it was yer birfday everybody should be nice ter yer.'

Polly couldn't believe it. There were little cakes and fishpaste sandwiches and a lovely red jelly. In pride of place in the middle of the table stood a bowl of fruit. Shirley's twin brothers, Thomas and Terry, were there: they were about the same age as Billy. Shirley's eldest brother Ron was helping his dad at the market. And Vera, her older sister, was out shopping. Baby James began to cry and Mrs Bell took him out of his pram.

'D'yer wanner 'old 'im, Polly?'

'Oh, please.' She cradled him in her arms and gently kissed his forehead. ''E's lovely, Mrs Bell. I'm gonner 'ave lots of babies when I grow up.'

'They're all right, I s'pose,' said Shirley. ''Cept when 'e cries in the night. 'Ere, at Christmas me dad's letting us 'ave a party. D'you two wanner come?' Without waiting for an answer she went on. 'Dad's gitting some new furniture for our front room on the never-never, and me mum's gonner light a fire in there.'

'We never 'ave a fire in our front room now. Me mum can't afford it,' said Polly.

Mrs Bell came waddling out of the scullery, proudly carrying a cake and singing, 'Happy birfday to you, happy birfday, dear Polly.'

Enthusiastically everybody joined in. 'Happy birfday to you.'

''Ere are, love. We've only got one candle, so 'urry up and blow it out,' said Mrs Bell.

'That fer me?' asked Polly in amazement.

'Yes! Yes!' they all shouted and nodded excitedly.

'Go on, Pol, blow it out,' said Shirley.

Polly looked at it in wonder. It wasn't a very large cake, and it didn't have white icing and pretty pink flowers on it like the ones in the shops, but it did have a lighted candle that flickered in the draught.

''Urry up and blow it out,' urged Billy.

Polly pursed her lips and blew hard.

'Yer should 'ave made a wish,' shouted Shirley.

'I did,' came the soft reply.

* * *

Christmas came and went. The whip was never returned to its rightful place above the mantelpiece, and it was never mentioned. But Polly knew where it was – in Harding's, the pawnbroker in Rotherhithe Street. Her mother had to pass the shop every day to get to work, Polly knew that, and she also knew Harding's was the shop Mrs Bell reckoned you got a better price from. She told Polly they had to keep things a year before they could sell them.

Ron Bell left school at Christmas and went to work with his father on the vegetable stall full-time. He always spoke to Polly whenever he saw her, giving her an apple at the market, or saying hello when she was playing with Shirley, who in turn would give her a friendly push, saying, 'I fink 'e's got a soft spot fer you. All I ever gits from 'im is a clip round the ear-'ole.'

Polly would blush. "E's only being nice cos of me eye,' she'd insist, 'that's a bit more than what our Sid does.' She tried to make it sound casual, but Ron did make her go all hot. After all, he was older than her, and with his dark hair slicked back he was very good-looking.

Whenever she grumbled about Sid, Shirley would stand up for him. 'Your Sid ain't ser bad,' she'd say after Polly's angry swipings at her brother. 'After all, yer eye was an accident. Me mum says yer shouldn't go frew life 'olding a grudge.'

In the spring when Sid was fourteen, he left school and went to work at the market. Mr Bell managed to get him a job on the egg stall. He bought himself some second-hand clothes and looked very grown-up in his long trousers, boxing anyone's ears who dared laugh at him. Sid and Ron, like Polly and Shirley, were always together.

One day after school, Polly and Billy rushed into the house. Polly threw herself on Grandad's lap, sobbing.

'Oh my Gawd, now what's 'appened? Whatever's the matter wiv yer?' Polly looked up at him, her face wet and dirty. Billy had a bloody nose.

'Oh Grandad,' her voice quivered. 'The kids at school 'ave

21

been calling me names again and Billy 'it this big kid, and 'e 'it 'im back.'

Her younger brother proudly cuffed his bloody nose.

'There, there love.' The old man affectionately patted her back as she buried her head in his chest. 'Now come on, dry yer eyes, tell me all what's 'appened.'

She sat up and wiped her nose on her piece of rag. 'The kids always call me Polly One-eye, and today, when I lorst the pin in me drawers, they started laughing and shouting and pushing me about, trying to pull me drawers down. They chased me and yelled, "Look at Polly Long-drawers." I couldn't run very fast cause they were 'anging down round me knees.' She sniffed and wiped her nose on her sleeve this time.

'I 'it one of 'em,' said Billy. Looking down at the floor he added, 'Then this big kid 'it me back and pushed me in the mud. I 'ope Mum don't clip me round the ear-'ole fer gitting mud all over me trousers – and look, me shirt's got blood on it.'

Grandad ruffled his hair. 'It's a good job yer ain't got yer front teeth yet, else 'e might 'ave knocked 'em out. Where was yer mate Shirley? She always sticks up fer yer, don't she? And if she bashed 'em they'd know all about it.'

'She 'ad ter stay in and write out lines again.'

'That girl's always in trouble. Wot she done this time?'

Polly half smiled. 'Talking in Assembly.' She sniffed. 'I don't like school, I'll be glad when I'm fourteen an' can leave.'

'Come on, let's see if we can git yer cleaned up a bit 'fore yer mother gits 'ome. She ain't all bad yer know.'

'I 'ate the kids at school, they're always making me cry.'

'Polly, fer Chrissake stop yer grizzling and go and wash yer face. Yer'll 'ave ter learn ter take a few more knocks and name-calling in this old world before yer much older, I'm afraid.'

Polly knew Grandad had told her mother about the incident, but it was never mentioned. To her delight, the following Friday her mother asked her if she would like to go to the factory with her on Saturday morning.

'Yer'll 'ave ter work a bit, and run a few errands, and yer

got ter git up early. No loafing about in bed.'

Polly was elated, and sharp at six the next morning she wrapped her scarf round her neck and plunged her hands deep into her coat pockets – she could go down a long way as the lining was torn. In the dark she skipped along the road beside her mother, becoming a little apprehensive when they crossed Tower Bridge.

'Come on, don't dawdle, we ain't got all day. 'Sides, it's bloody cold up 'ere.'

Polly stopped at the join in the road. 'What 'appens if all of a sudden it goes up?' Quickly she jumped over the crack, and running over to the iron railings looked down at the dark, murky, swirling River Thames below. 'I can't swim – we'd all be drowned like Grandad's mum and dad was.'

Her mother laughed. 'Come on, yer daft 'aporth. It don't suddenly go up, yer gits plenty of warning when a ship's coming through. A hooter sounds and a barrier comes down across the road, and you're not allowed on the bridge.'

'Oh,' said Polly looking behind her, still very unsure about it as they crossed into Mansell Street.

It was silent, dark and eerie when they entered the large building. Their footsteps echoed on the concrete stairs as they made their way behind the night-watchman, up to the workroom. When he switched on the lights, Polly stared in wonder at the rows and rows of sewing machines. Each one had a basket of unfinished clothes standing beside it.

Mrs Perkins went to a cupboard and took out a broom and a galvanized bucket. She put on her sacking apron, filled the bucket with water and began sprinkling it over the floor to settle the dust. 'Margaret,' she called over her shoulder as she began sweeping the wooden floor between the machines. 'Make yourself useful, put all these pieces of cloth inter that bin over there.'

Polly loved bustling around, picking up the pieces of material that were strewn over the floor. 'Look at this bit, Mum.' She held up a small scrap of cloth. 'It's the same as me frock the lady gave me. D'yer fink she might let me keep it?'

'Dunno, you'd better ask Miss Bloom when she comes in.'

It was just before eight o'clock when a lot of women arrived. They walked up to a large-faced clock that stood against the wall and, one by one, took a card from a rack at the side. They put it in an opening at the bottom of the clock, pulled a lever that rang a bell, took the card out and put it in a rack the other side. Polly stood open-mouthed watching them, completely fascinated. Some gave her a nod before they sat at their machines. They were all talking at once, then someone blew a whistle and all the machines started. Polly quickly put her hands over her ears: the noise was deafening. A tapping on her shoulder made her jump.

'Hello, young lady.'

Spinning round, she could barely hear the lady who beckoned her to follow her outside into the corridor. To Polly she was the most beautiful person she had ever seen. Her dark-brown eyes twinkled, her shiny brown hair was neatly bobbed to just above her ears, and the beads on her ears glinted like diamonds.

'You must be Margaret?'

Polly nodded and thought that this must be Miss Bloom. Guiltily, she screwed up the piece of cloth she had in her hand and hurriedly put it behind her back in an attempt to hide it.

'I've heard all about you from your mother. She's been very worried. I was sorry to hear about your eye, do you mind if I have a look?'

Polly shook her head. Suddenly she felt scruffy; she was aware of the large darns at the elbows of her cardigan, and she kept her arms behind her back. The welt of her jumper showed peg marks where it had been hanging on the line, and she knew the hem of her skirt was hanging down.

The lady bent down and a lovely smell wafted all round her: it was nicer than Shirley's sister Vera's scent. 'It doesn't look too bad.' She straightened up. 'By the way, did you like your dress?'

Polly nodded vigorously.

'Lost your tongue as well?' she laughed. 'Sorry, I didn't mean to be unkind.'

'That's all right, Miss.' She looked down at the floor. 'Me frock was smashing, fanks.' Shuffling her feet nervously, she brought the piece of material from behind her back. 'Can I keep this bit of stuff?'

'I should think so. May I ask what you're going to do with it?'

'Make a frock fer me doll.'

'Have you got a nice doll, then?'

'Well, she's a bit old. Me dad bought 'er a long while ago. 'Er frock's a bit scruffy.'

A telephone's shrill bell interrupted them.

'Excuse me a moment.' Miss Bloom disappeared into a small room and closed the door behind her.

Polly stood staring at the door that had the word 'Office' painted in big bold black letters on the glass part at the top. The roar of the machines seemed to melt into the distance as Polly took in her surroundings.

She was full of it when she got home, telling Grandad and Billy all about the factory, the rows of machines, and the women who worked on them. After dinner she couldn't wait to run in to tell Shirley.

'I fought Jews ain't suppose ter work on a Saturday. It's their Sabbath,' said Vera, not bothering to look up from her magazine.

'Mum says Miss Bloom only pops in ter make sure everyfink's all right. She didn't stay very long.'

'I'd like ter come wiv yer,' said Shirley.

'Well yer can't.'

'D'yer git paid?'

'Naw, course not, it's just sumfink ter keep me occupied, so me mum says. Why don't yer go and 'elp yer dad an' Ron on a Saturday? They'd pay yer.'

'No fanks, I don't wanner work on the market. 'Ere, your

Sid don't 'alf look posh in 'is trilby.'

'I fink 'e looks daft.'

'Well I don't.'

'That's cos yer loves 'im,' she giggled.

'No I don't, Polly Perkins, so there.'

'Come on you two, out the way, I'll 'ave yer dad and Ron 'ome soon, and they'll be dying fer a decent cuppa.'

Polly left Shirley and, on the way out, bumped into Ron.

''Allo Pol, all right then?'

She blushed and, nodding, ran indoors.

From then on, Polly went to the factory every Saturday morning. The women who worked on the machines really took to her, sending her out for errands, and sometimes when there was a 'apenny or farthing change, letting her keep it. Others gave her biscuits and pieces of cake. She was very happy and all week wished for Saturday to hurry up and come. With the scraps of cloth and trimmings Miss Bloom let her have she taught herself, with the help of some of the machinists, to make dolls' clothes.

'Yer know Polly, yer got a real flair fer that sort a fing,' said Mrs Bell, admiring a dress she'd made for Shirley's doll.

'I'm gonner work at the factory making frocks when I leave school.'

''Ere, d'yer fink yer could git me a job working there?' asked Shirley.

'Dunno, I'll 'ave ter ask Miss Bloom'

''Ere, what yer gonner buy wiv all the money yer gits?' and as usual Shirley went on without waiting for an answer. 'I knows what I'm gonner git. First it'll be a fox fur.' She pulled an imaginary fur over her shoulders and strutted round the room.

Her mother and Polly laughed.

'Then it'll be a posh ring.' She held out her hand and wiggled her fingers. 'Oh, and some smashing scent like wot our Vera's got.'

'You'd better git the job first, young lady,' said Mrs Bell.

'What's Vera's scent called?' asked Polly, knowing it wasn't as nice as Miss Bloom's.

'California Poppy. What you gonner git, Pol?'

'The first fing I'm gonner git is Grandad's whip back . . .'

Chapter 3

During the school's summer holiday, Polly was thrilled at being able to go with her mother to the factory on Tuesday and Thursday mornings as well as Saturday. With the odd scraps of material and trimmings Fred the cutter gave her, and with help from the women on the factory floor, she put bows and many extras on her clothes. Polly always made sure her hems were up, and tried to look as neat and tidy as she could, determined not to look scruffy again in front of Miss Bloom.

One morning she was called into the office. 'This is the young lady I was telling you about, Father.' Miss Bloom was talking to a fat, balding old man sitting at her desk.

Polly stood in the doorway, afraid to go in.

'Oh yes,' he said, not bothering to look up from the papers he was going through which were strewn all over the desk.

Polly's knees began to shake, and her mind raced. Oh my Gawd, she thought, 'e's gonner tell me orf fer pinching 'is stuff. But then Fred had said it was all right. She wondered why on earth she was being drawn to the man's attention.

'Sarah, make sure this order goes out on time. He's a valued customer and we don't want to lose him.' The man, well-spoken like his daughter, continued writing as he spoke.

Sarah Bloom picked up the order sheet he'd pushed to one side. 'Margaret, would you go over to Charlie's and get my father a tin of Zubes. He's got a tickly cough.'

'Yes, Miss.' She turned to hurry out.

'Just a minute,' she called after her. 'You need some money.'

She took a purse from her shiny black handbag and handed Polly a thru'penny piece. 'That should be more than enough. You can keep the change.'

That was the first of many errands she ran for Sarah Bloom. Although she often saw Mr Bloom coming and going, and he always appeared to be in a hurry, he nevertheless gave her a polite nod whenever they met. It seemed that she hadn't done anything to upset him after all.

All too soon the summer was over, and reluctantly Polly had to go to school, only going to the factory on Saturday mornings once again.

One Saturday lunch-time, after they finished at Bloom's, Polly and her mother collected their usual pie and mash from the eel shop. All the way home Polly felt restless and fidgety. She picked at her dinner for a while, then pushed her plate to one side and played with her fork. She got up from the table and sat in Grandad's armchair.

'What's up wiv yer? Fer Christ's sake sit up and eat yer dinner,' said her mother.

'I don't want it.'

'I'll eat it, Pol,' said Billy, quickly pulling her plate towards him.

'What's wrong? You was all right this morning.'

'I don't know, p'raps I've got Grandad's cold coming.' She looked miserable.

'Yer'd better 'ave a good dose of castor oil now, and a dose of syrup of figs 'fore yer goes ter bed.'

'I'm all right really. It's just that I don't feel like going to the market wiv yer. Can I stay 'ome?'

Her mother eyed her suspiciously. 'Well, all right. Anyfink 'appened?'

'What d'yer mean?' asked Polly.

'Yer'd know soon enough.' She took the dirty plates into the scullery. 'Billy,' she shouted. 'Git yer coat on, you can come wiv me.'

'Oh Mum.'

'Don't "oh Mum" me,' she said, walking back into the kitchen. 'Someone's got ter 'elp me carry the shopping.' She put on her coat and adjusted her hat in front of the mirror that hung over the mantelpiece. 'Margaret, if yer staying 'ere, you can do the washing up.' She picked up her shopping bag and added. 'Don't go worrying Grandad, 'e's none too well.'

As her mother left Polly thought, I hope Ron puts a couple of extra apples in Mum's bag like 'e does mine every Saturday afternoon. Now Sid was working, things were getting a little easier. They had eggs more often, and now and again they even had a scraping of margarine on their bread. A small bowl of fruit had stood on the dresser on Saturdays since the Bells had moved in next door, but it had to be eaten quickly as it soon went mouldy.

Polly sat quietly for a few minutes after hearing the front door shut then, unable to contain herself any longer, raced up the stairs, careful to avoid the sixth stair, the one that creaked. She didn't want to disturb Grandad. 'I wonder why he went to bed,' she mumbled to herself, ''e always sleeps in the armchair. I 'ope 'e ain't gonner die. 'E can't, not yet.' She stood on the landing outside his room, listening to his snoring. It made her laugh, and she put her hand over her mouth to suppress the sound that was ready to explode.

Polly began mimicking him; when he was told to shut up he always said, 'I never snore.' She suddenly thought how old her grandad was looking. She knew he *was* old – he had white hair, but he didn't laugh so much anymore.

Turning the handle of her mother's bedroom door, she held her breath as the old man's sudden bout of coughing startled her. When it went quiet again she slowly pushed the door open, a little at a time. Praying it wouldn't squeak, she squeezed through the narrow gap and took hold of the handle the other side. Once in the room, she put the flat of her hand against the door and, still holding the handle, turned it in order to close it quietly. Safely inside the room she ran her sweaty hands down

31

her frock, anxious not to let her grandad know she was upstairs. Out loud, she said, 'Don't worry, one day I'll make you laugh again.'

Then she went over to the dressing-table and sheepishly pulled open one of the small top drawers. It was the drawer her mother kept her 'personal things' in, as she called them, and they weren't allowed to go there.

Polly didn't read any of the letters or neatly folded papers. She knew what she was looking for. Quickly she put them to one side and, picking up a delicate lace handkerchief, put it to her nose and sniffed. It smelt of the lavender that came from a pretty pink satchet which felt all lovely and scrunchy when she squeezed it.

She lifted out a small square red box. Inside, on the red silk lining of the lid, the name 'Saunders' was written in gold. There was a split in the red lining where a ring once sat – but it was empty. Another long narrow brown box had the same jeweller's name written on its white satin lining – that too was empty.

She took out an old tin tea-caddy and tipped its contents on to the dressing-table. Glancing up at the door she hastily began rummaging through the bits of paper, tickets, and other odds and ends. Polly had seen Harding's pawn tickets many times. Sometimes, when the weather was bad and Mr Bell couldn't take his barrow out, Shirley had to take his best suit into Harding's. Not that Mr Bell ever knew. Mrs Bell would wait till he was at the pub, then she'd undo the screws on the bottom of the chest where he kept it under lock and key, remove the suit and screw the bottom back on again. So far he'd never found out, as somehow she'd always managed to redeem it and put it back before his Saturday night out. Shirley had once said, 'Fank Gawd 'e don't git called out ter go to a funeral or sumfink in the week. If 'e ever caught 'er 'e'd kill 'er.'

Shirley's words ran through Polly's head as she sorted through Harding's tickets. There were some for the vases and ornaments they used to have round the house, and one for the silk firescreen. There was one for a three-diamond ring, another for a watch, and one for a rolled-gold dropped pearl necklace. Then she found what she was looking for. A smile came to her face as she read the ticket for a silver-handled whip. She carefully replaced everything except that pawn ticket. Looking at it she wondered how long it would take her to save seven and sixpence, when all she had at this very moment was fivepence ha'penny. Tucking it in the back of the handbag Miss Bloom had given her, she felt sad, knowing it was almost a hopeless task she had set herself.

Polly and Shirley were growing fast, experimenting with hairstyles, trying to look like the women in Vera's fashion magazines, and, when Vera was at work, using her make-up.

One day, on their way home from school, they stood drooling over the posters outside the cinema. 'Be glad when we leave school and git a bit a money,' said Shirley, 'Look at the lovely frock Ginger Rogers has got on. Ron said 'e'll give me some money if I clean 'is boots fer a week, then I can go and see 'er and Fred Astaire. Why don't yer ask Sid fer the money, then we can go tergevver?'

''E won't give me the drippings from 'is nose.'

'Well, try ter be a bit nice to 'im.'

'Humm, I'd rarver be friends wiv a snake, and I ain't cleaning '*is* boots.'

'D'yer know, Pol, sometimes yer makes me feel really sick the way yer keeps on about Sid. 'Ere, why don't yer ask yer mum fer some money?'

'Could you see my mum giving me money fer the pictures? She makes enough fuss over 'aving ter buy me a new pair of shoes. I wouldn't git any if she didn't wanner be shown up when I goes ter the factory.'

'Wot about the girls at the factory, don't they give yer sumfink for running their errands?'

She looked away from Shirley. 'Sometimes they let me keep the change, and I gits the odd 'apenny, but not very often.'

Shirley slid her arm through Polly's. 'Come on. Let's git 'ome. Looks like I'll 'ave ter go wiv Vera.'

By the beginning of December 1934, Polly and Shirley were fourteen, and at last the time came for them to leave school.

Shirley grinned as she glanced anxiously over her shoulder at the women busy working on the sewing machines, then clattered down the concrete stairs after Polly. Outside in the crisp, cold air she shuddered. 'I'm a bit worried.' Her breath formed clouds of vapour in front of her mouth as she spoke.

'Wot about?' asked Polly.

'The forelady. She looks a bit of a cow, everybody seems ter be frightened of 'er.'

'Big Vi? She's all right if yer gits on wiv yer work.' Polly tried to sound knowledgeable.

'D'yer see the size of 'er arms? Wouldn't like ter git a swipe from 'er.'

'Well, behave yourself and yer won't.'

'It's a bit noisy in there.'

'You'll git used to it, you see.' Polly felt very grown-up and very confident advising Shirley like this.

'Ta ever so much fer gitting me a job,' said Shirley, slipping her arm through Polly's.

'Miss Bloom's nice, ain't she? I said she'd take yer on. It'll be a time 'fore yer allowed on a machine. She said we'll 'ave ter clear up and make tea, and fings like that fer a while.'

'I know. I 'eard,' said Shirley brusquely.

'I was only saying.' Polly pulled her thin coat tighter at her throat. 'Come on, let's git 'ome. This time next week we'll be working girls.'

'And on Friday we'll git a wage packet.'

'We 'ave ter work a week in 'and, remember,' said Polly.

'Oh yer, I forgot.'

Giggling, they ran up the road.

'Answer the phone, will you?' said Miss Bloom one afternoon

when Polly walked into the office with her tea.

'What me, Miss? I don't speak proper.'

She looked up from her papers. 'Just say, "Hello, Bloom's Fashions, can I help you?" That's all.'

Hesitantly Polly lifted the persistently ringing telephone off the cradle and tentatively holding it near her ear, whispered, ''Allo, Bloom's Fashions, can I 'elp yer?' Her face filled with horror when someone gabbled something, and she quickly held it out to Miss Bloom.

Polly was about to leave the office, when Miss Bloom beckoned her to stay. 'That was Margaret,' she said into the mouthpiece. 'A bit younger than you . . . Yes she is pretty.'

Polly blushed and looked at her feet.

'All right, we'll see you Friday evening. Bye.' She replaced the receiver. 'That was David, my young brother. He's at college and he's coming home for the weekend. Margaret, how would you like to work in the office full-time?'

Polly's face lit up. 'Could I, Miss?'

'You won't get as much money as the girls working on the machines.'

'I don't care.'

'You had better have a word with your mother first. I don't want to upset her.'

'What would I 'ave ter do, Miss – in the office that is?'

'Well you'd have to do some filing, answer the phone . . .'

At that Polly's face fell.

'Don't worry. I think we can sort out your dropped aitches. It'll be like another Eliza Doolittle.'

'Who's she, Miss?'

'A George Bernard Shaw character.'

'Oh,' said Polly, still none the wiser.

In May 1935, the street party that was held for King George and Queen Mary's Silver Jubilee was the most wonderful thing that had ever happened in Penn's Place. To Polly and Shirley it had been transformed into wonderland. There were flags everywhere, and the tables from the pub at the end of the road were full of cakes, jellies, and sandwiches. Even the wind was in the right direction, sending the factory's smoke the other way. Polly and Shirley sat next to each other and ate as much as they could. Billy was sick and Mrs Perkins got very annoyed with him for showing her up.

'Anyone would fink yer never gits anyfink like that in our 'ouse the way yer stuffed yerself.'

'Well we don't,' he retorted, quickly ducking when she went to clip him round the ear – he'd had years of practice.

'And as fer you, young lady, you didn't behave much better. I saw yer, four cakes yer 'ad on yer plate, greedy little cow. Now git on up ter bed.'

Grandad gave her a wink. His face was rosy, and his eyes sparkled. He had enjoyed himself sitting outside the pub supping the free beer.

'But Mum, Sid ain't 'ome yet.'

'Don't "but Mum" me, you've got ter git up fer work in the morning, remember? 'Sides, Sid's older than you, and brings in more money. Now orf ter bed.'

Polly smiled. Her mother was always going on about her not bringing in as much as Sid, but she didn't care now she was working in the office with Miss Bloom. She raced up the stairs, now she certainly had something to look forward to every day. Her job meant everything to her.

Throughout the year, Polly was happy, despite still being very self-conscious about her eye.

'Like yer new frock, Polly,' said Grandad one Sunday afternoon as she was getting ready to go out.

She smoothed the blue cotton over her hips. 'Made it meself. Miss Bloom lets me use the sewing machine in me lunch break. Shirley helped, she's a good machinist.'

'She's gitting ter be a fast little hussy if yer asks me. I've seen 'er in the yard whistling and shouting at all the blokes, and 'aving a smoke round the back. 'Ere, I 'ope you ain't wasting yer money on fags, me gel,' said Mrs Perkins.

Billy laughed. 'Where yer off ter, Pol?'

'Up the park.'

'Wiv Shirl?'

'Course.'

'You watch yerself, young lady. Don't wantcher bringing no trouble 'ome 'ere.'

'Oh, Mum.'

'Don't "oh Mum" me. I've seen wot some of these girls gits up ter.'

'Why is it always the girls? I don't 'ear yer go off at Sid fer staying out late.'

'Cos it's different wiv boys, it's the girls that always brings the trouble 'ome, that's why.'

Polly picked up her handbag. 'Anyway, I don't fink yer got nothing ter worry about, do you? Don't s'pose anybody fancies me – me only 'aving one good eye.' She swept out of the kitchen.

At work life was good for both her and Shirley. Shirley was on the factory floor, working on a machine, and had become very efficient. Meanwhile Polly, in the office, was trying very hard to speak like a lady. After work they walked home together, laughing and talking about the day's events.

''Ere, did yer see that lovely hunk of a bloke that brought the clorf in terday? 'E's new, ain't 'e?'

'Yes. Old Mr Cooper's retired. Where did you see him?'

'I was downstairs 'aving a crafty fag. Is 'e gonner do all Webber's deliveries now?' asked Shirley eagerly.

'Should think so. You wonner watch it. Just cos Big Vi's off sick, you shouldn't go sliding off. Miss Bloom will go mad if she catches you. You'll be going back on piece-work with this new order.'

'Thank Gawd fer that.'

'You won't go sliding off, then.'

'No bleedin' fear. Christ, yer'll 'ave ter drag me away from me machine then. Anyway, I knew I was safe, I saw 'er go out.

'Ere, find out 'is name,' Shirley gave Polly a playful shove. 'And if 'e's married.'

'Shirley Bell, you'll git me the sack, I'm not suppose ter keep the drivers waiting – just sign the dockets and send them packing.'

'Yer can send 'im packing in my direction any day.'

Although they worked in different parts of Bloom's, and Shirley was very popular with the girls on the factory floor, out of work the two friends were inseparable. Polly loved her job and was greatly liked by the customers, and nobody mentioned, or seemed to care about her eye.

'You meeting your mum tomorrow night?' asked Polly.

'Course, I always does on Friday. Why?'

'No reason.'

'Did yer wanner come shopping wiv us then?'

'No, no thanks.'

'What about coming ter the pictures ternight?' said Shirley as they were walking home from work. 'Lizzy on the presser was telling me that on the news they've got pictures of that Mrs Simpson.'

'OK. Where d'you fancy going, Odeon or Gaumont?'

'Not fussed, let's see what's on when we pass 'em.'

'I think the King is really good-looking. That Mrs Simpson must feel very special. Mind you, I don't know if I fancy her being Queen of England.'

Shirley began laughing.

'What's so funny?'

'You. 'Ark at yer, you don't 'alf talk posh now.' She nudged Polly's elbow.

Polly laughed. 'It's being in the office with Miss Bloom. And I might tell you we've got some very posh clients, so I do have to try.'

'D'yer really like it in there? Yer don't git as much money as us lot on piece-work, and yer don't 'ave as much fun as us, eyeing and shouting at all the lorry drivers.'

'No I know, but I love it. Mum nags a bit about me not

bringing home as much as you do. You get good money, you know.'

'I works bloody 'ard fer it,' said Shirley quickly, and then added with a laugh, ''Sides, they're not allowed ter give yer bad.'

'Oh I know, I know you're very good at the work. What d'you mean, they're not allowed to give you bad?'

'D'yer know sometimes you can be so dim. You know, they're not allowed ter give yer bad money,' she said slowly. Tutting and tossing her head she added, 'Don't worry about it.'

'Oh,' said Polly again as they stood outside the Odeon looking at the posters. 'I don't fancy this, do you?'

'No, don't like gangsters. Still it's a good fing we're both sixteen, now we can see an "A" film wivout asking someone ter take us in.'

Polly laughed. 'We didn't have a lot of trouble before. When was the last time you had to ask someone to take you in? Look at you, you look more like twenty than sixteen.'

Shirley smiled and preened in front of the chrome fascia. She loved being flamboyant and showing off. They both tried to wear fashionable clothes on their limited budget, but even with her flair for altering and adding, Polly still felt like a meek little mouse beside her friend, although she was the taller of the two.

Shirley, with her long dark hair now stylishly bobbed, had a small black hat perched on her head. She also wore thick make-up, unlike Polly, whose mother carried on if she put too much on. They both painted their nails to match their ruby lips. Shirley, being shorter, always wore very high heels, while Polly always wore a hat with an eye veil. As usual they continued walking home, talking and laughing.

Ron and Sid were leaning against the wall, deep in conversation, when the girls arrived at their gates.

''Allo you two,' said Shirley. 'What yer up to now?'

''Allo Ding Dong. Polly.' Ron gave her a slight nod. Ding Dong was his nickname for his younger sister. 'We're not up ter nufink,' he said, smoothing down his slick black Bryl-creemed hair.

Polly smiled and, feeling herself blush, quickly looked down. Since she'd lost the sight of her eye, all boys made her feel shy and ill at ease, unlike Shirley. Ron was always nice to her and seemed grown-up and worldly.

''Allo Shirl,' said Sid. 'You going out ternight?'

'Me and Polly's going ter the Gaumont.'

'Who wiv?'

'No one, just me and Polly. Why?'

'Well, girls, yer in fer a treat.' Sid flicked back his dark-grey trilby with one finger. 'Cos ternight we're gonner take yer ter the flicks. What d'yer fink of that?'

'Don't know,' said Polly regaining her composure and looking at her brother suspiciously. 'What's the reason?'

'Bloody 'ell. See what I mean. I try ter do sumfink nice fer 'er, and she still finks I'm up ter sumfink.'

'You forget I know you too well,' she said confidently, suddenly forgetting how uncomfortable she had been with Ron.

'Come off it you two,' interrupted Shirley. 'If you're paying then you can take us, but no hanky-panky, Sid Perkins. I know you, so just make sure yer keeps yer hands ter yerself, that's all.'

'What d'yer say, Pol?' Ron touched her arm.

She shivered with excitement. 'Well, all right then.'

That evening she was a little in awe of Ron. He was her first date. She had never been out with a boy before, and felt silly and giggly. Ron was nice to her, buying her sweets and ice cream, and she enjoyed his company. By the end of the evening she relaxed, and felt very grown-up when he kissed her goodnight.

After that they often went out in a foursome. She let him put his arm round her, but Ron never tried to put his hand up her skirt like she could see Sid doing to Shirley – not that Shirley objected, in fact her giggles told Polly she must have been enjoying it. Ron always kissed her goodnight, and they left

Shirley and Sid almost eating each other. Relations were improving between Polly and her brother, especially when they were out, as he was always good for a laugh. But she could never understand why Ron and Sid, who were forever in each other's company, always appeared to have plenty of money, even when the weather was bad and they couldn't work the markets.

It was the beginning of December, and on their way home from work Polly and Shirley were looking in the brightly lit shops along Jamaica Road.

'Wot yer gitting yer mum fer Christmas?' asked Shirley.

'Don't know, what you getting yours?'

'A pair o' silk stockings.'

'That's a bit extravagant,' said Polly.

'Well they're rayon, really.'

'That's not a bad idea. Mind you, I can't see my mum wearing silk ones.' They stopped and looked in a sweet shop. 'I s'pose I could get her a nice box of chocolates.'

'Yer, why not, then you could 'elp 'er eat 'em.'

'Don't think she'll like that. Still, we've got another week yet to think about it.'

'You coming inter our place Christmas night?'

'If you'll have me. I love your house with the big tree and all the decorations.'

'Well, wiv Dad on the market gitting trees cheap, and all the kids, Mum likes ter do sumfink. As Christmas Day's on Friday this year, d'yer fink we'll git paid Thursday?'

'Hope so, and I'm hoping we'll get a bonus as well.'

'D'yer know 'ow much yet?'

'No, I don't do the wages sheets till Wednesday.'

The following Friday night Polly was on her way home. It was cold and damp, but she felt a rosy glow inside. Every Friday evening since they had started work, Shirley had met her mum to go shopping with her, while Polly had gone straight round to Harding's pawn shop. She was grateful that Mr Harding had been so kind all these years.

She had begun paying off the loan four years ago when she used to run errands on a Saturday morning for the factory girls. Many times over the years she had been tempted to buy sweets or a small toy for Billy, but she had remained determined to get Grandad's whip back. She was getting a rise after Christmas, and with Ron now taking her to the pictures twice a week, she would be able to afford thru'pence a week from the shilling pocket money her mother was going to give her.

'Not long now, Grandad, only another six weeks and the whip is yours,' she said to herself as she walked light-heartedly out of Harding's.

On a Friday evening six weeks later, Polly and Shirley left the factory and stepped out into the cold, drizzling rain.

'Christ, look at this wevver,' Shirley said, fiddling with her umbrella. She pulled at her coat collar and turned to Polly. 'You look bloody pleased wiv yerself. Wot yer been up to?'

Polly was so excited that she almost told Shirley what she'd been doing all these years. She felt guilty at not confiding in her friend and, putting up her umbrella, said as they walked through the gates, 'Look, your mum's over there in that door-way.' She pointed across the road.

'Yer wonner come wiv us? Then yer can tell me wot's made yer look ser bloody pleased. It ain't this rain.'

'No, not this week. Perhaps next Friday I'll come with you.' Telling herself that at the moment it was still her secret.

She came out of Harding's and ran all the way home. As it had been raining almost all day, Polly was worried Sid might be in the house. She opened the front door and crept into the kitchen, pleased to see Grandad was alone. 'Grandad,' she whispered, afraid of startling him from his fireside nap.

'What is it? What's the matter? Oh, it's you, Polly.' He sat up. 'Git yer wet fings orf. What's that yer 'iding under yer coat?'

'Come upstairs, I've got something to show you.'

'Can't yer show me down 'ere?'

'No, someone might come in.' She anxiously looked at the door.

Reluctantly the old man struggled out of his chair and followed her. 'It 'ad better be worf it, that's all I can say.' His breath was laboured as he puffed up the stairs behind her.

In the safety of his room she closed the door. She waited while he sat on the bed and got his breath back, then with a great dramatic flurry she proudly produced a bag from under her coat, and took the whip from it. His eyes lit up.

'Good Gawd . . . 'Ow did . . .? Where did . . .? 'Ow did yer manage ter git that!' He held on to the wooden bed-end for support.

Polly knelt at his feet and laughed till tears ran down her cheeks. 'I've been waiting a long time for this moment. It's taken me four years and two months to pay it off.'

As he let his hand tenderly travel over his prized possession, tears filled his eyes. 'Oh, Polly love. I never fought I'd ever see it again. You're a good girl, but 'ow did yer manage it?'

She threw her arms round his neck and kissed his cheek. 'It's taken me a long while, but it was the least I could do – after all, you did pawn it for me.'

'Pawn shops only keep fings a year before they sell 'em, so 'ow come you got 'old of it?'

'When I first went with Mum to the factory on Saturday mornings when I was still at school, the women let me keep the change from the errands I used to run for them. I went to see Mr Harding, I explained all what had happened, and he was very kind and let me pay off a bit every week. Sometimes it was only a penny. But I was determined to get it back.'

'I bet 'e fought yer'd give up, then 'e'd 'ave your money as well as the whip. Those sort don't do nufink for love.'

'Well, he kept his promise.'

The old man held her close. 'God bless yer, Polly,' he croaked, trying to control his voice and emotions.

Her heart was full. 'I was hoping I could have got it before Christmas, but . . .'

'It's Christmas fer me.' He brushed a tear away with the back of his hand. 'It needs a good clean. Look at it, the 'andle's all black.'

'Don't let Mum see it just yet.'

'Whyever not?'

'Well she might go off at me for going down her things to get the pawn ticket, you know how she feels about it. Can you hide it up here somewhere.'

He laughed. 'I don't fink she goes down me drawers.' With great difficulty he knelt on the floor and pulled open the bottom drawer of the oak chest. 'I'll put it at the back of this one; it'll be our little secret.' Before hiding it away he turned to Polly and, still on his knees looked up and said, 'Will yer make me a promise, love?'

'I will if I can.'

'When I goes, make sure the first fing yer does is come up 'ere and git me whip and 'ide it.'

'But Grandad,' she interrupted.

'No, 'alf a mo', now just you listen ter me. I want you ter 'ave it. Don't let Sid or yer mother git their 'ands on it, cos if yer does that's the last you'll ever see of it, and I want it ter stay in the family.' He cast his eyes down and gently ran his gnarled fingers over the whip's handle again. 'This is all I've got ter give yer, love.'

'Grandad, don't talk like that, it'll be years 'fore you go.' She forced a nervous laugh.

'That's as may be.' He struggled to his feet. 'Now don't fergit what I told yer.' Taking her face between his hands, he kissed her forehead. 'Now let's git downstairs and lay the table 'fore yer mother gits in from shopping.'

Chapter 4

The Silver Jubilee celebrations in May 1935 had been the best thing that had ever happened in Penn's Place. Now, two years later, the party was happening all over again, only it would be even bigger and better than before. This time it was for the Coronation of King George VI and Queen Elizabeth, and everyone had the day off from work.

As soon as Polly finished washing up the breakfast things she rushed into Shirley. They laughed and giggled at the red, white and blue striped frocks they were wearing.

'You look like a barber's pole when you twist round,' laughed Polly.

'Fanks. You look like a skinny stick of rock.'

They laughed together; there was no malice in their comments.

For the past week they had been feverishly machining at every opportunity, pleased that Miss Bloom had let them make their frocks during their lunch breaks.

'Don't the street look smashing? Have you seen all the flags from the bedroom window?' asked Polly.

'Yer, but let's go and 'ave another look.'

They raced up the stairs and leaned out of the window, pointing excitedly at the sea of red, white and blue. Flags and bunting hung from every house and lamp-post.

'I fink it was a bit mean of Ron and Sid not ter take us wiv 'em.'

'Wonder why they wanted to go up West?'

'I fink Ron 'ad ter see someone. Oh look,' Shirley pointed up the road. 'Old Mrs Jarvis looks 'arf cut.'

'Bit early in the morning, even for her. Shall we go to the palace this evening and watch the King and Queen come out on their balcony?' asked Polly.

'Cor, that'll be great. I love those two little princesses, I'm gonner call my baby Elizabeth when I get married.'

'D'you want to marry our Sid?'

'No bleedin fear, I want someone wiv plenty of money. Wot about you, you gonner marry our Ron?'

'No, I'd like someone like . . .' she hesitated. 'Someone like David Bloom.'

Shirley's eyebrows shot up. ''Ave yer seen 'im then? Is 'e good-looking?'

'Dunno, I've spoken to him on the phone, he sounds ever so posh.'

'Fat chance yer got of going out wiv 'im then.' Shirley leaned further out of the window. ''Ere look they're putting the pub's tables down the middle of the road.'

'Come on, Shirl, let's go down and help put the food out.'

'D'yer know, me dad got quite a bit of money when he went round collecting fer the grub and drink. He said everyone chipped in.'

'That's good. Even me mum's been busy making sandwiches all morning,' said Polly, their feet clattering on the bare boards as they ran down the stairs.

'See that box of paper 'ats and blowers, I've got ter take 'em outside and give 'em ter the kids.' She stuck a hat on Polly's head.

Polly put one hand on her hip and sauntered up and down the passage. 'Well, what d'yer think?'

Shirley giggled. 'Looks bloody silly if yer asks me. Still, I don't care, I'll 'ave this one. 'Ere's a nice one fer Grandad.' She plonked a bright-red peaked cap on her head, picked up the box and went outside to join in the fun.

'I hope it don't rain,' said Polly, looking up at the sky.

'You can be a right Jonah at times,' said Shirley, passing out paper hats and blowers to the kids waiting to tuck into the mounds of food and jugs of lemonade. ''Ere, grab 'old o' these and give 'em ter the kids over on that table.' She passed a bundle of hats over to Polly.

Outside the pub at the far end of the road, barrels of beer had been stacked on trestles. Grandad, wearing his paper hat, wandered up and joined the local connoisseurs who were admiring the colour of the beer and sampling its taste with much discussion and scrutiny.

''Ere, look,' shouted Shirley, trying to make herself heard above the din the kids were making. 'Mr Jones 'as brought 'is gramophone out. Let's go and ask 'im if we can 'elp 'im wind it up.'

'I don't reckon he'll let us near it,' said Polly. 'See, he's standing guard over it.'

'Yer I know, but 'e's got ter go in sometime, ter 'ave a wee or sumfink.'

'Sometimes, Shirley Bell, you can be very crude.'

'Don't start talking all posh ter me, Polly Perkins,' she laughed and gave her friend a playful shove. 'Let's go and ask 'im if 'e's got any Al Jolson records.'

''Allo girls,' said Mr Jones, looking up from changing the gramophone's needle. 'Enjoying yerselves then?'

'Not 'alf. 'Ave yer got any Al Jolson records in that pile?' asked Shirley.

'Yer, somewhere.'

'D'yer want me ter look for yer?'

'No I don't, keep yer 'ands orf 'em – they're very fragile.'

'All right, all right, keep yer 'air on.'

As they walked away, Polly burst out laughing.

'What's ser funny?'

'You, telling him to keep his hair on. He's as bald as a badger.'

Shirley too collapsed with laughter. 'And 'e's miserable wiv it.'

47

Everybody joined in the dancing, singing and drinking, which went on till the early hours of the morning. When Ron and Sid returned to Penn's Place and joined in with the dancing, Polly and Shirley forgot about going to see the King and Queen at Buckingham Palace – they were enjoying themselves far too much.

At work, Polly had taught herself to type, and become very efficient. She was also very interested in the designs they produced, and loved the feel of the cloth, draping cottons, silks, and crepons over her shoulder to get the full effect of how they would fall. She also liked experimenting with the trimmings, and was busy going through the new season's designs with Sarah Bloom when Mr Bloom walked in.

'Well, what do you think of them?' he asked her.

'Quite nice,' said Polly.

'You don't sound too impressed.'

'Margaret was just saying she thinks she could save you some money.' Sarah Bloom looked up from the patterns.

'Oh yes, how?'

'If you didn't have covered buttons.'

His curiosity was aroused. 'On which one?'

Polly began sorting through the sketches. 'On this one, look,' she said enthusiastically. 'See, it would look good with gold buttons, sort of military like.'

Mr Bloom carefully studied the design. 'You know, young lady, you could be right. Sarah, phone Martha, find out what she'd charge me for one-inch brass buttons. Work out how many we'd need for the samples, and tell her I want them at a good price.' He turned to Polly. 'If it works out cheaper and looks better. I'll get you to go through all of this season's collection.'

'She already has.' Sarah Bloom smiled broadly. 'Show him your notebook, Margaret.'

Two weeks later, Polly was hurrying out of the office. It was late, and when all the machines stopped and the factory was quiet, her high heels sounded eerie as they echoed on the con-

48

crete floor. As it was Friday, Shirley had gone on ahead to meet her mother.

Running down the poorly lit corridor she quickly turned the corner and bumped into the best-looking young man she had ever seen. They both jumped.

'I say. I'm most dreadfully sorry.' He took her arm to steady her. He touched his trilby. 'You must be Margaret?'

She quickly looked up; in the dim light at the top of the stairs she caught sight of his dark eyes. Hastily she turned away, thankful she was on her way home and wearing the hat with the turned-down brim, which she kept pulled well down over her blind eye.

'I've heard all about you. My sister sings your praises all the time. You've even got Dad speaking favourably about you now you've improved some of his lines and saved him money.'

Polly could feel herself blushing. 'You must be David,' she said softly, not daring to look him full in the face.

'Sorry, I should have introduced myself.' He held out his hand. 'David, David Bloom.'

'Margaret Perkins.' She took hold of the outstretched hand. His long fingers curled round hers.

'That's a very pretty hat. Sarah said you always wear nice hats.'

Polly pulled her hand away. 'Thank you,' she murmured, holding her breath, waiting for him to say he knew why she was so fond of hats, but he only asked, 'By the way, is my sister still here?'

'Yes, she's in the office. We had a late order to get out. You know where it is, don't you?'

'Sure. I expect we'll meet again.' He touched the brim of his hat once more.

Polly hurried out of the building, grateful Shirley wasn't with her. Her heart and mind were pounding. Fancy having called herself Margaret Perkins, all posh like. She smiled. David looked even better than he'd sounded; he must be about twenty; he was certainly very good-looking and well-dressed.

49

Still, he should be with all his father's money. He'd seemed to know all about her. They must talk about her at home. She wondered if he knew she could only see out of one eye? There was no way of telling.

All the following week she wanted to ask Miss Bloom more about David, but the opportunity never arose, and she had to be content with her dreams.

Polly relaxed when Ron slipped his arm round her shoulders. Usually, whenever they sat together in the back row of the pictures, she sat upright. Tonight she felt different: it was probably to do with the two port and lemons she'd had before they came in, and it was a very romantic film.

He pulled her closer and she nestled her head against his shoulder. His lips brushed her cheek in his search for her mouth. He tried turning her head. Unsuccessful at that, he worked his way towards her ear and began gently nibbling it.

He jerked his head back and, spluttering, spat out the large button earring she was wearing. Polly giggled, and stuffed her handkerchief in her mouth to suppress her snorts of laughter.

'Shh.' The couple in front turned round and glared.

Shirley, who was sitting next to Polly, untwined herself from Sid, leant forward and asked, 'What's ser funny?'

'I've lost me earring,' whispered Polly.

'Well, wait till the lights go up, we'll look for it then.' She nudged Polly. ''Ere, 'e ain't swallowed it, 'as 'e?'

She shook her head, almost convulsed with laughter. For Polly, the romance had gone out of the evening.

When the lights went up, and after they stood quiet for the Anthem, they scrabbled on the floor looking for the lost earring.

'I've got it,' said Ron. 'Christ, look at the size of it, I could 'ave choked me bloody self.'

They were still laughing when they left the cinema.

'It's a nice warm night, don't let's git the tram, let's walk home,' said Ron, slipping his arm round Polly's trim waist.

'Good idea,' said Sid.

Sid and Shirley stopped under the railway arches, where the gas-lamp's glow didn't reach that stretch of road.

'You two go on,' shouted Shirley.

Polly knew what they would get up to; Shirley had boasted about losing her virginity months ago.

Out of sight of the others, Ron shoved Polly against the wall and began kissing her hard and passionately. His tongue forced her lips open to explore her mouth.

Polly was taken aback, and tried to push him away. Ron had never kissed her like this before. She didn't know if she liked it, and she wasn't at all sure of her feelings for him. She knew she was flattered and pleased he asked her out; Ron could have gone out with any girl. But had he been taking her out of pity? Had Shirley asked him to? Polly struggled. This, this was something new. 'Don't do that,' she gasped, freeing herself from him.

'Come on, Pol, be a sport.' He started undoing the buttons on the front of her blouse.

'What's the matter with you, Ron? Stop it.' She slapped his hand away.

'I should ask you wot's the matter. Why yer so bloody stuck up? Christ we've been out quite a few times now, and I've always behaved meself. If it 'ad been any other tart, I'd be 'aving a bit be now.'

Polly looked down. 'I'm not any tart. I thought you just wanted to go out with me.' She hesitated, 'I didn't think you only wanted to have . . .'

He laughed. 'Blokes don't take yer out fer nufink, yer know.' He turned away and, putting his hands in his trouser pockets, gently kicked the wall. 'What's wrong wiv me?'

'Nothing. It's not you . . . It's just that I feel you should love someone before you let them . . .'

'Don't talk a lotta rot. D'yer fink our Shirl loves Sid? Yer don't see 'er going all moon-faced over 'im, do yer?'

'Well, no, but Shirley's different to me.'

'Christ, yer can say that again.' He turned and wagged his finger in her face. 'You're gitting ter be a right little snob working in that office. Factory floor ain't good enough fer you. Remember, yer only like the rest of us – working class – so don't start getting any fancy ideas.'

Polly felt upset. 'I haven't. Just because I won't let you . . . I like you Ron, but I don't think I love you.'

He laughed. 'Yer don't 'ave ter love someone ter 'ave a bit. And 'ere, don't go giving me all that old twaddle about saving yerself fer yer wedding night.'

She wanted to say, 'Yes I am,' but knew he would laugh at her.

'Come orf it, Pol, there ain't nufink wrong wiv a bit of slap and tickle. I promise I won't go all the way.'

She thought about Shirley and the way the girls talked at the factory. Perhaps she was trying to be different? As Ron just said, stuck-up and silly. When he grabbed her arms, she tried to relax. He kissed her, and buried his head in her neck. 'Yer know I wouldn't mind marrying yer, if that's what yer wants.'

She shook her head and laughed. 'What?'

'I'm deadly serious, gel. Yer knows I've always been sweet on yer, and if that's what yer wants, well, why not?'

Polly bristled. 'That's not what I want.' She didn't want to hurt his feelings by adding, Well, not with you anyway.

''Ere, yer ain't got yer peepers on someone else, 'ave yer?'

'Course not.' She looked down, not wanting him to see her blushing.

'No, I don't suppose you would 'ave. Not many blokes like looking at yer, you only 'aving one eye. Yer know it's a bit creepy sometimes the way yer looks at people with that dead eye.' He laughed. 'Reminds me of a dead fish on a slab at the fishmonger's, yer know the way they look up at yer.'

Polly was devastated. She turned her head and he kissed her neck. She felt numb, and shivered despite the warmth of the evening. Tears stung her eyes. No one had ever said that to her before, not even the kids at school. They only called her Polly

One-eye. No one had told her she looked creepy. Like a dead fish's eye. Ron's words were going round and round in her head. Not many men would look at her. Come to think about it, no one else had asked her out. Perhaps Ron is my only hope of getting married, she thought desperately.

'Well, what d'yer say?'

'I don't know.' Polly's voice trembled.

'Yer wouldn't mind 'aving a place of yer own, now would yer?'

'Well no. That would be very nice.'

'And yer wouldn't be under yer muvver's feet all the time. She does 'ave a go at yer now and again, don't she?'

'Well, yes.'

'We'll find us a nice couple of rooms and furnish 'em all proper like. What d'yer fink about that?'

Polly didn't know what she was thinking. 'I don't know. Would you really want to get married?'

'Yer, why not. Might be a bit of a laugh 'aving our own place, and kids of me own.'

'I don't want babies just yet.'

'Na, I meant a bit later on. Come on, wot d'yer say?'

What if she said no. This might be her only chance of getting married and leaving home – she didn't want to be a spinster all her life. Ron wasn't so bad: he had quite good taste, was a snappy dresser, never seemed to be hard up, and she did like him.

'Come on, what d'yer say?'

'Well I don't know. It's a bit sudden.' All kind of thoughts were racing round in her head. Would her mother give her consent? After all, she was only seventeen. A place of her own. What if she had babies and had to give up work? 'I'll have to think about it.'

'Don't take too long, I might go off the boil,' he laughed. 'No seriously, Pol, I fink we could make a go of it. Yer not bad-looking, apart from yer eye. Tel yer wot, why don't we git engaged, just till yer got used ter the idea.'

'Well, all right, if you like then.'

'Well, that's settled, we're engaged.' He gathered her in his arms and kissed her. His mouth was harsh, demanding and aggressive. Slowly his hand travelled up her skirt. He fingered the tops of her silk stockings and began caressing her bare flesh. His hands were rough as they moved up and down her suspenders. She fought back the tears. She didn't want him – she didn't want anyone this way. Her thoughts went to her knickers. She wished she hadn't put her best French ones on. Her old elastic-legged bloomers would have been a lot safer.

She could feel his hardness pushing against her thigh. She longed to shove him away, but knew he'd get angry and probably hit her for being a tease. She groaned and wriggled in order to stop his hand riding up any further. He must have mistaken her groan for ecstasy, and her movements for a come on. He feverishly went up further and tugged at her knickers so hard that the button that held them fast at the waist, flew off, and they fell to the ground.

A froth of cream satin and lace lay at her ankles. Polly looked down and giggled nervously.

'Stop that bloody laughing,' he shouted and, grabbing her shoulders, shook her till her head wobbled.

She laughed louder. Tears ran down her face and hysterical sobs began to mingle with the now subdued laughter.

'Bloody 'ell, what's wrong wiv yer? What's so bloody funny?'

'I'm sorry, Ron.'

'So yer should be. If I fought fer one minute yer ...' He didn't finish his sentence, just stared in amazement as she stepped daintily out of her knickers, picked them up, and put them in her handbag.

'They cost me four an' eleven. I hope you ain't torn 'em,' Polly said primly.

'Christ, yer can't 'alf turn a bloke off. Come on, let's go 'ome.'

They arrived at their gates with hardly a word passing

between them. Ron held her gate firm.

'Ron, what you playing at? Open the gate.'

He pulled her round to face him. 'I meant it, Pol, when I said let's git married.'

She remained silent.

'I'll find us a nice couple of rooms. Yer'd like that, a place of yer own, wouldn't yer?'

A place of her own. If it was big enough, perhaps she could have Grandad come and live with her.

'Well, what d'yer say? We'll do all right, you see. Yer do like me, don't yer?'

'Yes, I like you, but I don't . . . I don't love you.'

'All that love stuff's fer the pictures. Christ, yer don't fink our mums and dads went in fer all that sloppy stuff, d'yer?'

She didn't answer.

'Well, that's settled then, we're engaged.' He took her into his arms and kissed her long and hard. 'Anyway, I fink yer a little smasher. Come up the market on Saturday and I'll git yer a ring.'

Chapter 5

Polly arrived home from work, and, without removing her hat and coat, plonked herself on the chair opposite Grandad.

'All right, Pol?' he asked tenderly.

She nodded. 'A bit tired, that's all.'

'Humh,' said her mother, without looking up from the peas she was shucking. 'Yer don't know the bloody meaning of the word. Yer don't call that 'n'ard day's work, do yer – sitting on yer arse all day long? Christ, the 'eaviest fing yer picks up is a phone. You wait till yer married and 'ave ter git yer old man's dinner every night. That'll give yer sumfink ter moan about.'

Polly twisted the three-diamond ring round and round her finger. 'Don't start on that again, Mum.' She stood up and peered in the mirror before removing her hat. She knew her mother wasn't too pleased about her getting engaged. After all, when they finally got to set the date to get married, she'd be losing a wage packet. 'I've been up and down those stairs dozens of times today, I feel like a flaming yo-yo. Been going over the new season's collection with Mr Bloom and Fred. So don't start nagging.'

'Don't you git lippy wiv me, girl. Gitting above yer station – that's the trouble with you, young lady.' Her mother snatched up the colander half-full of peas. They slid dangerously to one side before she righted them and stormed off into the scullery, slamming the door behind her.

Taking off her coat, Polly sighed. 'I can never do or say anything right in this house just lately.'

57

'Don't worry about it, love,' said Grandad. 'She's got ter 'ave a go at someone. Remember, it used ter be me before I let 'er pawn the whip.'

Polly anxiously put her finger to her lips. 'Shh.'

He grinned. 'She's fond of yer and don't want yer ter leave 'ome, that's why.'

'She's got a funny way of showing it.' She hung her coat on the hook behind the kitchen door.

'Don't fergit she'll be your money short when yer goes.'

'She's got Billy's money coming in now he's started work.'

''E don't git much in that tea factory.'

'No, I know, but he's only fourteen. I didn't get much when I first started.' She sat down. 'Why is it always me? You never hear her go off at Sid.'

'Well,' whispered the old man, quickly glancing at the scullery door. ''E is 'er little blue-eyed boy, so ter speak. And 'e does bring 'er in a few extra bob now and again from 'is wheeling and dealings.'

'I bring her things, sometimes.' Polly felt hurt. 'Only last week I bought her some flowers. To tell the truth, I'd like to know what Sid does get up to half the time.'

'Take my advice, love.' He kept his voice low, and with the tip of his finger touched the side of his nose. 'It pays ter keep this out of 'is business.'

It was at that very moment that the front door shut with a bang, and Sid rushed breathlessly through the kitchen and out into the scullery. When they heard the back door slam, Polly and Grandad looked at each other and began laughing. They went to the window that overlooked the back yard and watched Sid run towards the closet.

''E's in a bit of a 'urry, ain't 'e?' said the old man.

Polly grinned. 'Must be something he's eaten.'

'What's wrong wiv Sid?' asked her mother, wiping her hands on the bottom of her apron as she walked in.

Polly shrugged.

A loud rat-a-tat-tat on the front door silenced them, and

they looked from one to the other.

It was Doris Perkins who spoke first. 'Who the bloody 'ell's banging on the knocker like that?'

Polly made a move to answer the door, but her mother forestalled her. 'I'll go, and I'll give 'em a piece of me mind.' She disappeared from the room.

Raised voices came from the passage. Polly could hear her mother; the other voice belonged to a man. She stood by the door trying to make out what they were saying.

'What is it? What's going on?' asked Grandad.

Polly sat on the chair again. 'I don't know. I can't quite hear them.'

A few minutes later they heard the front door shut, and a grey-faced Mrs Perkins returned to the kitchen, accompanied by two policemen. One was tall, well-built and surly looking, the other was also tall, but thin.

Polly jumped up. 'What's the matter? What's happened?'

The surly one said, 'We've got a warrant for Sidney Perkins' arrest.'

'I told yer, 'e ain't 'ere.' Doris Perkins sat at the table.

Polly glanced over at Grandad and lifted her perfectly shaped eyebrows.

'What's 'e done?' asked the old man.

'He's wanted for questioning.'

'What about?' demanded her mother.

'A robbery.' The curt reply from the surly one showed he was the senior of the two.

Mrs Perkins smoothed out the brown chenille cloth they now had covering the table. 'I don't believe it. What's 'e supposed to 'ave pinched?'

'Where is he, Mrs? We know he's here, we chased him down the road.' The thin one didn't bother answering her question.

'Next door.'

'No he ain't, we've been in there.'

Polly looked alarmed. 'Is Ron Bell in there?'

59

'Dark-haired bloke about twenty?'

She nodded.

'He's in the bath. Been in there quite a while according to his mother, the water's nearly cold. His sister won't go out the kitchen so he can't get out.'

'Humm, shouldn't fink that'll worry 'im, or 'er come ter that,' said Mrs Perkins.

'Anyway, that's not answering my question. Where is he, Mrs?'

'Out back.' She waved her arm limply towards the scullery door.

They rushed through the kitchen, into the scullery and out into the back yard. Polly anxiously watched them shove open the closet door.

They returned to the kitchen alone.

'He won't get far. We know where they hang out.' The surly one tugged at the bottom of his tunic. 'We'd like to search the house.'

Doris Perkins stood up and leaned on the table, her knuckles showing white. 'Over my dead body. Yer not putting yer bleeding dirty little maulers inter my cupboards – or anywhere else in this 'ouse fer that matter.'

The policeman didn't flinch when she clenched her fist and shook it in his face. Ignoring her he undid the button on the top pocket of his tunic and removed a piece of paper. 'This is a search warrant, Mrs.' He waved the paper in the air. 'And if you interfere with the course of justice, then you could find yourself in the nick.'

'Sit down, Mum. I'll see to it. Where do you want to start?'

Her mother would not sit down. 'I'm not 'aving 'em creeping all over me 'ouse – poking their snotty little noses inter everyfink. I knows all about them, they'll pinch sumfink then swear blind it wasn't them.'

'Oh, so there's something worth pinching in here, then,' said the surly one, looking round the shabby room.

'Sit down, Doris, and let Polly see to 'em,' said Grandad wearily.

'Do as he says, Mrs,' said the thin one.

Reluctantly, she sank into the chair.

'Where do you want to start?' inquired Polly.

'Upstairs.'

They went from the boys' room to her mother's, pulling out all the drawers and tipping the contents on to the bed. Everything was dragged from the cupboards; they even looked under the beds.

'What are you looking for?' asked Polly.

'We're not at liberty to say. Whose room's that?' asked the thin one, pointing to the last of the three doors on the small landing.

'That's my grandad's. There's nothing in there.'

As they made a move towards it, Polly quickly stepped between them and the door. 'Do you have to pull everything out in there?' She was concerned at the mess they had made in the other two rooms but she was more worried about them finding Grandad's whip which was still hidden in the bottom drawer.

The surly policeman grabbed her shoulders and pushed her to one side. 'Get out the way. What you hiding in there? And look at me when I'm talking to you.'

Over the years Polly had perfected her habit of not looking at people full in the face when they were up close. 'There's nothing in there,' she protested loudly, bringing her mother running up the stairs.

'What they up to? What they doing now?' she shouted.

'It's all right.' As Polly moved and leaned over the banisters to reassure her mother, the policeman quickly pushed open the old man's bedroom door and began pulling everything out of the cupboard.

Polly and Doris Perkins could only stand in the doorway looking on.

'Look at the bloody mess yer making. Who's gonner clear up after yer?'

'Shh, Mum. It won't do any good you leading off.'

Methodically they went through the five drawers in the oak chest. Polly gasped when they tipped the contents of the bottom one on to the bed. Now everyone could see their secret.

'Well, well, well,' the thin policeman said. 'What have we got here? What do you make of this?' He handed the whip to his fellow officer.

'Humm, this is very interesting.'

'It's got a nice silver handle, anything like it on the list?'

The surly one twisted it round. 'I don't think so. It's heavy,' he said feeling the weight of it in his hand.

'Where did that come from?' screamed Doris Perkins.

Both policemen spun round.

'You've never seen this before?' He brandished the whip in her face.

'Yes . . . But . . .' she stammered.

'It's my grandfather's.' Polly hoped her voice sounded even.

'If you know all about it – how comes your mother don't?' He lightly tapped the palm of his hand with the whip, and walked menacingly towards Polly.

'She thought it was still in the pawn shop,' she blurted out.

'What d'you mean, she thought it was still in the pawn shop?' He slowly repeated every word.

'She pawned it, and I redeemed it,' said Polly quickly.

'You did what?' shouted Doris Perkins, pushing her way into the room.

'And you didn't tell your mother?' The surly policeman paid no attention to Mrs Perkins.

'No,' whispered Polly.

'Why was that?'

'I didn't want her . . . She might have wondered . . .' Polly fumbled for the right words.

'I think we'd better go downstairs and ask the old man what this is all about.'

In the kitchen, Grandad explained how he got the whip, why it was pawned, and how Polly redeemed it. Although they seemed reasonably satisfied, Doris Perkins was obviously not – she sat drumming her fingers on the kitchen table.

After searching the front room, kitchen and scullery, they went outside to look in the closet.

'You crafty cow.' Her mother narrowed her eyes and growled in a low whisper. 'How long ago did yer git that back for 'im? And where did yer git the money from?'

Polly sat at the table and didn't answer.

'She'll tell yer later, Doris.' The old man was agitated. He sat on the edge of his armchair, nervously tapping and smoothing the wooden arms.

'Yer must 'ave gone down me fings ter git the pawn ticket.' She sat staring silently at the whip for a moment or two then, jerking her head up, suddenly burst out, 'Yer must 'ave done that years ago.'

The policeman came back into the kitchen. 'There's nothing out there.'

'I told yer that from the start,' rapped Mrs Perkins, colouring with anger.

'When your son comes home, tell him to come along to the station, that's if he knows what's good for him,' said the surly one. He slowly looked round the room, then added, 'It might be to his advantage if he can help us with our inquiry.'

The thin one stood in the doorway waiting. His colleague was about to follow, when he hesitated. He picked the whip from off the table and slowly turned it over in his hand. 'Humm, this is very nice.'

The old man visibly froze in his seat, his eyes riveted on the policeman's hands. Casually the policeman tossed the whip back on to the table and only then did Grandad relax.

But the slamming of the front door seemed to let the devil loose in Doris Perkins. She picked up the whip and began thrashing Polly with it. 'You selfish little cow,' she screamed. 'All what I've done fer you. Just been a bloody skivvy in this

63

'ouse – and this is all the fanks I git.' She screwed up her eyes, and rage distorted her flushed face.

Polly put her hands over her head in an effort to protect herself from the frenzied attack.

'Stop it, Doris. Stop it,' yelled the old man. 'What's she done ter you?'

'Got yer bleedin' whip back, that's what she's done.' Every word was accentuated with another blow and Polly, shocked, was incapable of retaliating. The old man tried to struggle out of his chair, but was pushed down by Mrs Perkins' free hand as she moved round the table, lunging at her daughter.

Suddenly the kitchen door opened, and for a split second Billy stood in the doorway before leaping across the room like a tiger. He grabbed his mother's arm and yanked it upwards. She dropped the whip and rubbed her wrist and Polly staggered back, stunned. Fortunately, her mother's inexperience at handling the whip meant the thin leather thong had missed Polly most of the time, but she was still reeling with shock.

'What the bloody 'ell's going on in 'ere?' demanded Billy looking from one woman to the other.

Polly and her mother sank into chairs at the table. Polly was all eyes – even her blind one appeared to have life in it. Grandad lay back in his chair breathing heavily. Only their mother's sobs broke the silence.

'Well?' said Billy. 'Answer me someone.'

Polly couldn't control her shaking, and whispered slowly, 'The police have been here looking for Sid.'

'That's no big surprise,' interrupted Billy. 'What's 'e been up to? Did they find 'im?'

'No. He ran out back and jumped over the wall.'

'So. What's that to do wiv this?' He waved the whip at everybody.

'They searched the 'ouse,' said Grandad. 'Fink they were looking fer sumfink 'e'd pinched.'

'Did they find anyfink?'

He shook his head.

Their mother remained silent. Slowly she lifted her head, tears glistening on her cheeks.

'They found Grandad's whip,' said Polly.

'I can see that. Where did it come from?' He hesitated. 'Mum pawned it years ago.'

'I got it back.'

'What? How did yer manage ter do that? You was only a kid when yer 'ad to go in 'ospital and they pawned it. Where did yer git the money from ter pay fer it?'

Their mother wiped her face dry with the flat of her hand, and snapped, 'That's just what I'd like ter know.'

Polly looked down at her fingers twitching nervously. She began picking off the nail varnish. 'I started saving when I used to run errands for the factory girls on Saturday mornings. Sometimes they let me keep the change.'

'She must 'ave gorn down me drawers ter git the pawn ticket – nosy little cow.'

''Ang on a bit, Mum. Let 'er finish. How long did it take yer?' asked Billy in amazement.

'Over four years.'

'Over four years,' repeated Billy slowly, 'Well, I'll be buggered.'

'It's a pity yer didn't look after yer mother, and get some of my fings back fer me.' Doris Perkins' eyes were blazing. 'Lorst everyfink I did, looking after you lot when you were little. And you.' She pointed her long, bony finger at the old man. 'I've always been the one ter go out ter work, and go wivout since Tom died, not you. Oh no, you've 'ad ter stay indoors cos of yer poor bleedin' chest. What about my poor chest?' She jumped up and rapidly pounded her tightly clenched fist into her breast to emphasize her words. 'Out in all bloody weathers at six in the morning. Sod you and yer bleedin' chest, you could 'ave found sumfink if yer'd really wanted to. 'Ad ter bring you lot up on me own.' She sat down again, and her voice softened. 'Got nufink left of what Tom bought me, d'yer 'ear, nufink. Siddy's been the only one ter worry about me. Not you lot, oh no, too bloody selfish, that's your trouble.' She lowered her head on to her arms, and sobbed pitifully.

They all sat in stunned silence at her outburst. Polly stared at the top of her mother's head, unable to speak.

Gradually her mother's shoulders stopped heaving, and very slowly she brought her head up. She wiped her face on her apron and, choked with tears, said, 'All the lovely fings my Tom bought me, all gorn. Me engagement ring, me watch, and I 'ad a lovely gold necklace with a pearl that 'ung down.' She buried her head in her apron and wept.

Polly knew her tears were bitter tears. Years of pent-up emotions spilled from her mother's eyes unchecked. Polly felt an overwhelming wave of sadness and fear. If only her mother had told her, confided in her, not kept her at a distance all these years. Her guilt was engulfing her, her mind churning over and over. Had she been wrong to get the whip back? She'd had no idea it would open up this floodtide of anger and bitterness.

'What can we say, Mum?' Billy looked anxiously at his mother.

She raised her head and looked at him. Her eyes were red and swollen, she looked old and frail and vulnerable. 'Oh Billy.' She grabbed the whip from the table and Polly winced. 'All those two ever worried about was this bleedin' fing.' She threw it to the floor and went upstairs.

Polly knew there was no point in trying to comfort her – she would only be rejected.

The following day, Sid was arrested. Mrs Perkins would not speak to Polly, and only spoke to Billy and the old man when necessary.

Sid was tried in the Magistrates' Court. Some of the stolen goods were recovered, and the pawnbroker said it wasn't Sid who sold them to him. Yet somehow the police made sure Sid was involved. He was given nine months for assisting in the robbery, and the ill-feeling Mrs Perkins had for Polly continued. Polly couldn't help smarting at the injustice of it all, however sorry she felt for her mother. After all, Sid was the one who'd got himself into bother yet she was now the one her mother was angry with.

A week later Polly and Ron were sitting in the pub. He touched her hand. 'Let's git married, then yer can git out of there. Yer've been like a bleedin' wet week since yer muvver found the whip and Sid went in the nick.'

'I can't, not now. I don't think she'll ever forgive me for getting that whip back.' She twisted her engagement ring round her finger and, looking down at it, said, 'It must have been awful for her to have to pawn hers.'

'Let's 'ope yer don't 'ave ter pawn yours.' He squeezed her hand. 'I don't like ter see yer so upset. Let's git married soon? Wot d'yer say Pol?'

'I don't think she'll sign the consent papers, more so now she's not got Sid's money coming in.'

Ron sat back in his chair. ''E was a bit daft gitting caught.'

Polly looked up. 'What d'you mean?' Although she was cross with Sid for getting on the wrong side of the police she really didn't think he could be guilty of theft.

'Nufink. Come on, drink up, let's go 'ome.'

Chapter 6

At the end of January 1939, Mrs Bell had another baby.

'What you going to call her?' Polly asked Shirley as they hurried home from work.

'Judy, me mum's got a fing about film stars. Christ, it's bloody cold. It's freezing on the factory floor, what's it like in your office?'

'Not too bad.'

''Ere, will Sid be 'ome fer yer wedding?'

'I think so, Billy said he's hoping to get paroled or something before Easter. Anyway, he's not doing his full time.'

'That's good. I miss 'im yer know. 'E's always good fer a laugh.'

Polly didn't answer. The day the police had come to the house, and the miserable months that had followed, still held many unhappy memories for her. The tension between Polly and her mother had eased a little at Christmas when Polly gave her a carefully chosen present – a rolled-gold dropped pearl necklace – but the atmosphere in the house was still fraught. Sid would only make the quarrelling worse.

'I bet yer was surprised when yer mum said she'd sign the consent papers?'

'I think when she heard Sid was coming home, she thought it might be better if I was out the way.'

'Ron 'ad any luck wiv rooms yet?'

'No, we've got to look at some on Sunday, round Weaver Street.'

'That's not too far away, let's 'ope yer gits 'em.'

'Miss Bloom's going to bring me some swatches of wedding-dress material when she goes to the wholesalers.'

'Ohh,' Shirley wrapped her hands round her arms. 'It's ever so exciting. I think yer pattern is smashing, and it'll look real good in heavy satin – I can't wait ter be a bridesmaid.'

'Miss Bloom wants to use my design for some dresses.'

'Humm. I bet yer don't git paid for it, not like those fancy blokes who come up with those fancy patterns wot you make look better.'

'She is giving me the material for my dress, and yours. And she's letting me make them at work.'

'Yer, I suppose she's not too bad. 'Ere, won't yer feel a bit guilty walking down the aisle all dressed in white?'

Polly quickly turned on Shirley. 'No. Why should I? Would you?'

'Naw, course not. But I ain't a . . . You know?' She nudged Polly's arm. 'Ain't you and Ron ever . . ?'

Polly flushed. 'I wouldn't tell you if I had. Sometimes, Shirley Bell, you've got a lot of cheek.'

'I tells you what I gits up to.'

'Well, that's up to you. I just hope Grandad's well enough to give me away.'

'I 'eard 'im coughing the other night. It sounded real bad.'

'I worry about him.' Polly shivered. 'This wind's making me eyes water. I won't be sorry to get home tonight.'

'Me too. Christ, I hope me old man don't wanner drag me up the 'ospital ter see Mum and the new baby again ternight.'

It was a few weeks before the wedding, and Mrs Perkins had been busy getting Sid's bed ready for his return.

''Allo mate, all right then?' she asked when he walked into the kitchen and kissed her cheek.

'Not ser bad.'

'Margaret, take Sid's bag upstairs.'

Polly did as she was told; she knew there was no point in

making a fuss. Sid was sitting on the chair opposite Grandad when she returned to the kitchen.

'Wot was prison like?' asked the old man.

'Not ser bad, as long as yer kept yer nose clean.'

'D'yer fink yer'll git yer old job back, son?' asked Grandad.

'Yer, Ron's been ter see old 'Arry and 'e said it was OK. Christ, let's face it, there's more villains down the market than in the nick. And anyway, I ain't no villain. It was good of Ron ter find out fer me. 'E came ter see me a couple of times. That's more than some of me family did.' He looked over at Polly.

She went into the scullery and returned with the knives and forks.

'So, yer gitting 'itched then?' Sid asked her.

'Yes, Easter Sunday.'

'Yeah, so Ron said. 'E said yer got some rooms round Weaver Street.'

'Yes,' Polly's answers were polite but curt.

'Didn't fink it'd last this long.'

'Why's that?' Polly busied herself laying the table.

'No reason. Yer knows 'e's asked me ter be 'is best man?'

'Yes.'

'Well, wot yer got ter say about it?'

'Nothing, it's his decision.'

'Wot's 'is decision?' asked Mrs Perkins, coming back into the kitchen.

'Sid being Ron's best man.'

'Oh that. Don't know why yer in such a bleedin' 'urry ter git married.'

'Yer not up the spout are yer?' asked Sid.

'No I am not.'

'Well I fink Ron's all right,' said Grandad.

'Well you would, wouldn't yer?' said Mrs Perkins. 'She can't do no wrong in your eyes – yer finks the sun shines out of 'er arse.'

'I don't know why you're so against me getting married,' Polly said wearily.

Sid grinned, making his eyes disappear. Polly hated that look, it always reminded her of the day he flicked the fish bone at her.

'P'raps Mum finks yer could 'ave done better fer yerself.'

Polly felt herself go hot. 'I happen to be very fond of Ron. At least he doesn't worry that I'm blind in one eye.'

'I wondered when yer was going ter bring that up again,' said Sid, leaning back on the chair and picking up the newspaper.

Doris Perkins rammed the poker in the fire. 'It was an accident, and well yer knows it, but yer always got ter 'ave a little dig about it though, ain't yer?'

Polly didn't answer.

'This 'Itler bloke's 'aving a bit of a go,' said Sid, magnanimously changing the subject. 'I reckon we're all gonner finish up in the Army soon. Don't s'pose they'll be fussy who they take on.'

Polly went upstairs. She didn't like all this talk about war; she had enough of it in her own family, never mind worrying about it in the world outside.

The phone was ringing as Polly entered the office. 'Hello, Bloom's Fashions . . . Hello Miss Bloom . . .'

'Margaret, I can't get in till much later today, I've got to go over to the wholesalers – but father wants to see the new designs as soon as possible. Do you think you could bring them to the house this afternoon?'

'Well, I don't know.'

'It's very easy to get to our place. You get the underground to East Putney, then it's only a short walk to where we live. Oakhill, Number 195. Come over after the dinner break. Tell Violet I hope to be back at the factory before it's time for the girls to go.'

'All right. Do you want me to bring all of them?'

'Yes please, and Margaret, you can go straight home from our place. Bye.'

'Bye.' Polly put the phone down and sat on her chair. She smiled every time Miss Bloom said the name 'Violet' – there was nothing like the delicate little flower about the forelady. She was big, with arms like tree trunks. Shirley always reckoned she would crush her old man to death if she ever gave him a bear hug. Polly waggled her legs. 'I'm going to the Blooms' posh house,' she said out loud.

A few hours later Polly found herself staring at the large, impressive-looking red-brick building in front of her as she walked round the gravel drive. She mounted the steps, and before ringing the doorbell, checked that the seams of her stockings were straight.

The door was opened by a smart woman whose dark, grey-flecked hair was pulled back into a bun. Her deep brown eyes were alive and alert, and Polly could see she was Sarah Bloom's mother – the likeness was unmistakable. She smiled. 'Hello, you must be Margaret. Do come in.'

To Polly it was like stepping into another world. Her shoes sunk into a deep red carpet, and she quickly took in her surroundings. A mahogany high-backed seat was against one wall, and the wide staircase, with a dark wood balustrade that had a large acorn on the end, was against the other. There was a table which held the telephone, and there was a large mirror in a dark frame above it.

'Do go into my husband's office. It's that door there.' She pointed to one of the four doors leading off the hall. 'I'll just put the kettle on. I expect you would like a cup of tea, or would you prefer coffee?'

'Oh no, no thank you, tea will be fine.' Polly began pushing open the heavy door when raised voices caused her to stop.

'What are you worried about a war for?' It was Mr Bloom's loud voice.

'A lot of fellers are talking about going into the Forces and getting commissions.' Polly recognized David Bloom's voice.

'So, what's that to do with you?' asked his father.

Polly looked about her nervously. Mrs Bloom had gone into

73

the kitchen, and she didn't know whether to go into the room or not.

'I want to leave University and join the Air Force.'

'What?' The sound was like an explosion. 'Hell, now look what you've made me do,' shouted Mr Bloom.

'I've been taking flying lessons, and I've made up my mind.'

'You've done what?' The words were slow and full of anger. 'Now just you listen to me, son, and you listen good. I've spent a lot of money on your education, and you are going to be a lawyer – d'you hear?'

Polly strained her ears, waiting for David's answer. Her fingers were still wrapped around the door handle. Suddenly it was jerked out of her hand, and Polly jumped back. Mr Bloom stood in the doorway with his back to her.

'We'll have no more talk about wars, or the Air Force, in this house – do you understand?'

'What about what's happening to the Jews in Europe? All the suffering over there? Don't you feel anything for them?' David's voice coming from inside the room sounded full of sensitivity.

Polly quickly sat on the monk's seat and stared at Mr Bloom's back filling the door frame.

He stiffened, and for a few moments remained motionless. 'You of all people should know how I feel about wars. I abhor them.' He stepped back into the room, leaving the door wide open. 'Don't you ever forget that your grandparents, my mother and father, were killed by a German Zeppelin.'

Polly sat riveted as Mr Bloom went on. 'So of course I feel great concern for my fellow man.' He spoke very slowly, and in a low tone. 'But what I and my family worked for is very different and, to me, far more important.'

'Albie,' Mrs Bloom came out of the kitchen and called, 'Margaret's here.' Her voice was anxious.

Mr Bloom was already out of the room. He stopped and turned before climbing the stairs, his face red with anger. 'Take her into the office,' he said abruptly.

'Albie. What is it?' Mrs Bloom looked embarrassed.

'I've spilt some sherry down my shirt, I've got to change it. I'll be down in a minute.' He continued on up the stairs.

Mrs Bloom turned to Polly, who smiled weakly. 'I'm sorry about that. You go on into his office. David's in there, he'll entertain you for a moment or two till my husband comes down. I'll bring in the tea.'

Polly was flustered, and felt awkward at overhearing her boss's argument. She pushed the door open. The room smelt of leather and cigar smoke. It was manly. A large mahogany desk covered with patterns, papers and swatches, stood in front of one of the two long windows. At the other window stood David. She walked into the room.

David, with his hand resting lightly on the rich, heavy brocade green curtains was idly gazing out. He didn't move when she walked in. Polly followed his gaze. A long sweep of fresh green grass stretched from the house down to an orchard. The trees were covered with blossom, waving in the breeze, blowing the petals around like confetti. In the borders, daffodils were nodding and bending excitedly in the March wind.

Polly gave a little cough. David spun round.

'Margaret, I'm so sorry, have you been there long?'

'No, only a few moments. That's a lovely view.' She walked towards him.

'Yes it is, isn't it? The fun Sarah and I have had here over the years. Making snowmen in the winter, bonfires in the autumn. Chasing around on the grass.'

'You are very lucky.'

He turned. 'Yes, I suppose in a way we are.'

The door opened and Mrs Bloom walked in carrying a tray covered with a white lace tray-cloth. The tray was beautifully laid out with cakes, biscuits, and expensive-looking thin china. Polly couldn't help but compare it to her mother's thick cups.

'David, you haven't asked Margaret to sit down.'

'I was busy admiring your garden,' Polly said quickly.

'Yes, it is rather nice at this time of the year. Now, do come and sit down. Do you take milk and sugar?'

'Yes please, one.' Polly sat gingerly on the edge of one of the tan-coloured leather armchairs.

'Cake?' Mrs Bloom handed Polly a plate. 'We should have gone into the drawing-room, it's far cosier in there.'

'Oh no, thank you. I only came to deliver the patterns, I didn't expect tea.'

'Sarah said we were to look after you. She thinks very highly of you, young lady.'

Polly blushed and looked down as Mr Bloom walked in.

'Well, you didn't have any trouble finding us then, Margaret?' he said, taking the cup and saucer his wife offered.

Polly shook her head. She felt totally out of place. She was terrified she was going to spill her tea, or drop cake crumbs, or, even worse, choke. She noticed Mr Bloom looking angrily towards David.

'Sarah tells us you're getting married at Easter.' Mrs Bloom's smile was warm.

'Yes. Miss Bloom is letting me make me frock, er, dress at work.'

'I understand you designed it yourself?'

Again Polly could feel her face colour. 'Yes,' she said softly, and gulped down her tea. 'I think I'd better be going,' she announced the minute she'd finished. 'The patterns are on your desk, Mr Bloom.' She stood up, and so did David and his father.

'I fancy a breath of fresh air. Would you mind if I walked to the underground with you?' David took her cup and saucer.

Polly looked amazed. 'Well, well yes . . . Er, no . . . if you want to.'

'I'll just get my hat.' With that he quickly disappeared out of the door, and seconds later he stood in the doorway. 'Ready?' he asked.

Outside he held her elbow as she walked down the steps. On the pavement he quickly moved to the road side, so protecting her from the traffic. She was embarrassed and flushed with excitement. Ron never did anything so polite.

'I hope you didn't mind me coming along with you? You see I just had to get out of that house.'

She looked at him, interested. 'Why?' She was immediately cross with herself for asking such a prying question. He must have known she'd heard them arguing. So she added light-heartedly, 'You all seem very happy.'

'Well, I suppose we are in a way, but you see my father and . . . Did you overhear what . . .?'

'Well . . . Yes, some of it.'

'My father can be very . . .'

'I don't think you should be talking to me like this,' Polly quickly interrupted. Although she was intrigued, she said guardedly, 'It's very kind of you to walk me to the station, but after all, I am only one of your father's workers.'

David stopped. 'I find you very easy to talk to, and I find this so-called class thing ridiculous. University certainly changes a lot of your attitudes. Look, how about you having a drink with me? There's a nice little pub near the heath.'

'I don't know. It's a bit early.'

'Have you got to get home then?'

'Well, no . . .'

'That's settled, they'll be open by the time we get there.'

They continued talking about the weather, commenting on the colours of the flowers in the park, laughing at children playing, chatting about everything in general, yet nothing in particular.

Inside the pub, Polly stood in front of the inglenook fireplace and rubbed her hands together. The heat from the fire warmed her.

'Cold?' asked David.

'Only my hands.'

'What would you like to drink?'

'I'll have a gin and orange please.'

He laughed. 'Are you old enough?'

'I'm eighteen,' she said light-heartedly.

David walked over to the bar, and Polly settled herself at a table near the fire. She looked at her surroundings. This wasn't like the spit-and-sawdust pubs round her way. This was all oak beams and polished brass.

'It is a bit early, that's why it's empty,' said David, putting the drinks on the table and sitting opposite her. 'You should see it in here in the summer, you can't move.'

'It's very nice.'

'Margaret, the reason I asked if I could walk you to the station was because I need to talk to someone. I know I shouldn't bother you with my problems.'

She put her glass on the table and laughed. 'You've got problems. You live in that lovely house, go to University, and you think you've got problems.' She stopped and ran her finger round the rim of her glass. 'I'm sorry, I shouldn't have said that. It's not my place to . . .'

'No, I'm sorry, it's a family matter and I shouldn't involve . . . Well, you know what I mean?' His deep-brown eyes looked sad. 'But I would like to have the opinion of someone else.'

Polly suddenly felt pity for this rich, good-looking young man, and on the spur of the moment her thoughts went to Shirley. If she were here now, sitting in a pub with him wanting to pour out his sorrows, she would be like a cat on heat, all over him. 'David – you don't mind me calling you David, do you?'

'No, why should I?' He smiled. 'I love the way you hold your head on one side, it's very becoming.'

Polly blushed and quickly turned her head. 'That's because I can only see out of one eye.'

'I'm very sorry, I shouldn't have . . . It was very thoughtless of me.' He took a cigarette from the packet he'd put on the table earlier, and banged the end hard on the table. 'Sorry, cigarette?'

Polly took one and leaned forward for David to light it. She had no intention of going into details about her eye, and felt rather pleased that after all these years of holding her head on one side, someone should think it was becoming. 'Thanks.' She drew deeply on the cigarette. 'I am only one of your father's employees, you know. A common girl from Rotherhithe.'

He laughed awkwardly. 'But a very important one, I might add. Anyway, I don't think you're common, you are very nice, and I'm not a snob.'

'That's as may be, but you're upset at what happened between you and your father, and I don't think I should hear what you want to say.'

'Good God, girl, it's not that dramatic. Besides, you and your people are a little more down to earth.'

'You mean we call a spade a spade.'

'Well, yes. And I feel after talking to you that I could ask your opinion on something. You seem very level-headed.'

'Thank you.' She looked at her watch.

'I'm keeping you.'

'No, not to worry. Well, what is it you want my advice on. Come on, tell Auntie Polly.'

He laughed a little more easily this time. 'I'm glad you have a sense of humour. Well, as you know, I'm at University, and a lot of the chaps there have been training to fly. Well, today, just before you arrived, I told my father I wanted to quit Uni and join the Air Force. To cut a long story short he almost jumped out of his chair – that's how he came to spill his drink down himself – and had to rush upstairs to change his shirt. Would you like another drink?'

Polly shook her head.

'Well, back to the plot. No, joking aside. I feel that with the political situation as it is, we should be ready if anything happens.'

Polly looked alarmed. 'You mean a war? But Mr Chamberlain said . . .'

'We all know what he said, but can we trust Hitler? You forget I'm a Jew, and I can't forgive him for what he's doing to the Jews in other parts of Europe.'

'I've seen it at the pictures.'

'Yes, it is pretty horrific.'

'I heard you tell your father that.'

David toyed with his glass. 'I expect you also heard me ask him what he thought about the state of affairs . . .'

'Yes, and what he said I thought was very nice.' Polly sat back in her chair. 'Do any of your relations still live in Europe?'

'No, my great-grandparents came to England years ago.'

'Were they in the rag trade?'

'My grandfather was; he had a small bespoke tailor's in Whitechapel. That was before my grandfather and grandmother were killed. It was my father who wanted to expand, and so he started the factory. You can see why he's so against war. Not that I . . . Well, you know. I think we should be prepared. Anyway, Aunt Polly,' he leaned forward and peered at her, 'What do you think of my dilemma?'

She laughed. 'Sorry, I shouldn't laugh, but why don't you give it a little longer, just to see how things develop? There may not be a war, then you would have given it all up for nothing.'

'I don't know. You see I love flying.'

'You break up for the summer holidays like the kids at school, don't you?'

He nodded.

'Well then, wait till then, and if things don't look any different – chuck it. Are you going to work in the factory?'

'No, father wants me to be a lawyer.'

'Oh, very posh.'

He took hold of her hand and kissed it. 'D'you know, you are an angel. And I'll do what you suggest. That'll please Sarah as well, she's been getting a little cross with me lately – but that's another story.'

Polly pulled her hand away and giggled. 'Don't be daft. Look, I must go, thanks for the drink.'

'Seriously Margaret, thank you. It's nice to have someone to talk to who doesn't try to put their will over you.'

Polly looked puzzled. 'I can't imagine anyone doing that to you.' She stood up.

'I'll walk you to the station.'

On the train home her thoughts were full of David Bloom. He was nice, she found him easy to talk to, and she liked him. Could he possibly like her too? She told herself she shouldn't even be thinking such things and the minute she stepped into the Penn's Place kitchen she was brought firmly down to earth.

'Yer late, where yer been?' her mother shouted. 'Yer dinner's in the oven, must be all dried up be now.' Doris Perkins scowled up from the sock she was darning.

'Sorry about that, Mum. I had to go out.'

'Why didn't yer tell 'er next door yer'd be late?'

'I thought I'd be back in time,' yelled Polly from the scullery as she took her dinner out of the oven. She screwed her nose up at the unappetizing-looking meal.

'Where yer been then?'

Polly sat at the kitchen table. 'I had to go over to the Blooms' house.'

Doris Perkins' head jerked up. 'Hobnobbing wiv that lot now, are yer? Wot d'yer 'ave ter go over there fer?'

'I had to take some patterns.'

''Ave they got a smashing 'ouse?' asked Grandad.

Polly nodded, swallowed hard, and said enthusiastically. 'You should see it, the carpets, the garden, it's really lovely.'

'Where d'they live?' asked Grandad, his curiosity roused.

'Out Putney way.' Polly looked up when the kitchen door opened. 'Hello Ron, sit down, I won't be long.'

'Who lives out Putney way?' he asked.

'The Blooms. I've been over to their house this afternoon. I'll tell you all about it later. We still putting the curtains up tonight?'

'Yer, if they're ready?'

'I managed to finish them yesterday lunch-time.'

Two hours later Polly was standing on a chair when Ron walked into the bedroom. 'I love this place. We were ever so lucky to get it.'

'Got influence, ain't I?' He came over and ran his hand up her leg.

'Stop it,' she giggled. 'You'll have me fall off – and mind me stockings.'

'I'll finish putting 'em up if yer like.' He helped her down and, holding her close, whispered, 'That bed looks inviting.' He kissed her passionately, and she responded.

'Come on, let's try it out,' he whispered.

'I don't know.'

''Ere, yer ain't still gonner be funny about it, are yer?'

'But Ron . . .'

'Christ we're gitting 'itched next week. Yer ain't scared, are yer?'

'A bit.'

He began undoing her blouse. 'Come on Pol, I promise I won't 'urt yer,' he said softly, and gently pushed her back on the bed.

Chapter 7

Everybody had gone to the church. Grandad was in his bedroom putting the finishing touches to his attire.

Polly was sitting alone at the dressing-table in her bedroom, waiting for the car to come back from taking her mother and Shirley to the church. She pulled on the long point of the tightly fitting sleeve that covered the back of her hand. She ran her fingers over the silky fabric and turned her hand over to admire the row of tiny covered buttons that went from her wrist to her elbow. Sally, the finisher, had worked lovingly on these for many hours during her lunch breaks.

She adjusted the wax flowers of her mock orange-blossom headdress, and tenderly caressed the pearls she had carefully entwined through them. Polly had been very surprised, and touched, when her mother brought her own headdress from out of an old paper bag that had been tucked away at the back of the cupboard, and insisted that Polly weave the pearls in with her flowers. She never knew her mother had kept it hidden all these years, or was so sentimental. When Polly asked her about her wedding dress, she told her that it had long since been cut up for blouses. She felt sad thinking about that, and put in a few more kirby grips to hold her long veil secure.

'Wouldn't Dad have loved to be here today,' she whispered to the mirror. Leaning forward she peered at herself, and studied her blind eye. It didn't show so much now, and the family never mentioned it. Today was her wedding day. Did she really love Ron? What was love? Would she be happy? Her mum had said that at eighteen she wasn't old enough to know her own mind. Perhaps she didn't, but what other chance would she have had of getting married and leaving home if she had turned Ron down? He was good to her. They had furnished their two rooms and the scullery nicely. She was very lucky; some of the women at the factory only lived in one room, and they had a couple of kids.

Grandad came into the room and stood behind her. 'You look lovely.' He put his hands on her shoulders. She turned and kissed the back of the old, gnarled, brown-spotted hand. 'Yer mum looked nice in that posh 'at.'

'I'm glad you're giving me away,' she said.

'I feel very honoured.'

'I'm going to miss you,' she whispered.

'You're not living that far away.' He sniffed, and taking his new, snowy-white handkerchief from his top pocket, wiped his nose.

'Grandad. I bought that for show.'

'Too late. Come on, the car should be 'ere soon.'

Polly pulled the veil over her face and stood up. She smoothed down the shiny white satin that clung to her slender hips, making her look tall and elegant. Her veil, a froth of white net, fell to the floor. 'Do I look all right?'

The old man swallowed hard. 'Yer looks a little smasher. Now come on, pick up yer flowers.'

She laughed. 'These, my dear Grandad, are very expensive lilies – arum lilies.' She kissed his cheek.

'I don't care if they're bloody Jeanie's, Jeanie wiv the light brown 'air – now git a move on. Fank Gawd the weather's cheered up a bit. Look, the sun's shining.' He moved over to the window. 'Yer knows what they say, "'Appy the bride the sun shines on terday."'

As she arrived at the church Polly was thrilled to see Miss Bloom standing outside and, as she peeped through the porch, was surprised at the number of people inside.

Shirley looked very nice in her pale-blue satin dress, and she fussed around Polly making sure her veil and dress would flow out behind her as she walked down the aisle.

All the Bells were in the pews behind Ron, and most of the girls from the factory were on her side. She was pleased; she had been worried that her mum and Billy would be sitting alone. As the organ began playing, Ron and Sid moved into position, and Polly started to walk down the aisle. Billy turned, grinned, and gave her a wink. She smiled back at him. That had been another bone of contention – her mother had wanted Billy to give her away. Polly squeezed her grandad's arm; smiling, he patted her hand.

The wedding reception, with plenty of booze and noise, was being held in the Bells' house. After cutting the cake, Polly helped Shirley hand it round. As she passed Ron he grabbed her hand.

'Leave that, Mrs Bell.'

She giggled. 'Mrs Bell, sounds funny.'

'Let's go upstairs.'

'I can't. What will everybody say if we suddenly disappeared?'

'Me dad'll say bloody good luck to 'im. Yer gotter git out o' that frock. Come on, I'll 'elp yer.' He pulled her close.

Polly glanced across at her mother, but she was deep in conversation with Mrs Bell, and Shirley had just slipped outside with Sid.

'Me other frock's in me bedroom next door.'

'Come on, then, they won't miss us now Fred's gitting 'em going wiv 'is accordion.'

'Just going to change,' she mouthed to Grandad.

He nodded and gave her a wink.

They rushed out of the house and into the silence of the house next door. Ron closed the door behind them and, seizing her arms, kissed her long and hard.

'Polly, yer look smashing,' he croaked, nuzzling his head in her neck.

'Careful Ron, mind me veil. Let's go upstairs, then you can give me a hand to get out of this lot.'

'Cor, not 'alf.' Laughing, he raced up the stairs two at a time.

In the bedroom she sat at the dressing-table and, while she studied Ron through the mirror, she removed her headdress. He carefully undid the tiny covered buttons down the back of her dress; when he'd finished, he pulled her to her feet. She glanced in the mirror at their reflection. They did make a striking couple, he so dark against her blonde hair. Slowly he slipped the dress off her shoulders, letting it fall to the floor. He studied her for a moment or two, standing before him in her white cami-knickers.

'Christ, y'er lovely,' he whispered, before clumsily pulling down the thin straps to reveal her small white breasts. He began kissing them, and impatiently pushed her back on the bed.

Polly was a little apprehensive: this was her mother's bed. True, she was no longer a virgin since they had done it in the flat last week. But she hadn't thought it had been that much to rave about, although Ron had told her it always hurt at first. Perhaps this time would be better. She lay back and enjoyed the sensation of him exploring her body; cupping her breasts in his hands he kissed and licked her protruding nipples. It sent wonderful shivers all over her, and her stomach tightened as he tried to enter her.

'Relax,' he whispered stroking the inside of her thighs.

The couple of gins were helping her do that. This time it was far nicer, and now she was married she had no need to feel guilty. She wondered if Ron had been with any other girls; he seemed to know what to do. With her eyes closed she just let the pleasurable feeling wash over her. But, to her distress, she found it wasn't Ron's face that filled her thoughts. It was David Bloom's. However, as Ron kissed her again and she felt herself respond, she succeeded in banishing David from her mind. And afterwards she felt silly at having allowed herself even to contemplate the possibility of someone as grand as David Bloom.

* * *

On the whole Polly was happy being married, and five months later she still, thankfully, wasn't pregnant. Although she loved children, she didn't want any just yet and although Ron was keen that they carry on trying, she was less enthusiastic, both about the trying and the possible result. She loved being as they were: away from home and independent. They could come and go as they pleased, and no one would nag if they got home late. Furnishing her flat, and having Ron to cook and clean for was wonderful, and she didn't want anything to spoil it. Nor did she want to have to leave her job. There was a lot of talk about a war, and Grandad said that if the Germans started it again, it could be even nastier this time. Despite the doom and gloom about an impending war, Polly was determined she wasn't going to let it worry her. The summer had been warm and sunny, and tomorrow being the first Monday in August, they'd been given the day off. Perhaps she could persuade Ron to take her up the river and have a picnic.

She looked out of her bedroom window to see if Shirley was coming along the road. They were supposed to be going to Petticoat Lane. Ron had left home very early that morning – he said his dad had to see someone, and they would be going on to the pub for their usual Sunday-morning pint.

Impatiently she looked at her watch. It had gone nine, Shirley was late. If she left it much longer it wouldn't be worth going. Although she had prepared the vegetables, she still had to get back in time to cook Ron's dinner. Polly went into the kitchen, and was relieved a few minutes later to hear someone knocking on the front door. She ran down the stairs and flung the door open. 'You're a bit late, I didn't think you were coming.'

'I told yer yesterday I'd be 'ere.'

'You all right? You don't look too well.'

Shirley didn't answer. She rushed past Polly, down the passage, through the side door and out to the closet, with Polly following close behind.

Slowly she came out, wiping her mouth with her handkerchief.

'You look awful, what's the matter?'

'D'yer know, sometimes you can be so bloody fick. I've got a bleedin' bun in the oven, that's what's the matter.'

Polly put her hand to her mouth. 'Oh no, whose is it?'

'Whose d'yer bloody well fink? That bleedin' bruvver of yours, that's whose. I feel a bit better now. Come on, let's go upstairs.'

Polly looked at Shirley and felt a great pity for her. 'Does he know?' she asked, pushing the kitchen door open.

Shirley shook her head. 'Not yet. And don't you go saying nufink to 'im, or yer muvver.'

'Course not.'

'How far gone are you?'

'Four months.'

'What?' Polly quickly counted on her fingers.

'December,' volunteered Shirley.

'How have you managed to keep it to yourself all this time?'

'I've been all right till now, and I was 'oping it'd go away.'

Polly stood staring at her. 'I thought you didn't look too good the other day.' And almost speaking her thoughts said out loud. 'Our Sid's.'

'Yeah.'

'Will he marry you?'

'Shouldn't fink so. Anyway, can't say I fancy being tied to 'im fer the rest of me natural. And don't ask me if I've tried ter git rid of it.' Shirley slumped into a chair at the table. 'Christ, I've 'ad so many 'ot barfs I've very nearly burnt all the skin orf me arse, and I've drunk so much gin I was in a drunken stupor all last Sunday. And I've 'ad so much syrup of figs, I fought I'd finish up inside out.' Shirley laughed. 'Don't look ser shocked.'

Polly gently lowered herself down in a chair. 'What you going to do?'

'Me mum's a good sort. She don't want me to go round to that old Mrs Creasy, she's a bit of a butcher. She said she'll look after it, bring it up like one of 'er own. One more in the 'ouse won't make any difference.'

'What did your dad say?'

The grin disappeared from her face. ''E don't know yet. Mind you, 'e ain't got a lot of room ter shout – me mum was expecting our Vera 'fore she got married.'

'At least he married her. That brother of mine!' Polly began to get very angry.

'It takes two ter make a bargain, don't fergit.'

'You don't have to defend him for me. I know him too well, he'll go merrily through life taking what he can.'

'Stop carrying on. 'E ain't all bad. Don't fergit when 'e went ter clink 'e didn't squeal on your Ron.'

'Ron?' repeated Polly, somewhat surprised.

'Yer don't fink Ron's all sweet and innocent, do yer?'

'I . . . But . . .'

''Ow d'yer fink yer got this place and all this nice stuff?' Shirley looked round the neatly furnished room.

'I'm helping with the repayments on the gas stove,' said Polly, following Shirley's gaze, pleased with the way she had tastefully furnished their kitchen. It looked attractive with its green chintz curtains and the plain green chenille table-cloth. In the middle of the table stood an elegant cut-glass vase. It was a wedding present from the Blooms. Above the mantelpiece hung an oval mirror with coloured flowers climbing up the sides. That was from her family. Ron's mum and dad gave them all the lovely crockery that filled the glass cabinet. All the cups had handles, and everything matched. She knew he got it cheap at the market, but didn't mind that.

'I know, but 'e does as much wheeling and dealing as yer bruvver. In fact,' Shirley lowered her voice, 'I'd say 'e was the worst of the two.'

'What d'you mean?' She knew Ron didn't deny her anything for their tiny flat. There was the brand-new gas cooker in the scullery. In the bedroom she had a beautiful walnut bedroom

89

suite; it cost forty-seven pounds nineteen and eleven pence, and, as far as she knew, Ron was paying it off weekly. She loved it. It had a matching headboard with lights and pretty pink shades fixed to it, and they could switch off the light without getting out of bed.

'Shirley, what d'you mean, Ron's the worst of the two?'

''Nuf said. I'm all right now, come on, let's be off.'

Polly was home long before Ron. She hurriedly put the meat in the oven, and all the time her mind kept going over what Shirley had told her earlier on.

It had gone three, where was he? The pubs closed at two. She paced the floor, getting more and more angry as she waited for him to come home. Had he seen Shirley? Had Sid told him Shirley knew what he got up to? Was he involved with Sid?

Polly heard the front door shut, and she stiffened with temper. She didn't want stolen goods in her flat, or things bought with stolen money. She listened to his footsteps on the stairs.

''Allo love, all right then?' He walked in and gave her the usual kiss on the cheek. 'Dinner smells good.'

Polly didn't move.

'What's up?'

'Shirley's expecting. Ron, where did the money come from for all this?'

'All what?'

'All this furniture and stuff.'

'From the shop, yer knows that.'

'Where did the money come from?' she repeated more forcefully.

'From work. Yer know, the market.' There was a biting edge to his voice. ''Ere, what's all this about?'

'Was you with Sid when he did that robbery?'

'What?' His face contorted with anger. 'Who says I was?'

'No one. I'm only asking. I know you're always together. Ron, where did the money come from for the wedding and all this?' She waved her arm round the room. 'Did you get it honestly?'

'I told yer, I works fer it, so mind yer own business.' He laughed. 'What's this about our Shirley? Is it Sid's?'

She nodded. 'This *is* my business. Did you pinch it?'

'Who's been talking? Ding Dong? She gonner marry Sid?'

'No.'

'What's she gonner do then?'

'Your mum's going to look after it. Ron, you didn't answer my question.'

'That's just like 'er, don't care about anybody else, only 'er bleedin' self. Don't she fink our mum's got enough ter do wivout looking after 'er kid?' He sat at the table. 'Where's me dinner then? I'm starving.'

'Ron,' Polly raised her voice. 'You didn't answer my question.'

'Listen gel, what yer don't know about won't 'urt yer, so I've got nufink ter say.'

'I think you and me had better have a little talk.'

'What about? 'Ere, you're not finking of looking after 'er kid, are yer?'

'No, I told you, I don't want any children just yet.'

'Oh yes, I forgot, yer wants ter git on wiv yer career,' he said sarcastically.

'Well, yes.'

'I don't know why yer bovvers wiv a tin-pot firm like that. She didn't even 'ave the decency ter come in the church when we got married.'

'She's Jewish, perhaps she didn't like to. Anyway, she came to see me outside the church. And I happen to like working there.'

'Well yer would, wouldn't yer, just sitting answering the phone and doing yer drawings all day. Yer don't call that a day's work, do yer? And fer kangaroos as well. I'm surprised the blackshirts ain't busted their place up.'

'Don't say things like that, they are very nice people. Anyway, you used to be interested in my job, and the Blooms.'

'They ain't ever invited us ter their house, 'ave they?'

'Let's face it, Ron, we're not exactly in their class.' She laughed. 'You should have seen me when I had tea there, I was like a fish out of water.'

'Not in their class,' he mimicked. 'I may not talk proper, but I've got it up 'ere.' He touched his head.

'I sometimes wonder why you were so eager to marry me. Did you think, no you . . .'

'I married you,' he interrupted, 'fer lots of reasons. One, I wanted ter git out of me mum's 'ouse. Four boys in one room didn't give us a lot of privacy – me bruvvers are a nosy lot of buggers. And the other fing was that I wanted a wife who'd stop at 'ome and look after the kids.'

'You've got a long wait for the second one.'

'Yer know what they're all saying, don't yer? They don't fink I've got it in me. What's wrong wiv yer? Yer only seem to want it when yer 'alf cut and then I'm not ser sure. Even me old man said terday 'e wouldn't stand fer it. Told me ter prove meself a man, and carry on the family name.'

'He's got the twins and James to do that.'

'I'm a bloody laughing stock, I am.'

'Why? Because I want to stay at my job? We've only been married a few months, what did they want me to do, walk up the aisle in the puddin club?'

'You would 'ave if I'd 'ad me way.' He got up and went into the scullery. 'I've made up me mind, Pol,' he shouted. 'And you ain't gonner stop me. You mark my words, by this time next year we'll 'ave a kid running round 'ere.' Walking back into the kitchen he asked, 'Right, where's me dinner?'

'Get it yourself. I'm going out . . .' she yelled and stalked down the stairs thinking, half angrily, half amused that anyway there couldn't be a kid running around next year even if she were to fall now – they didn't start to walk till they were over a year old!

Chapter 8

'Hello Mum.'

Doris Perkins looked up from pouring out a cup of tea. ''Allo. What you doing 'ere this time a day? Where's Ron, next door?'

'No, at home.'

Sid didn't lift his head from the large, unappetizing-looking plateful of dinner in front of him. It consisted of shrivelled roast potatoes, a mound of yellow cabbage and meat. Polly couldn't identify the meat. It was dark brown and curled at the edges through being kept warm in the oven, seemingly for hours. A hard dark-brown ring of dried gravy decorated the rim of the plate.

'Any tea left in that pot?' asked Polly.

'What's wrong wiv Ron?' asked her mother.

'Nothing.'

'Why ain't yer at 'ome gitting 'is dinner then?'

She didn't answer, and took a cup from the dresser.

The clatter of Sid's knife and fork stopped, and he studied a piece of meat stuck on the end of his fork. He pointed it at Polly. 'Yer muvver asked yer a question.' He popped the meat in his mouth and the clatter of his cutlery began again.

'You two 'ad a row?' asked Mrs Perkins.

Polly nodded, and took a bite out of the piece of cake she'd picked up.

'Well don't fink yer coming waltzing back 'ere every time yer 'as a row, cos yer ain't. Go on, go back ter yer old man.'

'Where's Grandad?'

'Upstairs, and don't change the subject.'

'Is he all right?'

'Not too good. Where're yer going, young lady?'

'To see Grandad.'

'You come back 'ere. Don't you walk away from me when I'm talking to yer.'

Ignoring her mother, Polly went upstairs. She knocked gently on the old man's door.

'Who is it?'

Peeping round the door she said, 'It's only me.'

'Polly love.' He struggled to sit up, his face crinkling into a broad smile. 'Come over 'ere and sit down.' He patted the bed. ''Ow are yer?'

She kissed his cheek. 'I'm all right, what about you? You don't look very well.'

'I'm all the better fer seeing you.' He took hold of her hand. 'That's a pretty frock, yer looks very nice. Ron downstairs?'

She smiled. 'No, we've had a row – only a little one.'

He grinned. 'Don't s'pose it's the first, and it won't be the last.'

'Has the doctor been to see you?'

''E popped in yesterday.'

'What did he say?'

'Nufink new, just that me old pipes are wearing out. What about you? That's a nice little place yer got round Weaver Street.'

'I only wish it was big enough for you to come and live with us.'

'Go on wiv yer, yer don't want an old man like me 'anging round yer.'

'Oh yes I do.'

Their conversation was cut short when a knocking on the front door was answered, and Ron's loud voice carried up the stairs.

''Allo Mrs P, where is she then?'

Polly quickly kissed Grandad. 'I'd better go. I don't want him coming up here making a scene.'

Stealthily she made her way down the stairs, careful to avoid the creaking sixth one. She stopped at the bottom. Fortunately the kitchen door had been pulled to. Ron's voice was muffled. Polly crept along the passage and out into the warm sunshine, quietly closing the front door behind her.

She stood at Shirley's gate for a short while, pondering whether or not to go in. She decided against that; Shirley might well be having a nap after traipsing round Petticoat Lane all morning, and Polly knew Ron would go in there looking for her. She didn't want a to-do in there. Their flat was only a few streets away, and she wondered about going home or to the pictures. She looked at her watch. Half-past four – the big picture would have started by now.

It was a lovely afternoon, and walking along the road, swinging her handbag, she smiled to herself. Her yellow cotton frock hugged her slim figure, accentuating her small, round, firm breasts, and clinging to her hips. With the brim of her white straw hat pulled well down over her blind eye, she felt good.

How differently she dressed now. Miss Bloom gave her the pick of the frocks that didn't come up to Bloom's high standard, and at cost. Polly always made hers a little individual – adding something here, or removing something there, bringing plenty of compliments from customers. She was happy, and knowing she looked well-dressed gave her confidence, making her step light.

Her thoughts continued to run. She'd not done so bad considering she was only eighteen. She was married, with a nice home, and a good job she loved. Of course she'd love to be a designer, and earn lots of money, and see her frocks in the shops. She grinned. To be a bit like Sarah Bloom, really. Not like Shirley and the girls on the factory floor, who only thought of blokes and babies. But she daren't say anything to Ron or Mum, they wouldn't understand. Grandad would though. But then if there was a war, everything would change. She

95

shuddered. She didn't want thoughts like that filling her head on such a lovely day. She pulled her white lacy cardigan round her shoulders and muttered to herself, 'And I'm not going to give it all up and stay at home to have babies. Well, not yet anyway, whatever Ron and his family think.' Polly knew she could get round him in time.

The warm night air was still and sultry, and the bedroom window was wide open. The lace curtain fluttered gently when it caught a slight breeze. The bang against the front door startled Polly: she was in bed and must have dozed off; the book she'd been reading had fallen to the floor. She looked at the clock — it was almost midnight. Ron's bad language, and his fumbling to get the key in the lock, told her he was drunk. Quickly she turned out the light and pretended to be asleep. She didn't want a row at this time of night.

'Sod it,' he cursed, staggering into the bedroom and falling over a pair of shoes.

Polly cringed, and sneaked a look over the bedclothes. The sight of him hopping round the room on one leg, trying to take his trousers off, made her laugh. She quickly stuffed the sheet in her mouth to stop any noise escaping.

He kept losing his balance and falling to the floor. Finally he collapsed on top of the bed, and lay very still. Polly turned over and sighed with relief when the snoring began.

It was the pain that woke her. His fingernails were digging into the soft flesh of her breast, and it hurt. His other hand was getting tangled in her nightdress as he groped around the tops of her legs and over her flat stomach.

'Ron, what are you doing?' His full weight rolled on top of her; he was forcing her legs apart. 'Ron, get off. Stop it, you're hurting me,' she yelled.

'I told yer I was putting yer up the spout, and I'm starting right now.' He covered her mouth with his.

His beery breath made her gasp, and she twisted and turned in an effort to free herself. His nails dug deeper into her breast, squeezing it till she cried out in pain. He tried to enter her. Tensing her muscles, Polly brought her tightly clenched fists up, and pummelled his chest in an effort to push him away. He laughed, and sat back on his haunches, his straight black hair dangling over his face, hiding his eyes from her angry gaze.

Silently towering over her, he brought the back of his hand swiftly across her face.

Her teeth jarred; she was terrified he'd knocked some loose. She was too stunned to cry. The taste of the warm sticky blood oozing from the side of her mouth made her whimper.

'Now shut up and open yer legs, or yer'll git anuver one.'

Turning her head, she quietly did as she was told.

Polly was glad it was a bank holiday and she didn't have to go to work. The cold compress she'd been applying all day to the side of her face had helped to reduce some of the swelling.

Ron got up and left the house without breakfast, or any mention of last night, or her face. For most of the morning she was still in a state of shock. She was very angry with Ron, and felt very sorry for herself. She hadn't had a lot to do with drunks. Sometimes Billy and Sid had a drop too much and came home drunk, but they'd only fall about, making her laugh – they were never violent. Not that anybody would have dared to be in front of her mother.

Polly looked in the mirror again and gently touched her swollen face, 'What will Mum say when she sees this?' she said to her reflection.

Polly knew a lot of men beat their wives when they'd had a few drinks. Some of the women at the factory often came to work with black eyes. She wasn't going to be one of those cower-down women who lived in fear of their husbands. All day she plotted and planned. The next time Ron tried anything like that, she'd be ready for him, and give him the same treatment.

It was late when he finally came home, and she was in bed. He wasn't drunk, and quietly crept in beside her without a word. When his arm came across her, she automaticaly tensed and, slipping her hand under the pillow, tightened her grip on the poker she'd hidden under there.

'Good night love,' he whispered.

The following morning, Polly applied more make-up than usual in an attempt to hide the bruise, which was now a collection of multi-coloured hues.

'Christ, what 'appened ter you? Walk inter a bus?' was Shirley's reaction.

Sarah Bloom was a little kinder. 'I won't ask what happened, but it looks as if you have walked into a door.'

Her mother said nothing, but Polly noted the look of horror on her face when she brought in the tea.

For the next two days things were very strained between her and Ron, and she only spoke to him when necessary.

On Wednesday evening Ron was reading his newspaper. 'The news ain't ser good.' He looked up. 'Wouldn't be surprised if we didn't 'ave a war. I might 'ave ter go in the Army if they start calling up my age group. Market traders ain't exempt, yer know.'

Polly didn't answer and continued piling up the tea things on the tray to take into the scullery. She had her back to Ron and he didn't see the concern on her face.

Since her conversation with David Bloom before she was married, she had become more and more worried about the threat of war, and what was happening to the Jews. She had watched the newsreels with alarm when Oswald Mosley's blackshirts began smashing shop windows belonging to Jews living in Britain.

'It says 'ere we're all gonner be issued wiv gas-masks.'

Polly sat at the table. She was thinking about Grandad. He knew all about the fear and terror of being gassed.

'Did you 'ear me? 'Ow long's this silent treatment going on for? I dunno what yer making such a fuss about.'

She jumped up and caught sight of her reflection in the mirror. 'My God, you're an unfeeling bugger. Look, look at my face? Don't you think I've got enough of a handicap with me eye?'

'Yer, well. I'm sorry about that,' he mumbled. 'But I was only after me legal rights.'

'Your rights. I'm not one of your market tarts, you know.'

He laughed. 'No, they don't struggle.'

She tossed her head. 'I'm going to bed.'

Ron jumped up and grabbed her arm.

'Let me go.'

'No. Now just you listen to me, Pol. I'm yer 'usband, and it's yer duty.'

She pushed his arm away and went into the bedroom.

That night in bed he pulled her close. When his hands began wandering over her body, she bit her lip to stem the tears, and to stop herself from crying out with fear. She shuddered when he touched her – he couldn't have enjoyed his legal right to make love to her that night.

Walking home from work the following Friday, Shirley said, 'Yer know, yer been a right bundle of joy this week.'

'Well, what do you expect me to do – walk down the road singing? Your brother did beat me up you know.'

'Come off it, Pol, one little slap. Don't yer fink yer making a bit of a mountain out of a molehill?'

'It wasn't you he hit.'

'No I know, but I've 'ad a few off 'im in the past. Trouble wiv you is no one's ever laid a finger on yer before.'

'Sid has, and what about the time me mum hit me with Grandad's whip?'

'Oh yes, sorry. I forgot the one and only.'

'You don't have to be sarky.'

'Blimey, yer wanner fink yerself lucky. I've 'ad a good few 'idings in me time, I can tell yer. 'Ad the belt off me dad more than once, and the buckle end when 'e was drunk. Christ, I can remember when 'e gave me a wallop just fer giggling at the table.' She laughed. ''Ere, d'yer remember that time when we were kids and we sneaked off down the cemetery, and took all

99

the ribbons off those wreaths on that grave?'

Polly nodded.

'Well, I got anuver bloody good 'iding fer that. You were a crafty cow, you 'id yours. And I got anuver one fer saying the dead person buried under the ground didn't want 'em. By the way, what did you do with yours?'

'I was terrified me mum would find out so I hid them. Kept them for years, then I used them for trimming our dolls' clothes.' Polly smiled.

'That's better. Come on, Pol, cheer up. What was it over? Wouldn't yer let 'im 'ave a bit?'

Polly grinned. 'Something like that. But that don't give him the right to hit me.'

'You did say for better or worse, and me mum says you should always let 'em 'ave it. It's their right.'

'Don't you start. I'm fed up with being told what's his right, and my duty.'

'Sorry, I'm sure. Look Pol, who yer upsetting – only yerself. Tell yer what, let's go to the pictures ternight.'

'I don't know,' she hesitated for a moment or two then said cheerfully. 'Yes I will, come round about seven.'

'That's more like it,' laughed Shirley. 'Next time, bring yer knee up, that'll stop 'is capers.'

'That's what you should have done, then you wouldn't be looking so green round the gills.'

'Boody cheek!' Shirley's laugh was infectious, and Polly was soon laughing with her.

When she arrived home, a lovely bunch of flowers filled the cut-glass vase. Leaning against it was a note. It simply said, 'Sorry. Love Ron.' Polly smiled. He can be such a nice – annoying – bugger at times, but I suppose he means well.

That night when she got home from the pictures there was a box of chocolates on the table, and Ron was in bed. She knew he had an early start on the market the next morning, so she tried to be quiet. She made herself a cup of cocoa and sat pondering on the past week.

The kitchen door opened and Ron came in wearing only his pants. His hair was dishevelled, and she could see he'd been asleep.

'Sorry, did I wake you?'

He rubbed his eyes. 'I must've dropped orf. Pol.' He sat next to her. 'Pol, I'm really sorry about the other night. Yer know it was the drink?'

She didn't answer.

He took hold of her hand. 'I didn't fink I'd be like that. I always said I'd be different from me old man.' He kissed her hand. 'Don't let's be . . .'

She turned to face him. He looked sad. 'Only if you promise never to do . . .' She didn't finish the conversation as his lips were on hers.

'I promise,' he whispered pulling her to her feet.

She took his hand and, leaving her cocoa, went to bed.

Polly was disappointed when at work the following morning Shirley announced she wouldn't be able to go on their usual shopping expedition that afternoon. 'Why not?' she asked.

'Me mum wants ter go up West wiv Vera, and I've got ter stay in and look after the kids. Mind you, I could bring 'em round ter your place, but they'd be inter everyfink and probably wreck the joint.'

Polly always looked forward to her Saturday afternoon shopping with Shirley, and walking home she felt very sorry for herself. 'I think I'll go round to see Grandad, he always cheers me up,' she muttered under her breath. 'And Mum won't be home, she always goes to the market on Saturday afternoons.'

Polly left Weaver Street and was very surprised when she turned the corner to see Billy and Grandad walking towards her. 'What are you doing here?'

'We've come ter see yer,' said the old man, leaning heavily on Billy's arm, his every step laboured.

'What for? And what are you doing out of bed?'

He sat on a stone coping wall that flanked the row of terraced houses, his ashen face sweating with effort as he tried to regain his breath.

'I told 'im Pol, but yer knows what a stubborn old devil 'e is.'

'Can you manage to get to my place? It's a bit nearer than home.'

'Give me a while ter git me breath back, love.'

'That's funny, cos I was just on me way round to see you.' She looked at her brother. 'Why ain't you helping Mum at the market? And what have you got there?' She pointed to a shopping bag he was carrying.

He shrugged his shoulders. 'This is what this is all about.' He opened the bag. 'It's 'is whip. I 'ad ter git it down and out the 'ouse while Mum's out shopping. She's coming 'ome with Sid terday.' He looked at the old man. ''E wanted ter bring it round ter yer. Gawd only knows what she'll say when she gits 'ome.'

The old man's face broke into a smile. 'I expect she'll 'ave a bit of a go.'

'Oh Grandad, what did you go and do that for?'

'I wanted to be sure yer gits it. I've been busy doing a lot of finking just lately, and about that to-do we 'ad wiv the police that time, remember?'

'Yes, but that's all over now, and the whip's been back on the wall for ages.'

'Always said it was yours, didn't I?'

She nodded. 'But why now, today?'

He staggered to his feet. 'I feel a bit better now – I fink we can go on. It's a lovely day fer a walk.'

Polly came back into the kitchen from the bedroom. 'More tea, Billy?'

'Why not?'

Polly refilled his cup. 'I'm glad he's having a lie down. That was silly of him to come all the way round here.'

'Yer knows what 'e's like about this fing.' Billy took the whip

102

from the shopping bag. "'E's terrified Mum or Sid's gonner git their 'ands on it. All week 'e's been on about bringing it round ter yer.'

Polly smiled and turned the whip over in her hands, gently caressing the silver handle. 'He's a funny old man, but very lovable. Look, me and Ron can bring him back after tea if you want to get off somewhere.'

'Naw, that's all right. I'm not doing anyfink ternight anyway.'

'What, a handsome young man like you not going out with a girl from the factory?'

'Na, nobody will 'ave me.'

'I don't believe that. Well look, if you're not going out, why not stop and have a bit of tea with us? We always have egg and bacon on Saturday night.'

"'Ere, that'll be smashing. Yer got a nice place 'ere,' he said, looking round. 'And yer done it out nice.'

'Thanks. I've just had a thought. What about Mum? She'll be worried stiff when she finds Grandad missing.'

'No, it's all right. I told Shirley next door we were coming round 'ere, and if we're not 'ome first she said she'll tell Mum.'

'That's good. How's your job going?'

'Not bad. I fancy a change though.'

'What? You've only been there five minutes. Where're you thinking of going?'

He played with the sugar spoon, and without looking up said, 'I'm finking of joining the Navy.'

'What?' She threw her head back and laughed. 'You don't know the front end of a boat from the back. The most water you've ever seen is the Thames. Besides, you're not old enough.'

'Not yet I ain't. But I'm dead serious Pol. It looks like we're gonner 'ave a war, and I fought if I put me age up and got in now, 'fore they calls me up, I might be able ter git on a bit.'

'You don't think there's going to be a war, do you?'

'Dunno. Don't know nufink about politics. We just 'ave ter do as we're told. I s'pose if they say go to war, we just 'ave ter go. 'Sides, I fancy seeing a bit of the world.'

'Shirley was telling me her and her mother might have to be evacuated.'

'Why's that?'

'Well Mrs Bells got Judy and James, and they're both under five, so she can go with them, and as Shirley's expecting, she can go as well.'

'Will they 'ave ter leave 'ome, even if they don't want ter?'

Polly nodded. 'I think so. Shirley said the government wants all the children out of London.'

'Where will they go?'

'Don't know. I'll miss Shirley. We've been friends for years.' Polly made rings on the table-cloth with her finger.

'Well, let's 'ope there's no war then, but I still wanner go in the Navy.'

Polly stood up and picked up the cups and saucers. As she passed him on her way to the scullery she ruffled his blond hair. 'I know why that is, you want to see all those dusky maidens in their grass skirts and beads. I bet they don't all look like Dorothy Lamour.'

He laughed. His blue eyes twinkled as he leaned forward. 'D'yer know, I ain't fought about that.'

On the way home from Polly's, Grandad was very chirpy but he decided to go to bed right away when he got in.

'I'll be round to see you as usual tomorrow,' said Polly closing his bedroom door.

Downstairs Mrs Perkins was grumbling. 'I've always said that bloody whip will be the death of 'im. You mark my words.' She turned on Billy. 'Just 'ad ter frow all your bleedin' tea away. What the bloody 'ell did 'e want ter go out for? If 'e's so worried about that fing, 'e could 'ave waited till yer come round 'ere termorrer night, then give it to yer.'

'Yer knows what a funny old bugger 'e is,' said Billy.

'Yer don't 'ave ter tell me. Me and 'im 'ave been at logger'eads about that whip fer years.'

'We'll see you tomorrow, Mum,' said Polly, wanting to

make a quick exit. She knew that conversation would be going on for the rest of the evening.

Next day as usual on a Sunday evening, Polly and Ron went to see their parents. But when they met the doctor at her mother's gate, the colour drained from Polly's face.

He smiled sadly and shook his head. 'He was a brave old man,' he said, closing the gate behind him.

Polly ran up the stairs, looked at the mound under the sheet and cried out 'No!'

Ron put his arm round her shoulder; angrily she shook him away and fell to her knees. Slowly she pulled back the sheet.

His sparse white hair was ruffled and untidy. Without his false teeth his grey cheeks had hollowed, making him look old and haggard and bony. This wasn't her beloved Grandad, whose watery blue eyes lit up when she walked into the room. Picking up the weightless, brown-spotted hand, she held it close against her cheek. Tears ran down her face and on to the cold hand.

'Come on Pol,' said Ron softly. 'Yer only upsetting yerself, yer can't bring 'im back.'

She kissed Grandad's hand and carefully tucked it under the sheet, then threw herself on to his still body and broke her heart.

Chapter 9

Polly sat at the table staring at the wireless, unable to grasp this new situation. In the brief space of three weeks she couldn't believe so much could have happened, so many lives could have changed direction. First her beloved Grandad had died. Then yesterday, Shirley had been evacuated with her mother, James and Judy. Nobody knew where they were going. And now today, Sunday 3 September 1939, the Prime Minister, Mr Chamberlain, was telling the nation that war with Germany had been declared.

To Polly, Grandad dying was the biggest blow. She knew he was ill, had been for years, but he'd appeared in such good spirits on that Saturday evening when they took him back home. He had said he was tired, but that was understandable: it was the furthest he'd walked in years.

Was that only three weeks ago? Grandad had been taken bad the next morning, and Billy had had to go for the doctor. Nobody called a doctor out on a Sunday, unless . . .

Polly was heartbroken she hadn't been with him at the end. Tears stung the back of her eyes, and she looked at the whip now curled up on her wall above her fireplace. Would she be as possessive of it as he had been? Could it be an omen that whenever it was passed to someone else, the previous owner died? She quickly admonished herself for being stupid and walked over and turned the wireless off.

'Wot d'yer do that for? I was listening ter that,' said Ron.

'It's depressing. I don't want to hear all that.'

'What's a matter wiv yer? Jesus Christ. War's just been declared – we gotter know what ter do.' He jumped up and turned it back on again.

She went into the bedroom feeling miserable and tearful. She lay on her bed and thought about Shirley. On Friday night, after she had finished work, Polly had gone round to the Bells'.

'I've packed and unpacked this bag a dozen times,' Shirley had said, throwing a blouse on the floor. 'Sod that bloody Hitler. Buggering us about like this. I dunno what ter take.'

Polly sat on the edge of Vera's bed watching her friend. 'Just take what you need for now, and what you and your mum can carry. Make sure you've got clean drawers though.'

Shirley laughed. 'Don't wear 'em.'

'So that's how you got in that state. You should have worn tin ones.'

'Your brother would 'ave brought a tin opener wiv 'im.'

'Well, yes, knowing him I expect he would. But I thought he might have at least taken a bit of interest in the baby.'

'Don't start on that again. Yer know I'm all right on me own. Anyway, what was yer saying?'

'When you get settled, perhaps your dad could come to wherever you are, that's if it's not too far away.'

'Knowing our luck we could all finish up on a bloody island in Scotland.'

'I shouldn't think so.'

Shirley sat on the bed next to Polly. 'Wiv a bit o' luck we could all be back 'ome next week. That's if Chamberlain gits it right and there ain't gonner be a war.' Shirley, six months' pregnant, put her hand in the small of her back.

'You all right?'

She nodded. 'Just a bit winded that's all. Oh Polly, wot we gonner do?' She threw her arms round Polly's neck and cried.

Polly, who had been fighting back the tears, found them rolling down her cheeks. In all the years she had known Shirley she could never remember seeing her cry like this. 'Come on now,' Polly patted her back. 'You've got to keep cheerful.'

'I'm a soppy old fing.' She wiped her eyes. ''Ere, you tried yer gas-mask on yet? Talk about looking beautiful.' She laughed, but her eyes were still moist with tears. 'Well one fing, if there's a gas attack, we'll all look alike.' She blew her nose. 'You coming ter the station wiv us termorrer?'

'Yes, Miss Bloom said I could have the morning off. Not many of the women will be in anyway, most of them are seeing their kids off.'

'Christ, it's gonner be a right barrel o' laughs in there on Monday. Good job I'll be out of it.'

'I'm going to miss you.'

'Yer, me too.' She sniffed. 'Right, let's go down and git a cuppa tea, I'll finish this later.'

On Saturday morning, Polly had gone with Shirley and her family to the station. Mr Bell tried to be cheerful as he lifted James high up on to his broad shoulders, while Mrs Bell silently wheeled Judy along in her pushchair. They had looked such a pathetic bunch, all the children with brown labels with their names and addresses tied to their coats, and brown cardboard boxes containing their gas-masks slung over their shoulders.

There had been large crowds at the station, and it upset Polly to see so many children going away. Some of the younger ones were carrying their favourite toy, others were holding pitiful little bundles which some of the bigger boys were banging their younger sisters about the head with. Occasionally a mother would catch one of them and give him a clout.

The noise in the station had been unbelievable. There were kids everywhere: some were running about shouting, while others, who were hanging on to their mother's coats, were quietly crying. The sound from the tannoy trying to give orders was crackling and breaking down, and the steam from the trains only added to the confusion.

Shirley and Polly had kissed and hugged each other for as long as they could. They had both tried to be cheerful, but Polly had panicked when she lost sight of her friend when they boarded the train.

Suddenly Polly saw her: there she was, hanging out of a window she had managed to elbow her way to. 'I'll write as soon as we get settled,' she yelled as Polly edged her way nearer to the window. Polly put out her hand; Shirley, leaning out, grabbed it, and with tears running down her face, wiped her eyes with the back of her other hand, spreading her mascara all over her cheeks.

When the slamming of the carriage doors finally stopped, the guard blew his whistle, and Polly saw his green flag waving high above the sea of heads. Slowly the train moved forward. Polly had stood and waved until it had completely disappeared.

'Come on love, let's git on 'ome.' Mr Bell had put a comforting arm round Polly, and together they had pushed and jostled their way through the excited crowds of those waiting to leave, and the sad ones whose families had already gone.

Polly lay on the bed and cried at those sad memories. She felt so alone.

Suddenly a wailing noise filled the air, terrifying her. She ran into the kitchen, screaming, 'Ron, Ron, what is it? What's that noise?'

'It's the air-raid warning. Quick, let's git out of 'ere.'

They hurried down the stairs.

'Me handbag, I must go back . . .'

'Come on yer silly cow, we could all be killed if we stay indoors.' He grabbed her hand and they raced into the street, milling with the many other people who looked equally confused, their faces full of fear.

Some had stopped running to look up at the sky. Nobody knew what they were looking for, or where they were going, or what they were running from.

'Where're we going?' shouted Polly, hanging on to Ron's hand as he pushed his way through the congestion.

'The underground. They said it'll be safe down there.'

They had almost reached the entrance to the station when the long steady note of the all-clear filled their ears.

'What's that?' cried Polly, bewildered and frightened by this new sound.

'That's the all-clear, ducks,' shouted an old man. 'Not ter worry now, it's all over.'

'Come on, love, let's git 'ome.' Ron took her arm.

'I'm frightened,' she said clinging on to him.

'So's everyone else, Pol.'

That Monday morning the factory wasn't buzzing with the noise from the machines, it was buzzing with all the chatter from the women who were discussing the weekend's events in loud, excited, high-pitched voices. Polly looked over at Elsie Mann. She was sitting at her machine, crying, and Sally the finisher was comforting her. Polly knew Elsie had said goodbye to her four children on Saturday. She told Polly last Friday they were being evacuated.

'In some ways I'll be bloody glad ter see the back of 'em. Those free boys a mine can be right bloody cow-sons at times. I pity the poor cow that finishes up wiv 'em.'

But for all her talk, Polly knew she must be missing them.

Even Big Vi was subdued. Although her family had grown up and left home, she could obviously feel for her fellow workers, and wasn't in her usual hurry to get them working. Polly was surprised to see Sarah was in the office before her. 'What's going to happen now war's been declared Miss Bloom?' she asked.

'I don't know. Things should be the same for now. Though we have got to sort something out for the black-out later on. Did Shirley get away all right?'

Before Polly could answer, Mr Bloom came striding into the office. 'Sarah, and you, Margaret. If the siren goes, make sure all the girls get out as fast as they can. They'll have to go along to the underground for the time being, till we sort something out about a shelter.'

Polly nodded. She wanted to smile at this big, important man, with the cardboard box containing his gas-mask bobbing up and down on his bottom – the same as everyone else's.

Polly suddenly thought, War was a great leveller.

'I've been told they're going to build a public one at the bottom of the road,' said Mr Bloom.

'Sir, will we still be making frocks, er, dresses?'

'For the time being. I expect we'll soon be on war work, as will everyone else. Thank goodness I had enough sense to lay in a good stock of cloth. Sarah, we've got to get some sort of sticky paper or something to cover these windows. We don't want glass flying around all over the place, do we?'

Polly looked first at Sarah, then at Mr Bloom. He sounded so matter-of-fact and businesslike. 'Mr Bloom, you don't really think anything's going to happen, do you?' she asked.

'We have to take precautions my dear. Better safe than sorry.' He laughed: it was a false, unconvincing laugh. 'But as my accountant said last night, "Everyone's drinking champagne. Nobody's laying down port."'

Polly didn't understand that remark.

'Now, get those women back to work, we've got a lot of work to get out, and we've lost enough time already.' He left the office as he came in – in a hurry.

Polly sank into her chair. 'Miss Bloom, what's going to happen to all of us?'

'I don't know.' She walked over to her desk and went through the motions of tidying the papers. 'Like my father said, we've got to carry on as normal.' Polly noticed the quiver of emotion in her voice.

After that first false alarm, things were very much as normal, and they did carry on as usual, despite sandbags being piled everywhere, windows boarded up, and buckets of sand and water placed in strategic positions. Air-raid shelters began springing up like mushrooms. It seemed every house had to have one, much to Mrs Perkins' annoyance when the men finished putting one in her tiny back yard.

'You ain't catching me down that fing,' she said when Polly went out to have a look at the new shining Anderson shelter.

112

It was half buried in the ground, looking for all the world like a giant silver tortoise.

'Look at the bleedin' mess they've made. Mud everywhere. They've been trailing mud and concrete in and out all day. I'll 'ave ter scrub that lino up the passage. I'll tell yer, I've only got ter 'ave me bleeding washing-line break on Monday and fall in this lot, that'll just about put the tin 'at on it. Sid ain't none too 'appy about 'aving ter put all that earth back on top, are yer?'

'No, I ain't.'

'Mum, you'll be just like the rest of us if the worst comes to the worst and we have to go down them.'

Mrs Perkins bent down and peered in the dark void. 'I'll feel like a bloody rat creeping about down there. 'Sides, it's cold and damp, it ain't 'ealfy.'

'It'll be a bloody sight more un'ealfy, if yer stays up 'ere when Jerry comes over and starts dropping bombs on yer,' Sid scoffed.

'Don't say things like that, Sid. You know you can be a right Jonah at times. Where's Billy?' asked Polly.

'Don't ask. 'E can always find an excuse ter sod orf when there's work ter be done 'ere at 'ome.'

''E's 'elping old man Lucas,' said Sid.

'Mum, I've had a letter from Shirley. She's in Bristol.'

'Yer I know, 'er dad next door told me.'

'She said she's keeping well.' Polly looked at Sid. 'She wants a little girl.'

'What yer looking at me for? I asked 'er if she wanted ter git 'itched, she said no – so that's up ter 'er.'

'I hope you're going to send her some money now she can't work.' Polly was anxious for her friend.

''Er old man said she's working in the aircraft factory down there,' said her mother aggressively. ''Sides, I fink it was six of one and 'alf dozen of the other. Always seemed ter be a fast little bitch if yer asks me. Those Bells are a right old lot. Yer wants ter fink yerself lucky you never finished up in the puddin club 'fore you got married.'

'Our Pol's too bloody clever, or too frigid, fer that. This cold's getting ter me bladder, got ter 'ave a jimmy riddle.' Sid threw the shovel to the ground.

Polly walked away before she really lost her temper, and said something she might regret.

Shirley and Polly wrote to each other regularly. Shirley's letters were always happy, and she sounded as if she was having a good time. The Bells had moved on from the family they had been evacuated to. They had found themselves a three-bedroom house to rent. Shirley was working in an aircraft factory. It was long hours, but the money was good. There was an RAF camp nearby and, despite being pregnant, it seemed to Polly that Shirley's life was one long round of dances and dates.

'Our Vera's finking of going ter live wiv 'em. I reckon Dad will go down there before long. 'E was saying there's some smashing markets, and if 'e can git in on a couple of 'em, 'e'll give it a go. 'E might even take the twins.' Ron handed Polly the latest letter her father-in-law had brought her back.

She looked up from the letter. 'Who will look after the house up here?'

''E'll let that go.'

'What about you? What will you do about the market stall?'

'I reckon I'll 'ave ter go in the Army soon, so that'll take care a me.'

Polly looked alarmed. 'You're not volunteering, are you?'

'No bleedin' fear. No, I'll wait till I'm called up, I ain't no bleedin' 'ero.'

Mr Bloom welcomed a government order to make shorts for the Army and Navy. The younger girls on the machines were hysterical about it, and often sewed pieces of paper, with their names and addresses written on them, discreetly inside their shorts. Big Vi, Mr Bloom, and Sarah pretended not to notice what was going on.

At the end of November, Polly had a long letter from Shirley telling her about her new daughter, Elizabeth, who had arrived three weeks early. According to Shirley she was the prettiest baby ever born.

Dear Polly,

I hope this letter finds you as happy as me. I'm writing to tell you I've got a lovely little girl. She's got a mass of black curly hair and deep blue eyes. Mum says all babies start off like that. She really is lovely, Pol, you should see her dear little hands, and the dear little nails on her fingers. Funny, I never noticed these things on Mum's babies. Mind you, it didn't half hurt. I don't think I'll have any more. She can't half yell, and I won't be sorry to put her on the bottle when I get out of hospital. I'm going back to work as soon as I can; Mum's going to look after her. I've called her Elizabeth Margaret, the Margaret's after you. When you come down we'll have her christened. Will you and Ron be godparents? By the way, when are you coming down to see us? Don't leave it too long.

Love Shirl. XXX

PS. The girl in the next bed's a teacher, so she helped me with the spelling.

Polly wiped her tears. She missed Shirley so much, and how she envied her. Her thoughts went to how she could get to see her. Christmas was approaching, perhaps Ron would take her to Bristol then? Polly sighed, No, that was no good, her mother would want them to spend Christmas with her. But it wouldn't be the same this year without Grandad, and the Bells' big tree, and all the fun they used to have in the evening. The war had changed things so much.

'What yer drawing?' Ron peered over her shoulder as she sat at the table.

'Nothing. I was just thinking about the lovely frock Miss Bloom's having made for a big do they're going to. It's a bit like this.' She held up the paper. 'She's having it made in pale blue crepe. It'll look lovely on her, she's got the right figure for this draped look.'

'Yer know, yer quite good at this drawing lark.' He picked up the paper and studied it. 'Where're they going?'

'Some big hotel up West.'

'When?'

'The Friday before Christmas. Why?'

'Nufink, just taking an interest in yer work, that's all.'

'The whole family's going, including their son David. Miss Bloom was telling me he's leaving University and going into the Air Force.' Polly sighed and put her pencil on the table, thinking how handsome David would look in uniform. It was funny, she hadn't thought about him for a while – she must be feeling contented.

'Some blokes 'ave all the luck,' Ron said, 'and they still ain't satisfied. Christ, I wish my old man could 'ave sent me ter University. 'E couldn't even afford ter send me ter 'igh school. I'd swap University any day fer the market.'

Polly looked at him tenderly; she had never known he felt like that.

He sat at the table next to her. 'The way fings are going we will all finish up in the Forces soon. How old is 'e?'

'Don't really know – early twenties I should think. He's a bit younger than Miss Bloom.'

He looked at her sketch again. 'Yer know, I bet their do will be really sumfink.' He plonked the paper down on the table. ''Ow d'yer fancy going down ter see me old mum at Christmas?'

Polly sat dumbfounded. 'You mean it? Really mean it? Go to Bristol for Christmas?'

'Yer, why not? Now our Vera and the twins are down there, that only leaves the old man, and 'e's talking about staying down there. 'E reckons they've got some bloody good markets 'e can work.'

She jumped up and flung her arms round his neck. 'That would be the best present you could ever give me. I'm dying to see Shirley again, and baby Elizabeth. Shirley wants us to be godparents.' Suddenly Polly sat down, her face dropped. 'I can't go Ron.'

'Why?'

'Me mum. I've always been home for Christmas.'

'Yer I know, but that was 'fore yer got married. She can't expect yer ter go round there, not now. At least my lot know 'ow ter enjoy 'emselves. Christ, I know where I'd rarver be.'

Polly smiled. 'So do I. I'll tell Mum tomorrow. Though she won't be very happy about it, especially now Grandad's gone.'

'All the more reason fer yer ter git away. At least yer could always 'ave a laugh wiv the old man, even if 'e was a bit dotty over that fing.' He glanced up at the whip.

'Blooming cheek. Here, you don't think being daft runs in the family, do you?' She pulled a funny face.

He stood up. 'Come 'ere.' Ron held her close and kissed her. 'D'yer remember what yer said before we got married, about you not loving me?' He held her at arm's length.

She lowered her head.

He tilted her head up. 'Well, I've been finking. D'yer fink that might be the reason yer ain't fell fer a kid? Yer know, p'raps that's what makes yer . . . Yer knows what I mean?'

Polly jerked her head away from his hand. 'No, I don't know what you mean. You think it's my fault I haven't fallen?'

'There's no need ter git uppity. I only asked. Christ, let's face it gel, I've got it in me.' He rubbed his chin, and with a satisfied grin on his face added, 'Yer should know that be now.'

Guilt brought the colour to her face. 'I'm sorry Ron. I'm very fond of you. Perhaps it is love – I don't know.'

Ron sat in the armchair. 'Yer'll know soon enough when I 'ave ter go in the Army. I bet yer miss me then.'

She touched his shoulder. 'I will miss you. These past eight months have been good. Except for one or two little problems.

Still don't let's talk about you going away, let's talk about Christmas.'

He pulled her on to his lap. 'Yer knows what I finks? I fink yer sees too many films. Just because we don't 'ear bleedin' bells ring, and 'ave violins playing every time we 'as a bit, and you don't 'ave stars floating round yer 'ead, yer don't fink it's love. I'll tell yer Pol, you and me, we're all right.'

'You could be right. Perhaps what I feel for you is love – I don't know. Perhaps I do expect too much out of life.'

'The trouble wiv you is yer don't know what's yer want.'

'Oh yes I do. I know I want to see Shirley at Christmas, that's for sure.'

'Right, that's settled then. Find out when the trains go, and write and tell 'er ter meet us at the station.' He kissed her long and hard.

Polly didn't hear bells or violins, but she was happy.

'But you've always spent Christmas at 'ome.'

'I've got a husband now, and I've got to spend it with him. I remember a few months ago you told me off, said I shouldn't be round here – told me to go home to him.'

'That was different. Christmas is time fer families.'

'Well Ron's family now. 'Sides, you've got Sid and Billy.'

'Not got the old man though. I fought this year yer'd 'ave a bit more feeling.'

Polly sat in Grandad's armchair. She fondled the wooden arms; she always felt close to him sitting here.

'Shirley wants us to be Elizabeth's godparents.'

'Oh, so that's it. Made this a good excuse between yer.'

'No Mum. I'd like to go away with Ron. He don't get a lot of time off, and he reckons he'll be called up soon.'

Mrs Perkins jerked her head up. 'That means Sid might 'ave ter go.'

'He's a bit younger than Ron.'

'Not by much.'

'Mum, let me go to see Shirley, please.'

'Well please yerself. 'Ow long will yer be gorn?'

'We're catching a train early on the Saturday evening, as soon as Ron finishes at the market, and coming back on the Tuesday, Boxing Day. I've got to be at work the next day.'

'I see. Got it all worked out already then.'

Polly didn't let her mother see her smile. For her it was going to be the best Christmas she'd had since her dad died.

Chapter 10

'You're not going out tonight, are you?' asked Polly as Ron stood in front of the mirror slicking his hair down with Brylcreem.

'Only going out wiv Sid fer a quick one. You fergit I won't be seeing 'im till after Christmas.'

'So? You'll see him at the market tomorrow. Besides, you've just had a bath, you'll end up catching a right old cold, and Shirley won't thank you for going down there sneezing and coughing all over Elizabeth.'

He kissed her cheek. 'Don't nag. I know, yer worried I might find meself a nice-looking piece o' skirt, seeing as 'ow I smell like a ponce after gitting inter your barf water.' He sniffed the air and held his nose. 'Phew,' he laughed. 'This kitchen smells like a broffel.'

'I wouldn't know, I've never been in one,' said Polly, kneeling on the floor and ladling the bath water into a bucket. 'Bucket's full.'

'Look, why don't you come wiv us?' Ron picked up the bucket of dirty water and carried it into the scullery to throw down the sink.

'You know I can't, I've just washed me hair, and I've got the packing to do.'

He put the bucket on the floor beside her. 'You can do that termorrer, yer got all afternoon.'

'I've got to get some presents.'

Polly had a towel wrapped round her wet hair, revealing her

white neck. Ron bent down and kissed it. 'Yer know, I'm really looking forward ter Christmas, seeing me mum and Ding Dong again, and 'er baby. 'Ere, wot yer gitting me?' he asked as he continued emptying more buckets.

'I ain't telling. What you getting me?'

He touched his nose. 'Wait and see. Got yer sumfink really nice. Well, if I can't git yer ter come out fer a drink, I'll just 'ave ter go on me own. Yer nearly finished emptying that barf yet?'

'Yes, this is the last.' Polly stood up.

'Don't know wot time I'll be back. I might even see if Dad's going up Covent Garden straight from the pub. If 'e is, I'll go wiv 'im.' He kissed her.

'Well wrap up, and don't wake me up when you get home.' Polly closed the kitchen door behind him.

David Bloom helped his mother into the back seat of the car and tucked the rug round her legs. 'That all right?' he asked.

She nodded. 'Yes, thank you.'

'That was a lovely evening,' said Sarah, climbing in beside her mother. She pulled some of the travelling rug over her knees. 'I really enjoyed myself tonight.' She hiccuped.

'Sounds like it,' laughed her mother.

Sarah giggled and quickly put her hand to her mouth. 'You must excuse me, that champagne was wonderful.'

Mr Bloom eased his large bulk behind the steering wheel and started the motor. He wound down the window, drew heavily on his cigar, then tossed the butt out. 'It certainly was. Mind you, the whole affair could have been a lot better if this – this . . .'

'Your son,' interrupted David calmly.

Mrs Bloom leant forward and gently tapped his shoulder. 'Now David, don't go upsetting your father.'

'I wasn't aware that I had.'

'Why the hell couldn't you have been a little more . . .'

'What?' asked David abruptly.

'You know? More courteous to that nice little Mary Ritman?' asked Mr Bloom.

'I thought I was.'

'You didn't dance with her very much.' He took a quick glance at his son. 'Her father and I had quite a long discussion.'

'So I noticed.'

'Ahh, yes, well. We think, between us, of going into a very lucrative venture. Hey, come on my boy, cheer up.' He playfully nudged David. 'He owns a great deal of property, and with you acting as his lawyer, as well as being his son-in-law . . .' He laughed. 'Oh yes, it could be very lucrative indeed.'

The car hit a kerb and pulled the wheel from Mr Bloom's hands. He quickly righted it.

'Do be careful dear,' said his wife.

He leaned forward and peered into the darkness. 'It's this damn black-out, can't see a thing. These silly little slits in these headlight covers don't give any light at all. Thank goodness there's not a lot of traffic about.'

David remained silent. He wasn't about to drop the bombshell on his mother and father tonight. No, what he had to tell them could wait until after Christmas. In the comfort and darkness of the car he smiled, knowing that things wouldn't be going all the old man's way.

His mother was speaking. 'Do you know, Sarah's dress was the talk of the evening.'

Mr Bloom puffed himself up. Over his shoulder he said proudly, 'We got some new clients through that dress. It caused quite a bit of interest.'

'I know, some of them wanted to know who designed it.' Sarah gave a little giggle. 'I wouldn't tell them.'

'Who did?' asked her mother.

'The basic idea came from Barny, but it wasn't till Margaret finished with the design that it looked like this.' Proudly she smoothed her hands over the soft blue crepe.

'Is that all we go out for, so that you can be a walking advert for the firm?'

123

'Now David, that's not a very nice thing to say.'

'Sorry Mother. It's just that you lot seem to forget there's a war on.'

'Don't talk nonsense. Haven't I just been complaining about the black-out. Anyway, it won't last forever, and besides, we have to think of our future. We can't stand still and let everybody else get ahead of us – not in the rag trade,' said Mr Bloom.

'I'm glad I told Margaret I wouldn't be going into the office in the morning. I think I've had a little too much champagne.' Sarah was trying to ease the tension.

'That will make you sleep,' said her mother. 'Margaret seems a very capable girl.'

'She certainly is. I don't know what we would do without her.'

The conversation lapsed, and they finished the journey in silence. It wasn't long before the car turned into the gravel drive.

'I'll put the car away. Rachel, have you got a front-door key?' asked Mr Bloom as he stopped the car and they got out.

'Yes, somewhere in this silly little bag.' She walked on ahead, rummaging through her evening bag.

Sarah put her hand on David's arm and gently drew him to one side. 'Don't you dare say anything to upset Dad's Christmas. It can wait a few more days.'

Although they were Jews, their father, much to Sarah and David's delight, had always insisted they celebrate Christmas. It was only Mrs Bloom who was true to the letter of their faith.

'Ah, here it is.' Mrs Bloom brandished the key. 'All I've got to do now is find the keyhole.' She gave an infectious chuckle.

'Hang on, I'll help,' called David. He turned to Sarah. 'I have no intention of saying anything yet.' He strolled towards the house.

'Hurry up, it's cold out here.' Mrs Bloom hunched her shoulders, pulling her evening wrap tighter at her throat.

Mounting the steps, David wondered how he would go about telling them he'd left University, passed his medical, and would be in the Air Force this time next week.

Mrs Bloom pushed open the front door. 'Quickly, all inside before I switch the light on.' She pulled the thick black-out curtain across the door and flicked the hall light on. 'I'm just going up to change into my slippers.' She gave a long sigh as she kicked her shoes off. 'My feet are killing me. Put a kettle on for a cup of coffee, Sarah, there's a dear.'

Sarah went into the kitchen. David went along to the drawing-room and began raking the embers, and his father came in rubbing his hands.

'Put a log on the fire for now, that'll cheer the place up. Do you fancy . . .?' He hadn't finished when an ear-piercing scream came from upstairs. 'My God, that's your mother. Whatever's happened?'

They both rushed from the room, meeting Sarah at the bottom of the stairs. In the turmoil they all tried to climb the stairs together. Mr Bloom, with his sheer bulk, managed to push past them, and flew up the stairs, taking them two at a time.

Rachel Bloom staggered out of her bedroom, her face white as death. She clung to her husband and burst into tears.

'What is it? What's happened?' Sarah and David were both talking at once.

David pushed his parents, who were locked in an embrace, to one side. He stopped abruptly in the bedroom doorway, his eyes quickly scanned the scene. 'My God!' he yelled. 'Who the bloody hell did this?'

Sarah emitted a strangled gasp and clutched her hand to her mouth. The colour drained from her face.

David stepped inside the room. Clothes from the wardrobes were scattered over the floor. Drawers had been emptied on to the bed. The contents of his mother's powder bowl had been spilt over the dressing-table, and her jewellery box was empty. He stood surveying the disarray in his parents' room.

'I'll phone the police,' said Mr Bloom quietly as he gently eased his wife down the stairs. 'David,' he called over his shoulder as David rushed to the other rooms, 'don't touch anything.' He took Rachel into the drawing-room. 'Sarah, come down here and fix us all a good stiff drink.' He went back into the hall, picked up the phone, and dialled the police station.

In the drawing-room, Sarah sat with her mother on the long red velvet sofa. She plumped up the cushions behind her, and tried to comfort her.

'Right, the police will be here shortly. Where's that drink?' asked Mr Bloom.

Sarah pointed to the large glass of whisky on the table.

He picked it up and sat next to his wife, gently putting a reassuring arm round her. 'You'll have to let me know everything that's missing,' he said softly.

'They've been in every room upstairs,' said David, coming into the room. He looked around at the lovely silver they had on display. 'I've been in all the rooms down here and they don't seem to have taken anything.' He went over to the fireplace and aggressively kicked the log. Wild sparks shot out like arrows, blackening when they fell on to the tiled hearth. 'As far as I can see they must have got through the bathroom window and stayed upstairs. Probably didn't want to venture down here, in case someone was home.'

'I'd like to get my hands on the buggers, I'd chop their bloody hands off.' Mr Bloom stood up and walked over to the drinks cabinet and refilled his glass.

'Thank goodness we were all wearing our best jewellery tonight,' said Sarah.

Mrs Bloom raised her head, her lids blinked rapidly. Her make-up had streaked, making her look sad and vulnerable. 'They've touched all my belongings. They've had their dirty hands all over my nice things.' She gave a sob. 'I don't think I could ever wear them again knowing someone has . . .' She couldn't finish the sentence.

Sarah put her arm round her. 'Come on now.'

'Would you like a drink, dear?' asked Mr Bloom.

She shook her head.

'I'll make you a nice hot cup of cocoa, that might help you sleep,' said Sarah.

Mrs Bloom's head shot up. 'I couldn't sleep, not up there. Never again in that room, not now.'

'You can sleep in my bed, and I'll come down here.'

'What about your father? You've only got a single bed.'

'He can stay in your room.'

'No.'

'Rachel, be reasonable.'

She began to cry.

'Dad,' said Sarah, giving him an icy glance. She turned to her mother. 'Naturally you're upset. But it would only be for a little while.'

'No, we've never slept apart in all our years of marriage.'

Sarah looked up at her father. 'Well, couldn't we bring your mattress down here? Just for tonight?'

He nodded. 'I should think so, but we'll have to wait until the police have finished looking around.'

The police were kind and sympathetic. They spent two hours going over the bedrooms, asking what was missing, and taking notes. Through sheer exhaustion, Mrs Bloom had dropped off to sleep on the sofa. Sarah gently placed a blanket over her.

'Do you have to question her tonight?' She looked at the black marble clock on the high mantelshelf. 'It's half-past three. Can't it wait till tomorrow?'

A tall dark-haired policeman said, 'I should think so.' He addressed the rest of the family. 'If you could make a complete list of what's been taken, I'll collect it tomorrow and we can circulate it to the local pawnbrokers. They won't have a lot of time to get rid of it before Christmas, unless of course they have a fence lined up already.'

'I suppose we should think ourselves lucky. We were wearing most of the good jewellery,' said Mr Bloom. 'And of course we are well insured.'

'Did many people know you were out tonight?'

'I don't know.'

'Do you keep a lot of money from the business in the house?'

'No, in fact, very little.'

127

'I think that's all for now. Good night Sir, Miss.'

Sarah nodded, and Mr Bloom accompanied him to the door.

David sat in the chair and rested his head in his hands. 'How am I going to break my news to them after this?'

Sarah didn't answer, she only shrugged her shoulders in a long, exaggerated movement.

Chapter 11

Polly hung on to Ron's arm as they jostled through the barrier. 'This reminds me of the time we all went to Southend.'

'Yer, that was a good day. I don't fink we're gonner git a seat, not wiv that lot in front of us.' Ron strained his neck in an attempt to look over the heads of the crowd.

On the train they pushed and struggled past the many people in the corridor, looking for an empty seat.

The carriage doors slammed, the guard blew his whistle, and the train lurched forward. Ron quickly put his hand out to steady Polly. ''Ere, yer'll 'ave ter sit on this.' He pulled the old brown leather suitcase away from the side of the train. 'Didn't fink it'd be this crowded.'

'I expect a lot of people want to be with their families this Christmas,' said Polly, trying to make herself comfortable on the suitcase. The corridor was dingy and dimly lit, cigarette smoke hung heavy, and the smell of bodies filled the air.

'You must be tired working half the night, and all day,' said Polly, looking up at Ron.

'Yer, I was 'oping we'd git a seat, then I could 'ave got me 'ead down. 'Ow long did Ding Dong say it took ter git down there?'

'A few hours.'

'Christ, I'll be like a wet rag by the end o' the day.' Ron offered her a cigarette.

She shook her head. 'No thanks.'

'Did yer pack everyfink?'

'Yes, I've got lots of letters and cards from the women at work, Shirley will be pleased about that. And I've got all the cards and presents from us. Do you think Shirley will like that powder compact?'

'Should fink so. What about my present?'

'You've got to wait till Christmas morning – what about mine? What have you bought me?'

'I ain't telling,' he said indignantly.

'It had better be something good.'

He bent down and whispered. 'Yer better be grateful fer wotever yer gits, and if yer plays yer cards right, gel, yer could end up by 'aving me.'

Polly laughed. 'This is the best present you could give me.' She was so happy and excited at the thought of seeing Shirley and her baby in a few hours. 'Do you think Shirley will like Elizabeth's christening gown?'

'I should bloody well 'ope so. All the work yer put inter it. No love, it's really smashing. P'raps the next one yer makes will be fer our kid.'

Polly didn't answer, she still wasn't really sure if that was what she wanted. Now there was a war on, Ron could be called up soon. How could she cope bringing up a baby on her own? Besides, there was still her job. The noise and bustle of people pushing past made conversation impossible, so she leaned her head against the side of the train and let its steady rhythm lull her.

After a few hours and many stops later, the buzz amongst the passengers was that the next one should be Bristol. The train drew to a halt and someone was yelling what sounded like, 'Bristol, Bristol Central.'

The carriage doors had begun slamming and Ron opened the door and called to a sailor, 'Did 'e say Bristol Central mate?'

Polly looked anxious.

'Yes,' came back the reply.

Ron turned to Polly. 'Donner why they 'ad ter take all the

station's names away. Careful, mind the step.' Ron took her arm as she stepped from the train.

'Well, it's in case a German spy comes over, they'll know where they are.'

'I knows that, but yer've only got ter ask someone and they'll tell yer where yer are soon enough.'

'Yes, I suppose you're right.'

The station was in darkness. They followed the crowd through the barrier and out into the crisp, cold night. Ron and Polly stood looking around them.

'You sure Ding Dong said she'd be 'ere?'

'Yes, I told her what train we were catching.' Polly was beginning to sound panicky.

'Where's yer torch?'

'Here, in me handbag.'

'Well git it out then. Is this the right station?'

'Yes, I hope so.' Polly was turning this way and that, looking for Shirley. 'Why couldn't we have caught the earlier train with your dad? At least he knows where to go.'

'I told yer why. I said I'd clear up and put the barra away fer 'im.'

'You two still arguing?' Shirley's voice behind them came from out of the darkness.

Polly threw her arms round her, almost knocking her off her feet. Laughing and crying, they kissed and hugged each other.

'Where yer been?' asked Ron giving her a kiss on the cheek.

'Chatting up that good-looking sailor over there.'

'You haven't changed,' laughed Polly. 'It's so good to see you again.' She slipped her arm through Shirley's and shivered. 'Come on, it's freezing, let's get out of the cold. Is it far to your place?'

'No, about twenty minutes on the bus.'

'Where's the bus stop?' asked Ron.

'Just over the road. Come on.'

'Do we pass any pubs?' asked Ron.

131

'Yes. And Dad said ter make sure yer pass 'em, and ter 'urry up cos 'e's taking us ter our local.'

'So you heard, Ron, we *pass* them. Right, now lead me to that baby of yours.'

They left the station in a carefree and happy mood.

When they arrived at the house, after all the hugging and kissing from the Bell family, Polly went upstairs to look at Elizabeth lying contentedly in her cot.

'She's lovely,' cooed Polly, holding on to the tiny hand. 'I never thought Sid could produce anything like this. I bet my mum would love to see her.'

'Well, yes, I did all the producin', not Sid. She's mine, yer know.' Shirley bristled slightly.

'Sorry, that was a bit thoughtless. Yes, she is yours, and she's lovely, and look at you, you look smashing. Motherhood has certainly made you blossom.'

'Look at me belly.' She patted her stomach. 'It's gone back nice and flat. What d'yer fink of me 'air?' Shirley now did her hair in the latest style and the heavy fringe on her forehead suited her. She was still inclined to use too much make-up for Polly's taste, but that didn't matter, she was here with her.

'You look good,' Polly said smiling at both her friend and her little daughter.

'Me mum ain't gonner fank yer if yer go spoiling 'er while yer 'ere. She's the one that's gotter look after 'er all day while I'm at work.'

'You can't spoil babies with love,' said Polly, giving Elizabeth another kiss before leaving the room.

'Where did yer git that posh saying from?'

'Dunno. Yes I do, my dad used to say that to me mum when Billy was born. D'you know, I've never even thought of that before.'

''E must a been a nice man.'

'Yes, he was.' Polly paused. 'Now where's this bathroom? I've been dying to see it ever since you wrote and told me you had one.'

'In 'ere.' Shirley opened the door and Polly stood and stared in amazement.

'It must be wonderful not having to bring in the tin bath, or have the job of filling and emptying it with all the buckets. And not to have to all use the same water!'

'Yer, it's a bit cold up 'ere, I miss not 'aving me barf in front of the fire, but it's nice ter 'ave a bit o' privacy fer a change. This is your room. Me mum's borrowed a mattress and chucked the twins downstairs fer Christmas. 'Ere Pol, why don't yer come down 'ere ter live? Yer could get a job dead easy. And yer could always stay wiv us, we've got more room than we know what ter do wiv. And there's always plenty of dances and parties.' She looked towards the door. 'I'll tell yer sumfink. I fought it'd be dead boring down 'ere, but yer know wot? I'm 'aving the time of me life.'

Polly laughed. 'That's no surprise.'

Polly had already done a grand tour downstairs. She had seen the large kitchen with its well-scrubbed deal table filling the middle of the room, and a dresser covering one wall. There was a big old-fashioned range that, apart from cooking all their meals, warmed the room, making it feel nice and cosy. The two youngest had been playing on the floor in front of the fire; the heat made their faces red and rosy.

Shirley had told Polly that the front room was furnished with a few bits the previous owner had left. When Polly and Shirley walked in, the twins looked up guiltily: they had been busy feeling the presents under a tree that was decorated with tinsel and baubles left over from previous years. It looked gay and Christmassy.

'Leave 'em alone, yer little toe-rags,' said Shirley. Then, nodding at the high ceiling, 'Me and Vera made all the paper chains.'

''Allo Pol,' said Terry. ''Ere, yer knows that holly stuff Dad sells orf 'is barra? Well, it grows on dirty great bushes. Look, me and Tom went and picked some.'

'Is there some round here then?'

'Yer, not too far away. It's great living near the country,' said Thomas. 'Mind, it can't 'alf prickle.' He grinned. 'And we got some mistletoe. That grows on trees as well.'

'We went scrumping fer apples when we first moved 'ere,' interrupted Terry. 'There's lots o' country that's only a couple of stops on the bus – it's bigger than Blackeef.'

Polly laughed. Seeing the twins made her think of Billy and the tricks the three of them used to get up to.

In the dining-room was an oak table, and around it an assortment of chairs: some wooden, some padded, and some downright tatty. Leaning against the wall was the mattress that had been borrowed for the twins.

To Polly it was a warm, friendly house, and with all the Bells tearing about, it rang with noise and laughter. She put the case on the bed and began undoing it. 'This is a lovely old house,' said Polly looking round the room that she and Ron were going to use; like the other three rooms upstairs, it was big.

'The furniture ain't very posh. Dad got a few bits off the market, yer should see wot sum of these rich people chuck out. Yer bed, and that oak table downstairs, only cost 'im a couple a bob. Wot d'yer say about moving down 'ere?'

Polly sat on the bed. 'I don't know. I don't want to leave Bloom's. And what about Ron?'

'Dad's gitting on some of the markets down 'ere. 'E could work wiv 'im. 'Sides, 'e'll 'ave ter go in the Army soon,' she laughed. 'That's if 'e ain't got two left feet.'

'I must say it's very tempting.'

Ron shouted up the stairs. 'Ain't you two ready yet? They'll be closed soon.'

Polly looked at her watch. 'Look at the time, we supposed to be going to the pub?'

'Not 'alf. You should see some of the lovely blokes that gets in there, they come from the RAF station near 'ere. I 'ope ter find meself one of 'em before long.'

Polly smiled. Shirley hadn't changed.

The evening was one long round of drinking and laughing.

Polly hadn't been so happy in months.

The following afternoon, Elizabeth was christened in the church round the corner. To Polly's delight she didn't cry during the ceremony, and everybody admired the beautiful gown she had made for her niece. When they got back to the house, in true Bell fashion, the party went on till well into the night. To Polly it didn't seem as if food shortages affected the Bells. She knew her father-in-law had a lot of connections, and there was plenty of everything.

'All over Christmas they seemed to be eating, laughing, and getting drunk. When she and Ron made love, it didn't seem to matter that there was a war on. Polly was contented beyond words. Then all too quickly Christmas was over.

Soon it was Shirley's turn to stand on the station and wave goodbye to her friend. With tears streaming down her face she yelled, 'Write soon!'

Slowly the overcrowded train pulled away. This time Polly and Ron had managed to find a seat. They sat huddled together in the corner of the carriage, and he put his arm round her.

'Come on, wipe those tears.'

Polly blew her nose.

'All right now?' He lightly kissed her cheek.

She nodded and smiled weakly, cuddling closer. He can be so nice she thought. Perhaps this *was* love that she felt for him. She did know she was going to miss him a lot when he went into the Army.

'Wiv a bit a luck we might 'ave clicked this weekend.'

Polly blushed. 'Shh,' she said, undoing her scarf and quickly glancing round the carriage. 'It's warm in here.'

'What d'yer expect? It's packed. Blimey, now I know what a sardine feels like.'

She laughed and gently fingered the brooch at the neck of her dress. 'Thank you for my lovely present.'

'Only wish it was real.'

'I don't care if it's not, I still think it's lovely.'

'Ere Pol, you won't go wearing it ter work, will yer?'

135

'Why's that?'

'Well yer knows what a nosy lot o' buggers they are at that factory, and, well, I don't want 'em ter see it, that's all. Christ, they'll all want one, and I don't want 'em to 'ave the same as you.'

She smiled. 'You are a funny old thing at times.'

'Anyway, promise.'

'I promise, if that's what you want. D'you know, that was the best Christmas I've had since I was a little girl.'

'Let's 'ope we 'ave a lot more like that.' He pulled her close and, resting her head on his shoulder, she studied their reflection in the window. Outside the day was quickly drawing to a close.

The dim light in the carriage was switched on, and a guard shouted from the corridor. 'Could someone pull the blinds down in there?'

Ron reached across and pulled down the stiff green blind, securing the cord round and round on a button.

Their reflection had gone, disappearing almost as if they no longer existed. Polly shuddered and nestled her head against Ron again. She closed her eyes, the rhythm of the train rumbling over the rails mingling with her thoughts. If Ron got called up she'd be all alone. She knew she could never go back home to live, so should she go and stay at Shirley's?

But she knew deep in her heart it was Bloom's that had a bigger hold on her.

Chapter 12

On the Wednesday morning following the holiday, and before the machines thundered into life, the factory was buzzing with excitement. Everybody seemed to be talking at once about what they did over Christmas.

Polly was eavesdropping on Elsie Mann's conversation, which was frequently punctuated with her high-pitched laugh. She was telling some of the women how pleased she'd been at seeing her children over Christmas, and about the things her boys got up to in the country. It appeared they loved it, and had settled down well – much to Elsie's surprise, as she didn't think that much of the country, and was glad to get back home again.

'It was the bleeding birds and chicken's cock-a-doodle-dooing first thing every morning that got on our nerves. Me old man reckoned it was quieter in London.' She laughed uproariously at herself and the others joined in.

Big Vi walked over to the clocking-in clock. It was eight o'clock. Polly smiled and gave Elsie a wave as Vi blew her whistle and the machines roared, drowning all the chatter.

When Sarah Bloom came into the office she didn't look her usual cheerful self.

'Did you have a nice Christmas, Margaret?' she asked politely.

'Yes, thank you,' beamed Polly. 'Me and my husband' – saying that always made her smile – 'went to Bristol. We stayed with Shirley. She had Elizabeth christened.'

'Did Shirley like the dress you made for the baby?'

'She was over the moon, and Elizabeth looked lovely – she's a beautiful baby.'

'Now, now, we don't want you getting broody, do we?'

Polly smiled. 'Did you have a nice Christmas, Miss?'

Sarah turned away and pulled open the filing cabinet's top drawer. 'I'm afraid not.'

Polly didn't know what to say. 'I hope nobody was ill.'

'No, it was nothing like that.' She continued rummaging through the drawer. 'Have you seen that order for Mr Norman?'

'It's in the second drawer of your desk.'

Sarah sat at her desk.

Mrs Perkins brought in the morning tea, and Polly didn't pursue the conversation.

'Yer coming round ternight?' asked her mother as she passed her her mug.

Polly nodded, and picked up the ringing phone. 'Yes, Mr Bloom. Your father,' she said, handing the phone to Sarah.

'See yer ternight,' whispered Mrs Perkins, closing the office door quietly behind her.

'Yes, Dad . . . I think that's a very good idea . . . Yes, I'll leave early and pick them up on my way home.' Sarah replaced the receiver on its cradle, and picked up her mug of tea. She rested her elbows on her desk and wrapped her fingers around the mug. 'I've got to go shopping this afternoon. We didn't have a very nice Christmas; we were burgled on Friday night while we were at the dance.'

'How awful! I'm ever so sorry. Did they take much?'

'Some money and a few pieces of jewellery. Mother's more upset over someone going through all her belongings. I've got to go out and buy her new underwear. My father's taking her to Brighton for a few days while we have her bedroom redecorated. It might help to cheer her up. Poor Mother, what with that and David going in the Air Force next Friday . . .'

'He's left University then?'

'Yes. My father was none too happy about it.'

'I bet he'll look ever so smart in his uniform.'

'Yes, I expect he will.' Sarah finished her tea and returned to her normal businesslike self. 'Now we must get on. We should be getting a few inquiries about the dress I wore on Friday night.'

'Did it look nice?'

'Yes, and it felt good. That ruching you suggested just finished it off.'

Polly was typing when the phone rang again. Sarah answered it.

'Yes Sergeant . . . That's good news . . . Well, thank you.' For the first time that morning she smiled, though only briefly. 'The police have recovered my father's pocket-watch, and David's silver cufflinks.'

'Where did they find them?' asked Polly.

'In a pawnbroker's.'

'Is that everything that was stolen?'

'No. We won't see the money again, I expect that went over Christmas, and the rings were probably presents for one of their floosies.' She added brusquely, 'As was my pretty stemmed brooch.'

Polly stopped typing. 'What brooch was that?' She hoped her question sounded casual.

Sarah continued going through her papers. 'I don't think you've ever seen it. I don't wear it to the office, it's a bit fussy.' She looked up. 'Funny thing, I was going to wear it on Friday but it didn't go with my dress. It's very pretty, gold with green leaves, and with diamonds at the base of the stem. My father had it made for my twenty-first birthday. I'm very angry at losing that.'

Polly turned her head as she felt the blood drain from her face.

'Margaret, are you all right? Don't you feel well?'

'I'm all right, thank you. I just came over a bit funny.'

Sarah looked at her suspiciously. 'Are you sure you're all right?'

Polly blushed. 'Yes, thank you.'

139

For Polly, the day seemed to drag on forever. Sarah buried herself in her work, but there was none of her usual chatter and laughter greeting the customers when they walked in. Polly was aware of answering the phone, and of people coming and going. She tried to concentrate, but her mind was elsewhere and her actions automatic. Six o'clock couldn't come quickly enough.

The cold was biting when she left the factory. It had been snowing on and off all day; now it lay two or three inches deep and kicked over her shoes, making her feet cold and wet. Hurrying home she felt fed up and miserable, and mumbled to herself, 'And after we'd had such a lovely Christmas as well.' Pulling her scarf tighter at her throat, she bent her head against the wind. Tears from the cold mingled with tears of anger and disbelief as she went over and over the Friday night before Christmas.

Ron had been out almost all that night. He said he'd been to Covent Garden market with his father. Was she being unfair to him, suspecting him? After all, he did ask her if she wanted to go with him and Sid for a drink. She had said no, as she had just washed her hair and was busy getting ready for going away the next day. Would he have asked her if he and Sid had planned something? He did try hard to persuade her to go with him. Ron wouldn't have asked her along if they had planned it, surely, but then Ron was devious – he'd have known she would probably have had too much to do. What if they'd had a few drinks and Ron had told Sid about the Blooms going out that night? If she had gone with them, could she have stopped them . . .? Was it just a coincidence that Sarah Bloom's brooch sounded the same as the one Ron had given her? Was she jumping to conclusions? Her mind was full of when Sid went to prison, and what Shirley had told her all those months ago. Polly felt guilty at her thoughts: she couldn't even say the word 'robbery' in her mind.

Perhaps Ron hadn't been involved in the robbery itself. Had he bought it off someone without knowing it was a stolen, valuable piece? After all, he'd apologized for it not being real. But then why had he made a point of asking her not to wear it to work? Should she take it to work and show Miss Bloom? She tried to dismiss those thoughts. 'I'll know all the answers when I get home,' she muttered to herself.

She closed the front door and ran up the stairs. Bursting into the room she demanded, 'Ron, where did my brooch come from?'

He was sat by the fire. 'What? Christ, yer frightened the bloody daylights out o' me. Can't yer wait till yer gits in 'fore yer starts?'

She stood motionless for a few moments with her back pressed hard against the kitchen door. Her body was shaking as she tried to get her breath.

'Look, I've built up the fire. Git yer wet fings orf, I've got yer a nice cuppa ready. What's up? Yer looks like yer seen a ghost.'

Feeling ashamed at her thoughts, she took off her shoes and slowly moved away from the door. Silently she took off her gloves and put them on the table. She removed her hat, stuck the hat pin in it, and placed it next to the gloves. Ron stood behind her and took her coat. He put it over the back of the chair which stood in front of the blazing fire. Quickly the heat from the fire produced small wafts of steam from her damp coat. Unwinding her scarf she asked again, but casually this time, 'Ron, where did my brooch come from?'

'What, yer mean the one I got yer fer Christmas?'

She nodded.

'Why? Yer ain't lorst it already, 'ave yer? 'Ere, yer didn't wear it ter work, did yer?' He sounded agitated.

'No.'

'So what's this all about? And who wants ter know?'

'I want to know.' She stabbed her finger at her chest. 'It's me that wants to know.'

'Why? It was a present. Anyway, wot yer gitting all riled up for?'

141

'Did you steal it from the Blooms' house?'

He threw back his head and laughed. 'Wot?'

'I think you heard. Miss Bloom had a brooch with leaves and diamonds stolen last Friday.'

'They've been done over, and yer finks it was me? Now that's not a nice fing ter say.'

Polly was confused. Guilt was enveloping her. What if her thoughts were wrong. Would he tell her if he was involved? Perhaps he had bought it. 'Who sold it to you?'

'Oh, so now yer finks I got it from a feef?' He tried to look hurt. 'Where would I git the money ter buy somefink like that if it was real?'

Polly sat heavily in the chair. She studied Ron's face as he poured out the tea. He appeared totally unconcerned. I must be wrong, she thought, he wouldn't be this calm, he would have lost his temper by now and be shouting. 'Ron, where did it come from?' she asked, smiling sweetly.

'I'm buggered if I'm gonner tell yer. Yer finks I pinched it, don't yer? Well, fanks a bunch.'

'Ron, I'm sorry,' her voice took on a pleading tone. 'Please, just tell me where you got it – that's all I want to know.'

'Dunno what yer making such a fuss about a bit of paste and glass fer.'

'But it looks so good. Come on, tell me.'

'I ain't giving yer the satisfaction. If you don't trust me, who would? I'm going round ter Sid's. Yer coming round ter see yer muvver?'

'No, the snow's too thick, and I don't fancy getting wet again.'

'Please yerself.'

'Ron, wait. I'm sorry, it's just that . . .'

He pushed her aside, and waved his finger in her face. 'Just cos those kangaroos got 'emselves turned over, yer finks it was me. Yer suppose ter 'ave a bit a respect fer yer 'usband. I ain't staying 'ere all evening listening ter you going on about that bleeding brooch. Christ, I'm sorry I bought it. Now, if yer ain't

142

coming wiv me, I'm orf. Git out me way.' He shut the kitchen door with a bang.

She stood looking at the door for a few moments, her mind mulling over the conversation they'd just had. He said he'd bought it. Perhaps when he saw the weather he'd change his mind and come back and she could try to find out more.

Polly went into the bedroom and before switching on the light and pulling the black-out curtains, she stopped to look out of the window. There were no lights from the street's gas-lamps now because of the black-out, but there was a bright full moon. The falling snow looked like confetti furiously fluttering about. The moonlight reflecting on the rooftop's clean white snow contrasted with the black smoke from the chimneys, and added to the picture. Below the beauty, the road was a dirty, slushy mess, and people with their heads bent hurried to get home. She quickly pulled the curtains together and turned on the light. From her drawer she took the box containing the brooch.

'I'll study this in the kitchen, the light's better in there,' she said out loud.

Sitting at the kitchen table, she carefully examined the beautiful green and gold spray of leaves, with tiny white stones nestling in a bunch at the base of the stem. They really did look like diamonds. She turned it over and looked for the hallmark.

When Ron had bought her wedding ring, the jeweller had showed them what to look for. He'd told them, 'That's to prove it's real gold – they're not allowed to put it on anything but the real thing.'

There were lots of little scratches on the back – she hadn't noticed them before – but she couldn't see any hallmark.

Why wouldn't he tell her where it had come from? He could have said anything, like he bought it off a bloke in the pub, or at the market – anything. Polly felt ashamed suspecting him. Was she looking for something that wasn't there? Perhaps it was sheer coincidence that her brooch sounded like Miss Bloom's.

Carefully wrapping it in cotton wool, she put it back in its pretty cardboard box. She studied the box. It wasn't from a jeweller's, there was no name inside. It was more like those you get in Woolies. Ron wouldn't have bothered buying a box just to put a brooch in, he would just have wrapped it in a bit of paper. But perhaps he'd got it from the market; they sold things in boxes like that at Christmas. She sighed wearily. All in all, she didn't know *what* to think.

The alarm went off at six as usual. When it continued ringing, Polly put her hand out. 'Ron, Ron, wake up.' Patting the empty space beside her she quickly sat up and pulled the cord over the bed. The soft pink glow from the light on the headboard showed his side hadn't been slept in. She leaned over and banged the top of the clock to stop its incessant ringing. The silence was almost deafening.

'Ron,' she called out, making her way to the kitchen, hastily tying the cord round her thick blue wool dressing-gown as she went. She pushed open the door – it was just as she had left it last night. She shivered. 'It's freezing in here,' she muttered, going into the scullery and lighting all the gases on the stove to warm the room. Her heart was beating fast. Where was he?

She turned out the kitchen light before pulling back the corner of the black-out curtains a little to see what the weather was like. She smiled, thinking how quickly people got into habits, like putting out lights before opening curtains. The inside of the window was covered with frost. To Polly the patterns it made were lovely: if only cloth manufacturers could capture that. She studied it for a while before scraping off the ice with her thumbnail. She peered through the small hole she'd made. Outside, everything was muffled. A white blanket had turned London into a scene from a Christmas card. Everywhere looked so serene and beautiful it was hard to believe there was a war on.

Polly shuddered. 'I've got to go out in that lot. I'd better take some dry shoes to change into.' She talked to herself constantly as she got dressed and prepared her breakfast. 'I expect he stayed with Sid last night,' she said resolutely. Then worry took over again. Sid wasn't that far away, he could have come home. She stirred the porridge angrily as it bubbled on the gas. 'Unless of course he was too bloody drunk,' she spluttered to herself.

She was about to go out of the front door when she hesitated. She ran back in the bedroom and collected her brooch and tucked it into her handbag, thinking, On my way home tonight I'll pop into Harding's and find out what it's worth.

At six o'clock she hurried along to the pawnbroker's shop.

'Damn,' she said out loud as she tried the door. 'I should have remembered Thursday's early closing.' She trudged away, to find Ron waiting at home. He gave her cheek the dutiful kiss and, after taking her coat, handed her a cup of tea. 'Sorry I didn't come 'ome last night. Me and yer bruvvers 'ad a skinful. We were out celebrating.'

'Celebrating what?'

'Didn't yer muvver tell yer? Billy's going in the Navy.'

'No, she didn't.' Polly sat at the table. 'I didn't see a lot of her this morning, we've been very busy. Mind you, she didn't look very happy.' Then, suddenly realizing what Ron had said, added, 'Our Billy's not old enough!'

'Don't know about that, 'e must a' put 'is age up.'

'When's he going?'

'Saturday. Going to Portsmouf, wherever that is.'

'That soon? Why didn't she tell me?' Annoyed, she banged the spoon on the table. 'I seem to be the last to hear anything these days. I must go round to Mum. By the way, where did you sleep last night?'

'Slept wiv Sid. Blimey, 'e can't 'alf snore.'

'You've not heard yourself,' she said angrily.

Ron ignored her, reaching for his coat. 'I'll come wiv yer,' he muttered and they left the flat in silence.

When they arrived at her mother's house Ron went next door to see if his father was home. Polly pulled the key through the letter box and let herself in. 'Yoo-hoo, it's me!' she called.

Billy quickly opened the kitchen door.

''Allo Pol, yer've 'eard the news then?' Billy was clearly very excited about going into the Navy.

'I'd like ter know why yer ser bloody keen ter go,' said Mrs Perkins, glaring at him.

'I told yer, Ma, we'll all 'ave ter go soon.'

'Yer, that's as may be, but yer only a kid. I don't fink it should be allowed, taking 'em ser young.'

'We went over all that last night. I told yer I'm going as an apprentice.' He winked at Polly.

'And I'll be yer money short.'

'I told yer, Ma, I'm making yer an allotment.'

'What did you go and join up for, Billy? You're ever so young,' said Polly.

'I was fed up in that tea factory, and at least I'll 'ave a chance of learning a trade.'

'That's if yer don't git yerself killed first,' their mother said angrily.

'I was surprised when Ron told me. Mum, why didn't you say anything at work this morning?' asked Polly.

'Didn't see the point. 'Sides, I was too upset. I don't wanner see 'im go orf and git 'imself killed. It's bad enough 'aving ter listen ter the wireless and 'earing about all the ships that's gitting sunk.' Mrs Perkins stormed off into the scullery.

'I don't fink it's gone down too well,' said Billy as they listened to the crashing and banging coming from outside.

'You can't blame her. After all, you are the baby of the family.'

'Yer, I know, but let's face it, I ain't Sid.'

'No, that will really be a blow when he goes. By the way, where is he?'

'Next door. 'E said yer'd be over, and 'e knew Ron would go next door first ter see 'is old man. 'E said 'e wanted ter see Ron 'fore 'e came in 'ere.'

'Now what they up to?'

'Don't ask me. Sorry we didn't call fer yer last night, but it was a men-only do. Look, Pol, I'll tell yer what, we'll go fer a drink termorrer night, just you and me. What d'yer say ter that?

I'll meet yer from work and we'll go ter Lyons fer a bite.'

'That'll be smashing,' she said, ruffling his hair, trying to take her mind off Ron and Sid.

Mrs Perkins returned with the tea-pot. 'Margaret, would you come round 'ere straight from work Saturday, and come up the market wiv me? I'm a bit scared ter go on me own in case the Germans come over.' She glared at Billy. 'And wiv you away ...'

'Course I will. What time you off on Saturday, Billy?'

'Seven – in the morning.'

'Well I won't be seeing you off,' said Mrs Perkins. 'I've gotter go ter work.'

'No, I don't want anyone to.' He looked sad, and Polly felt guilty.

'Where are you going from?' she asked.

'Victoria.'

'Tell you what, if the snow's not too thick, I'll meet you at the underground and come up with you. I should be back in time for work.'

His cherub face broke into a grin, and he kissed her cheek. 'Thanks.'

Humm, she thought, looking at her handbag, suddenly everybody wants me. Which was all very well, but when would she get time to get the brooch valued?

It certainly wouldn't be this week ...

Chapter 13

The following evening Billy met Polly outside the factory and together they made their way to Lyons Corner House.

'These nippies always look down their noses at the likes of us,' said Billy, sitting at the table and looking anxiously around.

'Don't be daft, they're only working girls.'

'Yer, well, it's all right fer you, yer speak proper now. Not like me.' Billy leaned forward. ''Ere Pol, yer don't fink it'll spoil me chances of gitting on in the Navy, not speaking proper?'

'No, why should it?'

'Dunno.'

The waitress put the tray of tea and buns on the table.

'These buns don't look bad,' said Billy.

'I'm going to miss you.'

'I wonder wot I'll be doing this time next week?'

'Jankers, or whatever it's called in the Navy, if you don't keep your nose clean.'

They laughed and talked, and when they'd finished their tea, made their way to the Golden Eagle, their local pub. As usual on a Friday night it was full, making the atmosphere warm and friendly.

'Find a table while I git 'em in. You still on mother's ruin, Pol?'

She nodded, and smiled with approval at her younger brother as he disappeared into the throng at the overcrowded, smoke-filled bar.

Although only fifteen, and under age to drink, it didn't worry him. He looked older than his years, and was streetwise in a different way from Sid. He had filled out and was now taller than his sister.

Balancing the drinks, he elbowed his way back to the table. Giving her a boyish grin he eased himself along the seat. 'This time next week I'll be in uniform.'

'You put your age up, didn't you?' announced Polly, sipping her gin and orange.

'Well, could you see Mum giving me 'er blessing?'

'No, I suppose not. She's very upset you know. Didn't they want to see your birth certificate?'

'I told 'em me mum lorst it. 'Sides, I don't fink they worry too much if yer eager. You'll 'ave ter touch me sailor's collar fer luck.'

'Whose, yours or mine?'

'Go on, you ain't done so bad. Got yerself a good 'usband, and a nice little place.'

'You sound like some old man,' she hesitated. 'Billy, there's something I want to ask you.'

'Well, go on, ask away.'

Polly sat back. 'D'you know this is the first time we've been alone since that Saturday you brought Grandad round?'

'That was a bloody shame, 'im going like that. I fought a lot of 'im, yer know. Funny, after you got married we seemed ter git real close.'

'I really miss him to talk to, especially when I need a bit of advice.' Polly moved closer. 'Billy, does Sid still do a bit of pinching?'

He put his pint on the table. 'Shh, keep yer voice down, there might be some rozzers in 'ere.'

'I was only asking.'

'There's no need ter git uppity. What d'yer wanner know for?'

'I want to know if Ron goes with him.'

'I don't know.' He leaned forward and said in a loud whisper, 'And I don't ask. It don't pay ter know too much about our Sid.'

'What about Ron?'

'Dunno.' He touched the side of his nose. 'I likes ter keep this clean and out of other people's business.'

She took the small cardboard box from her handbag. 'Ron gave me this for Christmas.' She handed him the brooch.

'This is smashing,' he said. 'See, I told yer yer lucky. Is it real?' He turned it over.

'I don't know.' Nervously she glanced round the bar. 'You see, the Blooms – you know, the people me and Mum work for – well, they were robbed just before Christmas, and one of the things taken was a brooch like this.'

''Ow d'yer know it was like this?' He handed the brooch back to Polly.

'Miss Bloom described it to me.'

He took a swig of beer and, wiping the froth from his mouth with the back of his hand, laughed. 'And you fink Ron bought it off someone who 'alf-inched it?'

'Or him and Sid pinched it.'

'Come orf it Pol, Sid and Ron?'

'It's not the first time, is it?'

'No I know, but grant Ron wiv a bit a common. Even if they 'ad nicked it, 'e wouldn't be daft enough ter give it to yer fer Christmas, now would 'e, seeing 'as 'ow yer works wiv the daughter? 'E's not that fick.'

'I don't know. I thought about that, but you know what Ron's like, he does daft things sometimes – likes to make a bit of a show. Wants everybody to think he's a good bloke and all that.'

'Well, 'e is.'

'I suppose so. But where does he get all his money from? He never seems to be short of a bob or two, even when the weather's bad and he can't get to the market. Mind you, he makes out to me he's broke, but I've seen his wallet. And you should have seen what he spent at Christmas. Flashing his money about in the pub like a toff, he was.'

'Christ, Pol, I fink yer making sumfink out of nufink. 'Sides,

I didn't bring yer out ter talk about yer old man. Come on, drink up, I'll git yer another.'

'Sorry.' She put the box back in her handbag and rummaged around for her purse. 'Here y'are.' She gave Billy half-a-crown. 'Have this one on me. I'll have the same again.'

'Fanks. Now look who's flashing their dough about.'

'Go on with you.' Polly gave her brother a playful push.

Billy picked up their empty glasses. ''Ere look, 'ere's Ada ter tickle the ivories.'

The old lady carefully wedged her pint of beer on the top of the piano, and when she'd made herself comfortable on the tatty piano stool, began belting out some well-known songs. Everybody joined in, singing their hearts out, while the glass on top of the piano danced up and down without spilling a drop.

It was well past nine o'clock when Ron and Sid came pushing their way through the crowd. Ron was rubbing his hands together and blowing on his fingers. 'Fought we'd find yer still in 'ere,' he shouted, trying to make himself heard above the din. 'Right, what's yours Billy, the usual? Still on the gin, Pol?'

She nodded. Her face had a rosy glow, and she was getting very giggly.

'Got anuver celebration,' announced Sid, putting two pints on the table and plonking himself down on the bench seat. 'Move up gel, let Ron git in.'

Ron handed Polly her gin.

'What have you got to celebrate?' she asked her brother.

'Go fer me medical next week, I'm going in the Army.'

She laughed. 'Well Ron, that only leaves you to protect us now.'

'Sorry Pol, but I'm orf wiv Sid fer a medical next week.'

She put her glass on the table. 'I might have guessed it. Like bloody birds of a feather you two are. I'm surprised you didn't marry him instead of me – you spend more time with him than me.'

'It ain't allowed, Sis,' said Sid, laughing. ''Sides, 'e snores.'

'Now don't git all upset.' Ron put his arm round her. 'Come

on, love, just fink, you'll be 'aving a regular bit o' money coming in every week, not like now wiv the weather ser bad we can't git the barras out. 'Sides, we'll 'ave ter go sooner or later. Our country needs us, and all able-bodied blokes between nineteen and twenty-seven are being called up anyway. So it might as well be sooner.'

'Who says all blokes of your age have got to go?'

'It was in the paper, Pol,' said Billy.

'Anyway, what makes you think you're able-bodied?'

'Cheeky cow,' laughed Ron. 'I expect you were too busy reading about the rationing, and 'ow much meat yer gonner git old Bert the butcher ter give yer over yer ration, ter worry about me gitting called up. Now come on, drink up. It's your turn ter git 'em in, Sid.'

By closing time they were all very merry.

'See yer at the station in the morning, Pol,' Billy said cheerfully kissing her cheek.

'At least the snow's eased off a bit now,' she said as she waved goodbye. She and Ron left her brothers at the corner and staggered home.

'The room's going round and round,' she giggled, tossing her shoes in one direction and her frock in the other. She sat on the edge of the bed and removed her silk stockings. She stood up and her pink silk camiknickers clung to her well-shaped body.

Ron was shedding his clothes all over the floor. He twirled his socks above his head and threw them across the room, turning to catch sight of Polly.

'I hope I get up in time to see Billy off in the morning,' she said, lying on top of the bed.

'Don't worry about that now,' he gasped clambering beside her. 'Now, I'll show yer if I'm able-bodied or not.'

Polly giggled, and his rough hands grabbed her close to him, exploring her body as if it was something new. He kissed her eager, open mouth with lustful passion. Breathlessly she clung to him when his lips travelled down her slender neck, slipping the thin straps of her camiknickers off her shoulders to reveal her firm white breasts.

'Christ, dunno if I can make it after all that beer,' he panted.

'Just keep on trying,' she whispered, all her worries about brooches and robberies and wars gone from her mind.

An overwhelming sadness came over Polly as once more she walked into the railway station. A few weeks ago it had been Billy, now it was Ron's turn. As usual the station smelled of coal and steam, and a voice on the tannoy was shouting inaudible orders. It was buzzing with hundreds of service men in various coloured uniforms, all loaded with backpacks and kit-bags. They, along with the many civilians, were all pushing their way through the crowds.

She clung to Ron's arm, terrified of being separated from him. She didn't want him to go. Many women and a few children were waving goodbye and crying. Tears stung Polly's eyes as he held her tight, crushing her to him. He took her face in his hands and kissed her warm lips hard, before disappearing on to a crowded train. She stood wondering if he could find a window from which to wave; they all seemed to be full of bobbing heads.

Suddenly she caught sight of his shiny black hair, and waved furiously. He pushed his way to a window and grabbed her outstretched hand.

'I'm gonner miss yer, Pol.'

'I'm going to miss you,' she sniffed.

The guard blew his whistle and waved a green flag. Slowly the huge engine shunted forward. Polly quickened her pace as the train moved.

'I love yer, Pol!' shouted Ron.

She ran a few yards with it as it gathered momentum, then, snatching her hand back, said softly, when he was well out of earshot, 'I love you, Ron.' She waved and blew kisses until the train snaked out of the station and was out of sight and lost forever; it was then that her tears fell.

I hate railway stations, she thought to herself as she turned to leave. I always seem to be saying goodbye to someone. But at least she'd had one stroke of luck. When Polly had first heard Sid was going to join up she had panicked, terrified her mother might ask her to come back home to live – the last thing she wanted. So when Sid's medical revealed he had flat feet and couldn't go into the Army, Polly had been as overjoyed as their mother. Life wasn't all bad, she reflected, as she walked back to their cosy flat. At least she had her own home to go to.

Polly wrote long and often to Ron. He wasn't the best of letter writers, but she was glad he made the effort, even though his letters were often heavily marked by the black pen of the censor.

She also wrote to Billy. When he managed to get home for a weekend they went out for a drink. He looked very handsome in his uniform, and Polly was proud to be with him, but he didn't stop talking about the Navy and his mates. He was obviously very happy.

Sid had to go into a factory doing war work. After his free and easy life at the market, he wasn't too pleased at having someone watch over him while he worked.

'Bet you're having a good time with all the girls, though,' said Polly one night.

'Yeah, not 'alf, got some right little darlings working there, and they're not shy about sharing their rations wiv me. Mind you, I 'ave ter watch it if their old man's due 'ome.'

'Don't you let Mum hear you talk like that.'

'She don't worry about me, I can do what I like ser long as I bring in a bit extra fer 'er. I might be able ter git you a bit o' extra sugar if yer like.'

'All right then,' Polly agreed. She knew Sid was still up to his old tricks, but if it meant she could have sugar in her tea all week, she didn't care, not now.

She was grateful her days at Bloom's were busy. They still made a few dresses, and Polly was asked to alter Barny's original patterns to save as much cloth as possible. Barny, like most of the other young men who used to come and go, had been called up. Only Fred the cutter remained, too old for the Forces. Carefully he'd go over the designs with Polly, showing her how to cut and get the best out of a pattern, explaining the weave of the cloth, and how to ensure that a hem didn't drop, or the material fray. She would take a pattern home and spend all evening working out ways of improving it. For Polly this was the best part of the war; she was doing something she loved.

Most of their work now came from the government. 'From shorts to shirts and anything in between,' was Mr Bloom's favourite saying about his war effort.

But Polly was lonely. She missed Ron and Billy, and visited her mother when there wasn't any work to bring home – anything to get out of her tiny flat. Nowadays she found it less of a comfort. At times she felt the walls were closing in on her. It was quiet, almost eerie now the old lady downstairs had gone to live with her daughter. She missed going to the pub, and sitting on her own in the pictures wasn't much fun. She had never mixed with the factory girls very much – except when they had all gone on the firm's outings, or Shirley had dragged her along with the crowd for a drink – so she didn't feel she could ask any of them to go out with her; besides, some of the younger ones had left to join up or go into war work. Polly worried that she might have to go, if they made it compulsory. The thought appalled her: she hated the idea of leaving Bloom's.

It was Friday night and Polly hurried out of the factory. She had decided to go to the pictures.

''Allo, love.' Suddenly Ron stepped out of the dark doorway, making her jump.

She threw her arms round his neck and kissed him long and hard. 'Why didn't you tell me you were coming home? Let me look at you.' She pinched his cheek. 'You've put on weight. How long a leave you got?' She tucked her arm in his.

'I've only got this weekend.'

'Is that all? Still, never mind, we'll enjoy ourselves.'

'Polly, it's embarkation leave. I'm going abroad.'

She stopped and looked at him. 'Where to, Ron?'

'I don't know.'

She was upset at the thought of him going off to heaven only knew where and didn't know what to say. 'Come on,' she said, pulling herself together. 'Let's get home and have a bit of tea.'

''Ow yer managing?'

'Not too bad, I've only got meself to worry about.'

'I've got a ration card, so you won't 'ave ter go short.'

All through the weekend there was a strange atmosphere between them. Although Polly had thought many times about Ron coming home, and had planned all kinds of things, somehow it was different. She would find herself looking at him; she didn't like his short hair, and he seemed to have changed. He was certainly a lot tidier. At times they moved around the flat like strangers, then they were lovers again. Polly resented the fact that Sid spent every evening with them. She wanted to be alone with Ron, but instead the weekend was one round of boozing, which went all too quickly.

Very early on Monday morning, Ron left the house, alone. He didn't want Polly to come to the station.

Once more she felt very lonely.

When she first read Shirley's letter, she couldn't believe it. She danced round the room waving it in the air. Shirley was coming to stay with her for Easter, a whole weekend together.

For days Polly cleaned and polished everything till it shone. The girls at the factory who hadn't gone into the Forces, or were doing war work and knew Shirley from before the war, were pleased.

'Tell 'er ter come in on Saturday when we finish work, then we can all go ter the pub fer a sandwich,' said Betty, who used to work on the machine next to Shirley. Shirley still had many friends, unlike Polly who didn't have any now Shirley had gone. It occurred to her now more than ever just how alone she was. She knew part of it was through being in the office; Shirley had told her most of the girls thought she was stuck-up. When Shirley used to relate to her some of the goings-on that took place out of work, Polly appeared shocked, although really she enjoyed their bawdy jokes, and the lurid descriptions of the girls' love lives. Sometimes she envied their clothes, their peroxide hair, and fancy jewellery, and would have loved to go out with them. But she was never asked for herself, and only went with them when Shirley took her along. Ron's words often came back to her. Perhaps he was right, she thought bleakly, I may well look sinister – frightening people off with my dead eye.

On Good Friday morning, Polly sat waiting impatiently on the platform for Shirley. When she got off the train and they caught sight of each other, they screamed out, kissing, crying and hugging like a couple of schoolgirls.

'You're still wearing too much make-up,' said Polly, teasing her friend with her disapproval.

'Fanks a bunch. I come all this way ter see yer, and yer still nags. Let's go ter Lyons fer a cuppa. I'm parched.'

'That's a good idea, then you can tell me all your news.'

They strolled arm-in-arm out of the station and into the warm early spring sunshine.

'D'yer know, that train was packed. Tell yer what, there was a lot of good-looking blokes on it, and it wasn't 'alf fun being all squashed up tergever.'

'Shirley, you haven't changed.'

She laughed. 'If anyfink, I've got worse. Mind you, some of the packs these blokes 'ave ter carry about wiv 'em don't 'alf git in the way. And yer 'as ter watch where they stick their rifles.' She pushed open the door. 'I'm dying fer a pee, back in a mo.'

Polly sat down, removed her gloves, and smoothed then out on the table.

A waitress in the usual black dress and white lace cap came over and asked her what she wanted.

'A pot of tea for two please. Have you got any cakes?'

'No, we sold out first thing. We've only got buns left.' The waitress looked about her and whispered. 'They ain't got many currants in 'em.'

Polly laughed. 'Not to worry.'

'I'll have a bun,' said Shirley joining her.

'Make that two buns please,' said Polly. Leaning forward she asked eagerly, 'How's Elizabeth?'

'Great, she sits up and tries ter say "Mum". She likes a lot of attention; Mum reckons she's worse than the rest of us put tergever.'

'I'd love to see her again.'

'P'raps you can come down in the summer.'

'I could try.'

'Anyway, what yer got planned fer the weekend?'

'It's home first, then I thought we'd have an early tea, then go up West.'

'That sounds good. I've missed London.'

'It's not the same. No bright lights since the black-out, and they've taken Eros away.' Polly patted Shirley's hand. 'I've really missed you.'

The waitress arrived with the tray.

Shirley pulled her hand back. 'Don't be daft. Is there still plenty of blokes up the West End?'

'I think you'll find a few. Mostly servicemen now. Don't you go leading me astray. Remember I'm a married woman.' Polly stirred the tea in the pot. She put the strainer in the cup and began to pour. 'Just look at this, it's like gnat's water.'

'I fink it's cos there's a war on, remember,' chided Shirley.

'Hark who's telling me. You forget my husband's gone off fighting somewhere.'

'Mum was a bit upset when you wrote and said Ron 'ad gone abroad. Dad said there's a lot of trouble in Europe – not that I bovver wiv that sorta fing. How is 'e, d'yer 'ear from 'im much?'

'Not a lot. I think he's all right, I don't get any letters for ages then I get a couple together. He can't say very much, and I don't know where he is as most of the letter's blacked out by the censor. I'll show you what I mean.' She took a letter from her handbag and gave a page to Shirley.

'Looks like a kid's scribbled all over it. Ahh, I didn't fink me bruvver could be so romantic.'

Polly snatched the letter back. 'That's all you're going to see.'

'The twins signed on last week.'

'No? What for?'

'The RAF. Mum said she's glad James ain't old enough ter go – she gits a bit tearful over 'er boys. Our Vera's 'aving a baby, so she's come ter stay wiv us now Sam's in the Navy.'

'That was a bit sudden, your Vera getting married so quick.'

'Well, you know wot us Bells are like.'

'Yes, fast little hussies. So you've got another houseful now. I envy you lot.'

'Good job we've got a big 'ouse. There's still room fer you down there.'

'It could be very tempting, seeing Elizabeth and you,' Polly said wistfully.

'Come on, drink up, and let's git off before I 'ave yer crying in yer tea-cup.'

Once again, with arms linked, they walked out into the spring sunshine.

The following morning, Polly quickly quietened the alarm clock and slipped carefully out of her side of the bed, hoping to avoid waking Shirley, who was lying on her back with her mouth wide open. Polly put her hand to her mouth to stop her giggles, then swiftly moved it up to her thumping head when she bent down to retrieve her slippers. 'They must be right under the bed,' she mumbled. 'And they can stay there.'

In the kitchen she groped in the cupboard for the Andrews. 'My God, we shifted a few last night,' she groaned. 'I don't think we disgraced ourselves. Oh, this lino's cold,' she grumbled to herself out loud as she padded barefoot around the scullery, filling the kettle and making toast.

Polly was sitting at the kitchen table when the door opened. She looked up and laughed. 'You don't half look a mess.'

Shirley nonchalantly brushed her hair away from her face and peered at Polly through screwed-up, black-rimmed eyes. 'Fanks. I bet you didn't look ser good 'fore yer got yerself done up ready fer work.' Her voice was thick with sleep. 'Any tea left in that there pot? Me mouth feels like sandpaper. Where's yer fags?' she rasped.

Polly pointed her toast. 'On the mantelpiece.'

'See yer got yer grandad's whip.' She grabbed the cigarettes and matches and flopped in a chair at the table. Her pink celanese dressing-gown parted, revealing the deep cleavage of her soft white breasts. ''E was a nice old man.'

'Yes he was. I still miss him.' Polly filled a cup with tea and pushed it towards her. 'Sugar and milk's there, but if you want any toast you'll have to make it yourself, I haven't got time. OK?'

Shirley held on to the cup with both hands and nodded slightly. She put her hand to her head. 'Me bloody 'ead.'

Polly stood in front of the mirror adjusting her hat. 'Come to the factory just before one. Miss Bloom won't mind you coming up a bit early. We'll have a sandwich in the pub with the girls, then we'll take Mum to the market. Shirley, are you listening?'

She drew long and deep on her cigarette. 'Don't shout. D'yer 'ave ter be ser bloody cheerful first thing in the morning? By the way, you up the spout yet?'

'No, Ron thinks it's my fault.'

'Why's that?'

'Don't know. He reckons he tries hard enough.'

Shirley laughed, then groaned, 'Oh me 'ead.'

'I don't think it's funny. What're you laughing at?'

'I was just finking, if yer can't fall, just fink of the fun you can 'ave.'

'You forget I'm married. It's over a year now.'

'Yer, I know, but remember there's a war on, and while the cat's away and all that . . . Get stuck in, gel, I bet 'e is. 'E could be in France wiv all those oh-la-la French bits.'

161

Polly scowled at her. 'Shirley, you can be so crude at times. Anyway, d'you fancy going to a dance tonight?' said Polly, changing the subject.

'Yer, where shall we go?' And as usual, without waiting for a reply, Shirley added, 'What about good old 'Ammersmif?'

She hesitated. 'It's a bit far.'

'Yer must be joking. Yer know it's worth it. By the way, any chance of a new frock from the factory?'

'I don't know, I'll have to ask Miss Bloom. We've got some seconds left over from the last order – I expect we could find one your size. We have to take them to pieces now and try to make some good ones out of them.'

'How's that good-looking brother of 'ers? 'E still around?'

'No, Miss Bloom said he's a pilot in the RAF now.'

'I bet 'e'll break a few 'earts then. Where's 'e stationed?'

'Don't know.'

'I 'ope 'e comes down our way. Cor, that'd start the tongues wagging if I walked in wiv 'im on me arm.'

'You can dream, ducky.' Polly ran her hand down her left leg to straighten the seam of her stocking. 'If you want to borrow anything, just help yourself. I'm off. See you later.'

'Don't work too 'ard.'

Polly's steps were light as she went to work. She even jumped over the crack in Tower Bridge, and she didn't care who saw her . . .

Chapter 14

Polly stood in the office gazing out. The early spring sunshine was straining to come through the green netting that covered the window. The sound from the outside traffic was deadened. She twisted her wedding ring round and round. Today was Easter Saturday. A year ago, though not to the day, she had got married. Grandad had still been alive then. Now it was April, and the country had been at war for almost eight months. Apart from Ron being abroad, and one or two other problems like rationing and the black-out, things hadn't been as horrific as everyone had forecast.

Polly looked at her watch. It was almost one o'clock. I expect Shirley will be late as usual, she thought to herself as the phone rang. It was for Sarah Bloom. 'I'm afraid Miss Bloom isn't here at the moment . . . No, not till Tuesday. OK. Thank you.' She replaced the receiver and peered through the criss-cross strips of brown paper Mr Bloom had insisted they stick over the office door's glass panel, to prevent it flying about in the event of an air-raid.

Shirley had arrived and was busy talking to the girls on the machines. She caught sight of Polly and waved, then made her way to the office. Pushing the door open, she poked her head round and asked, 'All right if I come in?'

'Course.'

'Where's Miss Bloom?'

'She's gone. She said you can have one of the dresses if it fits you, but we can't do any alterations here.'

'Did she say 'ow much?'

Polly thoughtfully rubbed her chin and, imitating Mr Bloom said, 'To you, my dear, a pound.'

They laughed.

'Yer know, yer gitting ter sound more like one of them every time I sees yer. The frocks still kept downstairs in the basement?'

Polly nodded. Suddenly the dull drone of the machines stopped. The noise of chairs scraping on the wooden floor followed immediately.

'Must be one o'clock.'

The door burst open and Betty popped her head round. The babble of women's chatter, high heels clattering, and the ping of the clocking-off clock drifted into the office. 'See yer in the Arms, Shirl,' she called, and disappeared.

'Wait till they've finished rushing down the stairs, then we'll go down and have a look at these frocks. You can try one on if you like. Fred said he don't mind waiting a while to lock up.'

After the girls left, they went downstairs. Polly opened the stock-room door and pulled on the light.

Shirley hung back. 'This place always used ter give me the creeps when yer opens the door and yer on yer own. I always fink sumfink 'orrible's gonner run past yer leg.' She stepped inside the dimly lit room and looked around. 'What's 'appened ter all the bales of clorf that used ter be stacked up over there?'

'They've all been used.'

'Cor, I remember the fun we used ter 'ave behind them. Some of those delivery boys were a bit of all right.'

Polly tutted. 'No wonder you finished up in the family way.'

Shirley looked hurt. 'We didn't git up ter nufink like that. So, when yer gitting more stock?'

'We can't, not at the moment. I'm a bit worried, that's all we've got left. I don't know if Mr Bloom will keep all the staff on.'

164

'I fought you was busy wiv government orders.'

'We are, but I reckon Miss Bloom could do without me.'

'Well in that case you can come down ter Bristol and work in the aircraft factory wiv me,' she grinned. 'Right, where's these frocks?'

Polly pulled a dust sheet off from a rail of dresses.

Shirley slowly flipped through them. 'I like this one, an' it looks about my size.' She pulled out a green linen dress with short sleeves, and held it at arm's length.

'Try it on, it's your colour, and that cross-over neck should suit you. I like the way you're doing your hair now.'

'It's all the go, wings up at the sides, wiv a bang. I'm surprised you ain't let yours grow – put a bit o' peroxide on it, it'll do wonders for yer. Yer'll 'ave ter let me 'ave a go at it one of these days.' She took off her coat.

Polly stared at her, and gasped out loud. 'That's my brooch.'

'Yer I know, yer don't mind, do yer? I found it in yer drawer. It's the one Ron gave yer fer Christmas, ain't it?'

Polly's throat went dry, but before she could answer, Shirley went on as always.

'Don't worry, I'll look after it, I won't lose it; if I do I'll git yer anuver. It'll look nice on this frock.' She held the dress against her.

Polly was speechless for a few seconds. 'What do you mean, you'll get me another? Do you know where Ron bought it?'

'No, I s'pect it come from the market; but it looks good, don't it?' She patted the brooch, then turned her attention to the dress. 'I like this one, I'll try it on.'

'Well, be quick, then let's get out of here in case Miss Bloom comes back.'

'Why? Yer said it was all right.'

'Yes, yes it is, but the girls will be waiting for us in the pub.'

'Don't worry about them, they know wot I'm like when I gits sumfink new.'

'Hello Shirley, how are you? Margaret said you were coming in today.'

They hadn't heard Sarah Bloom open the stock-room door. They spun round.

'You're looking very . . .' She didn't move from the doorway. Immediately the colour drained from her face, the muscles round her mouth began twitching.

''Allo Miss Bloom.'

'Where did you get that?' she whispered. Her voice had a slight tremble as she tried to speak in a calm and level tone.

'Polly, I mean Margaret 'ere, said it was all right fer me ter 'ave a frock. I'll pay fer it,' Shirley babbled anxiously.

'Yes, yes. I didn't mean the frock, er, dress. I meant that brooch.'

Polly froze.

'Pretty ain't it?' Shirley touched it. 'It's Polly's.'

Sarah Bloom's eyes, wide and staring, quickly darted to Polly.

Polly's throat went dry. The whole of her body felt as if it belonged to someone else. It was as if she was watching this scene from a distance. All these past months she had been torn between believing and disbelieving Ron's word. After thinking about it for a long while, she had decided it would be an act of betrayal if she had the brooch valued. And what could she do if it was Miss Bloom's? She couldn't send her husband to prison. When Ron had gone into the Army, she had put it out of sight at the back of the drawer, and had forgotten about it, till today. Now her best friend was wearing it, and her worst fears were being confirmed. She could hear Shirley's voice echoing round in her head.

'You all right, Miss Bloom? Yer look ever so pale.'

'Take it off.' It was a command, not a request.

Shirley's dark marble-like eyes flicked from one to the other. She noticed the fear on Polly's face, and clearly sensed something was wrong. 'Why d'yer wanner see it?'

166

Sarah Bloom tried to smile. 'I'd just like to look at it, it looks very good.'

'It's only a cheap paste . . .'

'You heard me,' Sarah Bloom's voice rose. 'Take it off at once.'

Shirley covered it with her hand, she looked annoyed. 'Why? It ain't nufink ter do wiv you.'

Polly stood motionless, like a statue. She couldn't speak; as her face paled it became expressionless.

'Polly, say sumfink.'

'Just do as she asks,' she croaked.

Slowly Shirley undid the pin and handed it to Sarah, who almost snatched it from her.

She turned it over in her hand. Her eyes smouldered. 'Margaret, where did you get it from? My father had this specially made for me, to his design, so I know it's mine.'

'Yours?' said Shirley in disbelief.

'Sarah.' David Bloom's voice came from outside in the corridor. 'Sarah, hurry up, I haven't got all day.'

'I'm here, in the stock-room,' she called over her shoulder, her voice shaking with emotion.

'Have you got that order form Dad asked . . ?' David came into the room. He filled the doorway, and in his uniform he looked taller and more handsome than Polly remembered.

'Hello Margaret, how are you?' His face broke into a smile, and he looked genuinely pleased to see her. He took off his smart Air Force officer's peaked cap, and quickly ran his fingers through his tight black curls. 'As you can see, I made it. Your advice was . . .'

Sarah turned to face him. 'My God, what's wrong with you? You look like you've seen a ghost.' Before she could answer he continued, 'Oh no, don't say the rats have come back, after all the money Dad spent on . . .'

Sarah moved in front of him. She said nothing and opened her clenched fist. The diamonds caught the light from the naked bulb that hung low from the ceiling on a single brown flex. They danced like fire in the palm of her open hand. She handed it to her brother.

'Where did this come from?' He studied it, and slowly turned it over. His black brows furrowed. 'Isn't this one of the things that was stolen? Where did you find it?'

'We didn't find it,' said Sarah. 'Shirley was wearing it.'

'It ain't mine. It's Polly's,' blurted out Shirley.

'Who's Polly? Oh sorry, you mean Margaret?' asked David, confused.

'She didn't find it,' said Sarah. And turning on Polly asked, 'Did you?'

Tears trickled down her face. Polly's world was crumbling all around her. Her thoughts were in uproar. Fear was overriding them all. She would lose her job. Her friend, whose fault it was anyway, couldn't wait to tell. Why was she so nosy? How dare she rummage through Polly's things. Now she would have to tell on her husband.

David Bloom walked towards her. 'Well?' he said in her face. His voice was flat. 'Where did it come from?'

She remained silent, clenching her teeth till her jaws ached.

'Please tell me. Don't make me angry.'

Still she said nothing.

Grabbing her shoulders he shook her. 'Margaret. Answer me. Where did you get it? Who gave it to you?' He tightened his grip, and his brown eyes were fired with anger. She wanted to cry out in pain.

'Answer me,' he said, shaking her with every word.

'Stop it,' shouted Shirley, grabbing David's arm. 'It was her . . .'

Polly winced. 'It was Sid. My brother gave it to me,' she said hastily.

Shirley put her hand to her mouth. 'Polly,' she gasped.

'When did he give it to you?' asked David Bloom.

168

'Christmas, it was a present.' Polly's voice was weak and feeble.

'That figures. Sarah, telephone the police. We'll let them get to the bottom of this.'

'Polly!' yelled Shirley.

With tears running down her face she turned on her friend. 'You shut up.'

Sarah moved towards Polly, and with tears in her eyes said softly, 'You knew this was mine, didn't you? You knew. All this time, and you knew. All I've done for you, all the help I've given you. Why don't you say something?'

Polly was crying silently, unable to answer.

'I liked you, Margaret, very much,' said David quietly. 'And now I just feel betrayed.'

'We all do,' said Sarah. 'I can't believe you could have kept it, knowing it had been stolen from me. Why didn't you hand it to the police?'

Polly's sobs filled the stock-room.

'Come off it, Sarah, she couldn't have done that, not without implicating her brother.' David looked anxious.

'She could have thrown it away, thrown it over the factory wall, anything.' Sarah's voice rose with anger. 'Not kept it, not after she knew it was mine.'

'Did she know it was yours?'

'I described it to her in great detail after the robbery. She could easily have visualized it. You knew, didn't you? And all this time I thought I could trust you.'

David took hold of his sister's arm and led her outside.

Polly slumped down on a bale of cloth. She shivered, the basement felt cold, the smell of damp filling her nostrils. She put her head in her hands and wept bitterly.

Shirley lightly touched her shoulder.

Polly quickly shrugged her hand away.

'I'm sorry, Pol, really sorry. I didn't know. But what did yer go an' say it was Sid for?'

There was no reply, no loud crying now, just the gentle heaving of her shoulders.

They both looked up at the glass bricks above their heads when a pair of heavy boots went clomping past, filling the room with the noise.

'It wouldn't 'ave mattered if yer said Ron,' Shirley said quietly, shaking her head. ''E's overseas, fighting. But poor old Sid. 'E's already been in the nick. Gawd only knows 'ow many years 'e'll git if they pin this one on 'im and find 'im guilty. 'E'll kill yer when 'e finds out wot yer said – yer knows that, don't yer?'

Polly jerked her head up. She looked a mess, her face was red, and her mascara had run down her cheeks. 'Oh Shirley, what have I done? If Sid don't kill me, me mum will.' She jumped up. 'I've got to tell them the truth.'

At that moment David walked into the room. 'Oh yes, and what is the truth?' he asked, his voice cold.

'I lied.' She looked down at her handkerchief and began picking at it nervously. 'It wasn't my brother who gave me the brooch, it was my husband.'

The sound of Sarah's high heels on the concrete stairs preceded her. 'I'll tell Fred not to wait, we can lock up. We don't want too many people knowing about this,' she said, standing in the doorway.

'Margaret's just told me it was her husband, not her brother,' said David.

Sarah paused and slowly moved forward. Her face was set in a grim fashion as she bit on her lower lip. 'He's overseas.' She turned to Polly. 'You know, you're a very clever young lady, switching the blame to him just to save your brother. Although I must say I'm surprised at that after what he did to you as a child. But it's too late, anyway. I've told the police and they're picking him up right away – then they're coming here, for you.'

Polly felt the room spinning. She quickly sat down. What was happening to her? Why was she made to suffer all these injustices? She didn't ask for a lot out of life. What on earth would happen to her now? And what would Sid and her mother do to her when they found out?

'I'm sorry,' she whispered.

'So am I,' said Sarah Bloom. 'So am I.'

Chapter 15

The prison sentence of twenty-eight days was, the magistrate said, to make an example of Polly for receiving stolen goods. He added that she would have got more if she hadn't been so young.

Young. Nineteen might be young to him, but to Polly it felt as if she had lived a lifetime. And the sentence seemed to go on forever.

The small cell, the prison warders, and the lack of privacy all helped to make her days long, shameful and miserable. She had to work in the laundry. It was heavy and dirty, and she hated it. Handling other women's smelly washing, surrounded by steam and noise from the huge machines all added to her discomfort.

When at last it was over and the huge gates slammed shut behind her, Polly shuddered, even though the sun felt warm on her face as it filtered through the streets on that early morning.

She stood for a moment or two breathing in the fresh, clean air, then she walked away – free. Tomorrow was the first of June. A new month, and a new life, for she knew she had to start again; there could never be any going back, not now. She hurried towards the bus stop, not turning to look back at the great ugly building she'd been locked up inside. 'I think I'd rather do meself in than go back in there again,' she mumbled under her breath.

It was after the workmen's rush hour, so the bus was empty. When the conductor came up for the fare he looked at her knowingly, making her feel dirty and tainted. She told herself she must try to forget that part of her life, that it was over, but she knew she would never forget it – or forgive Ron. Through him she had lost her job, and Miss Bloom's trust. Even her mother had disowned her for accusing Sid and making her lose her job at the factory. Polly looked through the green anti-splinter mesh covering the bus windows, but she wasn't seeing anything. She drew long and hard on her cigarette. What was she going to do?

Finally reaching the safety and comfort of her own flat, she paused and leaned against the door for a while, grateful to be home. A few letters were strewn over the passage floor; picking them up she quickly glanced at the envelopes, took them upstairs and put them on the table without opening them. 'Nothing from Billy,' she said out loud. 'Right, first things first,' and, filling the kettle, put it on the gas for a welcome cup of tea.

She threw the two letters from Ron to one side, unopened. At this moment all feelings she had for him were dead. After making herself a pot of tea, she sat at the table and mulled over her fate. It was his fault she had been sent to prison. He should never have given her that bloody brooch. Why did he always have to put on a show?

There was a letter from the landlord telling her how much rent she owed, and the one from the furniture shop was on the same theme. She pushed them aside, picked up her cup and propped her elbows on the table. 'Where am I going to get the money to pay these?' she said out loud. Her gaze wandered to the whip curled up over the fireplace. Her lip trembled. 'Oh Grandad, what am I going to do? I've no job, and Mum won't have me back, not now.'

She laid her head on her arms and let the weeks of pent-up hate and fear flow from her eyes while her thoughts travelled back to that black day in court.

Her mother, in the witness box, had pointed her long bony finger at her and, narrowing her eyes, had shouted, 'You've always been jealous of Sid. Always 'ad it in fer 'im ever since yer lorst yer eye. That was an accident, and yer knows it, yer scheming little cow. Yer been waiting fer years ter pin sumfink on 'im, ain't yer? Yer knows full well he wasn't wiv yer old man the night the Blooms got done over.'

When Shirley told the judge it was Ron who gave Polly the brooch, he must have believed her, and her mother, and the pawnbroker, who said it wasn't Sid who sold him the gear.

Miss Bloom had told the judge how Polly had suddenly changed her mind and said it was her husband, serving overseas, who had given it to her. He asked Polly why at first she had tried to implicate her brother.

She could only whisper. 'I don't know.'

The police had been eager to get their hands on Sid again, but when he told them that after closing time he went home and Ron went off to meet his father to go to Covent Garden, they could find nothing to connect him with the robbery, so Sid got off scot-free. Then when the judge heard that Miss Bloom had described the brooch in detail to Polly after Christmas, and she remembered her reaction, he sentenced her for receiving.

Through her tears, Polly had looked across at Sarah Bloom, who had quickly turned away. Polly was sure she had seen tears in her eyes.

A pang of conscience brought her back to the present. It worried her. What if her mother had been right, and Sid wasn't involved. Had she been looking for an excuse to get her own back? How long would he have got if he'd been found guilty? He'd already been in prison; it could have been a couple of years.

She shuddered. The fear and horror she had felt in prison had been like a nightmare, she had never felt as terrified as she had in that dreadful place. What must it be like for men, some of them locked up for years? She was so confused.

She looked again at the bills, and then back at the whip. 'Grandad, my life's in such a mess, what am I going to do?'

She caught a whiff of the prison's carbolic soap clinging to her skin. 'First I must have a bath,' she said out loud, and began filling the saucepans with water, and balancing them on the gas stove before going down into the yard to bring up the tin bath.

Over the years she had developed a liking for nice things, and one of Polly's luxuries was her sweet-smelling soap and perfume. It was the same as Sarah Bloom had been wearing the first day Polly went to the factory.

Sitting in the bath, she gently squeezed the flannel, letting the warm water trickle over her body. 'I wish this was Ron's neck,' she said, out loud, squeezing the flannel tighter. 'At this very moment I'd willingly swing for him, making me lose my job – and all my self-respect.' She groaned. If only she could see Miss Bloom, just to tell her – but tell her what? And where was she going to go? She couldn't go to Shirley's, not now; and besides, they were Ron's family, and she didn't ever want to see *him* again.

Relaxing in the warm, perfumed water, her mind went back once more to prison. Slowly a smile spread over her face as she remembered the last two weeks, the many conversations she had had with her cell-mate Brenda, and the things she'd told her. She'd certainly broadened her education! Brenda was about the same age as Polly, and was doing twenty-eight days for soliciting. Her tales about her exploits and encounters with clients had helped Polly to keep her sanity, and their giggles would bring the warders shouting for them to be quiet.

'I'm fed up with the bleeding rozzers down here,' Brenda had said. 'I'm going up North when I get out. Don't know why they can't make it all legal like.'

Polly, in her innocence, had asked, 'They couldn't do that, could they?'

'Why not, they do in other countries.'

'They don't, do they?'

Brenda nodded. 'They sure do. I've always fancied being a Madam meself.' She walked round the cell, waggling her hips in an exaggerated way.

'What's a Madam?'

'Christ, you're so bloody naïve. She's the one that sits in the warm and takes the money.' Brenda sat on her bunk. 'I've got to get away from London. They all know me and, besides, I ain't making enough dough to keep meself in silk stockings.'

'You could always go in a factory.'

'You must be bloody joking.' She leaned forward and said earnestly, 'D'you know, on a good night I can make well over a couple of quid. Go on, tell me what sorta factory pays that kind of money?'

'A day?' said Polly in amazement.

'No, a night, stupid. Here, Polly, why don't you come up North with me. You ain't got nothing to lose down here as far as I can see.'

Polly was shocked. 'I couldn't do that sort of thing, not . . .'

'I don't mean go on the game. Christ, I've got enough competition, I don't need you adding to it. No, I'm going to join the NAAFI.'

'The NAAFI? No, I couldn't leave London, what if Billy, my young brother, comes home?'

'Well, think about it.'

Over the few weeks they were together, Brenda had asked her more than once to change her mind and go up North with her when she got out.

Polly shivered as the bath water cooled. She stood up and wrapped a towel round herself. I don't suppose she'll even bother to come and see me when she does get out next week, she told herself.

She turned on the wireless. The announcer was reading the news and, only half listening, she made herself another pot of tea. She was sitting at the table when he said something about British Forces being evacuated from Dunkirk in anything that floated.

Her thoughts went to Billy. She hoped he was safe. It didn't sound like things were going too well with this war. The news-reader's voice droned on, but she still couldn't really concentrate on what he was saying. Her thoughts kept going back to

177

her husband. If Ron was one of those trying to get out of France, he'd push every other bugger out of the way and make sure he got on a boat!

She looked in the mirror, pushing her hair back to study her pale face. Over the years, her little-girl blonde hair had darkened; often she had been tempted to peroxide it as Shirley suggested. She leaned forward. 'I suppose now's as good a time as any to change my appearance, as well as my life,' she said to her reflection.

She took a jug from the cupboard and began emptying her dirty bath water into an enamel bucket. 'Tonight I think I'll go to the pictures and try to cheer myself up.'

For a week Polly wandered the streets, not knowing what to do or where to go. She knew she had to get a job, but at the moment she didn't feel like facing people. And what if they wanted a reference from Bloom's? She could scarcely expect Miss Bloom to give her a good one.

Once or twice she had gone to the top of Penn's Place to look at her old house. One day she saw her mother hurrying along to the market and Polly had quickly dodged round a corner. There was no point in attracting her attention. If only Grandad was still alive, she'd thought then, full of despair. She could have sneaked in and had a little talk with him.

Lazily Polly turned over, aware of the sun streaming through her bedroom window. Last night had been very warm, so she had pulled back the black-out curtains and opened the window before getting into bed. She looked at the clock and let her thoughts go to Bloom's. Eight: the machines would be starting up now. Everybody would be chattering about what they did over the weekend, and who they'd been out with. With a sob she turned over again. What had she got to get up for?

A banging on the front door made her sit up. Who was knocking at this time of the morning? Could it be the landlord wanting his rent? Or could they be coming for the furniture that wasn't paid for? Polly slid back under the sheet and shut her eyes tightly, hoping and praying they would go away.

The thumping on the knocker continued. A female voice called out, 'Open up. It's me.'

Polly sat up again and cocked her head. She was unable to place the voice. 'Go away,' she shouted.

'Polly, Polly, it's me. Let me in.'

Excitedly Polly jumped out of bed and hung out of the window. 'I'm coming,' she yelled and, pulling on her dressing-gown, she raced down the stairs. Flinging open the front door, she threw her arms round an astonished Brenda, crushing her to her and half lifting her off her feet. 'You came,' she said breathlessly.

'Here, hang on. Bloody 'ell, what's up?'

'I'm so pleased to see you.'

'I can see that.'

'You look very nice.'

'Well, this is a bit better than prison gear.' Brenda's pretty elfin face broke into a smile as she smoothed down the pale-blue floral cotton dress that clung to her hips, seductively going in and out in all the right places. The low-cut front of the sweetheart-shaped neckline was pushed out by her firm, rounded breasts, revealing a glimpse of the deep cleavage hidden below. Her long, well-shaped legs were clad in fine silk stockings, and cream high heels added more inches to her five feet three. On top of her lightly hennaed hair was a tiny cream straw hat with a long veil draped artistically round her throat. Polly's skilful eye noted that it was all expensive stuff; Brenda looked as if she had just stepped out of a dress shop instead of prison.

'Ain't you going to ask me in?'

'Of course, come on.' Polly was almost jumping up and down with excitement. She ran up the stairs. 'I live up here,' she said over her shoulder.

Brenda picked up her suitcase with one hand, and Polly noticed the fox fur hanging over the other. At the top of the stairs she put the case down and rubbed the palm of her gloved hand.

179

'Me landlady's chucked me out. All right if I stay with you for a bit?'

A huge grin spread across Polly's face as she nodded enthusiastically. 'Course. Fancy a cup of tea?'

'Not half. It was packed on the bus. I ain't used to being out this time o' day.'

'How long you staying?' shouted Polly from the scullery.

'Don't know, not long, I've got to earn some money.'

Polly came back into the kitchen. 'So have I. Look at that lot.' She waved her hand at the letters propped up behind the clock on the mantelpiece. 'They all want money, and I don't know how I'm going to pay them.'

Brenda looked up, nodding at the whip on the wall. 'That's nice. Belong to your old man?'

'No, it was me grandad's.'

'That handle silver?'

'Yes.'

'What's it worth?'

'Don't know, but I could never sell it.'

Brenda stood up and carefully began removing the many pins from her hat.

'That's a lovely hat,' said Polly.

'Should be, cost me a bloody fortune. Still, you've got to look the part in my job otherwise you could end up with a lot o' riff-raff.' She studied her hat for a moment before putting it on a chair. Patting her hair, she added, 'I was a bit up-market, you know.'

Polly laughed. 'I can just see you walking down Oxford Street swinging your handbag and waggling your bum.'

They laughed at that.

Brenda sat at the table. 'It's a good way to earn a few bob. D'you know, I bet I can earn more in a night just laying on me back than you took home all week.'

'Is it that good?' asked Polly, pouring out the tea and pushing the cup and saucer towards her.

'Well, it ain't what you call hard work.'

'Are you still going up North?' asked Polly.

'Yeah, I'm getting too well-known down here. 'Sides, I fancy a change of scenery, and I feel I'll have to do me bit for the country before long. I don't want them to call me up to go in a factory or the Land Army.' She threw her head back and laughed. 'Here, can you see me milking a cow?'

Polly shook her head laughing. 'What exactly will you do up there?' she asked.

'I told you. There's this big army camp in Yorkshire, and I've been thinking of joining the NAAFI.'

'I've seen the posters about it. What will you do?'

'Serve in the canteen, or in the shop they've got on the camp.'

Polly sat mulling it over. 'Can anyone work there?'

'Should think so. 'Sides, I hope to make meself a few bob on the side.'

'What, with the soldiers?'

'No, the officers – bloody squaddies don't earn enough fer me.'

'Will they still let you work there even if you've been in prison?'

'Look ducks, there's a war on. I don't think they'll worry that much. It's not exactly a military secret, how to make a cheese roll.' She looked over her shoulder and put a finger, with its long red-painted nail, to her matching shiny red lips. 'Shh, p'raps it is, depends on what they put in 'em. Here, fancy being caught by the Germans and being tortured for the secret of the ham sandwich. I'm a coward, I'd tell 'em.'

They fell about laughing and Polly felt happy for the first time in ages. It was good to have someone to talk to. 'How much will it cost to go to Yorkshire?'

'Dunno. I've got a few bob tucked away.' She lifted her skirt revealing a ten-shilling note stuck in the top of her stocking. 'Anyway, we can always get on a train with a platform ticket, and if the inspector gets on you can hide in the lav. 'Sides, with so many people getting on and off the trains they won't notice little old me stuck in the middle of a crowd – I can blend in and hide behind some big strapping sergeant. Got any more tea in that pot?'

'You blend in,' that's a laugh,' said Polly. 'You'll stick out like a sore thumb dressed up to the nines like that.' She refilled the tea-pot. 'Wouldn't they give you a train ticket if you joined down here?'

'Dunno, but I want to find out all about it first.'

Polly shrugged. 'That's not helping me to solve my problem,' she said, sitting down at the table.

'Well, why don't you come with me?'

'What about me flat and all me nice furniture?'

'It's all in your old man's name, ain't it?'

Polly nodded. 'Yes, but . . .'

'Well then, you ain't got nothing to worry about. Just pack your clothes and go. But first of all, fancy going to the Palais tonight?'

Polly hesitated.

'I'll pay,' said Brenda.

'Oh no, it's not only that. I feel a bit self-conscious about me eye in those sort of places. It wasn't so bad when I went with Shirley, we used to have a few dances together.'

'Well I ain't going to bleeding dance with you,' spluttered Brenda.

Polly looked embarrassed.

'Sorry love, that was a bit thoughtless. Tell you what, why don't you wear sunglasses like the film stars do? It'll make you look all mysterious like. And put some colour on your cheeks – you looks like you've just come out a prison.' She rubbed her hands together. 'P'raps we'll be able to pick up a couple of punters and earn ourselves a few bob.'

Polly looked horrified. 'What, go on the game?'

When Brenda smiled, two small dimples appeared in her rouged cheeks. 'Well, it ain't exactly going on the game.'

'But I'm married. I couldn't do anything like that.'

'Don't talk daft. At least you're not new to it . . . Besides, when needs must – and it's better than starving.'

'I'm not *that* hard up.'

'Not yet. Why be faithful to that old man of yours – it was through him you went to prison, wasn't it?'

'Well . . . Yes.'

'Anyway, I thought you'd had enough of him.'

'Yes, but . . .'

'No buts about it,' interrupted Brenda. 'He's probably having it away with some foreign tart right now.'

'I don't know. I don't think I could.'

'Well, why don't we find out?'

Polly hesitated. 'Have we got to bring them back here?'

'Not if you don't want to. We can always go in a shop doorway. That's one good thing about the black-out. But remember to ask for the money first.'

Polly was taken aback. 'How much do I charge?' she asked, as much out of curiosity as anything.

'Well, let's see, as it's outside and a bit rough, I think you should get five bob.'

'Five bob?'

'If he haggles make it half-a-crown. Oh, and a word of warning, if you ever has it in the park, get him to put his coat down first – grass stains are a bugger to get out.'

Chapter 16

Polly was nervously fidgeting with her gas-mask case. The usual noise and hubbub of a railway station was going over her head. Once or twice soldiers rushing past almost knocked her over with their backpacks. When she bent down to shuffle the two suitcases closer together, a sailor, with his kit-bag over his shoulder, pushed past and gave her a wink. She tried to look above the sea of people, mostly in uniforms, for Brenda. Suddenly she caught sight of her and waved frantically to catch her attention.

Brenda pushed and shoved her way through to Polly, waving two platform tickets under her nose. 'I've got 'em,' she said, picking up her case. 'The machine was empty, so I had to go to the ticket office. The old man asked me if I was seeing me boyfriend off. When I said yes, the cheeky bugger gave me a wink and asked me what I was doing tonight. He was old enough to be me dad.

Polly smiled weakly. 'What platform?'

'Number six, over there.'

They moved forward and became part of the crowd of men and women in uniforms of all colours, and of girls in pretty summer dresses, tearfully seeing their husbands and boyfriends off. Some were just lolling about, while others were locked in a deep embrace, completely oblivious to the outside world. Many people were rushing to catch trains, some with bewildered, worried looks on their faces, their movements hampered by suitcases or kit-bags.

Polly looked up at the big clock hanging from the iron girders above her head, slowly ticking the minutes away. 'What time does the train leave?' She had to raise her voice to make herself heard.

'Half an hour. We'd better get right up the other end so we can blend in.'

Polly laughed. 'You make me laugh with your blending in. All the blokes keep giving you the eye.'

'I'm hoping someone's going to take pity on us and give us a hand with this case. It weighs a ton, and if I ladder me stockings, I'll go mad.'

'The way you're wiggling your backside you'll get more than a hand. 'Sides, have you thought how we're going to get through the ticket barrier with these? What are we going to say if they ask us why we've got cases and only platform tickets?'

'Sometimes, Polly, you're so thick. If we flutter our eyelashes we can get someone to carry our cases through, and we can just stroll along behind.'

'You won't catch me fluttering my eyelashes – that'd make 'em run a mile.'

'Stop being daft. Look, here's someone, I'll push me way nearer to him.'

Polly wasn't as optimistic as her friend, and the old brown leather suitcase banging against her leg was making her feel miserable and uneasy – but Brenda had winning ways. The young man took their cases on to the platform, and they walked through the barrier with no trouble at all.

After all the pushing and shoving to get on the train, they still couldn't find a seat, so they had to stand in the corridor, Brenda crushed hard against Polly. They had their legs astride their cases, and Polly gave a great sigh of relief when the train finally pulled out of the station.

'See, I told you it'd be OK with a platform ticket,' whispered Brenda, as she tried to edge herself and her case further along the corridor.

Polly followed close behind. 'We've still got to get out of

the station at the other end,' she hissed.

'Don't worry about that, not with all these soldiers to help us.' She smiled up at a tall sergeant in Army uniform, who pushed her case next to his kit-bag.

'Here you are love, park yourself on this.' He gave his kit-bag a kick.

Polly managed to get her suitcase next to Brenda's and tentatively perched herself on it. 'How long have we got to be cooped up like sardines?' she asked, moving slightly so the door handle didn't stick in her back.

'Where you off to?' asked the sergeant.

'Catterick. Do you know it?' asked Brenda breathlessly.

'Know it? Blimey, half the bloody train's going there. You two joining the ATS?'

'No, we're in the NAAFI,' she lied.

He bent down and slid his arm round her shoulder. 'In that case I'd better look after you if I want a nice fresh cup of tea in the mornings.'

'You won't be getting it in bed, that's for sure,' laughed Brenda.

He laughed with her. 'That's a pity. Fag?' He pulled a packet of cigarettes from his tunic pocket.

'Thanks. You want one, Polly?'

'Please.'

The sergeant gave her a nod and a wink. She felt herself blush and pulled the brim of her shiny navy-blue straw hat down further over her blind eye – she was still very conscious of it – and drew heavily on the cigarette when a light was offered. She leaned back against the side of the train; the general hubbub and the click-clacking of the wheels as they rushed over the track gave her time to think. Brenda was busy chatting to the sergeant as if she had known him for years – but then that was Brenda's way. Living with her over this past week had made Polly realize what different worlds they lived in.

Her mind went back to the disaster behind the Palais when she had had her first lesson in 'the trade', as Brenda had called

187

it; her first attempt at being a Pro. Pro – that was a laugh: the only fellow she fancied and managed to get outside was drunk and incapable. Still, so were most of the blokes inside, and Polly knew she wasn't exactly sober.

Her 'client' had pushed her into a doorway. Immediately one hand had gone up her skirt, grabbing her thighs, while the other hand had torn at the buttons at the top of her dress. 'Here, take it easy, mind me buttons,' she protested, and slowly began undoing them for him.

Brenda had told her to wear something they could get off easily. 'They don't want to spend half the night looking for it, they could get browned off and go on home,' she'd said.

So it was the pale-blue button-through frock and French knickers. Ron always liked that frock and made a big thing about undoing the buttons whenever she wore it. At that moment she almost thought fondly of Ron as she looked around the corridor for somewhere to stub out her cigarette.

The sergeant must have been watching her. 'Give it here, love.'

She passed him the end of her cigarette smeared with red stain from her lipstick. 'Thanks.'

What would Ron say if he knew I'd tried to go on the game, and – with Brenda's help – bleached my hair? she wondered. He'd probably say she looked a right tart; he'd more than likely try to kill her, or at the very least give her a bloody good hiding. Still, it was his fault she'd lost her job in the first place and finished up in prison. She settled back and let her thoughts return once more to what should have been her first and only customer.

The fellow had kissed her mouth with long, ardent kisses. Pulling her breast from her bra, he'd begun fondling it and, although it was a warm night, Polly had stood frozen to the spot. He quickly took his hand down from up her knicker leg and fumbled with his flies. Terrified, she waited for him to enter her. Suddenly she realized she couldn't do this sort of thing. She pulled away and looked down. Shaking her head she whispered, 'I'm sorry.'

But he was too concerned with himself to take much notice of her. 'Sod it,' he muttered. 'Hang on a bit. I'll be all right in half a mo'.' He was desperately trying to revive his limp John Thomas.

Polly began to laugh. It was just a nervous giggle at first, but when he said, 'Could you give me a bit of a hand?' she shrieked almost hysterically. 'I'm sorry – but when you said, give me a hand . . .' Tears rolled down her face and she fell back against the shop door holding her sides. 'I'm sorry.' She wasn't sure if she was laughing with relief, fear, or the drink.

Fortunately the young RAF lad could also see the funny side of it, and started laughing with her. Tidying himself up he said, 'Got brewer's droop – not to worry. Come on, love, let's go and have another drink. Perhaps we can give it another go when I'm on leave again.'

Polly had done up her buttons, smoothed down her clothes and straightened her hat. She'd slipped her arm through his and they staggered, arm-in-arm, to the nearest pub.

The next day she had had the curse, but anyway she'd decided by then that Brenda's so-called easy money really wasn't for her.

For Polly, the uncomfortable train journey dragged on and on. Brenda was enjoying every moment of it, being surrounded by servicemen offering her cigarettes and whispering in her ear, causing her to laugh loudly and flirt outrageously.

Once more the train began slowing down. The journey had been full of stopping and starting. The sergeant had told them earlier that the delays were probably due to them giving priority to Service personnel on the move. Now he looked out of the window and announced, 'This is it, girls.'

As the train puffed into the station, most of the men gathered up their belongings. Polly and Brenda were almost flattened against the side of the train when it stopped and they all jumped out.

'Come on,' yelled Brenda, hobbling along on her high heels and dragging her suitcase behind her. 'We've got to get in the middle of this lot.'

Somehow, much to Polly's relief, they managed to get through the barrier with only their platform tickets, and on to a bus that was going to the camp.

Once there, they wandered outside the perimeter for a while.

'Well, what d'you think?' asked Polly.

'I don't know.'

Polly was hungry and beginning to get angry. 'Don't say we came all this way for nothing.'

Brenda ignored her. 'I'll go and have a word with that fellow over there,' she said and breezed off. When she came back, she was all smiles. 'Come on, we've got to go to the office. That nice young lad's given me directions.'

'We could be a couple of spies,' muttered Polly.

'Don't talk daft, I told him all about us.'

'So much for security!'

They found the office and were interviewed by a mountain of a woman who looked as formidable as the prison warders. They had no difficulty in getting jobs, and were taken to a Nissen hut and shown where they were to share with twenty other girls.

'You're down the end with Maisie and Joyce,' said the young girl escorting them as she pushed open the door. Down each side of the hut were rows of neatly made beds, with their heads against the walls and their feet pointing towards the centre. Beside each bed was a small cupboard and a wardrobe; at the far end, towards which they were striding, were two armchairs.

'Blimey. They don't exactly go mad on the furnishings, do they?' said Brenda, as their feet echoed on the brown lino.

'You'll get used to it,' said the young girl, leading them on past a well-polished black stove squatting in the middle of the hut. 'Those are the best beds to have in the winter – it's perishing in here.' She waved her arm at the stove. 'Put your cases on the bed, you can empty them later. First you've got to collect your uniforms.'

They did as they were told and followed the girl on a tour of the NAAFI.

'You two are on the six-till-two shift,' said a woman sitting at a large desk. Her thick-framed glasses dangled on a chain round her neck. 'You start in the morning.'

'Six?' repeated Brenda.

'Yes, six in the morning.'

Polly noted poor Brenda turned pale at that, but said nothing. This could be almost as bad as prison, though at least they were being paid.

When they finally returned to their quarters, their new roommates were there.

'Hello, I'm Joyce.' A tall, well-built girl with brown eyes and peroxide blonde hair walked over to them. 'That's Maisie in the armchair. She was a librarian in London, and you can't get her nose out of a book.'

Maisie looked up and smiled. She was a small, thin, mousy sort of girl. 'Hello,' was all she said, and returned to her book.

'I'm from Oxford,' announced Joyce. She sat on her bed and took a bottle of red nail varnish from her bedside cupboard.

'That's a posh place,' said Brenda knowledgeably. 'By the way, I'm Brenda and that's Polly,' she said, opening her case. 'Which wardrobe's mine?'

'That one.' Joyce waved the nail-varnish brush at the one nearest Brenda.

'Thanks.'

'I hope you haven't got too many clothes, they're not built for large wardrobes.'

They finished unpacking and put their cases on top of the wardrobes. Joyce had finished painting her nails and was busy flapping her hands in order to dry them. 'D'you two dance?'

'Course. Why, is there a dance here tonight?' asked Brenda enthusiastically.

'There's one nearly every night,' said Joyce. 'It's all right if you're not on the eight-till-two shift; that one can be a real killer.'

'Eight at night till two in the morning?' said Polly.

Joyce nodded.

'We're on the six-till-two tomorrow,' said Brenda, sitting on the bed next to Joyce. 'What's the talent like round here?'

'Not bad, not bad at all.'

Polly observed that Maisie looked up at that remark and quickly looked away. She walked over to her.

'Whereabouts in London do you come from?' she asked.

'Poplar.'

'I come from Rotherhithe. I used to work near Whitechapel. Have you been up here long?'

'Since Christmas.' Maisie carefully placed a bookmark in her book and closed it.

'Do you like it here?'

'It's a job. When they closed all the libraries I was out of work, and I'm not trained for anything else. What did you do?'

'I worked in a dress factory.' Polly looked down. 'They were running out of work so I had to find something else. I didn't want to go in the Forces or on the land.'

'Me neither.'

'It's not too bad here – we have a cinema, and ENSA shows,' said Joyce. 'Ciggy?'

'Thanks.' Polly took one of the cigarettes Joyce was handing round and leaned against the wall. She gazed out of the window at the rows of huts, suddenly scarcely able to believe where she'd ended up. So much had happened since Christmas, just seven months ago. She'd been happy then. She didn't know *what* she was now.

It only took a few days for Polly and Brenda to settle down. The hours were long and the work hard, but they were, on the whole, kept busy enough not to feel homesick.

Polly lay on the bed staring up at the ceiling; she knew the others would be in soon. This was one of the few days they all met up: usually they passed like ships in the night, all working on different shifts. The door opened; it was Joyce.

'You look done in, Pol. You all right?'

Polly eased herself up on one elbow as Maisie walked in

wearing a towel wrapped round her head, turban-like. Her dressing-gown, a pale shade of blue, was discreetly fastened up to the neck, she was carrying her sponge bag. 'Go and have a nice bath, you'll feel better then,' she said, putting her washing things in her cupboard.

'At the moment me feet won't let me,' said Polly.

The door burst open and Brenda came quick-stepping in. 'Who's coming to the dance tonight?'

'I don't know where you get your energy from.' said Polly.

'Come on you poor old married woman, look alive,' said Brenda, still dancing round the room. 'All the blokes out there are just waiting to take us in their arms.'

'Don't forget, Polly, we're outnumbered about twenty to one,' said Joyce.

'That's just the sort of odds I like.' Brenda flopped on her bed and kicked off her shoes. 'Christ, me feet feel like great blobs of blancmange.'

'I'm not surprised, look at the heels on those,' said Maisie.

'Shh. Don't tell anyone. I can't walk around too long in those flatties. 'Sides, no one would see little old me behind the counter.' Brenda moved to the edge of her bed and gently began massaging her stockinged feet.

Maisie sat on her bed. 'Are you going tonight, Polly?'

'I should think so, are you?'

'No. I'm not very good at it. Joyce has been trying to teach me, but I think I've got two left legs.'

Brenda jumped up. 'Joyce, wind up your gramophone and we'll give Maisie a lesson.'

They were fortunate: Joyce came from quite a well-to-do family, and her father had brought her up in his car, so she had brought her gramophone and records with her.

'Maisie, push those chairs under the window, and slide your bedside cabinet over here next to ours. I'll push your bed next to Joyce's. There, that gives us a bit more room.' Brenda was a good organizer and, despite their aching feet, they all joined in to give Maisie – who still had her wet hair in the turban towel, and was wearing her dressing-gown and floppy slippers – her dancing lesson.

Two weeks later Polly finished her shift and wandered back to the billet. On the few occasions when she had the luxury of being alone, Polly wondered what her mother was doing, and several times she imagined she saw Ron standing at the bar, or in the queue waiting for his dinner. Once she rushed up to a fellow who had his back towards her, thinking it was Ron only to be disappointed when he turned round. What would he say if he got stationed up here? She expected he knew what had happened from Shirley, or Sid, especially if he'd gone back home. Polly's steps became slower and she took a packet of cigarettes from her overall pocket. All of a sudden fear gripped her. What if he were injured, or had been taken prisoner? Or even . . . No matter what she felt for him, what he'd done to her, he was still her husband. Perhaps Shirley would know where he was. How she'd love to hear how Shirley was getting on – and Elizabeth, she'd be crawling by now. Would she ever see them again? she wondered. Should she bury her pride and write?

It was a warm evening, and she decided to sit on the grass for a moment or two and let her thoughts wander. She often thought about the Blooms and, now the war was beginning to be a reality for Britain, with air battles over the south coast, she wondered if David Bloom was involved. Perhaps he wasn't even still alive: a lot of pilots had been killed.

The soldiers talked about losses all the time, and the news-reels didn't help alleviate Polly's fears either. Sometimes she worried over a young, fresh-faced youth who looked a little like Billy, and was off to God knows where.

Billy. Where was he? She had written and told him about going to prison, but never received a reply. Had his ship been involved with the evacuation at Dunkirk? Could he write? How could she find out if he was still . . ? Her thoughts just wouldn't let her think of Billy as dead.

A couple of girls went past, giggling. This was such a different life for her. She was mostly happy and, despite the odd quarrel, which didn't last for very long, the four girls had struck up a good relationship. They had a lot of fun, and they laughed a lot. Together they'd taught Maisie to use make-up, and done her hair in a fashionable way, and her dancing lessons were always a great source of enjoyment.

Polly lay back and pulled at a piece of grass. Her mind straying from one subject to another. Brenda was very popular and earned herself plenty of extra money from her 'overtime', as she called it. Apparently, she charged according to rank. Polly had decided after that night at the Palais that she wasn't cut out for that sort of thing. Although some of the fellers tried it on, she didn't let them go too far. And, to her relief, people had got used to seeing her lifeless eye; she'd get the odd one asking about it, but on the whole nobody bothered. The dancing and drinking had become part of her life, and she was having a good time. There was another dance tonight. She looked at her watch; if she went now, she'd have time for a bath before the others came back.

Several hours later Polly was wandering about, yawning. The dance had been a good one. Her head felt muzzy; she had knocked back quite a few gin and oranges.

Joyce came in and fell back on the bed. Maisie was getting undressed.

'See you kept your passion killers on again tonight, Maisie.' Joyce raised herself up on one elbow – she loved teasing her. 'Didn't anyone want to see your hankie?'

The pocket in their issue knickers was a standing joke for the fellows, and the girls.

Maisie was still terribly shy, and quickly turned her back on the other two. She undid her bra and hurriedly slipped her nightie over her head before removing her big khaki knickers.

'What about you, Joyce, did you lose yours?' asked Polly.

'Me? I wouldn't go out in those.'

'I know that – but did you lose them?'

'Not half. Lost 'em before the interval this time.'

195

Maisie tutted. 'Honestly, Joyce, haven't you got any morals?'

'No, they went out the window with me knickers.'

Polly and Joyce fell about laughing.

'Don't make me laugh, me head hurts,' said Polly, holding her forehead.

'Here, did you see who Brenda waltzed off with tonight?' said Joyce.

'No, who?' inquired Polly.

'Only one of the top brass. She should get quite a few bob out of him. She's very clever you know – have you seen the way she works?' Joyce had stripped off and was standing in front of the mirror admiring her body.

'Don't forget she's a professional,' said Polly.

'What d'you think, d'you think I could sell this lot?' Joyce cupped her breasts in her hand; Maisie blushed and turned away.

'Brenda's got some lovely clothes,' said Maisie, climbing into bed. 'You know, she lets me borrow some of her frocks. She's very kind.'

'We know,' they both shouted together.

'Christ, you tell us enough times,' said Joyce. 'You don't look down your nose at *her* and what she gets up to.'

'She's nice to me,' said Maisie, sounding hurt.

'It's a pity, Joyce, that we're too tall for her clothes,' said Polly, pulling the sheet over her head and hoping to avoid an argument at this time of night. 'Hurry up and turn out the light, I've got to get some sleep. Remember I'm on the early shift again in the morning.' Sometimes, it just felt as if life would go on like this forever. And, at the moment, Polly didn't really care if it did.

Chapter 17

Sunday 1 September 1940 was a wonderful, warm, sunny day, and David felt elated as he drove home in the car he had managed to acquire. He was humming quietly to himself, letting his mind wander, thankful to be alive after all the sorties he had been on.

For weeks he had hardly slept as the Luftwaffe came over the south coast in droves, and every day could have been his last, although those thoughts never entered anyone's head – at least, if they did you never spoke about it. For days now the tannoy ordering you to scramble had been silent. Now, with Yvonne at his side, he was on his way home to show her off to the family and, despite the small nagging feeling he had at the back of his mind, he was happy, very happy.

Yvonne's blonde, sleepy head rested lightly on his shoulder; her expensive perfume filled his nostrils. He still couldn't believe his good fortune. She was here, with him. That had indeed been his lucky day when, as Ginger's best man, he had met Yvonne, Mary's bridesmaid. As soon as David saw her he was besotted with her.

It was early afternoon when he brought the car to a halt in front of the house.

Yvonne stirred. 'Are we here already?'

'Yes, my darling.' He gently kissed her cheek. Then he bounded up the steps, his face wreathed in smiles, and turned the key in the front door.

Pushing it open, he was surprised to see Sarah rush at him

from the drawing-room. Her eyes, red from crying, were under-lined by fatigue and lack of sleep; her face was ashen. 'Where the hell have you been?'

Before David could answer she snapped, 'I've been trying to get in touch with you since yesterday – your CO said you were on a forty-eight-hour pass.'

David turned and took hold of Yvonne's arm. As they walked into the hall David said, 'Sarah, this is Yvonne.'

Completely ignoring her, Sarah threw herself into her brother's arms and sobbed.

He patted her head, mystified. 'My God, Sarah, what is it?' Gently he eased her away from him. 'Sarah?' His tone was sharp now – 'What's happened?'

Tears ran unchecked down her face as she looked up at him. 'It's Dad. He's dead.'

They were both aware of a gasp of breath as it left Yvonne's glistening ruby lips. Nobody spoke, and David's face took on the colour of stone. His mouth opened and closed but no sound came out. He collapsed on to the monk seat and buried his head in his hands. Yvonne remained standing, changing her hand-bag from one gloved hand to the other. She gave a little cough.

David looked up. Sarah was wiping her eyes.

'When? How? I can't believe it,' he stammered.

'I'm sorry, David, that wasn't how I wanted to tell you. But . . . I was angry, very angry, that I couldn't get hold of you.'

'When did it happen?'

'Yesterday. It was his heart.'

'What time?' asked David in a quiet whisper.

'About eleven o'clock.'

There was another gasp from Yvonne. 'Oh no.'

Sarah looked at her.

'Where's Mother?' asked David, interrupting and quickly changing the subject.

'She's upstairs with him.'

'He's still here?' said Yvonne in a shocked voice.

'It's a Jewish custom,' said David in a blank voice. Then,

198

pulling himself together added, 'Sorry, I haven't introduced you. This is my sister Sarah.'

'Hello, I'm pleased to meet you.' Yvonne removed her long white glove and, with a jangle of bracelets, held out her hand.

Sarah took the long-fingered pale hand that was offered.

'I'm sorry you've arrived in the middle of our grief.'

'I'm sorry about your father, especially now that . . .'

'I'll take Yvonne into the drawing-room. Perhaps you could go on up and tell Mother I'm here.'

Sarah nodded and slowly made her way up the stairs.

David ushered Yvonne into the drawing-room, quickly closing the door behind him.

'What's the big idea, interrupting me when I was about to tell your sister about us?' she demanded.

David stood with his back against the door. 'I hardly think this is the time or the place to tell them.'

Yvonne looked around. 'They've got to know some time.' She wandered over to the window. 'This is a lovely room. And garden,' she said, giving it a quick glance before settling herself on the sofa. Draping her bare arms along the back, she gently caressed the deep red velvet upholstery. 'This is very nice too. David, I think this is as good a time as any to tell them. After all, you are now the man of the house. And, as far as I can see, it is utterly delightful.'

She smiled at him and for the moment David was filled with love for this incredibly beautiful creature lounging there, inviting him to seduce her. He longed to take her in his arms and kiss her, but his sense of duty stopped him. 'I must go up to Mother. Wait here, and help yourself to a drink.' He pointed to the drinks cabinet.

In the darkened room, he kissed his mother's cheek. They clung to each other in their anguish. No words were said; words were not necessary.

They parted and she patted his hand. David bent over his father and kissed his cold forehead. Tears filled his eyes as he gazed down in disbelief at his father's peaceful face. Guilt and anxiety overwhelmed him. 'Please forgive me, Dad. I didn't know.'

Sarah took his arm. 'Of course you didn't,' she whispered. 'How could you?' She led him out of the room and they stood in silence at the top of the stairs for a moment or two.

David spoke first. 'I can't believe this has happened.'

'Can you stay for a few more days, at least till after the funeral?'

They moved away from the bedroom and spoke in loud whispers, not wanting to disturb their mother in her sorrow.

'I don't know. I'll have to phone my CO. It could be out of his hands.' He looked towards the bedroom door. 'You see the problem is, I've got to go to Scotland tonight. That's why I got this forty-eight-hour pass.'

'Scotland, what are you being sent up there for?'

'To train new pilots.'

'I would have thought you would have been more useful down here.'

David looked at his sister in surprise. 'I've done more flying hours than my CO likes. He thinks I should be off before my luck runs out, and before they run out of experienced pilots who can train the youngsters.' He ran his fingers through his thick black hair. 'Do you honestly think I want to leave all my . . .'

Sarah shuddered and took his arm. 'I'm sorry, David, that was a damn stupid, wicked thing for me to say. Of course we want you to be safe. I don't know why . . .' Her eyes filled with tears.

'You have been under a lot of strain.' He kissed her cheek. 'Come on, wipe away those tears. How are you managing?'

Sarah did as she was told. 'Not too badly,' she sniffed. 'If you're not going to be here, I'll have to make all Dad's arrangements. I'm a little worried about the factory, and if I'll be able to manage on my own.'

'Let's cross that bridge when we come to it.'

'It would have been nice to have had Margaret around.'

'Is she out of prison yet?'

'Yes. David, don't get angry.' Sarah looked at her fingers. 'I think I'd like her to come back and work for us.'

'What, after what happened? I daresay that could have had some bearing on Dad, you know.'

'Shh, keep your voice down. I thought you liked her.'

'Sorry. I do, I mean I did. But after what happened . . .'

'It wasn't her who did the robbery. She was in a very difficult situation. And she has paid for . . .'

'Yes I know,' interrupted David. Like Sarah he didn't like the idea of having been responsible for Polly's going to prison. 'But do you honestly think that's wise? And what would Mother say?'

'I don't know. I just know I need someone else there.' She leaned against the wall. 'I'm going to miss Dad.' A single tear trickled down her face.

David held her close. 'Look, even if I don't approve, if it's going to help make your life any easier, why don't you get in touch with her?'

'I've tried before. Just to try and patch things up. I think she's moved away.'

David stiffened. 'Oh. Well, let's go downstairs.'

'David, surely your CO will let you stay for your father's funeral?'

'I don't know. I can only ask.'

'Why didn't you come home yesterday? Or shouldn't I ask?'

David put both his hands on the banister and looked over. 'Sarah, there's something I have to tell you.'

'She's very pretty.'

'Yes, she is. You see Yvonne and . . .'

The bedroom door opened and Mrs Bloom came out. 'David, are you stopping for tea?' She began walking down the stairs.

'Yes, of course, Mother.'

'Sarah, give me a hand, we'll just have a few sandwiches. Is that all right with you?'

'Yes, don't worry about us.'

'Us?' Mrs Bloom stopped midway down the stairs.

'Yes, Mother. I've brought a young lady home with me.'

She gripped the handrail. 'Oh dear, whatever must the poor girl think. Do we know her?'

'No.'

'I'd rather not see her, not today. Sarah, you, David and his young lady can have your tea in the drawing-room.'

'What about you?' asked Sarah.

'I'll stay in the dining-room if you don't mind.'

'But I do mind,' said David. 'Please join us.' He looked down on his mother's neatly coiffured, greying hair. In her plain black dress with pearls at her throat she retained the air of dignity he'd always found rather awesome.

Not moving from the stair she turned and faced him. 'How long will you be home?'

David looked uneasy. 'I should really go back tonight. I'm supposed to go to Scotland on a sleeper – it's booked. I'm phoning my CO to see if I can get compassionate leave.'

'Scotland, that's a long way.'

'I've got to train new pilots.'

'What about your young lady, where does she live?'

'Yvonne lives at Windsor, but at the moment she's busy filming in London. Look, can't we go downstairs, I don't like standing here talking.' He looked towards the room where his father lay.

Suddenly the drawing-room door opened and Yvonne came out. 'Oh, I'm sorry, excuse me, but could I use the bathroom?'

'Do forgive me, young lady, I'm afraid we are not on our best behaviour today.' Mrs Bloom walked to the bottom of the stairs.

David looked at Sarah, who simply shrugged her shoulders.

'Mother, I'd like you to meet Yvonne.'

Mrs Bloom took her hand and permitted a small smile to remove the worry lines from her face. 'Hello, my dear.'

'I'm very sorry to hear about . . .'

'The bathroom's there, second door on the left,' said David, quickly interrupting and pointing the way.

'Is it all right to come up?' she whispered.

'Yes,' David nodded.

Yvonne went up the stairs, and the family carried on down.

'She's very pretty,' said Mrs Bloom. 'Perhaps you are right, David. Your father wouldn't like it if we lowered our standards, and I must not shut myself away. So yes, we will all have tea together.'

Mrs Bloom and Sarah went into the kitchen, while David waited in the hall for Yvonne.

She came out of the bathroom and stood at the top of the stairs. As she descended, David's eyes travelled up the well-shaped, silk-clad legs, teetering on high heels that added another five inches to her dainty five foot two, and on to the tiny waist held in by a wide white belt. Her slender neck rose from above her full, round breasts. David shuddered with pleasure.

She smiled, her blue eyes twinkled, and her scarlet lips parted seductively. When she reached the bottom of the stairs, she tossed her blonde hair and linked her arm through his. 'Darling, I've been thinking, perhaps you are right. I don't think today is a good day to tell them. Look I've put my ring in my handbag.' She held up her ringless left hand, and he kissed it.

David couldn't sleep as the train rushed through the blackness of the night, thundering past nameless and deserted stations. His thoughts were in a turmoil. What a weekend.

When he'd tried to phone to get an extension of leave, he was told his CO couldn't help as he was in transit from one camp to another. David knew he could be courtmartialled for being absent without leave from his new camp, and though he had tried to phone Scotland, it had been impossible. He lay in his bunk, gazing up at the dim lightbulb encased in a wire cage, unable to believe so much could happen in one weekend. His thoughts went to Yvonne, standing on the platform and waving him goodbye. She had attracted plenty of attention and scores of wolf-whistles as she blew kisses to him till the train carried him out of sight.

Yesterday he had been happy, blissfully happy; today he was in the depths of despair. And he couldn't even attend his father's funeral. 'Damn this war,' he said out loud. Sarah had been wonderful; he'd left her to organize everything. Why did I have to be moving camp this weekend, of all times? He punched his pillow and let his thoughts wander to Saturday. His wedding day.

He closed his eyes and summoned up a picture of Yvonne, a Gentile. She'd looked ravishing as she peeped out from under her large-brimmed white straw hat, her white silk dress clinging to every curve.

If only his father could have seen her, David felt sure he would have deep down approved, even though on the surface he wouldn't have been able to accept Yvonne as his son's wife. If only his father hadn't been so pig-headed, they could have had a proper wedding with all the family attending, not a brief ceremony in some bare registry office.

Yvonne had been as eager as him to get married, and when he had phoned her and told her he'd got a forty-eight-hour pass, she had gone immediately and got a Special Licence. Darling Yvonne, but if only it hadn't been this weekend.

How could he tell his mother and sister that, about the time his father died, he was being married?

Chapter 18

It was Sunday 8 September 1940, and all morning the camp had been buzzing with the news of yesterday's terrible air-raids on London. Everybody crowded round the wireless trying to listen to the latest bulletin.

'This could be it,' said one young lad. 'Reckon he'll be invading soon.'

Polly spun round. 'Don't say things like that.'

'He could be right, love,' said another.

They had all seen newsreels about the horrific raids on other ports and cities but, until now, London had been spared.

Polly went about her duties in a dream. How could she find out if her mum was safe? At the end of her shift she hurried back to the billet and began writing her a letter.

'What are you doing here?' asked Polly, looking up in surprise as Maisie walked in. 'You should be at work. Maisie, what's happened?'

Maisie was pale and drawn. Without a word she took a small scrap of paper from her pocket and handed it to Polly.

'Oh my God. Oh Maisie, I'm so sorry. Where did your mum and dad live?'

'Priory Road, near the docks,' she sobbed.

'How did you find out? Who told you?'

'My brother managed to get through on the phone. He lives in the next street.'

'Did you speak to him?'

She shook her head. 'It seems he's been trying all morning

to get through. He told Miss Beckett most of the lines are down, and a lot of the phone boxes have gone.'

'It sounds as if it's pretty bad down there. You going home?'

Maisie nodded and wiped her nose. 'That's if there's anything left of home. Miss Beckett said I could go right away.'

'Will you come back?'

'I don't know, it depends on what I find.'

'Have you got enough money for your train fare?'

'Yes, thanks,' said Maisie over her shoulder as she pulled her suitcase from off the top of her wardrobe and began packing it.

Polly lit a cigarette and walked over to the window. 'What train are you catching?'

'I think there's one about two. Why?'

'I'm coming with you.'

'Why? I'll be all right. Besides, Miss Beckett won't let you go, not just like that.'

Polly stubbed her cigarette out aggressively in the ashtray. 'She will when she hears that my mother lives in Rotherhithe, just round the corner from the docks.'

Once more the train was stationary. During the past hour, it had been stopping and starting for no apparent reason, and Polly guessed they must be in, or approaching, London. She was becoming fidgety; she couldn't look out of the window for familiar landmarks because of the black-out.

They had been lucky enough to get a seat in the overcrowded carriage, and the first part of their journey had been in bright, warm sunshine. Polly had laid her head against the window, and as they passed through the lovely countryside of Yorkshire, so green and peaceful-looking, she had devoured its beauty. The sheep and cows had been contentedly munching the grass, while the trees and telegraph poles rushed past, singing with the rhythm of the train as it rumbled over the rails. It must have been hard for some of the people living there to realize there was a war on, and that innocent people like Maisie's mum and dad were being killed. Polly looked across at Maisie. Understandably she hadn't been very talkative; she had been reading most of the time – although how she could see in the dimly lit carriage was a puzzle to Polly.

A corporal was standing in front of Polly; she quickly cast her eyes down when she realized he was staring at her. She noticed the floor looked as if it hadn't been swept in months. It was dirty and littered with cigarette ends, sweet wrappers and various other bits of paper. She glanced across at Maisie who was wedged, mouse-like, between the window and a sad-looking middle-aged woman, whose eyes never strayed from her knitting. The click, click, click of her needles became almost deafening at times.

Gradually the eerie sound of a distant air-raid siren filled the air. It sent shivers down Polly's back. Maisie looked up; with trembling hands she closed her book. Fear was written all over her pale face. The knitting needles stopped clicking for a brief moment, and the woman raised her sad eyes and took a quick breath between her teeth. When she lowered her eyes again, the knitting became more intense than ever.

The train shunted forward, catching most of the standing passengers off-guard, causing them to fall forward.

'Sorry, love,' said the corporal, regaining his balance and taking up his stance astride his kit-bag once more. 'Sounds as if Jerry's coming over again tonight.'

Polly didn't look up; she was terrified he would fall on top of her.

Very slowly the train moved forward, and when it stopped again someone was shouting, 'Everybody out. End of the line. Everybody out.'

Quickly Polly and Maisie grabbed their suitcases from the rack and joined the many others pouring through the ticket barrier.

Outside there was a tremendous noise from people rushing past, fire engines, and ambulances. Polly was trying to focus, trying to find familiar landscapes looming up out of the black-out. She took a deep breath: after being cooped up in that smoky, congested atmosphere for hours on end she was hoping to fill her lungs with fresh air. She coughed as the smell of dust and pungent, acrid smoke caught in her throat. The stinging taste burned her tongue.

'Oh my God.' Maisie stopped and pulled at Polly's arm. 'Look over there, the sky's red with fire.'

Polly turned and looked with disbelief at the glowing sky. She put her suitcase on the ground and gazed at the horrifically beautiful sight.

A man wearing a tin hat with 'Warden' written on the front came up behind them. ''Urry up, you two,' he shouted. 'Git yerselves down the underground, it ain't safe up 'ere.'

'I've got to get home,' said Maisie.

'Where's 'ome love?'

'Poplar.'

'Yer might not be able ter git over there ternight – the only fing running is the underground.'

'That doesn't go near my mum's,' said Maisie.

'Best git yerselves below then.'

They could hear the sound of guns putt-putting in the distance. Looking up, they could see stiff, pencil-like white ribbons from the searchlights stabbing the sky. Back and forth they went, stretching and sweeping, searching for enemy planes.

Polly and Maisie followed the sign to the underground, running as fast as they could on their high heels, puffing under the weight of the suitcases banging against their legs.

'Look at all these people,' said Maisie as they stood on the top of the escalator and were slowly lowered below ground.

Down on the platform, Polly was astonished to see it packed with people sitting or lying on the ground. Some had brought mattresses with them; others, with babies and young children, were settling them down for the night. The young ones cuddled their favourite toy, while babies sucked on a bottle or at their mother's breast. Older children were running about noisily, shouting and falling over feet, ignoring the tirades of abuse which followed their clumsy antics.

The noise from the trains, children and general chatter was almost deafening. Polly put her case down and looked around. Maisie was close by her side.

'Let's go right up the other end, it might not be so crowded.'

Maisie nodded her approval.

They scrambled over legs, bodies, and other objects, and made their way to the far end of the platform. It amused Polly that in the midst of all this chaos, some families were playing cards, eating sandwiches, and enjoying a bottle of beer, totally absorbed in what they were doing, completely oblivious of what was going on around them, almost as if it was a day at the seaside on a Bank Holiday Monday.

They carefully folded their coats, placed them on the floor and sat on them, watching all the comings and goings, completely fascinated by their new surroundings. There was just enough room for people to get on and off the trains that came thundering to a halt after pushing the air from the blackness of the tunnel at the other end of the platform.

'All right, Dad?' A young woman came and sat between Polly and an elderly man.

The old man looked up and nodded. 'Where yer bin? Fought yer'd lorst yer bleeding way.'

Polly moved a little further and pushed her case behind her to make more room for the woman.

'S'all right, love, I'm only skinny, don't take up much room.' She scrabbled on to the floor and turned to the old man. 'Been gitting yer this lot, ain't I?' She rummaged in her shopping bag and brought out two milk bottles full of a pale, brown-coloured liquid. ''Ere are.' She handed her father a sandwich.

Polly suddenly realized how hungry she was, and her stomach began gnawing and rumbling. The sandwich must have affected Maisie the same way: she sat forward and watched the old man slowly chomping his way through the great doorstep.

'Is there anywhere we can get something to eat?' Polly asked her new neighbour.

'Yer, there's usually a bloke on the up-line wiv a few bits. Yer'll 'ave ter 'urry, 'e sells out pretty quick.'

''Ere, yer aint't put no sugar in this tea.' The old man took his head out of the chipped white enamel mug which his daughter had filled with the pale-coloured liquid.

'Oh, sod it. Fergit me bleeding 'ead if it wasn't screwed down. Still I was in a bit of a 'urry. 'Ere ducks, d'yer fancy a drop of tea?' She offered Polly one of the half-empty milk bottles. 'Give yer mate a drop as well.'

'Thanks.'

'I'll have mine when I get back. I'll go and see if I can get us something to eat,' said Maisie, picking up her handbag.

Polly watched her carefully pick her way over the prone bodies. She turned to her neighbour. 'What's it like out there?' She nodded in the direction of the exit.

'What, yer mean on top?'

Again Polly nodded.

'Ain't yer seen?'

'No, we've just got into London. Been travelling nearly all day, from up North.'

'It's a bloody mess. The sods 'ave made it a bloody shambles up there. A lot o' these down 'ere 'ave only got wot they stand up in. So far, touch wood' – she touched the top of her head – 'we've been lucky. The 'ouse is still standing.'

'Up ter now,' interrupted the old man frostily.

'D'yer come from round this way?' asked the daughter.

'Yes, well, Maisie's from Poplar. She had a phone message from her brother telling her that her mother's and father's house was bombed.'

'They dead?'

'Yes.'

'Oh, that's a shame.'

'I've come back cos my mum lives in Rotherhithe.'

'That got it bad,' nodded the woman.

Maisie returned, clutching two cheese rolls. 'I was lucky, this is all he had left – got no butter on them though.'

They munched on the rolls as if they were to be their last, sharing the half bottle of cold tea the woman had kindly offered.

Gradually, the hubbub quietened down. Most of the kids had settled, and many of the old folk had nodded off; some were snoring loudly, completely oblivious to the trains coming and going. They could hear muffled explosions, and once or twice the ground gently heaved and rocked, causing the dust to drift down slowly, but nobody seemed unduly worried.

Polly felt her lids drooping. Eventually her head fell forward, making her jump.

'You all right?' asked Maisie. She was wide awake and still reading her book.

'Can't you sleep?' whispered Polly.

'No. I feel awful being so near home, yet so far away Pol,' she said softly, 'I've never seen a dead person, have you?'

Polly nodded. 'Yes, my grandad.'

'Did . . . he look all right?'

'Yes. He died natural like.'

'D'you think Miss Beckett could have got the message wrong? D'you think they might still be alive?'

'I don't know. I wouldn't like to say.' Polly shuffled uncomfortably. She couldn't possibly offer Maisie any hope.

Maisie leaned her head against the hard wall and sighed. 'I'm sure my brother wouldn't have phoned if they were safe.'

'Try to have a doze. Close your eyes, it'll help make the morning come quicker. It always worked when I was little,' whispered Polly.

'I don't know if I want morning to come. I don't know if I really want to find out what's happened.' Maisie gave a muffled sob.

Polly felt helpless and sad. She knew how her friend was feeling for, at that moment, she felt just the same.

Polly too leaned back, and her thoughts drifted to her mother. What if anything had happened to her? Guilt filled her mind, and under her breath she said a silent prayer. 'Please, let her be safe.' All at once she felt completely alone. She didn't know where Billy or Ron was, or if Sid was still living at home. Maybe he had shacked up with one of his so-called lady friends from the factory. Why was I so pig-headed when I came out of prison? Polly thought. I could have gone and seen her, just to say sorry. That's all it needed. Or I could have written. But Polly knew why she hadn't done these things. It was because her mother had said in court, while she was under oath, that she would never forgive her for trying to implicate Sid.

Another train came rushing to a halt. It was almost empty. Polly looked at her watch. That must be about the last one tonight. A faint smile came to her lips when her thoughts strayed to Shirley, remembering the times when she and Polly had caught the last train, sometimes just by the skin of their teeth. They'd had some good times, especially when they'd gone out in a foursome with Sid and Ron. She let her mind drift to her husband. They had been happy most of the time; life hadn't been too bad with him. If only he . . . I wonder if my flat's still there? she thought suddenly.

A child crying further along the platform reminded her of Elizabeth. Dear Shirley, at least they should be safe down there in Bristol. She was her only hope of finding out where Ron was – assuming he'd bothered to write to them. As the lights were dimmed her thoughts continued. When she got time she'd write to Shirley. Life was too short now to hold any grudges . . .

Chapter 19

Polly woke with a start when a train stopped. There was a steady drone from the people all around them who were beginning to collect their belongings together.

Maisie had slid down the wall and was curled up in an awkward shape. She too had been sleeping, and looked bewildered when she opened her eyes. 'What time is it?'

'Half-past five,' said Polly, trying to straighten her leg.

'That all? My mouth feels like a sewer.' She went to sit up. 'Oh, me back.'

'Me leg's gone to sleep,' said Polly, gently rubbing it, trying to coax life back into it. 'I'm dying for a pee. Look after the cases, Maisie, while I go and find the lav. I'll try and find out what's happened, see if I can see what buses are running.' She stood up and stamped her numb foot on the ground.

The skinny woman next to Polly sat up. 'Every uvver bugger will be trying ter git in these bogs,' she advised them. 'Yer best bet is ter go up top. The raid's over be now. They don't come over much in daylight.'

'Not yet 'e don't,' said her father aggressively.

Polly and Maisie thanked her and picked up their suitcases.

'Good luck, gels.' She lowered her voice, and with a knowing look added, 'I 'ope yer finds everyfink's all right.'

They said their goodbyes, made their way along the platform, went up the escalator, and out into the early morning gloom. They stood in silent horror, gaping at the destruction and confusion all around them. Although it was still quite dark, the glow from last night's fires lit up the scene. People, heads bent, were carefully picking their way over the rubble and hose-pipes that covered the streets and seemed to snake off in all directions, while fire engines appeared to be rushing about, ringing their bells, but getting nowhere.

The women who had just left the underground with their prams loaded with bedding were having difficulty pushing them along the debris-strewn roads – much to the children's delight as they bounced up and down on top.

Smoke billowed up in great black clouds, temporarily blocking out the rising sun. Mingling with the smoke was dust from a building that could no longer stand alone. It fell to the ground, defeated.

Polly looked in amazement at the great piles of concrete that were once houses; houses that were once somebody's home. Broken pieces of furniture littered the empty rooms, curtains flapped forlornly in the glassless windows. Shops were battered and blasted; shops that were once somebody's living now had their contents spewed out all over the road. It looked as if some giant hand had picked all this up and thrown it down again.

A lump came to Polly's throat. It was sad, very sad. 'I didn't think it would be like this,' she whispered.

'It's awful,' said Maisie. 'The air is enough to choke you. Polly, I'm going to try to get to my brother's. What are you going to do?'

'I'm going to me mum's.'

'Look, if you . . . Well here's my brother's address, and if you don't have anywhere to stay . . . Well, I'm sure you'll be made very welcome.'

Polly took the piece of paper she held out, then clutched Maisie to her. For just one short second they both appeared very small, and very vulnerable.

They didn't speak, it wasn't necessary.

Maisie picked up her case and walked off in the opposite direction to the one Polly would need to take. Polly looked down at the piece of paper, and tears gathered. She realized she had never really got to know Maisie. Now she understood what a kind, sincere person she was – someone who really cared, even in the midst of her own distress.

There were no buses going in Polly's direction, and it took her hours to get anywhere near to Penn's Place. Because of the many diversions, she appeared to be going round and round in circles. Unexploded bombs, blocked roads, falling masonry and crumbling buildings were all obstructions barring her way, and familiar roads and landmarks had disappeared into gaping craters.

Many times she stopped and felt her heart go out to a grandmother or grandfather, mother or father, whose eyes were glazed and staring, their faces full of anguish, as they watched men digging at what once must have been their home.

She felt even more distressed when she saw a body which had just been recovered and was lying by the ruins of a house, covered with a sheet. The wife or mother was kneeling beside her loved one, crying, while a young child played with pieces of concrete, concrete that was probably once part of their home.

Ambulances and fire engines were racing around everywhere, urgently ringing their bells, trying to get to people who needed them. Polly stumbled over hose-pipes, past men who looked dirty and tired, worried and gaunt, men who perhaps had been digging for many hours, searching and listening for any small sound that would spur them into yet more feverish activity. The dust and dirt got up Polly's nose and into her mouth, and her feet were beginning to hurt horribly.

Although she knew the area very well, many times she had to stop to get her bearings – and her breath back. Everything looked so different. Great gaps in houses revealed secrets never seen before: gardens filled with masses of colour, or back yards bursting with piles of old rubbish.

When she turned into the next road she suddenly realized that Weaver Street was nearer than her mother's house. If it's still there, at least I'll have somewhere to leave this damn case, she thought to herself and her step became lighter. But her heart sank when she turned the corner and looked down what was once Weaver Street.

All that remained of the neat row of terraced houses on the side of the road where she had lived was a row of empty shells. All the walls between the houses were still standing, save for a few near the end which had been completely demolished. The other side of the road had vanished.

Slowly she staggered on till she stood in front of what was left of her dear little flat. Tears ran unchecked, streaking her dirty face.

She looked up at what had been her bedroom. The glass had gone from the square window, which stuck up on its own. It looked like an unfinished building with the window added as an afterthought, complete with curtains. Curtains which now hung in tattered ribbons waving pathetically in the slight breeze. She remembered the fun she and Ron had had when they first put them up before they were married – the night she lost her virginity.

The roof had gone completely and through her tears she could see the rubble inside was piled high, right up to the window sill. Her pride and joy, her beautiful walnut dressing-table and wardrobe which she had spent hours polishing, was now splintered and broken, like a heap of matchwood.

She moved slightly to see into what was left of her kitchen. There, still hanging miraculously on the wall over the fire-place, was the mirror the family had given them as a wedding present. The mirror that held a thousand secrets was cracked and broken, looking sad and helpless as it hung lopsidedly on its chain. Ron always went mad even if it was just a little bit crooked; he couldn't stand it. What would he say if he was here now? Heartbroken she sat on her case and cried pitifully.

'My home,' she sobbed out loud, 'that was my home.' But there was no one around to hear her. It was as if Weaver Street had died.

Finally Polly struggled to her feet and looked up at the sky. 'Don't worry Grandad,' she said, her chest heaving. 'It's all right. I've still got your whip safely in here.' She touched the side of her case, thankful that at the last minute, just before she had left home to go up North with Brenda, she had taken the whip off the wall and stuffed it into her suitcase. At least she still had something left from the old life.

The shock she got in Weaver Street was nothing compared to the shock she received when she turned into Penn's Place. The middle of the road had completely disappeared, gone. A pile of tangled wood and rubble was all that remained of Numbers 13, 15, and 17.

The Bells' old house, her mother's, and the Rays' – a quiet couple who used to live in Number 17 before the war – had all ceased to be houses.

Her legs turned to jelly as she got nearer. She could see calm but intense activity going on. Ordinary men, as well as wardens, were frantically digging and throwing great lumps of concrete over their shoulders. Others, sweating, with soot-streaked faces, were bent over, holding timbers with their backs while more men burrowed beneath them with their bare hands, like dogs searching for a bone.

In a daze Polly wandered towards them.

'Git out the way, gel,' yelled someone. 'There ain't nufink ter see.'

She dropped her case and scrambled over the debris, oblivious to their shouts.

'Git out the bleeding way, can't yer?' shouted another.

'Can't yer see this bleeding lot could cave in any minute.'

Still she ignored them as she hastened her step. She fell over and tore her stockings, her leg began bleeding, her hands smarted and tingled when she brushed the dirt and grit from them, but she clambered on.

A man grabbed her. ''Ang on, gel. What yer after?'

'When did this happen?'

'Last night.'

'Me mum. That's me mum's house.' She tried to wriggle free.

217

'Oh my Gawd. Look love, come over 'ere out the way. You'll do no good gitting in their way.'

Still pulling away from him she asked softly, 'Is anybody under there?'

'We don't know yet. We 'ave ter keep looking just in case. Someone did say there was an old woman who lived 'ere on 'er own. She could be trapped in the shelter.'

An old woman. Could that be her mother they were talking about? It was all so difficult to take in.

Finally Polly was reluctantly led away. Someone found a chair in the wreckage that was still sound, and she sat in the road watching them dig for what seemed a lifetime. Waiting and hoping.

Last night, he had said. If she had managed to get home, would she now be buried under this with her mother? And where was Sid?

How she wished things had been different. If only her mother had been more like other mothers. If only she had kissed her, put her arms round her for no reason, taken her on her knee and cuddled her. She did before Dad died, but only when he was there. Grandad had always said she was jealous at the affection he showed to Polly. The only time she kissed her in all those years was when Polly went into hospital and when she got married.

Polly sighed deeply. Perhaps part of it was her fault. As she'd grown older *she* could have been the one to make the first move, show her mother how she felt. 'I promise, Mum, if you're all right, things will be different after this,' she said under her breath.

It was almost midday when the shout went up.

'Quiet. I think I 'eard sumfink. I fink there's someone down there. Be quiet.'

A hush fell over the rescuers. All ears were strained as the men knelt down and put their heads to the ground and listened.

Polly prayed like she'd never prayed before.

'There's someone down there, and they're alive,' shouted a man. 'Jump on yer bike, Bill, and git an ambulance.'

Bill raced off on his bike, bumping over hose-pipes, struggling to keep the bike upright.

Polly held her breath as she watched the men slowly enlarging the opening to the trapped victim. Gently and skilfully, they lifted the person's head. Polly strained her neck to see who it was. She wanted to go nearer, but the men were huddled round. She watched a man put his fingers down the injured person's throat.

'Give 'er a drink, Al, 'er airway's clear.'

It was a woman. Tears filled Polly's eyes, she wanted to rush to her, just to see if . . . But she knew she would be in the way. She had to be patient. As she watched and waited she marvelled at these men. Only a year ago they'd been ordinary people going about their ordinary everyday work. Now they were saving lives like professionals.

The man they'd called Al came up with a bottle of water and gently wet the woman's lips whilst others worked painstakingly to throw the great chunks of concrete and wood aside. Finally the survivor was brought out and laid on the ground.

Polly didn't recognize the woman's clothes, and she couldn't make out who it was. She was afraid to ask. Afraid now to go near, in case . . . Half of her didn't want to know, but the other half was screaming out for her to take a look. She moved closer. The tight circle of men parted as she asked in a quiet tone. 'Is it me mum?'

One of the men put his arm round her shoulder. 'Come and 'ave a look, love.'

The woman lay bruised and bleeding. One of her arms was twisted at a funny angle, her leg was a red, pulpy mass, and she was covered with grey dust and soot. The shallow undulating rhythm of her chest, and the flickering eyelids, were the only indication that she was still alive.

'Mum!' Polly cried out, and fell to her knees. 'Mum, oh Mum.' She gathered her carefully in her arms and gently rocked

219

her like a baby. 'I'm here, Mum.' She put her lips to her mother's cheek.

'Margaret.' It was barely above a whisper. She didn't open her eyes, but a faint smile quickly flicked across Doris Perkins' cut and bruised face.

Polly brushed the dirt and soot from her mother's face. She removed her tortoiseshell hair slide and put it in her pocket. Glancing down she almost smiled through her tears when she saw her mother's pale pink celanese knickers which she always wore pulled down over her knees, exposed to the world. She would have gone mad if she knew strange men had seen them. Polly took off her coat and placed it over her mother's legs. Her lisle stockings were in tatters, and she had lost one of her shoes.

Her mother drifted into unconsciousness. The ambulance came, and Polly sat holding her hand all the way to the hospital.

Polly sat in the hospital, waiting. She was surprised that in all the hustle and bustle, someone had bothered to put her old brown leather suitcase in the ambulance. Outwardly she seemed calm, but her mind was in turmoil. A muddle of thoughts – fears, doubts, and even ideas for the future – raced through her head, but nothing was registering. She was numb.

She didn't know how long she had been in the room. She wasn't really aware of other people. She knew some were crying, while others, like herself, just sat and stared at the comings and goings, hoping and waiting.

A nurse walked in. 'Mrs Bell,' she called. 'Is Mrs Bell here?'

Mrs Bell? That was her, Polly realized. She'd almost forgotten her married name. She stood up, flushed and trembly.

'Ah, Mrs Bell, would you come with me please?'

In a daze, Polly followed the nurse into a small room. On the table was a neat pile of her mother's dirty, blood-stained clothes.

The nurse picked up a pencil and turned it over and over in her fingers. 'I'm very sorry.'

Polly jerked her head up.

'I'm very sorry. Your mother had very severe internal injuries. I'm afraid she never recovered consciousness.'

Polly couldn't believe it. All she wanted to do was tell her mother she was sorry. Now she'd gone. Bring her back, her thoughts were screaming. Let me say I'm sorry. She mustn't go without her knowing I love her. Bring her back, I want to hold her.

The nurse was saying. 'Do you want her clothes?'

Polly shook her head.

'Here is her wedding ring, and the necklace she was wearing.'

Polly took the brown envelope. The necklace spilled out in her hand. It was the one she had given her mother all those years ago. Rolled gold with a drop pearl. She was wearing it. It was hidden under her clothes. Polly had never known it meant that much to her.

She lay her head on the table and cried. Bitter tears. Tears of frustration and anger. Tears for all the wasted years. If only her mother had cradled her in her arms and sung nursery rhymes to her like her dad used to years ago.

'Pretty Polly Perkins of Paddington Green . . .' The rhyme was going over and over in her head. Suddenly Polly realized that Polly Perkins too had died. She had gone forever, and only grown-up Polly Bell remained . . .

Chapter 20

Polly left the hospital in a state of shock. After filling in several forms, the nurse had asked her if she would like to see to the arrangements about burying her mother. Polly explained she hadn't anywhere to live, and didn't know what to do. The nurse had been very understanding and told her not to worry: her mother could be buried with the many other victims. She also told Polly they would be holding a memorial service in the hospital's chapel on Sunday morning, and perhaps she would like to come along?

Polly thanked her and wandered out into the warm September sunshine. She had no idea where she was going, or what she was going to do. Where was Sid? He should know about Mum. What if he said she should be buried with Dad? Who would pay? All her mother's insurance policies must have been in the shelter. She hadn't the faintest idea how she'd be able to lay her hands on what she'd left.

She felt alone and miserable; there was no one she could turn to. She had Maisie's kind offer, but would they want her? Her with her own grief in the midst of all their tragedy?

London seemed full of noise and distractions, but Polly didn't see or hear. Shirley's name kept invading her thoughts as she walked along aimlessly, her suitcase, which now felt like a ton weight, banging listlessly against her leg.

The sign on the street toilet advertising a wash and brush up for twopence suddenly made Polly feel very dirty. At least it was open and she could tidy herself up and change her stockings. She went down the iron steps: it felt wonderfully calm and tranquil here, below the ground.

''Allo love, yer can leave yer case 'ere if yer wants ter go ter the lav.' The attendant greeted her kindly.

'I didn't think there would be anyone down here,' said Polly, wallowing in the quiet of the clinical, white-tiled room. She looked in her purse for a penny.

'Raids or no bleeding raids, some of us 'ave ter go out ter work. Those of us wiv a 'ouse still standing 'ave still gotter find the rent, and feed ourselves, even if it is all bleeding rationed.' The attendant took Polly's penny. 'I was 'opping mad this morning,' she went on, as if she'd known Polly all her life. 'Our butcher goes down our tube station, and last night 'e gave me the whisper that 'e was gonner 'ave a bit o' liver in 'is shop terday. I went along there first fing, and d'yer know wot? Bloody 'Itler bombed it last night, so Gawd knows where me liver finished up.'

She dropped the penny in the slot at the top of the highly polished, shiny brass box, turned the handle, and pushed open the door to reveal a white porcelain toilet. 'A bit o' liver would 'ave made a nice change. I'd like ter know why we can't git liver like we used ter. They still breed animals wiv 'em, don't they?' Laughing, she took a cloth from the pocket of her floral overall, wiped round the wooden seat, and held the door open for Polly.

After Polly had handed over another two pennies, changed her stockings, washed the dried blood and dirt from her cut leg, combed her hair, and put some make-up on her clean face, she felt a lot better. 'Is there anywhere round here I can get a cup of tea?' she asked the woman, who was now sitting in the corner busy knitting what appeared to be Army socks.

'There's a bloke over the road who comes wiv 'is stall and stands outside the station – that's if 'e ain't been blown ter bits in the night, or sold out.' The knitting didn't stop.

Polly looked at her watch. 'What time do you shut?'

''Bout six, p'raps a bit before. Gotter be 'ome 'fore the raids start.'

'That gives me half an hour. Do you live far?'

'No, only round the corner.'

'Could I leave my case here while I try to get something to eat? I haven't had much since yesterday.'

'Course yer can, love. Where yer going after that? Yer going away?'

'Not till Sunday.' Polly didn't want to tell her why.

'Oh,' said the old woman, her voice sounding slightly offended as she carried on knitting.

'My flat was bombed, and I'm going to stay with a friend,' said Polly, feeling she should offer some sort of explanation. 'She won't be home till Sunday.'

'Oh,' said the woman again. This time her tone implied that she was satisfied with that. 'Where're yer going after yer got yerself sumfink ter eat?'

'Probably spend the night down the underground.'

'Safest place, an' all. Me and me daughter goes down there. Yer 'as ter git down our one early ter get the best place. 'Ere, d'yer know sometimes we 'ave a right old laugh, and a sing-song. Well, yer gotter do sumfink ter keep yerself cheerful, ain't yer? Yer a long time dead.'

Polly only nodded and half smiled.

'Right, now be orf wiv yer then, and don't worry about this.' She took Polly's case and put it in a small cupboard behind her chair.

Polly found the man with the stall, drank the so-called tea, and gratefully munched her way through two huge doorsteps of bread and jam. She hadn't realized how hungry she was, or how long ago it had been since she had had a good meal, but then food had been the last thing on her mind.

She collected her case and made her way to the underground station where she had slept the night before. She thought that if Maisie had had a similar experience to her today, she might well make her way back here. Polly settled down at the far end of the platform again. One or two people nodded in recognition. The old man and his daughter hadn't arrived, and she wasn't sure whether or not to save them a place; she didn't know if they were regulars.

Polly put her hand in her coat pocket and took out her mother's hair slide. For as long as she could remember, her mother had worn it just above her left ear. The same hairstyle, probably the same hair slide. Polly's fingers clasped round the small tortoiseshell object, and she lay her head back against the wall. The slide, her wedding ring, and the necklace, were all that was left of her mother. Tears trickled down her face. She never knew the necklace that had been bought to heal so much pain was cherished so dearly. She must have worn it all the time.

Polly's lids blinked rapidly as she tried to stem the tears. She was pleased to be away from people; she wanted to be alone. Her thoughts did go fleetingly to the old man and his daughter – they still hadn't arrived. The older folk and the children were beginning to settle down, and the quiet between trains was wrapping itself comfortably around her. They didn't seem to have sing-songs in this underground, or not tonight, anyway.

The following morning, Polly took her suitcase and made her way back once more to the public toilet and her little old woman. She knew she could safely leave her case there, and perhaps get away from all this death and destruction for a few hours, go to the park, anywhere.

A thick chain and padlock held the big black wrought-iron gates firmly together. She looked up the road, hoping to see her new-found friend come waddling towards her. There was the usual hubbub from fire engines and ambulances, and all the trauma and devastation from last night's raid, but it didn't shock her quite so much now. Was she getting like all the others and becoming immune to the situation?

She sat on her case and waited for half an hour, then amongst all the stench of fire, broken sewers and gas, the smell of cooking sausages wafted her way. She hastened her step towards the tea stall she had been to the night before. The man was hanging out a sign which said, 'Business as usual.'

'Excuse me. What time does the lady open the toilet?'

''Bout eight.' The thin-faced man laughed. 'Why's that? 'Ere, yer ain't breaking yer neck are yer, love?'

Polly smiled and shook her head. It was now nine o'clock. 'Is she ever this late?'

'Not as long as I've been 'ere these, what, must be all o' ten years.' As he turned the sausages, so Polly's stomach turned.

'Could I have a sandwich and a cup of tea please?'

'One sausage sandwich coming up. Reckon she must a' bought it. I 'eard they done Rapp Street last night, that's where she lived.' He handed Polly her sandwich and tea, shaking his head. 'Pity, she was a nice old dear.'

An ARP man came up to the stall and the owner began serving him. The man removed his tin hat and wiped his dirt-streaked face with a greyish handkerchief. 'Got it bad round Tower Bridge way last night,' he remarked, banging the white masonry dust from his navy-blue jacket.

Polly finished her breakfast and walked away, her thoughts filled with that friendly old woman knitting Army socks. Why wasn't she down the underground when the planes came over? What about her daughter? Were they still alive, or possibly buried under a pile of rubble like her mother had been? And what about the man on the tea stall, casually accepting that she could be dead. Someone he had known for ten years. What was happening to people that they could so easily accept death? What about the father and daughter who didn't come down the underground last night? God, I hope they're not dead, she thought. Yesterday it was her mother, today it could be any one of these people – or all of them.

'I must get away from all this,' she mumbled to herself. She didn't want to go back to the NAAFI just yet. As soon as the service was over on Sunday, she'd go to Shirley's. She'd finally made up her mind. She wasn't really aware of which direction she had taken, or where she was heading. As she walked along, the words of the ARP man came back to her.

'Got it bad over Tower Bridge way last night.'

227

I wonder if Bloom's factory's still there? Heavy-footed, she wandered on, amazed that some of London's familiar landmarks were still standing. In the background stood St Paul's, solid, strong and defiant. Grey smoke from many of the burning buildings and docks blurred its outline, making it squiggly in the heat haze. When the sturdy steel girders of Tower Bridge came into view, Polly's heart leapt.

The years dropped away as she recalled the first time she crossed it with her mother, on her way to Bloom's. A faint smile came when she remembered how she had jumped over the crack, terrified the bridge would open up and drop them into the murky River Thames below, swallow her up and drown her, like it did her great-grandparents many, many years ago. She had had a lot of bad dreams and nightmares about that bridge; now it stood proudly over the Thames like a great symbol and she was glad of it.

Today she had no need to cross it; there was nothing left for her on the south side of the water. Involuntarily, she found herself walking towards Mansell Street.

Standing at the far end of the street, the sight of Bloom's factory, windowless and blasted, made her feel sad. She remembered the time it had taken for her and Miss Bloom to stick up the green mesh and strips of brown paper which Mr Bloom had insisted on having over the windows. Now they had gone, leaving only empty spaces to gaze out like sightless eyes, deep and mysterious, over the road. The large sign that hung between the floors, announcing 'Bloom's Fashion House. Manufacturers of Fine Dresses', was only suspended at one end, swinging low and at a dangerous angle, almost defying gravity.

Two people, a man and a woman, were picking their way across the road. They disappeared inside what was left of the building.

Gingerly Polly went closer. Stumbling over the rubble, she could see the factory was in an unsafe condition. Getting nearer she could see the roof had caved in. Part of the floor, which her mother had spent years keeping clean, and which had been home to the rows and rows of noisy sewing machines, had crashed to the ground below. A lump came to her throat. Many of the machines lay broken and battered. Twisted and contorted lumps of blackened iron and steel sprouted in the dust. Some brick walls had fallen, while others were balancing on girders. Some of the twisted metal had navy-blue cloth draped on or caught round it. Polly guessed they must have been making shorts for the Navy. Some of the larger pieces of material stirred pathetically in the late September breeze. Other smaller pieces tugged aggressively to get away but, finding themselves trapped, surrendered.

Putting down her case, she stared up in amazement at the office door with its glass still surprisingly intact. It swung back and forth, opening up on to a void. We must have stuck that paper on really well, she reflected ruefully. Tears filled her eyes when she thought of all the good times she had had working in the office. The designing, learning to type, Miss Bloom teaching her to speak properly. She remembered the remark Sarah'd made about Eliza Doolittle all those years ago. Now she understood what she'd meant.

Voices came from inside the building. She recognized them and immediately turned to go.

'Margaret,' shouted a female voice. 'Margaret, is that you?'

She stopped, and slowly turned to face Sarah Bloom.

Sarah was hurrying towards her, stumbling, almost falling over in her effort to get to Polly. She put her case down and they embraced like long-lost sisters.

'Margaret, oh Margaret, what are you doing here?' She held her at arm's length, there were tears in her eyes and a sob in her voice.

Before Polly could answer, she hugged her again. 'It's so good to see you. Why have you got a case with you?'

Old Fred Baker came floundering across the concrete-strewn yard. 'Polly love, how are you?' He held her close.

Tears ran down her face; she couldn't speak.

Sarah lightly touched her arm. 'Come and have a cup of tea,

229

Charlie's is still open.' She half laughed and wiped away a tear. 'It's all boarded up as he hasn't any windows, but he makes us a pot of tea.'

Five minutes later they were sat in Charlie's, drinking tea and bringing each other up-to-date with everything that had happened during the past six months.

'Where have you been staying since you came back to London?' asked Sarah.

'I've been sleeping down the tube.'

'So where are you off to now?'

'On Sunday, after the church service, I'm going to Shirley's – you remember Shirley Bell?'

Sarah nodded.

'I must go to the service, that's the last thing I can do for my mum.'

'I'm very sorry to hear about your mother. It's a terrible war. How is Shirley?'

Polly played with the spoon. 'I don't know.'

'But I thought . . .'

'She doesn't know I'm coming. I never wrote to anyone after . . . But I haven't anywhere else to go. I don't know where Sid is, and my brother Billy's in the Navy. I did write to him but I've never got any answer.' She continued looking down and playing with the spoon, nervously turning it over and over. 'I don't even know where Ron is, or if he's alive. I think he was at Dunkirk.'

'That was a terrible thing. A lot of young lads died there,' said Fred sadly.

'Fred,' said Sarah quickly.

'Sorry. Another cup of tea Polly?'

'Yes please.' Polly hesitated and swallowed hard, and as Fred left the table whispered. 'I was ever so sorry about your brooch.'

It was Sarah's turn to be embarrassed. 'I'm sorry you had to go to prison. We should have sat down and talked about it, not phoned the police like we did, but at the time I was furious.'

'I can understand that.' Polly looked away. 'But you know

I wasn't involved, don't you? I just didn't know what to think when Ron gave me the brooch and so I did nothing, and then it all blew up in my face.' She glanced nervously at Sarah.

'That's what we thought,' she said quietly.

'When I came out of prison,' she went on, 'I was very angry and I didn't want to see anyone I knew – so I didn't write, not even to me mum. Now it's too late to say . . . I could be the only one left.' Polly sniffed.

Sarah gently patted her hand. 'What are you going to do? Are you going back into the NAAFI?'

Polly blew her nose. 'I don't know.'

'Here we are ladies.' Fred put the tray on the table.

'Thanks Fred.' Polly took a thick white mug from off the tray. 'That was a shame about Mr Bloom, he was a nice man.'

'Yes, yes he was,' said Sarah.

'What're you going to do about the factory?' asked Polly.

Sarah put her elbows on the table, first she looked intently at Fred, then at Polly. 'Well, we've got an idea. We've seen a lock-up under the arches we can rent for now, and we think we can salvage some of the machines. That's what we were doing earlier on, looking to see what was worth saving. It will be a lot of hard work – thank goodness Fred here is good with machines.' Sarah's enthusiasm was infectious. 'I've been to see Violet, you remember the forelady?'

Polly nodded.

'Well she has managed to contact some of the women, and they are willing to work at home, providing I pay them a good rate. I'm buying some second-hand treadle machines from a friend.'

'They should think themselves lucky,' interrupted Fred, ''aving a sewing machine at 'ome, and the work brought to 'em and taken away again.'

'Shh, Fred, I'm very grateful to them. At least I'll be able to keep the government order.'

'You still making shorts?' asked Polly.

'Yes, and lots of other things besides.' She stopped and put her hand on Polly's arm. 'Why don't you stay here and join us?'

Polly looked surprised. 'What? Oh, I don't know. No, I couldn't.'

'Why not?'

'Where could I live? My flat's gone. Besides . . . No, I couldn't.'

'Margaret, come and stay with us. You can have a room in our house, we've got more than enough rooms.'

'What? What would your mother say, especially after . . . No, I couldn't do that. Besides, what about your brother? I don't think he likes me.'

'David, I'm sure he does. Anyway, he's in Scotland, and he's married now, so he'll be setting up his own home when this war's over. I know Mother won't mind – in fact we often discuss you.'

Polly visibly bristled.

'In the nicest possible way. I'm always saying how much I could do with you at the factory. I've missed you.'

'Haven't you had any bombs on your house?'

'No, we've been very lucky, touch wood.' Sarah touched the table. 'So you see, it's my duty to look after you.'

Polly smiled as the tears flowed once more. 'If you think it will be all right. It would be lovely to work for you again.'

'Not for, with.'

Polly sniffed and fumbled for her handkerchief. Was her world beginning again?

Chapter 21

It was late afternoon. Polly and Sarah were excitedly chatting as they made their way to the Blooms' house. They discussed the state of the war, the bombing, and the plans Sarah had for the factory.

After the usual delays and diversions, which they knew were now going to become part of their daily lives, they finally reached the road where the Blooms lived.

Polly hung back reluctantly. 'What if your mother won't have me in the house?' she asked.

'Don't be silly, she'll be as pleased as I am to have you around.'

Sarah opened the front door and called, 'Come and see who I've got with me.'

Her mother came from the kitchen, wiping her hands on a towel. At the sight of Polly, she stopped in her tracks, and her face turned a deathly white.

Polly turned to Sarah, 'See, I told you it wasn't a good idea.' Her hand flew to the latch.

'No, Margaret, don't go.' Mrs Bloom's whisper was low and hesitant, but she quickly recovered. 'I'm sorry, it was the shock of seeing you standing there.' She looked at Polly's case. 'Are you staying round here?'

'Well I've . . .'

'I'll tell you all about it later, Mother,' interrupted Sarah.

'Oh. Would you like a cup of tea?'

'Of course we would. Margaret, give me your coat.' Sarah

moved round her and edged her away from the front door.

'Go in the drawing-room, I'll bring the tea in,' said Mrs Bloom.

When Sarah pushed the door shut behind her, Polly said in a loud whisper, 'I don't think I'd better stay, your mother's not all that pleased to see me.'

'I'll go and have a word with her, wait here.' Without removing her hat, she disappeared from the room.

Polly wandered over to the window. The view was the same from here as from Mr Bloom's study. She remembered the drink and talk she'd had with David on that evening so long ago: before she got married; before her mother died; before the war.

The sweeping lawn and flowerbeds still looked immaculate, but now, in the autumn, there were no nodding daffodils. The sun was swiftly dropping out of sight, and the leaves were turning various shades from green through to red.

She glanced around the room. On a small table in a heavy embossed silver frame stood a photograph of David. She went over and picked it up.

'He looks very handsome in his uniform, doesn't he?' said Mrs Bloom from the doorway. She placed the tray on the coffee table and sat on the sofa.

Polly immediately put the photo back on the table. 'I'm sorry, I didn't mean to . . .'

'That's all right. We're very proud of David.' There was an edge to her tone.

Sarah came back into the room. 'Margaret, I've told Mother you are going to stay here.'

Polly noted Mrs Bloom didn't look up from the tea she was pouring. 'I'll only stay till I find somewhere to live.'

'Do sit down, Margaret. I'm very sorry to hear about your mother.' Mrs Bloom handed Polly a cup of tea. 'This is a wicked war, killing and maiming innocent women and children.'

Polly felt uncomfortable. She was waiting for Mrs Bloom to welcome her to her home, but she didn't. She could feel the tension all around her. Polly finished her tea and, gathering up her handbag, said, 'Miss Bloom.'

'Call me Sarah, please. If we're going to work together . . .'

'I don't think this is such a good idea,' interrupted Polly. 'I'm sure I can find somewhere to stay, the YWCA might be able to help, or the Salvation Army. It will only be till Sunday, till after the church service, then I can go down to Shirley's.'

'Sit down, Margaret.' Mrs Bloom's voice was forceful but kind, and Polly instantly obeyed. 'When Sarah told me she had invited you to stay here, I must admit I was against it, almost outraged. But she has explained how you've lost your mother and how you can help her at work so, reluctantly, I've agreed. However, after what happened in this house I will make no excuses for my not being completely happy about it.'

Polly opened her mouth to speak, but no sound came out, so she hastily closed it again.

'Sarah also told me that you think your husband was at Dunkirk, and that your younger brother is in the Navy.' Mrs Bloom stood up and wandered to the window. With her back towards them, her voice softened as she continued. 'We have been very lucky so far. David is safe in Scotland and we still have our home.' She turned. 'I understand that your home, as well as your mother's house has been bombed and you have nowhere to go.'

Polly shook her head.

'Well in that case we can offer you a bed, and as Sarah wants you to help get her get started again . . .'

'See, what did I tell you,' interrupted Sarah. 'Come on, I'll show you to the guest-room.' She stood at the door waiting for Polly.

At the top of the stairs, she pushed open a door. Polly followed her into the room. Sarah went over to the window and closed the curtains. 'We've been fortunate enough to avoid the worst of the bombing so far. When the siren goes we go under the stairs.'

Polly looked about her. The highly polished dressing-table

235

and wardrobe were darker than hers had been. The green chintzy curtains fronting the black-out material matched the bedspread and covers on the armchair. Her shoes sank in the sage-green carpet. It was all very tasteful.

'This is a lovely room.' She looked at Sarah. 'Are you sure it's all right for me to stay? I don't want to come between you and your mother.'

'Of course. Besides, when she gets to know you, she'll be just as thrilled as I am at welcoming you back to the fold. Like the prodigal son.'

'I know who he was.' Polly smiled. 'I remember it took me a long while to find out who Eliza Doolittle was.'

Sarah's face lit up, and Polly's brow furrowed.

'What about your brother? What will he say about me staying here?'

'I know he felt as bad as I did at the time and when he hears what's happened to your mother . . . And as I said before, if he thinks you can help me keep the business running, I know he won't mind. I'll drop him a line later. Now, how about a nice bath?'

'That would be a real luxury the way I feel at the moment.'

'There's plenty of bath salts and things in there, so I'll leave you to have a nice old soak.'

'Miss . . . Sarah,' said Polly. 'Thank you very much. I'll never . . .'

'Go on with you,' Sarah looked away. 'That's the bathroom.' She pointed to a room across the landing.

'Just a minute.' Polly rummaged through her handbag. 'Here's my ration book.'

That night after dinner the sirens went and they sat under the stairs. Sarah was excitedly outlining her plans to Polly, who sat with her hands and jaws clenched. She was terrified, and strained her ears at the distant sounds.

'Sarah, do you honestly think it's wise trying to get started again with things as they are?' Mrs Bloom looked apprehensive when a bomb falling far away caused a slight tremor, and a small dusting of plaster landed in her lap.

'Could you see Dad sitting back waiting for the war to end?'

Mrs Bloom tutted and looked at Polly. 'She's so much like her father, and whatever I say won't make the slightest bit of difference.'

Polly was worried. She hadn't been above ground during a raid before, and was only half listening to the conversation. 'Is it safe under here? Shouldn't we go to a shelter?'

'The warden said this was as good as anywhere. It's a very well-built house. Besides we're waiting for a Morrison shelter to be delivered,' said Sarah cheerfully.

'What's a Morrison shelter?' Polly winced and looked anxiously about her, her face full of fear when the dull thud of another far-off bomb sent more small clouds of dust fluttering down.

'Don't look so worried,' said Sarah, putting down the list of figures she had been adding up.

Polly jumped and screwed up her face when the crack of an ack-ack gun filled the air. 'That sounded as if it was right outside.'

'It's probably miles away by now,' said Sarah, totally unconcerned. 'They rush about with them on the backs of lorries. One minute they're outside the door, the next, they've gone. You were asking about Morrison shelters. Well, they fit under a table, and our large dining-room table is just right, so the man said.'

'They look like a cage. I shall feel like a wild animal cooped up in one of those,' said Mrs Bloom with a shudder. But Polly was amazed at the well-ordered way they put the mattress and bedding neatly on the floor. As the evening wore on, the flasks of hot coffee were most welcome, as were the cheese sandwiches.

'You're very well-organized,' she said when Sarah asked her, during a lull, to rush upstairs and help bring down another mattress.

'We need to get on top of every situation,' she answered efficiently. 'Right, these are for you, Margaret – I hope you don't snore.' She passed Polly over some blankets.

'I don't think I'll be able to sleep, let alone snore,' said Polly, wrapping herself up.

'We'll see about that. After all, you've had a busy day, and, believe me, you'll have a lot more busy days in front of you if I can get hold of one of those lock-ups.'

'Is there any problem?' asked Polly.

'Well, there are a lot of people looking for premises to start again, and some can afford a lot more key money than I'm prepared to pay.'

'Now come along you two, settle down,' said Mrs Bloom. 'No more talking. Good night.'

Polly lay thinking. Yesterday her mother had died and she had no one, now, today, a whole new life was opening up. Once again she couldn't believe how quickly her fortune had changed.

The following morning Polly and Sarah went to Mansell Street. When they arrived, Fred was already rummaging amongst the rubble.

'Morning, Miss.' He raised his cap. 'Polly.'

Cheerfully they both said, 'Good morning, Fred.'

'Found anything worth saving?' asked Sarah.

'I think there's a good machine over here. I've managed to get a lot of bits of concrete off it. Come over and take a look.'

They clambered over the debris behind Fred.

'Here, Miss, what d'yer think? I can cannibalize some of these others that are a bit past it if we need spares.'

'Fred, you're a genius. Look, you two carry on looking for anything you might find useful, while I go and see about this lock-up.'

Sarah returned a few hours later with a big smile and two men wheeling a wheelbarrow. She dangled a key in front of Polly and Fred. 'It's all settled. We can move into Number 14 right away.'

'Good for you, Miss,' said Fred, shaking her hand.

Polly couldn't control herself. She rushed up to Sarah and

threw her arms round her neck, and once again the tears started. 'I'm so pleased for you,' she blurted out.

Sarah patted her back. 'Come on now.' She pushed her away. 'Look at your face – it's covered with dirt.'

Polly took her handkerchief from her pocket and wiped her eyes. She looked at her hankie. 'I see what you mean,' she sniffed. 'Sorry about that. Now it's our turn to show you something. Come over here.'

They walked behind a wall that was noticeably unstable and dangerous.

'Look.' Polly pointed to a pile of the large industrial cotton reels, a pair of scissors, and a large box of pins. 'And look what we have here.' She threw back a piece of cloth and revealed her typewriter. 'It's got a few bent arms, but Fred here said he can straighten them.'

They laughed, and the thought suddenly struck Polly that, in the midst of all this death and destruction, they could get excited over finding a few reels of cotton and a typewriter.

'Come on Fred,' said Sarah. 'Let's get these machines you want saved over to Number 14. Bill here and his mate said they'd give you a hand.'

Fred whispered to Polly. 'I bet that's cost her a bob or two.'

'This place wants a damn good clean,' said Polly when she walked into the lock-up half an hour later. 'D'you think Charlie would lend us a bucket and broom?'

Sarah was wandering around, looking into all the corners. 'I don't see why not. Just put that machine down anywhere,' she said to Bill and his mate.

Fred followed with a bagful of bits and pieces. 'Found some more spares,' he said to Sarah.

'I think it's time for a cup of tea, then we can ask Charlie about borrowing his broom.'

For two days they dug, rummaged and salvaged anything they felt they could use. The lock-up was swept and cleaned, and four good machines installed. They were elated when they found two bales of cloth that were almost intact.

'We only need to take a few feet off this one,' said Polly excitedly, partly undoing one of the bales of pale-grey jersey. 'Any pieces we have to cut off we'll wash and use for trimming.'

Sarah smiled. 'You sound just like my father; he was always on about wasting cloth. Are you sure there's not some Jewish blood way back in your family?'

They laughed. They were both very happy.

'Just look at my fingernails,' wailed Sarah that evening after she had taken a bath. She was sitting on the floor in front of the empty fireplace. Fortunately it was still too warm for a fire. The government had warned them to use coal sparingly, as it was going to be in short supply this coming winter. Sarah was wrapped in her blue Turkish dressing-gown; she had a towel twisted turban-fashion round her wet hair, and was hugging her knees like a child. Her face was shining, and her cheeks had the look of well-scrubbed rosy apples, which made her dark eyes glisten.

'What do you expect? Honestly, Mrs Bloom, you should see your daughter scrabbling around like an old totter.'

'Just hark who's talking,' laughed Sarah.

'If you ask me, it sounds as if both of you are enjoying yourselves, but you must be careful, and don't do anything silly, it's not worth it.'

'Don't worry, Mother, we are very careful,' said Sarah smiling broadly.

Polly relaxed, and lay back against the red velvet sofa, revelling in the luxury of her surroundings. Things were beginning to get a little less tense between Mrs Bloom and Polly, and she secretly hoped her life as it was now would never end. 'Sarah, have you given any more thought to that cloth we found?' she asked.

'No, my main worry at the moment is ensuring we keep the government contract. Come on, let's get the flasks and sandwiches ready. Jerry will be coming over soon.'

* * *

240

'Well?' asked Polly, when Sarah came back from the Ministry the following afternoon. 'Are we still going to be able to make shorts?'

'Yes. I told them about Violet and Elsie working from home, and that we were starting up again – the man seemed satisfied with that. So Bloom's is now back in business.'

'Great,' said Polly, her face wreathed in smiles.

'Congratulations,' said Fred, shaking Sarah's hand.

'How have you two got on today?' she asked.

'We found some of Barny's patterns.' Polly hurried over to an old desk Sarah had bought off some old man, and brought out the bundle of tattered paper. 'I reckon I can still use them. That jersey would look good made up in some of these.'

'We'll have to see about that. We need the work from the government first. Let's get the money from that contract before we start worrying about dresses. Violet and Elsie will want paying once the cloth is delivered, not forgetting Fred. I've got those treadle machines going in on Saturday, and I can't expect Mother to finance us forever.'

'Yes, perhaps you're right.' Polly smiled. 'You know what I'm like when I get hold of a pattern and some cloth.'

'I think we might have a bit of trouble finding a shop to take any stock at the moment.' Sarah rubbed her eyes with her thumb and forefinger. 'I'm tired, I think we'll call it a day. Margaret?'

Polly spun round at her tone.

'Don't look so worried. Tomorrow I'm going to take Mother to our synagogue.'

'But I didn't think you were, you know . . .'

'We're not good Jews. I haven't been to a Shul for years. Mother is far more a practising Jew than Father ever was. David always used to say Father was only a Jew when it suited him – he was probably right. Anyway, I thought I'd tell you, I won't be working tomorrow.'

'That's all right. I'll come over and help Fred.'

'Don't worry, Miss,' said Fred cheerfully. 'I'll make sure the machines are installed and running.'

On Sunday morning Polly carefully crawled out from under the stairs, hoping to avoid waking Sarah and her mother. She quickly washed and changed into her only suit. It was black velvet, and she was very proud of it. She was in her room, just putting the finishing touches to her make-up, when Sarah popped her head round the door.

'You were very quiet,' she said, yawning and ruffling her hair.

'I didn't want to wake you or your mother. I thought I'd leave early in case I have a job to get to the hospital.'

'Mother's getting you a cup of tea and toast, so you had better come down and have it, otherwise you'll be in her bad books.'

'That's nice of her, I'll be right down.'

Mrs Bloom was waiting in the kitchen. 'Good morning, Margaret,' she said kindly. 'Pour yourself a cup of tea while I see to the toast. I must say you look very smart this morning.'

'Thank you. This is the only thing I've got that's black.'

'I'm sure Sarah could have found you something – have you seen inside her wardrobe?'

'I've told her she can have anything she wants,' said Sarah, walking into the room. 'We're about the same size, and anyway, I'm sure she can alter anything to suit her.' She reached across the table for the tea.

Polly smiled. 'This suit was always a standing joke between me and Shirley; she had one as well. We were both so hard up after we bought them. I've sponged mine down with vinegar water so many times it doesn't know if it's a suit or a plate of fish and chips.' She sniffed her sleeve. 'I hope it doesn't smell.'

Mrs Bloom laughed. 'I can't smell anything.' A serious look came over her face. 'What time is the service?'

'Eleven. Although the underground goes almost there, I'm giving myself plenty of time in case the roads are blocked.'

She got up from the table, went into the hall, and put on her black hat with the eye veil. After adjusting it, she checked the seams of her stockings, picked up her handbag, and left.

Her journey was, to her relief, uneventful and, when she arrived at the hospital, she was very surprised at the number of people filling the small chapel. Two or three times she quickly glanced around, hoping that perhaps Sid had learned of his mother's death and would be here. Still more and more people joined the congregation, till there was only standing room.

Had all these people lost a loved one in this past week? Polly felt terribly sad. The swing from misery to happiness had been so dramatic in just one week that it had almost obliterated the pain of losing her mother.

The vicar's clear voice was condemning the pointlessness of war. A wave of emotion swept over Polly, and she buried her head in her hands and wept.

Chapter 22

Over the following weeks, Mary and Betty, two of the women who were at Bloom's before the bombs destroyed the factory, worked hard. Working conditions were far from easy: the air-raids forced them to run frequently to the shelter, and they would swear out loud when the cotton broke, or when they were plunged into darkness because of a power cut. Sometimes, just for a laugh and to ease the tension, they'd pull on a pair of the larger shorts they had been making over their slacks, and swagger round the work-room. Occasionally they'd put their names and addresses in the odd pair like they used to, and a couple of times, much to their amusement, they received a reply.

Sarah and Polly worked on the machines when they could. They were desperate to hang on to the government contract. The two outworkers, Violet and Elsie, were also contributing to ease the work-load, and Fred was kept busy repairing the machines and keeping them in running order.

By the time the weekend came around Polly and Sarah were always exhausted, relieved to have a respite from the struggle to keep up with their orders. One Sunday Polly was sitting quietly at the breakfast table reading the paper when Sarah walked in.

'Sunday is the only day we get to read a paper right through. What's the news today?'

Polly folded the newspaper, put it to one side and pushed the tea-pot closer to Sarah. 'It's these U-boats I'm worried about.' She clasped her hands round her cup and stared into space. 'I wish I could find out if Billy's safe.'

'You still haven't heard from the War Office?'

'No, they didn't hold out much hope as they have got so much work. They told me that now I have a permanent address I would hear if he was dead, as apparently I'm his only living next-of-kin they've got on record. You know I wrote to the address they gave me.'

Sarah nodded. 'What about your other brother? Is he in the Forces?'

'Sid? No, he didn't pass his medical, he's got flat feet.'

Sarah laughed. 'I'm sorry. That always sounds so funny. I wouldn't have thought that would have stopped the boys from going into the Forces.'

'It does sound daft, I know, but the Army must have its reasons.'

'What does he do?'

'He used to work at the market, but I can't find out anything about him. I've been to the market he used to work and seen some of his old cronies. Most of the boys have been called up and it's the mothers and fathers who are running the stalls now. Those that are left, that is. It's terrible when you ask after someone and you're told they are either dead or in hospital, or have just disappeared like Sid.' Polly stared into her empty cup. She swilled the tea leaves round and round, trying to make patterns and faces in the bottom of the cup.

'I expect he'll turn up one day,' said Sarah.

'Well, yes, bad pennies always do.' Polly sighed. 'Enough of this doom and gloom. Sarah, what're you thinking of doing with that cloth we managed to salvage?'

'I don't know offhand – any ideas?'

Polly sat forward. 'Yes. Christmas is coming, so what about making it up into a few dresses? There's not a lot of good stuff on the market, so you shouldn't have any problem shifting them.'

'I don't know. We've got a lot of work on.'

'We've got that spare machine Fred managed to get hold of.

Couldn't we get it over here, then I could do some in the evenings before we crawl under the table.'

Sarah laughed. Getting into the Morrison shelter still gave them a laugh as they pretended to be animals in a cage. 'I don't know, I'll have to think about it.'

'Well don't be too long, otherwise Christmas will have come and gone.'

'Who's talking about Christmas?' asked Mrs Bloom, patting and smoothing down her wavy hair as she walked into the kitchen.

'I was,' said Polly. 'I'm sorry, I forgot, you don't recognize it.'

'We do,' said Sarah, 'because of my father.'

'Yes,' said Mrs Bloom wistfully. 'He liked Christmas.'

'He made money out of it,' laughed Sarah.

'Sarah, that's not very kind. He was very good to you.'

'Yes, I'm sorry, Mother.'

'What were you saying about Christmas, Margaret?'

'I want Sarah to let me make a few dresses out of that grey wool jersey we found.'

'That's a nice piece of cloth, it would look lovely made up.'

'I know.'

'So, what's the problem then?'

Sarah refilled her cup. 'We haven't any patterns.'

'Yes we have,' said Polly eagerly. 'Remember we found some of Barny's old ones.'

'But they're all tatty.'

'I suppose they are. It's a pity we can't get hold of any tissue paper, then Fred and I could have a go at making new ones, using Barny's as a guide.'

It was Sarah's turn to sit up. 'I could go round to some of the other manufacturers and see if they can help.'

'That would be great,' said Polly enthusiastically.

Mrs Bloom smiled. 'You know it gives me such pleasure to see you both carrying on the business, in spite of all the problems and setbacks.' She hesitated, then added softly, 'Your father would be very proud of you, Sarah.'

'You forget, Mother, I couldn't do it without Fred and Margaret. With her flair for design we could go a long way.'

Suddenly Polly Bell felt very important. It felt good to be needed and appreciated: since her grandfather died no one had really made her feel like that. It was a wonderful sensation.

Three weeks before Christmas they had twenty dresses ready for Sarah to take round to the shops.

'Margaret, they are really lovely,' said Mrs Bloom. 'You are a very clever girl – there's not two exactly alike.'

'Bloom's Exclusive Fashions,' said Sarah, proudly holding one of the dresses against her. 'This one just happens to be your size. Do you like it, Mother?' She lifted one of the long sleeves.

'I think it's lovely,' purred Mrs Bloom.

Polly laughed. 'See, what did I tell you, Sarah? I knew this one was you, Mrs Bloom.'

'Mother, Margaret and I would like you to have it for Christmas.'

'Oh I couldn't – not take the stock.'

'Don't be silly,' said Sarah. 'You must have something new. Remember David hopes to be here with Yvonne.'

Mrs Bloom visibly stiffened. 'Oh yes, but whatever we wear she'll upstage us. I'll get the tea.'

'Doesn't your mother like your brother's wife?' asked Polly after Mrs Bloom had left the room.

'Unfortunately for both of them, the first time they met was the day after my father died. Mother's only met Yvonne once, and she was very upset when she found out David had married a Gentile. That was against my father's wishes – he had other plans for him. Mother still doesn't know David was married on the day Father died.'

'How awful.'

'Poor David, he was devastated. The letter I had from him was so sad; I don't think he will ever forgive himself. You must never tell Mother,' Sarah added quickly.

248

'I wouldn't dream of it. It'll be nice for you to have them here at Christmas. Perhaps they will get to know each other better.'

'Perhaps.'

'I was thinking of going to Shirley's.'

'Oh, must you? I'm sorry, of course you must. How is your little god-daughter?'

'Elizabeth.' Polly smiled. 'Shirley said she's into everything – quite a handful as far as I can gather.'

'I'm pleased you decided to write to Shirley.'

'So am I.'

'She still hasn't heard from your husband?'

Polly blushed. 'No, he was never the best of letter writers.'

'It's a shame the War Office can't help you.'

'If I know Ron, he's probably done a bunk,' Polly said bitterly.

'Are you sorry you never had children?'

'No, not really. It would have been difficult, what with one thing and another.'

'You probably wouldn't have gone to prison,' said Sarah.

Polly looked up surprised. That was the first time since she'd come to the house that it had been mentioned. She just smiled sadly, and said nothing.

The following week Polly was very upset to receive a letter from Shirley telling her that her mother was none too well, and that Elizabeth had the measles. 'I was really looking forward to seeing them,' she said, looking up from the letter. 'She's asked me to go down after Christmas, perhaps for the New Year. That's if Mrs Bell is well enough. Would that be all right?'

'Of course. I'm sorry to hear her news,' said Sarah.

Polly continued to scan the pages of Shirley's letter, when suddenly she gasped.

'What is it?' asked Sarah.

'It's Ron's address.'

'Where is he?'

'I don't know. Shirley doesn't say, just that he's written to me but his letters have been returned and he's worried about me. He must still be abroad as it's a PO number.' Polly bit her lip nervously. She knew she ought to try to write to him, to try at least to make contact with Ron. He was her husband, after all, and perhaps they could eventually sort out their differences. Quietly she folded Shirley's letter away, her mind troubled once more.

At the fourth attempt Polly finally managed to put in writing all that had happened to her this past year. With her elbows resting on the dressing-table, she chewed on the end of her pen thoughtfully. God, was it only last year they had gone to Shirley's? Only a year ago that she'd had the best Christmas since her dad died. Only a year ago that the good old-fashioned Christmas at the Bells' had been full of loving and laughter, and only a year ago that Ron had given her that brooch, the brooch that changed her life. At this moment it seemed more like a lifetime away. Would she ever find out if Ron had bought that brooch or stolen it? And did he know she'd been in prison because of his gift?

She popped the letter into the envelope and stuck it down. As she gazed round her room her spirits lifted. She still couldn't believe her luck. She was happy living here, and in such a short time she felt at home. Polly propped the letter against the dressing-table mirror and went down to dinner.

On Christmas Eve, David and Yvonne arrived. There was the usual kissing and hugging from his mother and sister. Polly stood in the background and stared in wonder at David's wife.

She was beautiful. Her well-cut fur coat and the heady scent of her expensive perfume filling the hall made Polly feel totally insignificant. Yvonne's soft blonde hair, falling on her shoulders when she removed her matching fur hat, was immaculate. Her skin was flawless, her figure perfect as, when David had taken her coat, she smoothed down the soft pink wool jersey dress that clung to every curve. Her sparkling china-blue eyes made Polly very conscious of her own blind eye. She could understand why David had gone against his father's wishes to marry this gorgeous-looking creature.

David removed his cap and ran his fingers through his thick black curly hair. He was so good-looking, and his smart RAF officer's uniform added to his attraction. When they settled in the drawing-room he was charming and thoughtful. As he served them with drinks, he hung on to every word Yvonne whispered.

Polly's eyes were drawn to David, and once or twice she caught Yvonne looking at her quizzically. She almost sensed Yvonne was dying to ask her about her eye, and she quickly turned away.

'David, darling, would you be a sweetie pie and pop upstairs for my wrap?' Yvonne asked in her breathless, little-girl voice.

'Are you cold, my dear?' asked Mrs Bloom.

'No, not really, but I do like something round my shoulders.'

David was out of the room and back in a flash. Sarah raised her perfectly shaped eyebrows at Polly.

He placed the white gossamer shawl lovingly round Yvonne's shoulders, and then sat next to Polly. 'I was very surprised when Sarah wrote and told me you were living here,' he said.

Polly stiffened. She hoped that he was too much of a gentleman to discuss the past. 'Your mother and Sarah have been very kind to me,' she said.

'Sarah's been telling me about the dresses you designed and made up with the cloth you managed to salvage.'

She smiled. 'I had a lot of help from Fred, and Sarah.'

'But it's you that has the talent,' insisted Sarah.

'And the enthusiasm,' said Mrs Bloom. 'You should have seen her, machining away till all hours.'

'Till Jerry came over and we had to crawl into our cage,' said Polly, embarrassed at these accolades.

'Darling, my glass is empty,' interrupted Yvonne.

David jumped up and took her glass.

'Do you work?' asked Polly.

'Yvonne is an actress,' said David proudly.

That figures, thought Polly, looking at all the make-up and the fluttering eyelashes. 'Are you on the stage?'

'No, I'm in films.'

'Oh, I go to the pictures a lot. What have you been in?'

'Unfortunately, up till now I've only had bit parts, though they've been speaking parts, of course. My agent is holding out for the lead in a really good film. It's being shot in Scotland, so I'll be near David.' She looked at David, and Polly couldn't decided whether the look was one of real love, or if she was just a very good actress.

Polly glanced up at the French carriage clock that stood in the middle of the mahogany mantelshelf. It was ten o'clock. 'Would you excuse me? You must have a hundred and one things to talk about.' Polly stood up.

David turned. 'You don't have to go on our account. It's much too early.'

Polly laughed uneasily. 'Down here in London we make the most of going to bed early. You never know if you're going to finish up under the table, and I don't mean through drink.'

'I hated sleeping in those horrid shelters. Thank goodness the raids have eased off and we can go to our own bed.' Yvonne gazed up at David who, after an uneasy glance at his mother, awkwardly ran his finger round the inside of his collar.

'Good night all, and I hope I don't see you till the morning.' Polly quietly closed the door behind her.

She sat at her dressing-table and looked at herself in the mirror. The way Yvonne had studied her had disturbed her, stripping away the fragile confidence she had built up. She had felt dowdy and out of place: all evening she had carefully watched every word she had said for fear of the wrong word or phrase slipping out. Polly picked up the letter she had written to Ron and never posted. She turned it over along with her thoughts.

What will he say when he knows I'm living with the Blooms for the time being? she wondered. She couldn't stay if David and his wife came to live here. So far David hadn't mentioned anything about that awful day at the factory, or about her going to prison although he had behaved a little oddly at first. She wondered if he'd told Yvonne about the robbery? Polly put the letter back against the mirror and got into the luxury of her soft bed, hoping tonight her sleep wouldn't be disrupted.

Christmas Day was wonderful. Polly was surprised that the Blooms celebrated Christmas in the same way as Gentiles. The expensive presents and the lavish meal, despite the rationing, was something Polly had never experienced before. She guessed they would eat well. People that came to see Mrs Bloom always seemed to have something in their bag, and Polly always made a discreet exit from the room if they started talking business.

Polly and Sarah finished the washing-up and joined the others in the drawing-room. The black-out curtains had been drawn but the light hadn't been switched on. The fire crackled merrily in the hearth, giving the room a cosy glow and lighting up David's fine features. He looked just as handsome in civvies as he did in uniform. Polly quickly sat down next to Mrs Bloom, afraid someone would read her mind.

Sarah switched on the light and sat next to David; for Polly the spell was broken. Sarah was bubbling with her plans for expansion. 'I'm thinking of renting the lock-up next door to the one we already have. I've managed to buy two more machines.'

'What about workers? Can you get them?' asked David.

'So far. Margaret has managed to contact a few of our previous employees and they seem keen to work for us again, but if they start to call women up it may be difficult, although they won't be able to take those with children, will they?'

'I shouldn't think so, but they could send them to factories that are doing war work.'

'Last week I managed to get hold of some more salvaged cloth from Solly. You remember him, David? So between making shorts, we'll be able to turn out a few more dresses. Got to keep that side of Bloom's going.'

'You sound like Father,' said David with genuine enthusiasm. 'He'd be proud of you, Sarah.'

'I hope I can build the business up again,' she said modestly. 'Mind you, I couldn't do it without Margaret.'

'Perhaps you should make her a partner. After all, if she's that kind of an asset, someone might steal her away.'

Polly laughed. 'I don't think so, David. I'm far too happy working for Sarah. What about you, aren't you interested in the business?'

'No, not really. I love flying more than anything.'

'Thanks,' said Yvonne curtly.

'After you of course, darling.'

Yvonne smiled and looked coy. 'I thought we were going to have some more drinky-poos, and a sing-song, not talk about silly old business all evening,' she cooed.

'Sorry,' said Sarah. 'That's my fault, and very ill-mannered of me. What would you like to drink? David, put a record on the radiogram for now – it may need a new needle – later on I'll get on the piano and we'll have our sing-song.'

'Put on that new record that I like,' said Mrs Bloom. Her face was flushed, and she looked happy.

The rest of the evening was perfect. The drink flowed, and they all relaxed and enjoyed themselves.

Mrs Bloom was the first to leave the room. 'I'm going up now,' she announced.

'We'll be up when we've finished this round,' said Sarah, shuffling the cards. They were playing rummy now.

Mrs Bloom kissed her son and daughter, and pecked Yvonne's cheek. When she got to Polly, Polly hugged her.

'Thank you for such a lovely day,' she whispered.

Mrs Bloom blew her nose. 'It was my pleasure, my dear.'

After a while, Polly and Sarah went to bed, leaving David and Yvonne sitting in front of the dying embers. At the top of the stairs, Polly kissed Sarah's cheek. 'You've been so good to me, I'll never . . .'

'Go on with you,' interrupted Sarah. 'It's the drink making you all silly and sentimental.' Hastily she turned away and went to her room.

Polly's room, the guest-room, was situated between Sarah's and David's. She lay on the bed looking up at the pure white ceiling. This was so different from the stained one in Penn's Place with its bare bulb hanging low on the brown flex. Tears filled her eyes. Their house in Penn's Place, like her mum, wasn't there any more. Here a pretty green frilly shade covered the bulb, like the pink one she had had in Weaver Street. That's not there any more either, she sniffed, as the tears trickled slowly down into her ears. She glanced across at the dressing-table. I must post that letter to Ron, she told herself. A feeling of guilt suddenly swept over her. She was wicked making him worry about her, when, here she was in this comfortable room, living in luxury, while he could be spending Christmas any-where, even down a wet and muddy fox-hole. Her head was full of thoughts, and her mind returned once more to Weaver Street. They'd been happy there. She recalled the times they made love. Love: she still wasn't really sure of the true mean-ing of the word. She fleetingly thought of when she was in prison. He hadn't worried about her then. But she quickly dis-missed those dark memories and the questions in her mind. All she wanted to remember at this moment were the good times. Sarah was right she realized, through the haze of tears and memories, the drink was making her all sentimental.

She heard David and Yvonne coming up the stairs. Yvonne was giggling: she's had more than enough to drink, mused Polly. Now if only Ron had one fraction of David's charm. She smiled. Perhaps things would have been very different. Her lids became heavy, but the smile remained.

A few minutes later a slamming door made Polly jump. She sat up; she had been in a deep sleep. Her head felt muzzy through drink. She was disorientated. Had the siren gone and she'd not heard it? Surely someone would have woken her and made sure she had gone downstairs. She cocked her head and strained her ears. The house was silent.

There was a bang like something hitting the wall. Then she heard Yvonne shouting . . .

Chapter 23

'Shh, darling. You shouldn't have slammed that door, you'll wake the whole house.'

'So what?' She put the whisky bottle and glass she had brought upstairs on the dressing-table.

'Well, they haven't had many nights in their beds just lately, and . . .'

'I don't give a damn,' interrupted Yvonne, waving her arms as she staggered round the room. She swayed uneasily and held on to the bed-end for support.

'Come along, darling, let me help you into bed.' David looked longingly at his lovely wife as he held her arm.

'Leave me alone.' Yvonne shook herself free. 'I can manage perfectly well. Thank you.'

'If you say so.' David removed his silk dressing-gown and stretched out on top of the bed. 'You've had too much to drink again,' he sighed, remembering the scene they'd had in her flat the last time he was home.

'You like it when I've had a little drinky-poos,' she purred.

David was lying on his back with his hands under his head. He watched her sit at the dressing-table and pour herself another drink. She took a cigarette from the silver box and, through the mirror, offered him one. He shook his head. With the cigarette dangling from her scarlet lips she stood up and kicked off her shoes. They banged against the wall as she sent them flying across the room.

'Yvonne, be quiet.'

'I won't. D'you know that's the most boring bloody Christmas I've had in my life,' she yelled.

David raised his head in surprise as Yvonne stubbed her cigarette out aggressively in the ash-tray.

'To think we could have gone to Justin's party and on to a night club. Instead we have to sit and listen to the Ink Spots singing "Whispering Grass" over and over again because Mummy likes it.'

'I'm sorry, Yvonne. I thought you wanted to spend Christmas with my family.'

She plonked herself down at the dressing-table and poured herself another drink. 'Want one?' She held out the glass.

'No, and you don't want any more either.'

'I'll have as much as I like. I've been a good little girl all evening, patient and polite, now I need something to calm my nerves. Bloody Ink Spots.' She walked round the bed. 'Then, if that wasn't enough, we all had to sing while your sister played the piano, and that was only after we'd been through all the talk about the business. My God, what a bloody boring lot.'

'Please, Yvonne, keep your voice down.'

'Ah yes, we don't want to wake Mummy darling, do we?'

David raised his voice and said sharply, 'Yvonne, please be quiet and get into bed.'

She threw her head back and laughed. 'Why's that, so that you can have your wicked way with me?' She put her empty glass on top of the oak chest of drawers and tottered across the room. Slowly she turned to face David. Swaying her hips in long, exaggerated movements, she undid, inch by inch, the long zip at the back of the black crepe dress which was moulded to her body. First, and very dramatically, she removed her left arm from the long, tight-fitting sleeve, then she proceeded to roll the right sleeve down her arm. Carefully and deliberately she let the dress slither down her body till it lay in a crumpled heap at her feet. Wearing only her black camiknickers, she daintily stepped out of her dress.

'Is this what you want?' She seductively ran her hand up and down the creamy bare flesh above her stocking tops.

David ached for her but hated her at the same time.

'You like this, don't you?' she teased, kneeling on the bed, revealing her deep cleavage. She cupped her breasts. 'That's all you think I'm good for, don't you – a good lay.'

David feasted his eyes on her body, wanting her, longing to feel her soft skin. 'Yvonne, I love you,' he croaked. 'But don't say things like that, it makes you sound cheap.'

Her laugh was raw and caustic. 'Oh, come off it. You knew I'd been around before you married me, so don't play the innocent hurt husband to me.'

David needed her, desperately, hungrily, but he loathed her when she was drunk and behaved like this. He knew it would end in tears, as it had the first time he had heard her openly admitting to what she had done in order to get a part in a film. 'Come on, you've had too much to drink.' He slipped off the bed and grabbed her arm.

She pulled away. 'What about you? Have you had too much to drink? Think you're man enough for me? I'm ready for it, but do you think you can make it?' She laughed in his face.

'I don't like it when you're in this mood,' he scowled.

'Don't you get all high hat with me. If you don't like me in this mood, well then, leave me alone, or better still, go next door.' Her voice had risen to screaming-pitch. 'Perhaps you fancy a bit of rough for a change? Try your luck with one-eyed Kate next door – she fancies you.'

'What?' shouted David angrily. He knew if Margaret was awake she would hear every word. He lowered his tone. 'Yvonne, shut up and stop talking in this ridiculous way. It's late. Get into bed and don't be so stupid.'

'Huh, that's a laugh, you calling me stupid. Oh I know you only want a great-looking dumb blonde hanging on your arm. It does your ego the world of good when I get whistled and ogled at.'

'That's not true.' But David knew that, above all else, he was physically attracted to her.

'I noticed you didn't take a lot of interest when they were discussing the plans for the factory. What if they make a go of it? Where will you stand?'

'I told you before, I intend to make my own way after this war, I don't want any hand-outs, or to take over the business. After the way Sarah and Margaret have worked, and what they've achieved, they deserve their success.'

Yvonne looked at David contemptuously. 'Do you honestly think you'll be as attractive to me on the dole? And out of uniform?'

'If you love me, it shouldn't make any difference.'

She laughed. 'My God, you are naïve . . . And what about you suggesting your sister offer one-eyed Kate a partnership. You must have made her day, and I bet Sarah was relieved when she refused.' Fluttering her heavily mascaraed eyelashes, and mimicking the way Polly always held her head slightly to one side, she said in a sickly sweet voice, 'I don't think so David, I'm far too happy working for Sarah. *Balls*.'

'Yvonne, you've had too much to drink.' He tried to edge his way nearer to her.

'Leave me alone,' she yelled. 'You're so damn polite, you make me sick. Why can't you say "pissed" like the rest of us? Can't you see she fancies you? The way she looks at you with that one eye of hers, it's like a soulful dog. Christ, she gives me the creeps, *and* she's been to prison. I bet your mother didn't want her living here. You'd better watch her, especially when she comes up here on her own. She could be robbing us.'

David turned white with anger and shouted, 'Yvonne, please be quiet.' He knew Margaret must be awake by now. How could he stop Yvonne? He gritted his teeth, and clenched and unclenched his jaw. It took all his strength to stop himself from slapping her face, but he decided to take the calm approach. 'My darling, I've told you before not to drink so much.'

'I'll do what I bloody well like.' There was a sob in her voice. She looked up at him, and her eyes filled with tears. 'I'm sorry.'

He moved closer and whispered softly, 'Why do you do it? It makes you become so unreasonable.'

'Oh David,' she murmured feebly as the tears began to fall.

He put his arm round her shoulders, and she laid her head on his chest. 'Come on now.'

'David. I talk like this because I love you and I'm afraid of losing you.'

'You'll never lose me.' David kissed her wet eyes and cheeks; when he found her mouth, it was open and eager for his. They lay back on the bed. He slipped the thin straps holding her camiknickers off her shoulders and caressed the beautiful body that belonged to him – and all other thoughts went out of his head.

Next door Polly cringed as she lay under the bedclothes listening to Yvonne end her tirade. *One-eyed Kate. One-eyed Kate.* The words were pounding in her head like someone beating a drum. How dare that silly little cow say such things? She wondered if Sarah and Mrs Bloom could hear her. They were such nice people; why must Yvonne be so loud and rude. Polly's heart went out to David. The humiliation of it. Poor, dear David. Perhaps Yvonne wasn't so daft. Yes, it was true, she did like him, but didn't think it showed. Polly knew he was out of her league, and besides, they were both married. She lay listening. Thank goodness the shouting had stopped. It was quiet, and she could only guess what was happening. She put her hands over her ears, not wanting to hear any more as she fought her feelings of jealousy and unhappiness.

Early the following morning, Polly put her suitcase on the bed and began putting a few of her belongings inside. She knew she had to leave this house; she was causing trouble for David and she was beginning to be afraid that her feelings for him were growing too strong. She would go to Shirley's. She started trying to think of some sort of excuse to give Sarah and Mrs Bloom for her hasty departure.

She knew David would be bringing Yvonne's breakfast up on a tray, as his wife didn't like to be seen first thing in the morning, at least not until she had completed her make-up. She didn't want to face Yvonne again; perhaps if she went now she could leave a note. But she needed a cup of tea first. Her mouth felt like a sewer.

Polly went quietly down the stairs, hoping the rest of the household were still asleep. She filled the kettle and put it on the gas stove, then wandered into the drawing-room and gazed out of the window. Looking at but not seeing the long sweep of lawn that led to the trees at the bottom of the garden. Trees that had been stripped bare of their leaves by the keen winter winds. Stripped bare, as Polly's confidence had been last night, by Yvonne's words. She loved the Blooms, and she loved living in this house. She didn't want to leave them, or her work. When David touched her arm she jumped and swung round.

'I'm sorry, I didn't mean to startle you.'

For a split second his touch made her fumble for words. She quickly looked away. 'Oh David . . . It's you. I didn't hear you come in. Is Yvonne . . .'

'No, she's still in bed. Rather a bad hangover, I'm afraid. We'll be leaving this morning as soon as she's ready. I have to get back to Scotland. I only managed to get a four-day pass. Margaret, about last night. I'm . . .'

'Don't say anything.'

'But I must. I'm sorry. I know you heard.'

She turned to look out of the window. 'Don't let it worry you. I've been called quite a few names in my time.'

'I'm truly sorry.' He bent his head. 'I wouldn't want to hurt you.'

Polly was upset and angry. Angry with Yvonne, angry with David for bringing her here, and she didn't care what she said any more – she was going to get out of their lives.

'You did once.'

'Margaret.'

'You don't have to worry about me, I'm leaving. I'm going down to see my friend Shirley.' She tried to sound light-hearted. 'You must remember Shirley, she was the one who shopped me.' Polly knew she was being unfair and hurtful but she couldn't stop herself. She screwed up her eyes, to stem the tears that were imminent. She ploughed on, regardless. 'They're my kind of people,' she said. 'Besides, I could see it in your face when you first walked in on Christmas Eve that I was an intruder. You didn't know what to say to me. The last time we met you were all for sending me to prison. I may be an ex-con, but at least I like to think I've got more manners than your wife.'

He pulled her round to face him. She looked into his dark brown eyes, soft and full of concern. 'I'm sorry for that, at the time I was angry at the grief the burglary had caused my mother. Margaret, you can't go.'

Polly shivered with pleasure at the forceful way he held her arms.

'Say you won't leave on Yvonne's account, please . . . I'd like . . .'

'Ah, there you are.' Yvonne stood in the doorway. The light shining through her flimsy white dressing-gown revealed a pair of perfectly shaped legs.

Guiltily Polly and David jumped apart as Yvonne walked into the room, the white of her breasts showing above her lacy nightdress. She was shaking with rage. Her face was devoid of make-up and her hair a mess.

'I told you she was still a thief. Look.' She produced Polly's whip from behind her back.

Polly leapt forward. 'Just what the hell do you think you're doing with that? You've been going through my case!' she yelled.

Yvonne took a step backwards. 'When I saw your suitcase on the bed I guessed you were packing. Thinking of running off, were you? I wanted to make sure you were only taking what belonged to you – and I found this.'

'Why you nosy little˙...'

The shouts brought Sarah and Mrs Bloom running from the kitchen.

'What the hell's going on in here?' asked Sarah. 'And what are you doing with Margaret's whip?'

'You know about this?' She brandished the whip. A flush started at Yvonne's breasts, and quickly went to her face.

'Yes. It belonged to her grandfather.'

Polly sat on the sofa, shaking. 'She must have gone through my things,' she whispered. 'That was right at the bottom of my case.' The cumulation of events in the past twelve hours brought tears to her eyes.

Mrs Bloom sat beside her and put her arm round Polly's heaving shoulders. 'Yvonne,' she said quietly, 'I think you owe Margaret an apology – first for last night, and now this.'

David went to speak, but his mother held up her hand. 'Oh yes, we all heard you last night.'

Yvonne looked at David, and without moving said in a defiant tone. 'Phone for a taxi, then come up and help me pack.' She threw the whip to the floor. 'That handle's solid silver. I'd like to know how her grandfather got hold of it.' She stormed out of the door.

David picked up the whip and placed it on the coffee table. 'I'm so sorry.'

He was about to follow his wife when Sarah called, 'David.' It was a command. 'Come into Father's den. I want to have a word with you.'

They left the room, quietly closing the door behind them.

Mrs Bloom took hold of Polly's hand. 'Why were you packing, my dear? You're not thinking of leaving us, are you?'

Polly sniffed and nodded. 'After what Yvonne said last night, I don't think ...'

'Margaret, you'll do no such thing. I want you to stay and, after all, it is my house. Sarah and I have been having a little talk, and she has something important to ask you. Besides, you have got to get me a new kettle.'

Polly looked up in surprise. 'Oh my God, I forgot.'

'It burnt dry while you were talking to David.' She smiled. 'But, if that's all the damage that has been done today, well, we can live with that, can't we?'

Chapter 24

'Well, what do you think?'

'It's very kind of you, Sarah, but I couldn't,' said Polly humbly.

'Why not?' inquired Mrs Bloom.

'Give me one good reason,' said Sarah.

'I've got no money to put into the business for one thing. Besides, what about David, and Yvonne?'

Sarah stiffened. 'I had a word with David before they left, and he's all for it. And as for you not putting any money in, it's your ideas I want. We'll work out a way for you to buy a share of the company later – you can do it gradually, through your wages.'

'But why do you want to make me a partner?'

'Security. You could go places when this war is over and I'm selfish enough to think that if you are part of the firm, nobody will be able to steal you away.'

Polly laughed nervously. 'Oh, but I wouldn't . . ..'

'Oh yes you would. If someone offered you the right money and a good position, you'd be off like a shot.'

'Sarah and I have spent a while discussing this. And you seem to be happy at work, and at home here.'

'Oh I am,' Polly said enthusiastically. She sat on the sofa and looked from one to the other. 'I can never thank you enough for taking me in, especially after what happened.'

'That's all in the past now.' Mrs Bloom looked embarrassed. 'You must try and forget about it.'

Polly sat grinning. 'I can't believe this is happening to me.'

'Well it is,' said Sarah. 'Now, how about a nice cup of tea?'

'I'll put the kettle, no, the saucepan on.' Mrs Bloom smiled. 'This has been a funny day,' she said, walking out of the room.

'Sarah, what about David and his wife?' asked Polly.

'I'm afraid Yvonne didn't do a lot to make herself very popular. Poor David, now he's torn between his wife and his mother.'

Polly shook her head. 'I still can't believe it. Me, a partner in Bloom's Fashions.'

Sarah laughed. 'With only one lock-up under the arches at the moment. Bloom's Fashions isn't as prestigious as it used to be – but give it time.'

'Thank you, Sarah. You'll never regret it – I promise.'

Christmas was over, and everybody was back at work. They were all feeling a little more relaxed now the air-raids had eased off. Sarah was telling Fred that Polly was to become a partner.

''Ere, we gotter call yer Mrs Bell now?' asked Fred, looking slightly put out.

'No, don't be daft. I'll always be Polly to you and the girls.'

'Are yer gonner change the name? 'Ere, yer could call it Bell's Blooms. Or what about Bloom's Bells?'

They laughed. 'We could call it Bell's Bloomers with all the shorts we're making,' said Sarah.

'I don't think we'll bother about changing the name. Let's wait and see if I can make the grade first. Right, we've stood around long enough, it's back to work.'

'Humm,' said Sarah to Fred. 'Looks like we've got a bit of a slave-driver here. What do you think?'

'Yer could be right, Miss, yer could be right.'

'Go on with the both of you,' laughed Polly, knowing that deep down she couldn't be happier.

On the Sunday night after Christmas, Polly woke with a start. 'Oh no, not again,' she wailed out loud.

'Come on Margaret, downstairs.' Mrs Bloom was banging on her bedroom door.

'Coming,' she yelled, pulling on, over her pyjamas, the slacks and jumper which were always on the chair at the ready. She grabbed her gas-mask and handbag and joined Sarah and her mother in the Morrison shelter, under the large mahogany dining table.

The anti-aircraft guns started almost as soon as Polly crept in.

'I haven't done any sandwiches or filled the flasks,' said Mrs Bloom apprehensively.

'Well, we have been a little complacent these past few weeks,' said Sarah, making herself comfortable. 'We've got out of the habit.'

'Let's hope it doesn't last too long,' said Polly. 'It was such a luxury sleeping in a bed again. I didn't want to leave it . . .' Her voice trailed off as the long low whistle of a bomb passed over. They quickly put their heads down, and with their hands over their ears, prayed.

One by one they gradually brought their heads up. In the gentle glow of the small paraffin lamp a look of amazement was etched on all their faces.

'It must be a time bomb, or a dud,' whispered Mrs Bloom, almost as if she was afraid the sound of her voice would make it go off.

The words were barely out when another long low whistle was heard. This one was much louder, and they knew it was coming for them. Desperately they tried to flatten themselves on the floor. The bomb hit the roof with such a tremendous bang and clatter that it sounded as if the house was collapsing all around them. Mrs Bloom let out a scream. 'My God, what's happened?'

'It sounds as if it landed on the house.' There was a quiver in Sarah's voice.

Suddenly they were all struggling to get out from under the table, and as Polly was last in, she was first out. She opened the dining-room door. 'Quick,' she screamed. 'There's smoke and flames coming out of David's room.'

'You get back under the table, Mother,' ordered Sarah. 'Margaret, grab that bucket of sand.' She raced up the stairs, slopping water from a bucket that had been strategically placed in the hall.

Polly snatched up one of the buckets that had been filled with sand: the government had instructed that every household should have one ready for just such an emergency.

'I'll get more water,' said Mrs Bloom, hard on their heels.

Sarah kicked the bedroom door wide open, and proceeded to throw the bucket of water into the room, which appeared to be full of leaping, spluttering flames. The rest of the house was quickly becoming filled with smoke, and Sarah was choking and coughing with the acrid fumes.

Polly rushed to the bathroom to refill the bucket. Mrs Bloom was right behind her with a bowl of water. Jostling each other in their haste, slopping the overflowing containers, they managed between them to keep up a constant chain.

'The firemen must be taking all the water,' yelled Mrs Bloom as the water from the tap began to dwindle. 'What are we going to do if their hoses are connected to our supply and it stops?'

'Pray!' cried Sarah.

But the water held out for long enough and gradually, as the flames subsided, they moved in closer.

'It's David's bed,' shouted Sarah, her voice full of panic. 'The bomb's on David's bed.' She grabbed the bucket of sand. 'I'm going to try and smother it.'

'I'll help,' said Polly, making her way into the bedroom. The smoke caught in her throat and made her gasp for breath.

'Be careful,' called Mrs Bloom.

'I'm going to wrap it in the bedclothes, and throw it out of the window,' croaked Sarah.

'I'll give you a hand.' Polly, on her way to the window, looked briefly at the red-hot tube of metal, spitting and spluttering like a giant firework. She tripped over one of David's shoes as she flung open the window.

They struggled to wrap the bomb in what was left of the mattress and bedclothes, fighting and battling to cover the flames. Finally they staggered to the window and hoisted it on to the sill. When the smouldering bedspread caught on the curtains and wouldn't go through the window, Polly picked up the shoe she had trodden on earlier and smashed the glass. In a shower of sparks, the bomb and bedding disappeared.

They were busy stamping out the small pockets of flames, when a warden raced into the room with a stirrup pump.

'Everything all right in here?'

'Yes,' said Sarah, brushing her hair back from her dirty face.

Polly looked up at the stars shining through the hole in the tiles. She was amazed that most of the roof was still intact; in fact the hole was comparatively small. Her gaze travelled on and out of the window. 'No it isn't,' she yelled. 'The damn mattress has got caught on the trellis. Look, it's beginning to set it alight!'

They all dashed for the door. The warden was first out of the bedroom, with Mrs Bloom following. He must have let the hose of his stirrup pump trail on the floor. Suddenly there was a loud scream as Mrs Bloom lost her footing and she and the warden tumbled down the stairs together. Polly and Sarah leapt down after them and Polly helped the warden to his feet, while Sarah went to assist her mother.

'Don't move me,' she cried out in pain as Sarah went to help her up. 'I think I've broken my leg.'

'Oh no,' said Sarah, kneeling on the floor beside her. 'Which one?'

'The left. Look, leave me, put the fire out in the garden before it gets a hold.'

'She's right,' said the warden. 'You come with me, Miss, and give me a hand with the pump. Your sister better stay here with your mother.'

Polly followed the warden.

271

'It's a bloody awful night,' he said grimly as they raced into the gloom. 'Jerry must be sending over everything he's got. He couldn't get us down with his high explosives, so now he's trying to burn us down – been mostly incendiaries tonight. The bastard. Begging yer pardon. Look, if yer phone's not working I'll go along to the ARP post and try and get an ambulance for yer mother.'

Polly didn't bother with explanations as she fought to keep the stirrup pump in the bucket of water while they extinguished the flames. When the warden felt it was safe to leave they walked back into the house.

'I'll try the phone,' he said. 'It may take a while to get an ambulance – they're all out at the moment.' With the receiver to his ear he banged the bar up and down. Next to him lay Mrs Bloom, a cushion under her head, and covered with a blanket. Sarah knelt by her side and Polly noticed her wince whenever she touched something. 'Here, let me look at your hands,' she said.

'They're all right,' Sarah replied quickly, pulling them away.

'Margaret,' said Mrs Bloom, 'I think Sarah has burnt herself.'

'Sarah,' said Polly forcefully. 'Let me look at your hands.'

Like a small, naughty child, she held them out. Polly cautiously opened them. Sarah took in a breath.

'My God,' whispered Polly.

'You'd better go with your mother,' said the warden, looking over Polly's shoulder. 'I've got to go to the post to phone; yours is out of action.'

'I'll pack a few toilet things for you both,' said Polly.

'I can't go,' said Sarah. 'I'm sorry, Mother, but someone has to stay here and clear up this mess, and make sure it doesn't all flare up again.'

'And what's wrong with me?' asked Polly.

'Well, nothing, I hope.'

'Well, go along with you. Besides, what can you do with those hands? You take Mum . . .'

Mrs Bloom quickly looked up.

'I'm sorry, your mother.'

'No, don't apologize,' she smiled. 'Mum sounds rather nice.'

Polly knelt down and kissed her cheek. She swallowed the lump in her throat. 'You've been like a mother to me.' She stood up. 'Sarah, you've got to go along and get those hands seen to. Don't worry about anything here, I'll clear up as much as I can, and if you're not back I'll go along to the factory to make sure everything's fine over there.'

'Thanks, Margaret.'

'You're shivering, must be shock. I'll pop up and get your coat.' Polly ran up the stairs. Sadly she looked into David's bedroom before getting a coat for Sarah. What a mess, she said to herself as she gazed around.

It was a while before the ambulance arrived.

'Is this the house with the broken leg?' The ambulance man looked up the stairs at the wet carpet. 'That looks nasty. Anyone else hurt?'

'Sarah's hands,' said Polly.

'It could have been worse. We could all have been in our beds,' said Sarah.

'Right, Missus, let's be having you. We'll make you as comfortable as we can, but I warn you we could be in for a bumpy ride.' He was busy putting a splint on Mrs Bloom's leg. He turned to Sarah. 'There's hose-pipes and fire engines all over the place. The bugger. Oops, sorry Mamm. He seems to be chucking over everything he's got left.' They lifted Mrs Bloom on to the stretcher, and Polly tucked the blanket round Sarah. 'He won't win this war,' said the man, skilfully manoeuvring Mrs Bloom into the ambulance. 'Churchill's told him that.'

'I'll be back as soon as I can,' called Sarah.

'Don't worry about anything. Just you look after yourself, and your mother.' Polly stood watching the ambulance disappear. She closed the door and leaned against it. She suddenly realized how quiet it was. The droning of the planes and the gunfire had ceased. In all the confusion, she had forgotten there was a raid on. I suppose this is how blokes feel when they're in a battle, she thought. They don't have time to think about it till it's all over.

The sound of a dripping tap brought her back to reality. 'Oh my God,' she yelled, rushing up the stairs. 'All the taps have been left open. The firemen must have put the water back on.' She left the bathroom, and the smell of smoke filled her nostrils. She wandered into David's room.

Through the curtainless and broken window she could see many fires all around them; in some of the houses it looked as if they had got out of hand. Polly noticed that the very edge of the sky was tinged with light: dawn was breaking at last.

'It's been a long night,' she whispered, glancing round the blackened room. 'Where do I start?' She leaned out of the window, and in the half light she could see the burnt and sopping wet mattress hanging limply over the trellis. Bedclothes were scattered over the lawn – it was a pathetic sight. She turned away, continuing to talk out loud to herself as a form of comfort. 'Well, this won't get the baby a new bonnet,' she scolded herself. 'Better put the kettle, the new kettle, on the gas – that's if we've got any gas. If not, it's on the primus again.' They were getting used to being without gas after a raid, and had learned to adjust accordingly.

After a cup of tea, Polly took David's clothes from the wardrobe. The smell of smoke was hanging heavily on them. Fortunately it was only the bed that was badly burned; the varnished headboard had blistered and bubbled. The wardrobe and other items of furniture were only singed or had burn holes. She placed his clothes all round the picture rail in her room.

She felt guilty going through the drawers in the large oak chest. Touching his shirts, socks, and underwear made her feel as if she was prying into his personal things. As she put them in the linen basket, she knew she was doing the right thing – they all had to be washed. She was staring at the lovely beige carpet when the all-clear sounded. Another night over, and they were all still alive. The carpet was burnt in places; it was wet and stained with water. 'There's not a lot I can do about that at the moment,' she said to herself then, looking in his dressing-table mirror, she started to laugh. 'Christ, I've gone and singed a bit of my hair.' Leaning forward, she shrieked almost hysterically. 'All my eyebrows have gone.'

It was midday before she finally finished washing down the paint and the room looked reasonable. I'll have to get someone in to put a tarpaulin over that hole, she thought, looking up. If it started to rain there'd be more mess.

At long last Polly sat at the kitchen table and drew long and hard on her cigarette. What a night, she reflected. Looking at her watch, she said out loud, 'I'll just finish this ciggy and my cup of tea, then I'll get ready for work. I wonder what I'll find over there?'

Chapter 25

The ringing phone sounded insistent and urgent as Polly pushed open the front door. She hurried across the hall and picked up the receiver. 'Hello. No Po . . . Margaret. Yes, she is, hang on a moment. It's David.' Carefully she handed Sarah the phone. 'Can you manage?' she whispered.

Sarah nodded as she gripped the receiver in her heavily bandaged hands. 'David,' her voice sounded light and cheerful. 'Yes, we're all fine. Sorry, I can't hear you very well, this line's very crackly. No, our phone was out of order. I'm afraid she can't. She's not here. No, she's all right, she's quite safe. She fell down the stairs with the warden and broke her leg, and she's in hospital. He was putting out a fire in your bedroom. An incendiary. No, not too bad. You mustn't worry about us. Yes, we will write and tell you all about it. I'll try, but I expect a lot of the lines are down. David! David!' Sarah looked at Polly. 'Damn we've been cut off.' She handed Polly the phone.

'It sounded very funny when you said your mother fell down the stairs with the warden,' she laughed. 'Poor David, he must be wondering what's going on down here.'

'Yes, he's worried sick. He's been trying to get in touch all day. He wondered why Mother wasn't here to answer the phone. Margaret, would you write and tell him what's happened? Mother said she would write, but I'd like him to hear from us.'

'Of course, you just tell me what you want to say. Did David mention Yvonne? I wonder if she's all right?'

'He didn't say.'

'Don't you think we should find out? Do you have her phone number?'

'It's in that book.' Sarah raised her hand and motioned to a black book on the telephone table. 'I'm surprised you want to bother after all the upset she caused you.'

Polly didn't answer as she dialled the number. 'You can talk to her,' she said, putting her hand over the mouthpiece.

'Do I have to?'

'Yes. You must tell her about your mother. She may want to visit her. Hello, is Yvonne there, please? Her sister-in-law.' She handed Sarah the phone.

'Yvonne, this is Sarah. I was ringing to see if you were all right after last night's raid. Oh, you were very lucky. Well, no. Mother's in hospital with a broken leg, we had an incendiary through the roof. David's. No, his clothes are OK. Well, if you get time.' Sarah's face was full of anger as she handed the phone back to Polly. 'That girl didn't even have the decency to ask which hospital Mother was in. All she said was that she would give us another ring if she gets time. Who answered the phone?'

'I don't know. Some man. He didn't say his name. Come on, into the kitchen and I'll make us a nice cup of tea, then I'll get everything ready for this evening. How're your hands?'

'Not too bad.'

'I didn't make such a bad job of pencilling in your eyebrows,' said Polly.

Sarah peered into the large mirror in the hall. 'Just look at the front of my hair. Do you think you could do something with it?'

'I'll have a go before we go in the shelter. Now go on upstairs and put some clean clothes on.'

'Thank's for coming to the hospital to see Mother,' Sarah said as she mounted the stairs. 'She was very pleased to see you.'

'Well, I was a bit worried in case you couldn't get home. It must be difficult getting money out of your purse with all your fingers bandaged.'

'It's not easy. I'm glad everything was fine at the factory. Being under the arches it should be fairly safe, except if there's a direct hit, of course.'

'Go on with you. Upstairs.'

In the chaotic aftermath of the bombing, it was difficult to believe that Christmas Day had only been one week ago. Now Polly and Sarah were sitting at the kitchen table and life was slowly returning to normal. Sarah carefully took the cup of tea Polly offered. 'What did the doctor say about your hands?'

'He was pleased with the improvement in just a few days.'

Polly smoothed out the table-cloth. 'We didn't get a lot of work done today.'

'That's not surprising.'

'They say that the bombs follow you about,' said Polly wistfully.

'I hope not, I'm hoping we've had our one and only.' Sarah sighed. 'But we're certainly having enough raids now. Will it ever end? I was very sorry to hear about Betty from the factory being killed.'

'Yes, she was nice. I must write and tell Shirley.'

'She will be disappointed you're not going to see her.'

'Well, I can't leave you, not now.'

'Thank you,' she smiled. 'What would I do without you?'

'I'll tell Shirley about Betty,' said Polly, quickly changing the subject. 'They used to have a lot of laughs together down in the basement.'

'The basement in Mansell Street. That seems a lifetime ago.'

'Come on, now, time to crawl into our cage.' Polly put the flasks, sandwiches and hot-water bottles under the table. She pulled a blanket round Sarah's shoulders.

'Do you fancy a game of cards?' asked Sarah.

'No thanks. Besides, how can you hold the cards with your fingers bandaged like that?'

'Yes, you're right. Do you want to sleep?'

'No, not really, not tonight. We really should wait till after midnight. Couldn't we just sit and talk for a while.'

'Why not?'

'Is there any chance of us getting more cloth?' asked Polly.

'Why?'

'I fancy making some more dresses. I'm getting fed up with shorts.'

'If I could get over to see some of my father's old associates, they may be able to help. I tell you what, I'll go to the synagogue on Saturday and see who's there.'

'Would that be all right? Going to the synagogue, that is?'

'Yes, besides, I feel I should give thanks for still being alive.'

'I know how you feel.'

The eerie sound of the siren filled the air.

'I hope it's not going to be too bad tonight,' said Polly apprehensively.

'So do I. I hope Mother's safe in hospital.'

'They have got good shelters.'

'I know.'

They sat quietly for a few moments. Each knew the other was reflecting on the past months. Polly still couldn't believe how things had changed for her. Her thoughts went to Ron. He should have got her letter by now, and they should soon be having an answer to the letter Sarah dictated to her for David.

She was still toying with her conscience as to whether to answer the letter she had received from David yesterday. She had read it so many times she could almost repeat it word for word. After first congratulating her on becoming Sarah's partner, the rest was full of apologies. He couldn't say enough times how sorry he was at Yvonne's bad manners. He tried to explain that she was under a lot of pressure from a certain producer, and this, with trying to please his mother, made her a little anxious, and she had unintentionally drunk too much.

When Polly showed it to Sarah, she made no comment.

Her thoughts drifted on. In the letter, David told her how cold it was in Scotland, and how beautiful it all looked. Lucky Yvonne, to be going up there, and to be with him. Perhaps, when she had to write for Sarah again, she'd be able to add a personal postscript.

'Margaret?' Sarah's voice interrupted her thoughts. 'Sorry, I didn't mean to make you jump. I've been wanting to ask you something for ages. Why do your friends call you Polly?'

Polly laughed. 'Well, are you sitting comfortably? This could be a long story.' She then began telling Sarah about her father and why he called her Polly. Without any interruptions from Sarah she went on to tell her about the family. Once or twice, the far-off sound of a bomb exploding or muffled gunfire silenced her. When emotions overtook her and she couldn't speak, Sarah asked no questions, and they sat together, giving each other strength as the evening wore on.

'I like the sound of your dad, and your grandfather,' Sarah said when Polly'd finished.

'Yes, they were nice.' She sighed. 'Do you feel like sleeping now?'

'No, not really, do you?'

Polly shook her head. In the distance they could hear the long low rumble of a bomb going off. 'Sounds as if someone else is getting it tonight.'

'Poor devils. Do you know, it's amazing how well we can manage with such little sleep.'

'When this war's over I'm going to get in a big feather bed and sleep for a week.'

'I bet you won't, you'll be with the rest of us, dancing and singing in the streets.'

'Do you really think it will be like that?' asked Polly.

'I should think so, if what I've read about the last war is anything to go by.'

'You're very lucky to have brains as well as beauty.'

Sarah laughed.

'No, honestly. I've often wondered why you've never married, especially with your religion and arranged marriages.

281

Have you ever wanted to get married, Sarah?'

'Right, it's my turn to tell you a story. Are you sitting comfortably?'

Polly shifted and nodded.

'I was supposed to get married, but that was a long while ago, when I was just twenty.'

'Go on with you, you're not that old.'

'Well, I won't see twenty-one again,' Sarah smiled. 'Anyway, it had been arranged that I should marry a friend of the family. His name was Peter. He was very nice and I was very fond of him, but I didn't love him.' Sarah shivered and pulled at the blanket round her shoulders. 'When I told my father I didn't want to marry him, all hell broke loose. There was a lot of shouting, and he threatened to throw me out of the house, and my job, and cut me out of his will. I think it was his pride more than anything that was hurt. Mother was wonderful – so was Peter. I sometimes wonder if he wasn't slightly relieved at the outcome of it all. I am a more dominant person than he was. If there had been someone else involved, I think things would have been very different – I know Mother wouldn't have been so kind.' Sarah stopped.

In the flickering paraffin lamp, Polly noted the sad expression on her face. 'Was there someone else?' she asked tenderly.

'No.'

'But you were fond of Peter? Didn't you feel that was enough to marry him?'

'No. We had grown up together, and Peter was sort of one of the family – brotherly, I suppose – and a bit old-fashioned. I didn't really fancy spending the rest of my life with him.'

'Are you sorry now?'

'No. I was at first when Dad was so frosty towards me. I was more upset at not being part of the business than about anything else. It was the best day of my life when I left college and went to work at the factory. Dad was against that, but I threatened to join his friend's firm, and that soon made him change his mind.'

'I've always admired you, but I never realized you were a bit of a rebel.' Polly sighed. 'Sometimes I wish I had been.'

'But I thought you and Ron were happy when you got married.'

'We were in our own way, I suppose. Our sort of people just drift into things. You're not really expected to think for yourselves, and I was only eighteen. Without a good education you can't get far.'

'What about you? You can't get much higher than being a partner in a business that makes shorts.'

They laughed. 'But that's only thanks to you.'

'Oh, I could see your talent, and I wasn't prepared to lose you.'

'More coffee?' Polly was feeling embarrassed. 'Have you had any regrets about not being married?' She filled the cup for Sarah and carefully handed it to her.

'Thanks. I did at first. But when Dad came round to my way of thinking, I soon got over it. Besides, I'm not over the hill yet, got another two years before I'm thirty, so there's still time.'

'I'm surprised you haven't got men friends lurking round every corner.'

'There have been one or two. David thinks I'm too fussy. Mind you, the doctor who's looking after Mother is very nice.'

'What did David have to say about you not wanting to marry Peter?'

'He was in full agreement with me. He too had a marriage arranged. It was just before the war. She was a lawyer's daughter, nice little thing. But she wasn't his type.'

'You think Yvonne is?'

'No. I think David is so besotted with the way she looks that he can't see any further than his nose.'

'But this is wartime, and we all have to grab at what happiness we can.'

'That's very true.'

'I still remember that time David took me for a drink and told me he wanted to join the RAF. I felt like an old auntie – me, giving him advice.'

'He told me about that. He's very fond of you, you know.'

Polly was pleased the light was low and Sarah couldn't see her reaction.

'He was very upset over the prison business.'

Polly jerked her head up.

'He felt so guilty over that.'

'What about you? Did you feel guilty?' asked Polly softly.

'You'll never know how much. The sleepless nights I had, thinking of you in prison. Knowing that we put you there. I tried to get in touch with you, but you didn't answer my letter.'

Polly looked surprised. 'You wrote to me? That must have been when I was up North and my flat got bombed.' She sighed. 'At that time I wouldn't have answered it anyway. I didn't want anything to do with anyone I knew – I felt so ashamed.'

'Well, thank goodness that's all behind us now.'

In a dark corner, the grandfather clock struck twelve. Sarah looked through the bars of the shelter. 'And that's 1940 out of the way. A Happy New Year, Margaret.'

'And to you. What a way to spend New Year's Eve.'

'Yes, I could think of a lot better ones. But now it's quiet out there, I think we could get ourselves a drink.'

'That sounds a very good idea. What would you like?'

'I think there's a drop of port left.'

Polly poured two drinks and crept back under the table.

'Here's to a safe and happy 1941,' Sarah said. 'And let's hope this war will soon be over.'

'I'll drink to that.'

They clinked glasses, and each said their own silent prayer.

Chapter 26

The winter dragged on, and it was a very cold Monday morning when Polly and Sarah walked into the factory.

Fred blew on his hands, and banged them against his side. 'Christ it's cold out there. I'm glad I'm not a brass monkey.'

''Ain't none too warm in 'ere,' yelled young Rosie, who had her long woollen scarf wound round and round her neck. Her fingers poked through the ends of her navy-blue mittens.

'Not a lot we can do about it I'm afraid,' said Sarah. 'I've been trying to get hold of another paraffin stove, but I've not had a lot of luck.'

Mary looked up from her machine. ''S'all right, Miss Bloom, we knows yer doing yer best.'

Fred took his coat off and hung it on the nail that served as a clothes peg. ''Ere Polly, I saw someone in the Arms on Saturday who said 'e knew yer.'

'Oh yes, and who was that?'

'Bloke called Sid. Yeah, that's 'is name. Said 'e's known yer fer years.'

Polly froze. 'Did he ask where I worked?'

'Yeah, I told 'im you're a partner in the firm now. 'E's coming round ter see yer.'

'Margaret, are you all right?' asked Sarah. 'You've gone very pale.'

'Yes, yes I'm all right. Did he say when he would be round?'

'Yeah, some time terday. You knows 'im then?'

She nodded.

'Would you like a cup of tea?' asked Sarah.

Again Polly nodded, and made her way to the small makeshift office in the far corner of the factory.

'It's your brother, isn't it?' said Sarah, when they'd settled down with a cup of tea.

'Yes. What am I going to do – I don't want to see him.'

'You've got to. What if he doesn't know about your mother?'

Polly sat down. 'He must know, but where's he been all this time?'

'Look, I'll stay behind with you if you want me to.'

'Would you? We could go to a pub. We don't have to bring him in here.'

'Why don't you want him to come in here?'

'I don't trust Sid.' Polly was worried. The last time she'd seen her brother was at the trial. What if he'd been looking for her and wanting to get his own back on her for implicating him? 'Why's he turned up now, now that I'm a partner?' she said voicing her thoughts.

'Perhaps he's been away.'

'Perhaps,' said Polly suspiciously.

All day she was on tenterhooks, looking at the door, jumping when anyone came in. The day dragged, and at six o'clock when it was time to leave, she picked up her handbag and went outside and waited for Sarah to lock up.

''Allo, Pol.'

Startled, she turned round.

'Y're looking a bit of all right. In partnership with this lot, I 'ear.' He inclined his head in the direction of the factory.

'What do you want?'

'That's nice, ain't it. Comes ter see 'ow me long-lorst sister is, and all she can say is, what d'yer want? Don't want nufink, do I?'

Polly didn't really want him to meet Sarah, but she knew it was inevitable.

'Hello, you must be Sid,' Sarah called over her shoulder as she locked the door. She began walking towards them. 'I'm Sarah Bloom.'

He touched his trilby. 'Pleased ter meet yer, I'm sure. That's wot I calls a nice welcome. Not like Pol 'ere.'

'You forget I know you.' Polly was seething. 'What do you want, Sid?'

'Look, Margaret', said Sarah soothingly, 'why don't we go over to the Red Lion? You two must have plenty to talk about after all this time. Besides, it's freezing out here.' Sarah hustled them across the road.

Inside the warmth of the pub they sat down. 'I'll get them,' said Sarah. 'Beer, Sid?' She took off her woollen mittens.

He nodded. 'Fanks.'

'Usual, Margaret?'

'Please.' Polly noticed Sid didn't argue about Sarah paying. As soon as Sarah was out of earshot, Polly said between clenched teeth, 'Well?'

'Wot she done to 'er 'ands?'

'We had an incendiary in the bedroom, and Sarah burnt herself.'

'I noticed the "we". Must be difficult wiv 'er fingers bandaged up like that?'

'They're not so bad as they were. At least she can hold some things now. Stop evading the issue. What do you want?'

Sid leaned back in his chair. 'What d'yer mean?'

'Come off it, Sid. Where've you been? And why have you suddenly turned up here? Did you know our house got bombed, and Mum got killed?'

He sat forward and fiddled with the ash-tray. 'Yeah, I 'eard.'

'Well . . . Where were you?'

'I was up Norf.'

'Doing what might I ask? Time?'

He leaned forward and spoke close to her face. 'Yer position ain't changed yer sharp tongue. Prison, now a partnership, and yer lives in their big 'ouse. Got it bleeding made, ain't yer?'

'I asked you where you were when Mum got bombed.'

'And I told yer, up Norf.'

Sarah came back, carefully balancing a tray of drinks.

'I would 'ave got them,' said Sid, standing up to help her. 'I didn't know about yer 'ands.'

'That's all right. I've got quite clever with these.' She held up her bandaged fingers and wiggled them. 'But I still can't hold a pencil yet; thank goodness Margaret can do all our correspondence.' She paused. 'Look, if you two would like me to go home, that's all right with me.'

'No, Sarah, we'll just have this drink and go. I haven't anything to say to Sid.'

'I might 'ave a few fings ter say ter you though, Sis.'

Polly was nervous and on edge. She didn't want him here. Why had he turned up now? She had a feeling he was going to be trouble. Polly ignored his remark, finished her drink and stood up. 'I'm ready, how about you, Sarah?'

Sarah emptied her glass. 'If you say so.' She shrugged her shoulders at Sid.

'We had another letter from David this morning,' said Mrs Bloom, waving it in the air as soon as they walked in. 'You must read it after Sarah,' she said eagerly to Polly. 'He is so pleased you are keeping him well informed.'

Polly smiled. His letters were beginning to mean a lot to her, and she was frightened that one day she would say something that would give him a hint of her feelings. She was anxious and restless all evening and her mind kept going back to her brother. What did Sid want? Thankfully, Sarah hadn't pursued the subject of Sid but nonetheless Polly watched the clock, and, after she'd made some cocoa, was genuinely pleased when it was time for bed.

'I think you two can risk going upstairs tonight,' said Mrs Bloom. 'After all, we haven't had any raids for a few weeks now.' She looked down at her leg. 'I'll be glad when this plaster's off, then I'll be able to get up and down the stairs a little quicker.'

Polly was grateful to be alone for a while, in her own room. That was another problem with this war: you never seemed to be able to get away from people. Often she would look out of the window at the long sweep of lawn that led down to the bare trees, longing for the warmer weather so she could wander, just her. To be alone with your thoughts was a luxury these days.

She picked up Shirley's last letter. They too had been having a lot of air-raids, but up till now they were all still safe. Perhaps I could go down there for a long weekend? she thought. It would be lovely to see her and Elizabeth again. She sat on the bed and scanned the pages once more. Shirley's mother didn't seem to be getting any better, but her dad was happy now he'd joined the ARP as well as working the markets. Polly smiled; he was a nice man. She folded the letter and got into bed. 'I'll ask Sarah about having a Saturday off later on,' she said, pulling the bedclothes over her head.

The following morning, Sid was outside the factory.

'What are you doing here?' asked Polly.

'Yer done all right, Pol. Always fought yer would.'

Quickly she looked around. 'Why are you here?'

'Fings ain't so good wiv me these days.' He blew on his fingers and rubbed his hands together. 'Ter tell the truth, I'm a bit brassic. It's a bit parky out 'ere.'

Polly opened her handbag and took a ten-shilling note from her purse. 'Here you are. And don't come back.' She turned to go.

Sid looked at the note. 'That old boy I met in the pub said yer doing all right.'

'So that's why you're here?'

'No. Fought yer might like ter 'ere 'ow Billy's gitting on.' He stuffed the money into his overcoat pocket.

'You know where Billy is?'

'Can I come inside? In the warm?'

Polly suddenly realized how untidy and dishevelled he looked. 'No. Wait here a minute.' She disappeared inside the factory, returning almost immediately. 'There's a café a few streets away. Let's go and have a cup of tea.'

Despite all the windows being boarded up, the café was still open. The large letters painted in red announced to all and sundry that it was business as usual.

After ordering, Polly sat at the table furthest from the counter, making sure nobody could hear them.

'When did you last see Billy?'

'Must 'ave been just before Christmas. 'E was up the West End.'

'Did he know about Mum?'

'Yeah, the Navy must 'ave told 'im.'

'How can I get in touch with him?'

'Aah, well, that might be difficult. Yer see 'e's on the Atlantic run. 'Ave yer 'eard from Ron?'

'I think Shirley has, I think he was at Dunkirk.'

'Yer 'e was. Me and 'im went out a couple o' times.'

Polly sat forward. 'You did? Was he all right?'

'Yer, I fink so.'

'What did he say about me?'

'Nufink much. ''E knew yer'd been in prison, and Mum fought yer'd gone down ter Shirley's.'

Polly sat and stared into space for a while. So Ron knew she had gone to prison. 'What did he say? Did you tell him about the trial?'

'I told 'im that at first you said it was me that give yer that bloody brooch.'

'What did he say to that?'

'Not a lot. 'E thought that was funny.'

'What else?'

'Nothing much.'

'Come off it Sid, he must have said something. Did he steal that brooch?'

''Ow the bleeding 'ell should I know. As I said, I left 'im outside the pub at closing time, and 'e said 'e was going to the market with 'is old man. Anyway, what makes you so sure 'e pinched it?'

'He wouldn't tell me where he got it from.'

'Well, that's Ron all over. I tell yer Pol I could 'ave knocked yer block off when the rozzers came round and carted me off.'

She played with the spoon. 'I panicked, I didn't know what I was saying.'

Sid fumbled in his pocket for a packet of cigarettes. 'Fag?' he offered.

Polly shook her head.

He drew long and hard on the cigarette. 'Well, you've always 'ad it in fer me, ain't yer?'

With her head bent she whispered. 'Well yes, I suppose I have.' She knew this was to be the end of the conversation, she would get nothing from Sid. Taking a pencil and paper from her handbag, she asked. 'Where are you staying?'

He clasped his hands round the steaming mug of tea.

'Well, at the moment you could say I'm of no fixed abode.'

'What d'you mean?'

'Well, the little lady whose bed I was sharing up to a few days ago was married, and 'er old man came 'ome on leave rather unexpected.'

'So you're in a bit of a state. No home and no job.'

'You could say that, but only for the time being. Yer see, I've got sumfink lined up, and it could be very lucrative. And of interest to your Miss Bloom, and you, now you're a partner.'

'I don't want anything to do with your shady deals.'

'Now, that's not nice. Besides, I fought yer wanted ter know 'ow ter git in touch wiv Billy?'

'I do.' She looked at her watch. 'I must get back to work.'

'Pol. D'yer fink yer can look after me clothes for a bit, just till I gits somewhere ter stay?'

Polly looked at her brother. 'I don't know.' Then she suddenly felt guilty, and remembered when she had walked the streets with nowhere to go. 'Well, all right then. D'you know, you frighten me at times.'

He laughed. 'Me frighten you. Why?'

'I don't know.' But she did know: it was because he always seemed to bring trouble into her life, and things were going too smoothly for her at the moment.

291

'Christ, 'ere I am, nowhere ter live and no money, and I frighten you. Do me a favour.'

Against her better judgement she said, 'Bring your things here, to the factory, tomorrow. And Billy's address and service number if you've got it.'

'Yer, I got it somewhere, but all yer gotter do is send a letter ter the Navy in London and they'll post it on ter 'im. See yer termorrer.' He got up from the table and sauntered out of the café.

When Polly arrived at work the next day Sid was waiting for her. He was carrying a battered old suitcase.

'Morning Miss Bloom.' He touched his trilby, and bowed his head slightly.

'Good morning, Sid.'

Polly moved between them; she didn't want them to start a conversation. 'I'll be in in a minute.' And when Sarah was out of earshot, added, 'Is this it? When are you picking it up?'

'Don't know, could be a couple of days, or even a week. So look after it, it's got all me prize possessions in there.' He handed her his case.

'What prize possessions have you got?' she asked, taking hold of his case and weighing it in her hands. 'Can't be much, it's very light.'

'Just mind yer own business. See yer when I gits back. And if yer plays yer cards right, I could be doing you and yer Miss Bloom a big favour.' He turned on his heel and left.

There hadn't been any sign of Sid for four weeks. Many times Polly had been tempted to open the suitcase that was tucked away in the far corner of the office. She often just sat and stared at it. What if something had happened to him? She ought to know where he was. But she tried not to show her concern, as she didn't want Sarah to know she was dying to see what was inside.

Her chance came one Saturday afternoon. Fred and the girls had gone home and Sarah hadn't come into work as she

292

had taken her mother to the synagogue.

She closed the door of the tiny office and lifted the case on to the desk. Removing the leather strap that held it together, she slowly pushed her fingers against the catches. They didn't move. She pushed harder. 'Damn him, he's locked it,' she said out loud, and banged the top. She looked round the office and, picking up a spoon, rammed the handle under the lock, forcing the spoon down – the catches clicked and she lifted the lid.

Not knowing what to find, Polly gazed in amazement at a couple of dirty shirts, some pants and socks, and a pair of shoes. It had struck her before how light the case had been, but she had forgotten in her eagerness to get it on to the desk.

Tentatively she sorted through Sid's meagre belongings. 'I wonder if this is all he's got,' she mumbled to herself. He'd been such a fussy dresser. Where had all his good clothes gone? She stopped. They must have been at Mum's house, she realized suddenly. She was overcome with guilt. She had to help him. As her mum would always say, 'Blood's thicker than water.' 'She wouldn't half have a go at me if she was here now, specially as I've got a few bob,' she said to herself, filled with remorse.

She took a pound note from her purse and put it in the bottom of the case. Her fingernail caught on something. Pulling it out, she found she was looking at a snapshot of Sid, Shirley, Ron and herself. Memories came flooding back. It was taken on the last Bank Holiday before the war, when they had all gone to Southend for the day. She didn't know he had it. He must have been carrying it around all this time.

Polly sat down and gazed at the photograph. They all looked so happy. Why did Sid have it? She would never have thought of him as the sentimental type. Who was it that he wanted to remember like this?

Ron was smiling up at her and tears began to gather in her eyes. Where was Ron? Was he still alive? Her letter hadn't been answered.

She put the pound note and the photograph back under the

clothes, closed the lid, pushed the locks down, put the leather strap round it and put it back in the corner, promising to herself to let bygones be bygones. She would help Sid all she could when he came back for his case.

It was the following Saturday when Sid walked into the factory wearing an expensive navy-blue suit, good shoes and shirt, and a neat Homburg.

'What d'yer fink of the togs, girls?' On the balls of his feet he turned a small circle in front of Mary and Rosie.

They giggled. 'Seems yer done all right fer yerself,' said Rosie. She knew Sid from the days he went out with Shirley.

'Me sister 'ere?'

'Na, she's out wiv Miss Bloom.'

'Tell 'er I took me case and I'll be in touch.' He touched the brim of his hat, picked up his case and left.

As soon as Polly walked in, she saw the case had gone. 'Did Sid collect his case?' she asked.

'Yeah, while you and Miss Bloom was out,' said Mary.

'Did he say if he was coming back?'

'Na. 'Ere, yer should 'ave seen 'im. All dressed up ter the nines he was.'

'What d'you mean?'

'Well, 'e 'ad on all this posh gear, a nice navy-blue suit – it looked real good – and nice shoes. Looks like 'e's come inter a few bob. 'Ere, yer should 'ave seen 'is tie.'

Polly sat at her machine and pondered on what Mary had told her. Where had Sid got the money from to buy new clothes in four short weeks, or had he left his good stuff somewhere before coming to see her? What was he up to?

Chapter 27

It was the first of March and, with the coming of spring and the raids easing off, everybody felt more relaxed.

'Four letters came for you this morning, Margaret,' said Mrs Bloom when Sarah and Polly stepped into the hall.

'Four!' exclaimed Sarah. 'Who's a popular girl, then?'

'I'm surprised we get any letters at all when you think of how many stations and post offices have been bombed,' said Mrs Bloom.

Polly picked the letters from off the hall table. Two of the envelopes had dirty smudges on them. She studied the hand-writing. Her face lit up. 'These two are from Ron,' she said excitedly. 'At long last. I wonder where he is?' She turned the letters over and put them underneath the others; she wanted to wait till she was alone before reading them. 'This one's from Shirley. And this is from David,' she said in a puzzled tone. 'Why has he written to me?'

'He said he was going to write and thank you for all the letters you wrote while I was incapacitated. He was very grateful for all your news. But now I've got these working again,' Sarah wiggled her fingers, 'even if it is only to type, he thought it only right he should thank you. But enough of my chatter. You must be dying to read your letters. Go into the drawing-room and I'll bring you in a cup of tea.' Sarah followed her mother into the kitchen. Although Mrs Bloom had had her plaster removed weeks ago, she still had a limp.

Polly sat on the red plush sofa and eagerly tore at Ron's

envelopes first, quickly looking at the date before reading either of them. After studying his scrawly handwriting she began reading the first one he'd written, which was the thickest.

My dear Pol,

I'm sitting here looking at your letter. It's great to hear from you after all this time. I can't believe you're still alive, and all what has happened to you since I last saw you.

I'm sorry to hear about your poor old mum. She wasn't such a bad old stick. She had her funny ways, but then we've all got them.

Me mate Jack lost his mum in the raids. I'm glad my mum's down in Bristol. We don't get a lot of news out here. I can't say where we are as the censor will blank it all out.

Shirley writes now and again, and said she hears from you. I bet her baby's getting big now.

So you're living in the Blooms' big house. You've done well Pol. Always thought you would. Shame the factory got bombed. We get the odd bit of news about what the bastard's doing to London. I reckon you're being very brave.

Have you heard from Billy? And what about Sid? He was lucky he wasn't at home when the bomb fell on your mum's.

It's a shame our flat's gone. Still, not to worry, after this lot's all over we can start again.

I'm glad Shirley gave you my address. She was worried as to where you'd finished up, and I've been worried sick, not knowing where you were, or if you've been killed, or you could have even been banged up in some hospital. I tell you Pol I was really dead worried. I may not have always shown it, but I love you and all your daft ideas. I can't put down what I'd really like to say as I hate the thought of someone else reading me letters before you get them. I did write a couple of times, but me letters came back address unknown, that must have been after the flat copped it.

I expect you read all about Dunkirk in the newspapers. I was lucky to get back from there. It was bloody hairy I can tell you. All that water, and you know I can't swim. I tell you Pol I've never been so frightened in all me life. When I got home on leave and found the flat empty, I was in a bit of a state, I didn't know you'd gone up North. I knew you'd be away for a long while as you'd taken nearly all your clothes, and your grandad's whip. I went round to your mum, but she said she didn't know where you'd gone. She thought you might be down at Shirley's. She said you didn't go round to see her after that nasty business with you going in prison. I didn't have time to go down to see Shirley, but I did write, and all's well that ends well.

Anyway girl, write soon. Us Service blokes like to get letters from home, it helps cheer us up. By the way it's . . . [The next line was blanked out by the censor.]

I really miss you Pol, and often think of the nights in our bed.

All my love, Ron.
XXXX

Polly looked through her tears at the letter. He didn't even say he was sorry about her going to prison. He never said it was his fault. She threw the letter on the sofa in anger and grabbed his second one. 'Perhaps he might have more to say about it in this one,' she mumbled to herself.

Dear Pol,

Well things are still much the same over here. Your second letter was great. Sorry to hear about the bomb and Miss Bloom's hands. Fancy them making you a partner, does that mean you get a share in the profits? Your old grandad would have been real proud of you, and what about Sid turning up like that. Good thing he wasn't in your mum's house when it got bombed. When you see him again, give him me best. We had a good time when I was on leave after Dunkirk.

So much for his worrying about me, thought Polly. It didn't take him long to get back out with his mates. She returned to the letter.

Mind you Sid's always been a crafty bugger, trust him to get out of going in the Army. I bet he's found himself a nice cushy little number, and a warm bed. Bet when this lot's all over he'll be a bleeding millionaire or something. A lot of the blokes here reckon those that are left at home are a right lot of shysters.

I didn't spend a lot of time in Blighty. As soon as me leave was up me regiment was shipped out here with all these bloody mosquitoes. I can tell you it's bloody hot here, and me poor old feet are really suffering, cramped up in Army boots day and night.

This is all I've got time for now. I know we ain't had a lot of time together this past year, but I promise when I get home I'll make it up to you.

Take care of yourself. Write soon. Don't let old Hitler get you down.

I love you Pol.

Love Ron.

XXX

Sarah came in carrying a tray loaded with tea things. 'Everything all right?'

'Yes. Ron's still abroad. He can't say where, but it's very hot.'

'Could be North Africa. There's been a lot of fighting over there.'

'He came home after Dunkirk and went to our flat, but I was up North. Sarah, he didn't mention anything about your brooch, or why I was sent to prison. He didn't even say he was sorry.' Polly stood up and walked over to the window. She gazed out on her favourite view. Spring was beginning to burst forth. The grass was very green and the bulbs were forcing their way through the cold damp earth, their buds full, waiting to burst into life. Down in the orchard, the soft pinks and white of the blossom would soon be turning the bare trees into a sea of gentle swaying colour.

'Well, perhaps he didn't like to stir things up again,' said Sarah, pouring tea into bone china tea-cups. 'After all, he has had a job finding out where you have been this past year, and if you were still alive.'

'That's what he said.' Polly turned from the window. 'If only I knew the truth. If only I knew for sure who took your brooch.'

'It's all in the past now, and you paid dearly for someone else. In some ways it might be better if you never know the truth.'

'I'll always suspect Ron, and my brother.'

'Come on, now, drink your tea before it gets cold. What about your other letters? What does Shirley have to say?'

'I don't know. I haven't read hers yet.'

Much later, in the seclusion of her own room, Polly sat and read Shirley's letter.

Dear Polly,

Sorry I ain't wrote before this, but I don't get a lot of time. We're working long shifts now.

It was a shame you couldn't come down at Christmas. Mind you I don't think you would have enjoyed yourself. Mum is still quite poorly. Betty got over the measles all right, but she wasn't very well, and she was so grisly. Talk about a miserable Christmas, a bit different to last year.

Fancy that David Bloom being married to a film star, I'll have to keep me eyes out for her. She sounds a bit of a bitch though.

I was sorry to hear about Miss Bloom's hands, and Mrs Bloom's leg. That bomb must have been nasty. So far, touch wood, we've been very lucky. There's been plenty round here but we can't be on Jerry's bombing run. Let's hope it stays like that.

It didn't help Mum when she got the news that one of the twins, Terry, has been reported missing. Dad's been in a bit of a state over it as well. What with that and the bad weather, he's really been getting the hump. He's thinking of going in a factory. I can't see it meself, all these years on the market, and him being his own boss. Gawd help us then.

Glad you wrote to Ron, his letters take a while to get here. I don't know where he's stationed, somewhere abroad, and what about Sid turning up out of the blue like that? He's always up to something, I wonder whose bed he crept out of?

Vera hasn't seen her husband for months. He used to manage to sneak home but he's been on these long Atlantic runs, that's what you said your Billy might be on. Good job she's living with us, she looks after Betty all day. Her, and Vera's Jane, are good company for each other. If she didn't look after Betty I'd have to give up work. I'd miss the money, and the company. We have a right lot of laughs, and still go to a lot of dances and parties, well, you can't let the war get you down, can you? There's a lot of talk round here that the Canadians are going to be stationed near here – that could turn out to be very interesting.

Write soon,
Love Shirley.
XXXX
From Betty XXX

'I do wish Shirley wouldn't call Elizabeth "Betty",' said Polly

300

out loud. 'Elizabeth is such a pretty name.'

She picked up her last letter. On impulse she held it against her cheek, then guiltily put her hand down, almost as if she was afraid someone would see her and be able to read her thoughts. And she couldn't help feeling she was betraying Ron, whatever he'd done to her. She read the envelope out loud. 'To Mrs M. Bell.' She turned the words over in her mind, and felt like she did when she was a child, always leaving the best till last. A smile spread across her face when she remembered how she used to save all the currants out of the spotted dick, and the skin off the rice pudding to savour and relish last of all.

Slowly she opened David's letter.

My dear Margaret,

I feel I must write and thank you for keeping me so well informed about my family these past months. You have such a wonderful sense of humour, and I always looked forward to your long, interesting letters.

Now Sarah is managing to use the typewriter I don't suppose I will be hearing from you, but if you ever feel like occasionally dropping me a line, I would be most grateful.

Polly stopped reading and mused dreamily. 'He would be most grateful . . .' She read on.

You are such a kind person, and hold no grudges at whatever life throws at you. I really value your friendship, Margaret, and hope we can keep in touch.

Polly hugged herself, delighted at his words. Then he changed the subject.

Yvonne came up here a while ago, but only for a week. Her producer was looking for a suitable location for his

301

new film. I was hoping I could have managed to get a little leave, and we could have gone walking together – there are some lovely walks around here – but it was not to be.

Humm, thought Polly, I bet she was glad about that. I can't see her tramping through the heather.

The scenery is wonderful at this time of year, but then Scotland is lovely at any time. When this war is over, you should try to take a holiday round these parts.

I am hoping to get home some time later this year. Yvonne's producer is getting married and I've been invited to the wedding – that's if I can get leave, of course. If I can make it I'll come to see Mother, and perhaps you can see your way to forgive Yvonne – even put in a good word to Mother – and we could all have a drink together?

Forgive me if I sound a little sorry for myself. It's funny, but I can always talk to you. Do you remember our chat before I joined the RAF? God, that was a long while ago.

Take care of yourself, Margaret, and if you feel like writing, please do so, as I always appreciate your letters.

Yours, very sincerely,

David.

Polly sat on the bed. He wants me to smooth things out between his wife and Mrs Bloom, she realized with a slightly sinking feeling. She wondered if Sarah had told him Yvonne never visited his mother while she was in hospital. His wife probably made up some plausible excuse to him. She could just see her looking up at him with those big, baby-blue eyes. Polly looked in the mirror and said out loud, 'David darling, I was so busy, I could never get away from the set till late, and you wouldn't want me to go racing across London in the black-out, now would you?' She fluttered her eyelashes.

But he had said he valued her friendship, she told herself, growing serious once more. But she wondered if he had any idea what she felt for him.

Polly decided to read the letter once again before going downstairs.

Chapter 28

''Allo girls.'

Polly looked up from her sewing machine. 'Sid, what are you doing here?' He looked smart and well-dressed in a belted camel-hair overcoat. He had always been taller than Polly and, with his slim physique and good looks, Polly could understand why he was never without female company. As she studied him for a moment or two, she could see the likeness between him and his daughter. He had never asked her about Elizabeth or Shirley. His dark-grey trilby was pushed slightly back from his forehead, revealing the front of his dark, well-slicked hair, and he seemed full of confidence. So different from the last time she saw him.

'Come ter see me skin and blister, ain't I?' He leaned forward and rested his hands on Polly's machine, and looked beyond Polly to Sarah, who was also working on a machine. 'And ter see you, Miss Bloom.'

'Me?' Sarah laughed. 'What do you want with me?'

'Well.' He looked over his shoulder suspiciously. 'I might have a little bit of gear you could be interested in.'

'We don't want any of your bent stuff round here, Sid,' said Polly indignantly. 'And if you must see me, I'll talk to you in the pub at lunch-time. Now will you please leave?'

'I can always rely on our Pol to make me feel welcome. And I was talking to the boss, not the oily rag.'

Polly's face flushed with rage. She stood up. 'I'm going next door to see how they're getting on.' She left in a temper, slamming the door behind her.

305

Sarah had managed to rent the adjoining lock-up, and now Big Vi, the forelady, and Elsie Mann, who used to work with them before the Mansell Street factory was bombed, and who had been working at home, both worked in the other workshop.

'Everything OK in here?' asked Polly.

'Yeah, except fer this bleeding cotton,' said Vi. 'It keeps breaking.'

'It might be the tension of your machine. I'll get Fred to come and check it. How's the children, Elsie?'

'Growing,' she replied with a smile. 'They're good kids, be all accounts. I get ever so many letters from 'em.'

'You must be pleased to know they're safe?'

'Yer, but I still miss 'em.' She returned to her machine.

Outside, Polly stood for a few moments wondering what Sid was up to. When she finally pushed open the door, he was walking through the factory, whistling and looking very pleased with himself.

'See yer later, gel.'

Sarah was in the tiny office. She was grinning and holding a swatch of pale-blue linen. 'What do you think of this?' She held out the cloth to Polly. 'It's salvage. Sid said he managed to get hold of a bolt, and thought of us. I think we can get it at a very reasonable price.'

'I bet he did. Did he say what lorry it fell off the back of?'

'He said it wasn't stolen.'

'You asked him that?'

'Certainly, and he assured me it was genuine salvage. He said it might have a few water-marks, but I told him how clever you are at making a silk purse out of a sow's ear.'

'I bet that went down well.'

'He's taking us to see it this evening. He's meeting us after work and we're going for a drink first. Come on, what do you think? I thought with summer coming along we could make quite a few smart dresses. It will be a change to work on some good cloth, and to make something other than shorts.'

Polly took the cloth and fingered it very gently. 'It's very good, got a lot of body. It would look nice in a princess design, flaring out just above the knee.'

'See, I knew you would like it.'

Polly threw the cloth on the desk. 'No, I'm sorry Sarah, I can't get involved in anything Sid does.'

'Oh, come on, we'll meet him tonight and discuss his terms, and we'll try to find out where the cloth came from.'

'I don't know.'

'It won't do any harm. Besides, I think your brother's rather . . .'

Polly shot her a glance that made Sarah's voice trail off. 'All right. I'll go with you,' Polly said tetchily, 'if only to keep an eye on him. But promise me that anything that looks the slightest bit fishy, you'll leave alone. I don't want any part of Sid's shady deals.'

'We are desperate for cloth. But I'll go along with your instinct,' said Sarah in a reassuring voice.

Polly continued machining, her thoughts racing. Was Sid involved in the black market? That would certainly account for his seemingly sudden change of fortune. Surely Sarah wouldn't have anything to do with knocked-off stuff. Polly quickly looked across at her smiling and singing along with the wireless. But then again Sid had told Sarah it wasn't stolen, and she had no reason to disbelieve him – after all she didn't know him as well as Polly. And to Sarah, business was business, and at the moment cloth was very hard to come by.

Sharp at six, Sid walked into the factory.

'OK girls,' he shouted, waving to the women on the machines. 'Yer ready, Miss Bloom, me mate's waiting fer us.'

'Where are we going?' asked Polly.

'Oh, you coming as well? We're going over ter see Reggie Woods. You remember 'im, Pol, 'e's got a wholesale business now.'

'You mean he's still pinching and selling?'

'Yer got a nasty little mind, always fink someone's on the fiddle, don't yer?'

307

'You forget I know you and your cronies.'

'Come on, you two, we can't stand here all night while you bicker.' Sarah picked up her handbag. 'Lead the way, Sid.'

Reggie Woods' wholesalers turned out to be his mum's back room in Peabody Buildings.

Polly smiled to herself and glanced round at Sarah, who was screwing up her nose as they groped their way up the dark and dingy staircase that smelt like a toilet. I bet she's never been in a dump like this before, thought Polly, noting the look of surprise on her face when they first arrived outside the old, red-brick buildings.

''Allo Sid. Pol. Come in,' said Reggie, opening the front door. 'Mind the black-out. Just stand still while I close the door, before I put the light on.'

He switched on the light, and the bare bulb threw a small circle of light on to the floor. It was just enough, in the small hallway, for them to see where they were going. Reggie led the way into his mother's sparsely furnished flat. Their shoes clip-clopped on the well-worn brown lino.

'Nice ter see yer again after all this time, Pol. Sorry ter 'ear about yer mum.' He shooed the cat off the wooden kitchen chair and beckoned at Sarah. ''Ere, Miss, take a seat.'

'Thanks, but I'll stand if you don't mind. I've been sitting down all day,' she said with a false laugh.

'Yes, it was a shame about Mum. Reggie, where did the cloth come from?'

'Didn't Sid tell yer? It's salvage, from one of the top West End shops.'

'Which one?'

'Christ, Pol, yer got a suspicious nature,' said Sid, flicking his grey trilby back with his finger. 'I can't remember the name of all the shops that copped it over there. Besides, we didn't exactly dig it out ourselves, did we, Reg?'

'No. Yer see this bloke I knows is in the ARP, and 'e told me the shop didn't want it, so 'e sold it ter us.' He looked at Sid for confirmation.

'That's right.'

'Where is it then?' asked Polly.

'In me mum's bedroom, I'll go and get it.'

A few minutes later he staggered back into the room, balancing a bale of cloth on his shoulder. He let it fall to the floor – as it fell, a cloud of dust billowed round their feet. 'It's a bit dusty, due ter the wall falling on it.'

Sarah bent down and began unrolling a little. She fingered the blue linen that at first was dirty and water-marked.

'Well, Miss, wot d'yer fink?'

'It looks quite good. How much would you want for it?'

'Is it good all the way through?' asked Polly, joining Sarah when she reached the sound material.

''Ow the bleeding 'ell do I know?' Reggie looked at Sarah. 'Begging yer pardon, Miss. I ain't unrolled it ter find out.'

'How much would you want for it?' asked Sarah again.

'Don't rightly know. What's it worf to you?'

'What did you pay for it?' asked Polly.

'I ain't telling yer that,' said Reggie.

Sarah looked pensive. 'Well now, let me see. You've no idea how much cloth there is, I suppose?'

'No, must be quite a few yards by the feel of it,' said Reggie.

Sarah lifted the end of the bale, and noted the weight of it. 'Yes, quite a few.'

Polly watched the cat-and-mouse game with interest. Had Sid and Reggie met their match? Sarah seemed to have regained all her usual composure.

'Could you get it over to our workshop?' she asked.

Reggie grinned at Sid. 'Should fink we can find someone wiv a barra, don't you, Sid?'

Sid nodded. 'Yeah, don't worry about that.'

'It's a long way to push a barrow,' said Sarah.

'Not ter worry, Miss. We got it 'ere, didn't we?'

'Out of a matter of interest, how did you get it here?' asked Polly.

Reggie threw a worried look at Sid. 'A mate of mine brought

it over,' said Sid. 'Now enough of this banter, d'yer want it or not? And if so, 'ow much yer gonner give us?'

'It looks as if there could be about fifty yards here.' Sarah bent down and lifted the end of the bulky bale of cloth again.

Reggie gave Sid a nudge.

'I'll give you – say I give you threepence a yard,' said Sarah. 'That's one pound ten shillings.'

'What? One bleeding pound ten bob?' exploded Sid. 'Come orf it, that's a good bit o' stuff. 'Sides, it'll cost us five bob ter get a barra.'

Sarah pulled on her gloves. 'That's my offer, take it or leave it.'

Sid jumped to his feet. ''Ang about. Don't let's be so 'asty. 'Ow about two quid?'

Polly followed Sarah to the door, amazed at her cool indifference.

'One pound fifteen shillings, that will take care of your expenses. Come along, Margaret.'

'Done,' shouted Sid. 'Well, give us the money then.'

'When I get the cloth.' Sarah closed the door behind her and began laughing. 'I thoroughly enjoyed that,' she giggled as she trotted down the stairs.

Polly tripped along at her side, worried. 'I still don't like it. Say it is stolen goods.'

'I don't think so. And it is nice cloth. As you said it will look really lovely made into a princess-style dress.'

The cloth duly arrived the following day, and Polly began cutting.

'It's great to have some good stuff to work on,' she said enthusiastically, trying to banish her reservations about where it came from.

'Humm,' said Sarah, who had her nose buried in the newspaper. 'They're going to start calling up women to do war work.' She folded the paper into a more manageable size. 'It says here that Mr Bevan is going to mobilize all the twenty- and twenty-one-year-old women for industry and the auxiliary services. As yet, married women with children will be exempt. While being trained for their new jobs in the factories, women will get one pound eighteen shillings a week.'

Polly put the scissors on the table and sat down. 'That means me. That's my age group,' she whispered.

Sarah looked up. 'I don't want you to go. I'll try and find out whether being a partner might make you exempt. After all, we are doing war work already in a way.'

'What about me eye? Do you think that might help?'

'I don't know. It's funny, I don't notice it at all nowadays. But we'll try and find out,' said Sarah, hastily gathering up the newspaper.

All day Polly's thoughts were on her future, and the possibility of her being called up. She didn't want to leave the factory, or move away from the Blooms'. And if she was sent away, she might never see David again.

At the end of March 1941, London was once again the target for Hitler's bombers.

'I'm getting fed up with all this,' announced Polly, as the wailing tone of the siren filled the air and they crept into their shelter.

'Aren't we all?' said Sarah. 'At least we should be grateful we are still alive.'

'I suppose so.' Polly sat staring into space. She couldn't just be thankful to be living from day to day. She was anxious about the future. And the thought of being called up to go in a factory to do war work was still uppermost in her mind.

Chapter 29

Once again the house and workshops had survived the early spring bombing campaign, and by the beginning of May things were looking brighter. The new linen dresses had been sold to the shops and, much to Polly's displeasure, Sarah had bought another bolt of cloth from Sid.

When Polly had to see her doctor about getting a certificate to prove she was unable to work in a munitions factory, she made a big fuss about her eye, and was made exempt.

'I've had a letter from David,' said Mrs Bloom, when Polly and Sarah returned home from work. She waved it around excitedly. 'And there's one there for you, Margaret.'

'Is it from David?' asked Polly quizzically.

'No, I don't recognize the writing.'

Polly picked up her letter. She didn't know the handwriting either. She turned it over before tearing it open. 'It's from Billy,' she yelled, sitting herself down on the monk's seat. 'It's from my young brother, Billy.' Tears filled her eyes. 'He's alive.'

'Is he all right?' asked Sarah.

Polly quickly scanned the two pages. 'Yes. He doesn't say a lot. He's had two letters from me. He's sorry about the flat and the Navy told him about Mum. He's pleased I'm living here, and when he gets home and some more leave he's phoning me.' She sniffed back the tears.

'Does he have our phone number?' asked Sarah eagerly.

'Yes. Funny, I don't know why – force of habit, I suppose

313

– but I always put it on the top of all my letters.' She wiped her face with the back of her hand. 'I must go upstairs.'

'Of course. I'll call you when dinner's ready,' said Mrs Bloom.

Sarah had begun reading David's letter. 'David says he might be able to get home soon.'

Polly was halfway up the stairs. She stopped and turned. 'Will he be coming here?' She tried to sound nonchalant. She had written as he had asked, and she had tried to make her letters friendly.

'He doesn't know if he will get the time. He's got to go to Yvonne's producer's wedding at Kingston.'

'That isn't that far away,' said Mrs Bloom, walking towards the kitchen.

'I'm sure he'll come to see us if he can,' Sarah called after her.

To Polly's amazement, two weeks later on the Friday evening, Billy telephoned. He told her he had a couple of days' leave and would be at Waterloo station about midday the next day, Saturday. He couldn't say much over the phone as he was in a public phone box, and there were a line of blokes behind him, banging on the glass to hurry him up.

The following day she was so excited she couldn't concentrate on her work. All morning she prayed Sid wouldn't turn up. He had been quite a frequent visitor to the workshop just lately, far more than she liked, and after all this time she wanted Billy to herself.

She left the factory at eleven, and made her way to Waterloo. The station was, as usual, filled with masses of jostling people. There appeared to be more servicemen and women than there had been when she'd been here before. She had arranged to meet Billy under the clock, and when Polly pushed her way through the crowds it seemed that everybody else had arranged the same thing. She looked impatiently around, then checked her watch against the large clock suspended above her head.

A piercing whistle made her and many other heads turn. She knew the waving hand above the crowd belonged to Billy. She pushed her way towards him, and with tears running down her face, held him tight. He crushed her to him; for a few moments no words were spoken.

Billy straightened his hat. 'It's good to see yer, Pol.'

She held him at arm's length. 'Let me look at you. You've grown! You're taller than me now. You look very well.' Polly fumbled in her handbag for a handkerchief and wiped away her tears.

'Go on with you. Mind you, could be the healthy life I lead. You don't look so bad yourself.'

They embraced again.

'Come on, let's go and have a cuppa,' said Polly, linking her arm through his. 'How long are you on leave for?'

'Got to go back tomorrow about lunch-time.'

'Where are you going to stay tonight?'

'I'll go to the NAAFI, they can always find you a bed some-where.'

'I can't get over how handsome you look in your uniform, and I'm not the only one – I can see all the girls giving you the glad eye.'

Billy laughed. 'You know what they say, Sis? A sailor's sup-posed to have a girl in every port.'

'Well, have you?'

'No. Unfortunately we don't get a lot of time to sort out the local talent. We're in and out of the docks before we 'ave time to draw breath. Mind you, there's always the ladies of the night hanging round when we dock, but I wouldn't touch them with a barge pole.'

When they'd settled themselves in a café Polly said, 'Right, now I want to hear all your news. Do you realize we haven't seen each other for nearly eighteen months.' She sighed. 'Eigh-teen months. It seems more like a lifetime.'

'Well, after I finished my training at Portsmouth, I joined a ship that was going back and forth to Portugal. I tell you, Pol,

315

that Channel can be a killer. Talk about sea-sick.'

'I thought sailors weren't sea-sick?'

'Don't you believe it. Do you know some of the regulars, real old sea dogs some of them are, been all round the world they 'ave, and they still bring up their boots.'

Polly laughed. 'Do you like the life?'

'I love it. Wouldn't do anything else, and I've got some real good mates. When I think of me working in that tea factory – I could never go back there. Do you think I talk proper now?'

'I did notice. Mum would be very proud of you.'

Billy bit on his bottom lip and played with the spoon in his saucer. He lowered his voice. 'I was ever so upset when I heard. She wasn't a bad old stick.'

'Funny, that's what Ron said.'

He jerked his head up. 'You've seen Ron?'

She shook her head. 'No, not since he was on embarkation leave just after he was called up. He was at Dunkirk, you know.'

'Poor sod. So was I. My God, we didn't get any sleep for days. We were backwards and forwards across the Channel, we picked up hundreds of blokes. Could even have picked up Ron. Not that I would have recognized 'im. Some of the blokes were in a right mess, almost dead on their feet some of 'em were.' He played with his spoon again. 'Seen some real 'orrible sights, I 'ave Pol. Anyway, how is Ron? Is he all right?'

'He seems to be. I think he must be somewhere where it's hot. Sarah . . . you remember Sarah Bloom?'

He nodded. 'Fancy you living at their house now.'

'Yes. I was very lucky they took me in. Well, she thinks he could be in North Africa.'

'Did you ever find out who pinched that brooch?'

'No, and I don't suppose I ever will. Anyway that's all in the past.'

'Was prison hard?'

'Not too bad, but dón't let's talk about that.'

'Sorry. What about Sid turning up like that? He was lucky

he wasn't in the house when Mum . . .'

'You know Sid. If he fell in a pile of you-know-what, he'd still come out smelling of roses eventually.'

'What's he up to now? Still wheeling and dealing? He ain't found himself a wife yet?'

'Not one of his own – someone else's from what I can gather. He pops into the workshop now and again. In fact I'm getting a bit worried: he's brought some cloth over and Sarah's been buying it. He says it's salvage, but I'm sure it's been knocked off.'

'Surely Sarah knows what she's doing?'

'I don't know. She thinks Sid's good fun.'

Billy laughed. 'What, Sarah Bloom and our Sid, come off it, Pol. Don't you think you're letting your imagination run away with you? They ain't been out together, have they?'

'No, but you should see how her face lights up when he walks in.'

'Well, let's face it, Sid's clock's enough ter make anybody grin. Maybe she likes a bit o' excitement, someone a bit different. When I get home again, perhaps Sid could come out with us? What d'yer say? It'll be nice ter get together again. After all, we are family.'

'Well, yes. We'll see. Anyway, that's enough about Sid. What about you? Have you been all right?'

'I've had a few near misses, but I'm OK.'

Polly sat back in her chair. 'I really can't believe this is happening. For months I've worried and wondered about where you were, then out of the blue I get a letter. Two weeks later we're sitting here, together. It really is good to see you, Billy.'

'It's good to see you too, Pol, and to know you're safe.' He reached across the table and patted her hand.

'You really do like the Navy then?'

'I wouldn't do anything else.' He sat back. 'D'you know, I've been to places I didn't even know existed. The States is really something – I tell yer, when this lot is all over I wouldn't mind settling down over there.'

'Vera Bell's husband's on the Atlantic run.'

'It's the lend-lease agreement we've got with the States. They won't get involved with our war, but at least they're helping us out with food and stuff. I could well 'ave been on his ship, or in his convoy. We all travel in convoys to protect the Merchant Navy ships from the Jerry subs: they're the ones that are bringing over our food.'

'Vera Bell's got a little girl.'

'No? How's Shirley's little un?'

'I haven't seen Elizabeth since the Christmas before last.' Polly looked wistful. 'I was supposed to go this Christmas, but Elizabeth and Shirley's mum were both ill.'

'Sorry to hear that. They all right now?'

'Yes, but Terry's been reported missing.'

Billy grimaced. 'That's a shame, I always liked the twins.'

They sat and talked for hours, drinking endless cups of tea, and going over the past eighteen months in fine detail, as well as reliving most of their childhood.

Polly looked at her watch. 'Have you got anything planned for this evening?'

'No.'

'How about going up West? We could have a meal somewhere if you like, then go on to a pub?'

'That sounds smashing. You know, you can't beat a good old drop of English beer.'

'Don't get too excited, I think they water it down up here to make it go round.'

'Blimey, they wouldn't do that down Portsmouth, the landlords would get lynched. Here, by the way, you haven't got a date or anything tonight, have you?'

'Only with you. Besides, I'm a married woman.'

'Does that matter today, with a war on?'

'I wouldn't like to say.'

When they left the pub at closing time, the siren began its mournful tune. Immediately searchlights scanned the sky, sweeping and criss-crossing above them. In the distance the sound of guns could be heard.

'Here we go again,' said Polly nonchalantly as they staggered along the road.

'Will you be able to get back home tonight?' asked Billy.

'I shan't bother. Let's go down the underground. If we pick the right one, we could end up having a good old sing-song.'

'That sounds a great idea.'

They rode up and down to a few stations, then found one that was not only having a sing-song, but a right old knees-up as well, as somebody had just got married. Bottles of beer were being passed round, and the man with the accordion knew all the latest songs.

It was well into the early hours before people began to settle down. Polly was sitting watching Billy dancing with a pretty girl. She smiled, her thoughts dulled through drink and fatigue. She looked around her. I wonder if this is the underground that the toilet lady and her daughter used to come down, she thought. A lump came to her throat when Billy sat next to her and put his arm round her shoulders. She wanted to shout to everybody, 'This is my little brother!' The rough serge of his uniform brushed against her cheek, her eyelids became heavy, and as she drifted off to sleep she wondered how long it would be before she saw him again.

The following morning, after tidying herself up and having breakfast at a coffee stall, they wandered along the Embankment. Last night's raid didn't seem to have caused that much damage. There were the usual fire engines and ambulances rushing around but as it was now a way of life nobody seemed outwardly bothered. Then it was time to go to Waterloo station.

He held her close before boarding the train. 'See you soon,' he yelled as the train slowly moved away.

She waved and waved till it was out of sight.

* * *

319

'Hello, Margaret, did you see your brother?' asked Mrs Bloom.

'Yes, thank you.' Polly was feeling sad as she looked in the mirror over the telephone table and removed her hat.

'We were worried about you when the raid started.'

'Oh, we were all right, we went down the underground. Sorry, I should have phoned, but you know how it is.'

'Of course – we understand. Did it do much damage up there?'

'I don't know, it's hard to tell which is new now.'

'Guess who came to see us on Saturday?' said Sarah.

Polly turned from the mirror as Sarah walked into the hall.

'David. He managed to get away from that wedding early.'

'David?' repeated Polly. 'Was Yvonne . . .?'

'Oh yes.'

'She looked lovely,' said Mrs Bloom.

'David said he was sorry he missed you.'

'Did they stay long?' asked Polly.

'Yes, they stayed the night. Well, they couldn't go back with a raid on,' said Mrs Bloom.

Polly tried to sound cheerful. 'I bet you were really pleased to see them both.'

'Yes, I should say so.'

'Even Yvonne behaved herself. I think she was under strict orders from David,' said Sarah.

'That's not a very nice thing to say, Sarah,' said Mrs Bloom.

'Why did they leave the wedding so early?'

'Oh, it turned out to be a very quiet registry office affair, with just David and Yvonne as witnesses. I think David was a bit peeved that he wasted a whole forty-eight-hour pass on it. And Yvonne wasn't very happy when she found out the press hadn't been invited. Come into the drawing-room and tell us about your weekend,' said Sarah, leading the way.

'I must go upstairs first and tidy up.'

'Yes, of course, I'll have a cup of tea ready for you when you come down.'

'Thanks Sarah.'

In the quiet of her room, Polly threw herself on her bed. Why, oh why did David have to come here the weekend Billy came home?

Chapter 30

On the night of 11 May 1941, London was again the target for Hitler's bombers.

In the comparative safety of the Morrison shelter, Mrs Bloom, Sarah and Polly sat terrified as the floor beneath them pitched and heaved. It silently rose and fell with every bomb that erupted near by. The sound of glass shattering and chimneys and tiles crashing to the ground merged with the resounding bursts of gunfire and exploding bombs.

'My God, we're going to be lucky if we get out of this lot alive,' whispered Sarah.

'Don't say things like that,' snapped Mrs Bloom. Her sharpness was totally out of character.

Polly patted her arm. 'Sarah didn't mean to upset you.' Her voice quivered with emotion and fear.

'I'm sorry Mother . . .' She stopped as first the scream, then the deafening sound of a bomb exploded quite near. In a split second it sent shock waves under the floorboards, and quickly they all lay flat with their hands over their heads, trying to make themselves as small as possible, waiting for the aftermath.

The french windows blew open and crashed against the wall. The glass shattered and the wood splintered, sending parts of the door across the room. The sound of the beautiful velvet curtains being ripped apart was dreadful. All around them plaster from the ceiling fell like snowflakes, and glass from the lamps tinkled gently as it fell to the floor.

No one spoke, and in the silence that followed the sound of

their heavy breathing turned to coughing as the air became heavy with dust and soot.

Fear rose like bile in Polly's throat. She felt she was choking. She was sweating, and began to panic as she fought for breath. She clawed at the neck of her sweater. Terror swept over her when a mixture of loud noises – buildings crashing and fire engines' bells – filled her ears. What if the roof falls in? We'd be buried alive. 'I've got to get out of here,' she mumbled.

'You're not going out there, not just yet, anyway,' yelled Sarah.

'I must, I can't breathe.' In the gloom, Polly started crawling and fumbling along the floor.

'Sit still and calm down.' Sarah's voice was a command, not a request.

'Come along, Margaret.' Mrs Bloom winced as another bomb fell close by.

'I don't think we've got any windows left,' said Sarah.

'I'm surprised the house is still standing after that,' gasped Polly, running her sweaty hands over her face. The taste of dirt and grit filled her mouth.

'I can't see what's happened,' said Mrs Bloom, coughing.

Slowly the dust settled. As the bright moonlight shone through the open doors, eerily lighting up the dining-room, they looked through the bars and tried to assess the damage.

Mrs Bloom began to weep softly. 'My home. My beautiful home.'

'There, there Mother, it probably isn't as bad as it looks,' said Sarah, trying to reassure her.

Polly peered out at the destruction. 'I suppose we should be grateful we're not all dead.' She too began to cry. 'It must have been awful for me mum when she was buried alive.'

'I'm sorry, Margaret. Yes, we should be thankful we're still here,' whispered Mrs Bloom.

For the rest of the night, as the moon slowly made its way across the sky, they sat and looked through the wide open space that had been the french windows, watching the sharp pencil-like rays of the searchlights sweeping the sky. The quick flashes from the guns looked like lightning in a summer storm, and the warm red glow from the many fires told them that a lot of people would not survive the night, and many more would be homeless.

Then, gradually, the edge of the sky lightened, and with the coming of dawn, the uplifting tone of the all-clear filled the air once again.

With faces gaunt and tear-stained, they crawled out of their shelter feeling dirty and exhausted.

The glass crunching beneath their feet made them stop in their tracks.

'Stand still, everybody, while I make sure it's safe,' said Sarah. 'We don't want to fall over things or have objects falling on our heads.'

'I'll go over and see if I can do something with the French windows while you make your way to the hall,' said Polly, picking her way towards the windows.

'Are you sure you feel up to it?'

She nodded. 'I'm all right now, but I don't think I want another night like that for a while.'

Sarah was pulling at the dining-room door. 'I can't get it open. It's stuck, I'll have to go round the front.'

'Have you got your front-door key?' asked Mrs Bloom.

'I'll have to make sure we've got a front door first,' said Sarah, laughing.

Suddenly they all joined in the laughter; a relieved, comforting kind of nervous laughter.

'When you've got the kitchen door open I'll come round and see about trying to make a cup of tea,' said Mrs Bloom.

'I'll get the dustbin, then we can fill it with all this glass,' said Polly, pulling down a stringy piece of curtain that had been left hanging.

All morning they toiled, clearing up glass, checking that any left in the frames was safe. Banging cushions to shake off the dust and glass; taking the rugs outside and giving them the same treatment. The soot, plaster and dust got up their noses, making them sneeze and cough. They felt dirty, despite wearing overalls and having their hair wrapped in turban-like scarves.

'I'm dying for that cup of tea,' said Sarah.

'I'm sorry, my dear, but I can't do anything about it. That kind ARP man said the water should be on soon, and he thinks the gas main will be repaired quite quickly. He has asked the WVS woman to call.'

At that moment there was a shout from the hall. 'Yoo-hoo, anybody home?'

They all hurried to the front door, which was miraculously still intact, glass and all. Sarah had managed to get into the house through the kitchen door as that had been blown open.

'Did you want tea?' asked the woman in the green uniform.

'Please,' they all said at once.

'Have you any cups left?'

'Yes,' said Mrs Bloom. 'Nothing in the kitchen has been broken, only the glass in the door.'

'This blast is a funny thing. Do you know, I think I could write a book when this war's over about some of the strange things I've seen. But enough of my chatter, I'll get my tea-pot. If you've got a flask handy, I can fill that for you as well.'

She returned carrying a huge, heavy, metal tea-pot. 'This is one of the worst nights we've had for a while,' she said, pouring tea into the largest cups Mrs Bloom could find. 'I've heard it's pretty bad round the docks way again. Those poor souls. They're all very brave, I think they deserve a medal for all they've been through. Right, that's your flask filled. If your water and gas isn't restored before the end of the day, I'll be back. Bye for now.' With that she was gone.

Polly began to laugh. 'She reminds me of a fairy godmother, flitting in and out like that.'

'In some ways she is a fairy godmother. What would we do without our tea?' said Mrs Bloom with her hands clasped round her cup, relishing every mouthful.

They sat quietly drinking their tea as if it were nectar.

'Do you think you two could manage without me now?' asked Sarah. 'I feel I should try to get over to the factory, just to make sure everybody's still safe.'

'Would you like me to go?' asked Polly.

'No, if you don't mind helping Mother.'

'Don't worry, we can manage,' said Mrs Bloom. 'But Sarah, please be careful.'

'Sarah, if there's a lot of damage, wait till we can get help,' said Polly.

'Of course. That's if the looters haven't got there first and helped themselves to everything.'

'I think all looters should be shot,' said Mrs Bloom venomously. 'Someone was telling me only the other day while I was queuing up for some fish that someone she knew was lying injured at the back of the house and the thieves were stealing her clothes from the wardrobe in the bedroom. It's terrible what some people will do, while others are risking their lives to help their fellow men.'

It was early evening, and Mrs Bloom was getting increasingly worried in case the raids started before Sarah returned home. Now the water and gas had been restored, Polly persuaded Mrs Bloom to take a bath before it got dark.

'You'll feel tons better. I know I did after washing all that soot and dust out of my hair.'

'It can't be a long soak now we're only supposed to have five inches of water, but I'll make the most of it,' she said cheerfully. 'We were lucky we got that man to board up the windows, otherwise it could be very draughty.'

Polly smiled, and made her way to the drawing-room. She could no longer look out on her favourite view as these windows were now covered with wooden boards, so she decided to take a walk into the garden. The telephone's shrill bell made her jump.

'Hello . . .'

'Margaret. It's me, David.'

327

Her face lit up. 'David. How are you?'

'I'm fine, what about you? Is Mother or Sarah there?'

'We're fine. Your mother's in the bath, and Sarah's at the factory.'

'Thank God you're all safe. I heard about last night's raid, and have been trying to get in touch with you all day.'

The line went crackly. 'David. David, are you there?'

'Margaret. I've been so worried about you.'

'I expect the lines were down, there's been a lot of damage.'

'I've been trying to get hold of Yvonne, but she's not at home. I would be most obliged if you could find time to give her a ring and tell her to phone me.'

'Of course.'

'Thank you.' The pips began to sound. 'Margaret . . .' His voice sounded urgent – they were cut off.

She slowly replaced the receiver on the cradle. She studied the phone for a few moments. I wonder what he was going to say. He said my name with feeling, and he said he'd been worried about me. She looked in the mirror. 'Don't kid yourself, girl – he meant he was worried about all of us,' she whispered to herself. 'Besides, look at you, how do you think you can compete with Yvonne?'

'Who was that on the phone, dear?' called Mrs Bloom from upstairs.

'David,' Polly called back. 'He was worried about you; he's been trying to call all day.'

Mrs Bloom came down the stairs in her navy-blue slacks and maroon sweater, ready for going into the shelter. 'I expect the lines have been down.'

'He asked me to try and get in touch with Yvonne.'

'I thought Windsor was quite safe?'

'So did I. Perhaps she's away filming or something?'

'I'll fill the flasks.' Polly was sure she heard Mrs Bloom mutter, 'Or something,' as she walked into the kitchen, but dismissed it.

Sarah returned before the evening raid started.

'Sorry I've been so long, but so many roads are blocked, and there are a lot of diversions on the underground because some of the stations have been put out of action.'

'I'll make some tea,' said Polly. 'Everything all right over there?' she asked over her shoulder as she filled the kettle.

Sarah nodded. She sat on the chair and removed her hat. 'We think we've got problems. You should see it up there. There's such a lot of damage, and people are walking around in a daze.' She stopped and swallowed hard. 'I've seen grown men sitting by the side of a pile of rubble, crying. And women looking bewildered were sitting on chairs in the road, their furniture piled up all round them.' She began playing with the spoon, tapping it on the saucer. 'I think a lot of people were killed last night.' She nervously began picking and studying her fingers. 'Violet and Elsie, and that new woman, Sheila, didn't come to work.'

'That doesn't mean . . . They could have been like us, clearing up the mess . . .' said Polly.

'Fred wasn't at work either.' Sarah stood up. 'I'll go and get changed, ready for tonight.' She left the room in a hurry.

Polly went to move.

'No. Let her be on her own for a few moments,' said Mrs Bloom. 'She'll tell us what's happened when she's ready.'

Sarah remained subdued for most of the evening. She was reading a book, but every time Polly looked at her in the soft light from the paraffin lamp, she could see Sarah's mind was elsewhere.

'It's quiet so far,' said Mrs Bloom, trying to ease the tension.

'Perhaps they won't be over tonight,' said Polly.

'Don't you believe it. After what they did last night I reckon they'll be in for the kill.' Sarah spat out the words.

'Has the factory gone again?' asked Mrs Bloom in a hushed tone.

'No,' said Sarah. 'That's the one good thing about being under the arches and having no windows.' She sighed, it was a long, deeply felt sigh. 'If only we had a café opposite us like Charlie's in Mansell Street.'

'Charlie's? What d'you want a café for?' asked Polly.

'Well, we could always leave a message there, and if some-one wasn't well, or anything had happened we'd . . .' Her voice trailed off.

'What's upsetting you?' asked Mrs Bloom.

Sarah began to cry. It was a soft gentle cry at first, then sud-denly the tears fell, rolling down her cheeks, smudging her mas-cara into two long, wet, black streaks that dripped off her chin and on to her hands. She wiped her face with her fingers. 'I'm sorry about that,' she whispered.

Polly realized that this was the first time she'd seen Sarah cry, really cry. After all she'd been through, with losing the fac-tory, the fire at home, and her hands, she had never really broken down. It upset Polly to see Sarah so distressed.

Mrs Bloom moved closer to her daughter and put her arm round the heaving shoulders. 'There, there my dear. Let it flow, let all the pain and hurt come out.' Sarah buried her head against her mother.'

No one spoke, and gradually the crying stopped.

'I'm sorry. I shouldn't have . . .'

'We all have our breaking point,' interrupted Mrs Bloom. 'Now, do you think you can tell us what has upset you so much?'

Sarah nodded. 'It's Fred. It's the not-knowing. If we had a café near us like we used to have Charlie's, well, we could leave messages, and meet each other. If someone was early, or I was late with the key, at least they would have somewhere to go. Fred's been with us for years.'

Polly thought about Elsie Mann and her children. What if she'd been killed? What would happen to them? Their father was in the Army, and anything could happen to him. Polly felt sad, but didn't want to show it. 'I reckon what's happened is,' she said in a down-to-earth manner, 'that Fred got there this morning and we weren't there to open up, so he got fed up with waiting and went off home.'

'You could be right.' Sarah smiled, screwing up her mascara-streaked face. 'But he could have slipped a note under the door.'

'He probably didn't think. You know what men are like,' said Mrs Bloom. 'Pass the flask please, Margaret. I'm going to have a nice hot cup of coffee, put my earplugs in, and get a good night's sleep. After last night, and all the work we've done today, I'm exhausted. And I suggest you two do the same.'

Polly and Sarah both looked at her and laughed. 'That's not a bad idea,' said Polly.

She drank her coffee, then took the small brown rubber earplugs the government had issued everybody with from her gas-mask case, popped them in her ears and pulled her blanket over her head. 'Good night all, and I hope I don't see you both till morning.'

Chapter 31

Fortunately none of the girls at the factory had been injured in the last big raid. It was as Polly had said, they had been too busy cleaning up their own homes and trying to make them secure, to get to work. Fred too was safe. He had been blown against a door and had hurt his hip, but other than that, everything was fine.

Spring turned into summer, and life gradually returned to normal. In June 1941, clothes rationing was introduced, which meant Bloom's Fashions would now get a small cloth allowance. So apart from the government contract, they could still produce dresses, which kept them all very busy.

Polly had another letter from Ron. It was more or less on the same lines as his other two, and although in her letters she had repeatedly asked him about the brooch, he had declined to answer. That just confirmed her belief that he *had* been involved.

Shirley had also written to say her mother wasn't getting any better, and she was worried about her dad as he seemed to spend more time fire-watching at the factory than anyone else. She also wrote enthusiastically about a Canadian she'd met called Ben.

Sarah and Polly also had to do their share of fire-watching, and when they donned their grey tin hats it always created great howls of laughter.

She hadn't heard from Billy in months. She was getting a little anxious about it, but Sid, who was always turning up at the factory like a bad penny, told her not to concern herself: he probably had a girlfriend who was more important. Polly knew that could never be: she and Billy had a very special relationship.

David had written twice, and his letters were very friendly. They both had the same sense of humour and, considering their different backgrounds, they found they could talk about a lot of things. He never said a great deal about Yvonne: it appeared she had been out of town, working during the big raid back in May.

The hot summer days slipped into the long shadows of autumn, and autumn into another winter. Life was very much the same for Polly, Sarah and Mrs Bloom. There were more and more shortages, and queuing was almost becoming a national pastime.

At the beginning of December it was announced that all women between twenty and thirty would be called up. Sarah hoped that, as the owner of a factory doing war work, she would be exempted. Then on 7 December 1941, Japan bombed Pearl Harbor, and America entered the war.

Polly was hoping to spend Christmas in Bristol, but as the holiday approached, didn't feel she could face the journey, what with overcrowded trains, air-raids and all the confusion that went with it. She was tired. The broken nights, fire-watching and all the extra work were beginning to take their toll.

'You certainly look peeky,' said Mrs Bloom when Polly told her.

'I feel awful not going to see Shirley, but I don't think I would be very good company.' She yawned. 'I must be off to bed.'

'You do that, my dear,' she said in a concerned voice. 'I'll wake you if there's a raid tonight.'

Christmas with Sarah and Mrs Bloom was a very quiet affair. The table didn't groan with food as it did last year and, much to Polly's disappointment, David didn't come home. But it did give her a chance to catch up on her sleep.

As the new year was welcomed in, everybody hoped that 1942 would see an end to the hostilities.

'Morning, girls.' Once again, Sid breezed into the factory. This time he was carrying a suitcase.

'Yer leaving us again, are yer Sid?' shouted one of the girls.

'Na. Got a nice bit o' gear 'ere yer might like ter see.' He rubbed his hands together after putting his suitcase on the cutting-out table. 'It's a bit parky out there.'

'Ain't none too warm in 'ere,' said Rosie.

'I'll always keep yer warm, gel.' He blew on his hands. 'See, got 'em all warmed up ready.'

'Go on with yer, Sid, yer'll git me a bad reputation.'

The other girls laughed.

'And I don't want any comments from you lot,' she shouted across at the other girls. 'Anyway, Sid, what yer got in yer case?'

He opened it and held up a skirt. 'Well, wot d'yer fink?'

'Very nice. 'Ow many coupons?' asked Sheila.

'To you, my dear – none.'

'What?' she yelled.

'What's going on out here?' asked Polly, coming out of the office. 'Oh, it's you. What do you want this time?'

'Brought along a little bit of me merchandise, ain't I? Fought Miss Bloom and some of the girls might like ter 'ave a perusal.'

'Where did you get it?'

'I've got me contacts. And it's all good stuff – genuine kosher. Where's Miss Bloom?'

'Out.'

'Wot a pity. I reckon she'd like some of this stuff.' He held up another skirt. 'This is just 'er style. I can just see 'er in this.'

'I've told you before, we don't want any of your bent gear in here.'

'Oh, come on, Polly,' shouted Sheila. 'Don't be a spoilsport. A lot of me coupons 'ave ter go on the kids, so I'm always looking fer sumfink fer meself.'

'Yer can always pick up fings down Petticoat Lane fer a few bob more and no coupons,' said Rosie. 'Got meself a nice coat the other Sunday.'

'Yer, well yer can try on coats, but I'd look a real Charlie, standing in the middle of the road in me drawers, trying on a skirt.'

'I dunno, could 'elp bring in the punters,' said Sid.

Sheila laughed her raucous laugh. 'Sid Perkins, you're a right one and no mistake. 'Ere, it's nearly lunch-time. All right if I try that navy-blue one on later?'

'Sure, that's if me skin and blister 'ere lets me 'ang around fer a while.'

Polly walked back into the office. She knew there was no point in arguing with Sid. He was very popular with the girls, and she didn't like to be too authoritarian when Sarah was out.

In the spring, Polly and Sarah were reading the letter from the Board of Trade, telling them about the new patterns they must use for all future dresses. They could only use a certain amount of cloth, and six buttons per garment. The hemline was to be shorter, and frills, trimmings and pleats were out.

'My God, no wonder they're calling it utility,' said Polly, studying the pattern. 'How are we going to show any of our own style if they've all got to look the same?'

'I know you, once you've got over the shock, you'll find a way of making them different. Anyway, we can't worry about that at the moment. We've got to bundle up that last lot of shorts. Fred has started altering the tension on some of the machines to take that new parachute silk. I'd like some underwear made up out of that.'

'Yes, it's lovely, but a swine to work on. And there's so much of it.'

'Don't knock it,' replied Sarah. 'Remember that's what's keeping us out of the Forces so far – touch wood.'

A few days after that, when they arrived home from work, Mrs Bloom met them at the front door. Her face was ashen.

'What on earth has happened?' cried Sarah, quickly bundling Polly and her mother into the hall.

'Margaret. This came for you this morning.' With trembling

hands she held out the buff-coloured envelope they all knew could contain a War Department telegram.

Polly couldn't find the strength to take hold of it. Her knees went weak, and she sank down on the monk's seat. Her hands almost refused to open it. Tears ran down her face as she read the few words over and over again.

'Who is it, Margaret?' whispered Sarah, sitting next to her.

She didn't answer. She just passed her the single sheet of paper.

Sarah quickly read it, then said to her mother. 'It's Ron, her husband. He's been reported missing.'

'I'm so sorry,' said Mrs Bloom.

'He could be all right. He could have been taken prisoner,' said Sarah. 'They don't say believed killed. I'm sure the Red Cross will do all they can to find out more for you. Tomorrow you must go to their office.'

'Yes, all right.' The tears had stopped. She appeared calm. Polly picked up her handbag. 'I must write to Shirley and her mum. Poor Mrs Bell, this is her second son to go missing.' She walked up the stairs in a dream.

In the solitude of her bedroom, she sat on the bed and reread the telegram over and over again. It still hadn't really sunk in. Once again the tears fell. 'Ron, oh Ron,' she wailed out loud. 'Why couldn't we have made things work? I did love you in a way. And we had some good times.' She lay back and looked up at the ceiling. The tears ran from the corner of her eyes and into her ears. Her body heaved with sobs. 'First me mum gone, and now Ron's missing. Who's going to be next?' She turned over and punched the pillow. 'When's this bloody war going to stop?' she cried.

The Red Cross said they would try and find out more for Polly, and she wrote a short letter to Shirley telling her the news. There didn't seem much more she could do after that.

Sid's only reaction to Ron going missing was, 'It could 'ave got too 'ot for 'im and 'e's done a bunk.'

Several months after she received the telegram there was still no news of Ron. One morning Polly was busy at her machine when she looked up and gasped out loud. Sarah was facing Polly, with her back to the door, but Polly's expression of horror made her turn round quickly.

'Why, hello, what are you doing here?' said a familiar voice.

The blood drained from Polly's face, and the memories of her past came flooding back. What did he want?

'Sorry, Miss, I didn't mean to startle you.' He was being polite this time.

'What have you come about?' croaked Polly looking up at the policeman who had arrested her all that time ago. She would never forget his face. He was now wearing civvies, and stood twirling his brown trilby round and round in his hands.

'Is there anything wrong, Officer?' asked Sarah. A flush swept over her face.

'Detective-sergeant now, Miss. No, not really. We're advising factory owners to be on their guard, and not buy anything off the spivs. There's a lot of black-market cloth being sold – stolen, most of it is. And there's a lot of clothes going into factories as well. You know the sort of thing, they ask for a few bob extra and no coupons. And we all know what you women are like for clothes.'

He laughed, and Sarah joined in, but hers was a forced laugh.

'I'll keep my eyes out for anything that looks the slightest bit suspicious,' she chirped. 'It's so nice to see you again after all this time, how are you?'

'Mustn't grumble. How's your mother and father?'

'Mother's fine. Unfortunately Dad died.'

'I'm sorry to hear that.' He turned and walked towards the door. 'Bye Miss,' he called over his shoulder to Polly.

'I'll show you out,' said Sarah, trotting at his side.

Polly stood and watched them laughing and talking in the doorway. Of all the coppers round here, it had to be him. No doubt he was asking Sarah all about her, and why she was working here.

For the rest of the day, Polly didn't really have much of a chance to talk to Sarah, she was singing along with the girls on their machines as the wireless blared out all the latest songs.

It was almost six o'clock and time to leave when Sid walked into the office. He didn't have his case with him this time.

'Hello, Sid,' said Sarah. 'What can we do for you?'

'It's what I can do fer you is more the question.' In his usual cocky manner he flicked his trilby back with his finger.

Polly was angry. She had been angry ever since that policeman came in. She had tried to find fault with everything, from the girls' work to the telephone people; anything she could vent her feelings on. She was also angry with Sarah for being so happy. The arrival of the policeman had upset her. It reminded her of her past. She was angry with Ron for not disclosing where he got the brooch: she might never see him again so she'd never know. And she was angry with Sid for breezing in and out of her life. Always up to something, and too streetwise to get caught.

'We don't want anything to do with you and your shady deals. So get out,' she said aggressively.

'Who's crawled in your nest?' asked Sid, surprised at her attitude.

'I'm afraid Margaret isn't too happy today,' said Sarah.

'Oh, got the dreaded curse then, gel?'

'Mind your own bloody business.'

'Language, gel, language. Blimey, yer must be upset, we don't often 'ear you swear.'

Sarah looked at Polly in surprise. 'What can we do for you, Sid?'

'Got some good cloth coming. I fink you're gonner like this.'

'We had the law here today,' said Polly, waiting for his reaction to that statement.

'So?'

'He was looking for stolen goods.'

'So?' he repeated.

'Thought you might be interested,' she said, tidying up her desk.

'No, not really.' He turned to Sarah. 'Anyway, d'yer fancy taking a butcher's at this little lot?'

'No,' said Polly emphatically.

''Ang on, 'ang about. It's not up ter you. I was talking to Miss Bloom 'ere.'

'I'm not interested in anything that's the slightest bit suspect,' said Sarah.

'This is all kosher. Got invoices ter prove it.'

Polly banged the drawer in her desk shut.

'I don't know,' said Sarah. 'I'll have to think about it.'

'OK,' he glared at Polly. 'But if it goes, it's your loss.'

'I'll take that chance,' said Sarah calmly.

'I'll call in the end of the week. Cheerio fer now.' With that he left.

'Sarah . . .'

'Before you say anything, let's get one thing straight.' Sarah's voice was angry. 'I'm no fool, and I don't need you to tell me what to do.'

Polly turned on her. 'Why do you encourage him? Why don't you send him packing? I always thought you had more respect for the law. You were quick enough to send *me* to prison.'

'That was a long while ago. Stop being a martyr. That part of your life is all over now. Things were different then. Remember there's a war on and we've got to make sure we stay in the fashion business. And if I can get hold of a little bit of salvaged cloth, then I will.'

'But what if it's stolen.'

'I'm not that stupid. I have contacts who tell me what has gone missing. I don't tell you everything, you know.'

Polly hung her head. Sarah's words had stung; she was hurt. Sarah had never spoken to her like that before. She thought that, being partners, they would have shared everything. The words her mother often used were drumming through her head. 'Don't go getting above your station girl,' they said, 'Don't go getting above your station . . .'

For the next few days, things were very strained between Sarah and Polly. When Sid came into the office later in the week, Polly walked out, waiting till he had left before going back. And Sarah didn't say anything about Sid, or going to see the cloth.

It was a warm September evening. They had just finished dinner and were sitting in the garden.

'I love this time of year,' said Mrs Bloom. 'Just smell the scent from those roses.' She sniffed the air. 'That's one of the few things that's not on ration now.'

'Sarah, do you fancy coming to see "Gone With The Wind"? I know there are long queues, but everybody says it's well worth it.' Polly began peeling an apple she had just picked.

'I don't know. When are you thinking of going?'

'I thought about tomorrow night.'

'I can't go tomorrow.'

'Oh, why's that?'

Sarah smiled. 'I have a date.'

Mrs Bloom was reading the paper, but at this her head shot up. 'May I ask with whom?'

'I'd rather not say.' Sarah glanced at Polly. 'Anyway, I shan't be home for dinner.'

Polly tried to control her anger. 'Well, I shall be going to the pictures straight from work, so don't worry about dinner for me.'

Throughout the following day, the atmosphere in the office was very uncomfortable, and six o'clock couldn't come quick enough for Polly. When Sarah walked in after changing her clothes, Polly couldn't help but comment.

'You look very nice,' she said, smiling nervously. 'Sarah . . . I'm sorry for what I said. I think a lot of you, and you've been very kind to me; it's just I would hate you to get hurt.'

Sarah laughed. 'That's all in the past now – and why should I get hurt?' She looked at her watch. 'Come on, hurry up or I shall be late.'

Polly stood at the bus stop watching Sarah cross the road. Who was she going to meet? Was it Sid? Why should he take her out? Was she going to buy cloth that might be a bit suspect? Even after that policeman had warned her. Why wouldn't she tell her mother? Or was she ashamed of going out with Sid? All these questions were turning over and over in Polly's mind as Sarah disappeared round the corner. Finally Polly's bus came along and, once upstairs, she lit a cigarette and stared at the mesh-covered window. When she arrived at the stop, she made her way to the cinema and joined the long queue. For well over an hour she slowly shuffled forward. She looked at her watch. She seemed no nearer the pay-box, and the big picture would be starting in half an hour; she didn't want to miss the beginning.

An old man in a navy-blue peaked cap with a little piece of gold braid at the front wandered up and down the queue, counting. Polly thought he was doing it just to put people off. His overcoat must have been made for someone else, as it appeared to be two sizes too big, but he was wearing his medal ribbons with pride.

Polly had read all the posters on the wall about the forthcoming attractions, and all the comments about the big film, and had studied the stills. She sighed and idly looked about her. She screwed up her eyes at a man in uniform standing on the other side of the road. He looked familiar; she stared at him deliberately. But no, it couldn't be.

He too turned and looked, almost as if he had been drawn to her gaze. He stopped, then hurried across the road towards her.

Chapter 32

'Margaret. Margaret. What are you doing here?'

Polly was stunned. She was sure her heart missed a beat. She couldn't believe this was happening as she looked up into David's dark brown eyes, and said lightly, 'I'm waiting to go into the pictures.' Then, regaining her composure, she asked, 'More to the point, what are you doing here? Are you on leave?'

'It's so good to see you,' he said, not answering her question. Then he looked along the queue. A faint smile lifted his face, and he bent his head nearer. 'Everybody's listening,' he whispered.

Polly quickly glanced round at the interested faces behind her.

'Look, why don't you come and have a drink with me?'

'But . . . I don't know. I've been standing here for well over an hour.'

'I have to go back later.' He appeared agitated. 'And I didn't want to go home.'

'Why not?'

'I can't go into details, not here. Come and have a drink.'

'I don't know . . . I really want to see this film.'

'You can go to the pictures any night.'

'Yes I know. But . . . I've been standing here rather a long while.' Polly hesitated. 'Why don't you come in with me? Then we could go for a drink afterwards.'

He shuffled forward with her as the queue moved. He looked hurt and took hold of her elbow. 'Please Margaret,' he whispered. 'I feel I need to talk to someone.'

Polly stiffened. His touch thrilled her, she desperately wanted to go with him.

'Please, Margaret.'

She looked up. He appeared worried. His eyes weren't laughing, and he seemed to be on edge. However, she didn't want to be seen as too eager to go with David, so she pretended to be torn between him and Clark Gable. But she made sure David won. 'Well, all right then,' she said when she'd finished her deliberations.

As they walked down the road he tucked her arm through his and patted it. 'You don't know how good it is to see you,' he said cheerfully.

'What are you doing in London? And why aren't you going home?'

'I'll tell you about it later, when we find a quiet pub.'

'What am I going to tell Sarah and your mother when they ask me about the film?'

'Tell them you met an old friend and went for a drink with them instead.'

'Not only do you stop me from seeing the best film that's ever been made, but you ask me to tell fibs as well.'

'It's not really fibs – I am an old friend, aren't I?'

She laughed, bursting with happiness, unable to believe her luck. She would have missed anything in order to spend an evening alone with him.

They found a pub, got their drinks, and settled themselves in a secluded corner.

David tossed his cap on a chair and, as usual, ran his fingers through his thick black curly hair.

She too longed to run her fingers through his hair. She knew it would be soft and springy to her touch. 'Right,' said Polly, leaning back in her chair, clutching her gin and orange. 'Now, I want to know what you're up to.' She suddenly felt alarmed, and leaned forward. 'David,' she whispered. 'You haven't run away from camp, have you?'

He smiled. It was a wide smile that showed off his perfect white teeth. 'No I haven't run away, as you put it. I'm in London on official business.'

'You mustn't tell me.' She looked around mock-furtively. 'Remember, "Careless talk costs lives".'

He laughed. 'There are so many things I like about you. No, I had to go to court today to give a character reference for one of my men who's got himself in a spot of bother. I got down here early this morning. I travelled on the sleeper, and that gave me time to go and see Yvonne before I went to court.' He sat forward and looked into his glass. He stared at it motionless for a few seconds.

'That must have been a nice surprise for her.'

'Yes, yes it was. Well, it certainly was a surprise,' he said harshly. 'Margaret.' He reached across the table and touched her hand. 'Margaret,' he croaked. 'I think a lot of you, and I value your friendship. A short while ago I was feeling miserable, angry, and very low. I couldn't have been more pleased than when I saw you standing outside the cinema. You're like a breath of fresh air.'

She laughed. 'That sounds like something out of a film.'

'I'm serious.'

'Oops, sorry, Sir.' She was trying desperately hard to keep the conversation light-hearted; she was terrified of showing her real feelings.

'When I arrived at Yvonne's house this morning I found her in bed with Justin.' It was said in a rush, without feeling, very matter-of-fact.

Polly was speechless.

'Did you hear what I said?'

She nodded. 'What did you do?' she whispered.

'The same thing as I did before – walked out.'

'She's done this before?' Polly's tone was one of shock.

'Many times, from what I can gather. Although I've only caught her once before. She tends to brag about it – it's supposed to be part of the system. The way to become a star.'

'You don't believe that, do you?'

'No, I don't. But I'm afraid my beautiful wife thinks her body should be shared.' He held his head in his hands.

Polly quickly moved to the other side of the table. 'David, oh David, I'm so sorry.' She put her arm round his shoulder. She wanted to hold him, comfort him, and above all, love him.

He looked up at her; his face was full of anguish. 'I can't love her any more. Not now, not after this. I forgave her once, but now I could never trust her. All the while I would be wondering whose bed she was sharing. Oh, I know we can all have little indiscretions, but this, this . . .'

'I don't know what to say.'

He kissed her cheek. 'I'm sorry. I'm always coming to you with my problems. Do you remember the night we sat in a bar and I told you I wanted to leave University and join the RAF?'

She nodded. 'That was before the war, and before I was married.'

'That seems like a lifetime ago. You were helpful then, telling me to wait. It was almost as if you knew what was going to happen.'

'Good old Aunt Polly.'

'Yes, I called you Aunt Polly then.'

'Yes, I remember feeling very flattered that someone like you should seek my advice.'

'I think I said at the time that you have a very different view of life, more down-to-earth.'

'Yus gov, we call a spade a spade.'

They laughed, and it eased the tension.

'David, what are you going to do?'

'I'll have to divorce her.'

'You can't.'

'I can't spend the rest of my life phoning my wife to see if my side of the bed's empty.' He spoke with venom and anger.

'Shh, keep your voice down.'

'Sorry. But I'm so angry. I felt like ramming Justin's teeth down his throat. There he was, lying there, in my bed. He's supposed to be a conchie – he doesn't believe in war. My God, neither do a lot of people, but that doesn't stop them fighting for their country, or dying for it. Not occupying someone else's bed and sharing his wife.' He stopped and noted Polly's sad face. 'I'm so sorry, Margaret, that was very thoughtless of me. I haven't even asked you if you've heard any more about your husband?'

'No, I haven't. The Red Cross are trying to trace him, they think he may have been in the Far East. He could be a prisoner-of-war.'

'I'm sorry to hear that. The Red Cross are very helpful. They'll tell you as soon as they find out something.'

'I know. David, what about your mother? She'll be heart-broken.'

'Oh, I don't know. She was never very fond of Yvonne. After all, we did get married without her knowing, and on the same day – and at almost the same time – as Dad died. I felt awful when I found out.'

'Yes, that was a shame.'

'So you see, when she hears . . .'

'You mustn't tell her any details. I know Sarah will understand, but please, use a bit of caution.'

His manner appeared pensive as he gently swirled the beer round in his glass. 'I did love Yvonne. But not now. I can see her for what she's really worth. It's not much.'

Polly looked at him. For the first time she noticed lines on his face. He looked tired. 'Where are you going to stay tonight?'

'I've got a sleeper booked. I travel back on the midnight train.' He looked at his watch. 'We have another three hours together. Do you fancy a walk?'

'Why not?' She finished her drink.

Outside they walked along to Piccadilly Circus.

'I wonder how long it will be before we see Eros again?' said Polly, looking up at the boarding that surrounded his plinth.

347

'Eros, the God of Love . . . But what a day that will be, when all the important statues are back in place,' said David, trying to be cheerful.

'Do you think this war will be over soon?'

His shoulders drooped again. 'I don't think so. I feel so frustrated being stuck up in Scotland after being in the thick of it a while back.'

'But somebody has to train the new pilots.'

'Yes, I know. But I'd still like to be up there fighting the bastards.' He kicked a stone; it rattled along the road before disappearing into a bomb site.

She wanted to hold him, love him, and tell him she didn't want him to fight. What if . . . The words wouldn't make themselves known in her head, and as if he was reading her thoughts, he said, 'Perhaps that was at the back of Yvonne's mind when she married me. Perhaps she thought she would be a widow with all . . .'

Polly turned on him. 'David, that's a wicked thing to say. I'm sure she loves you in her own way.'

'Maybe.'

Polly stopped and picked a daisy that was growing by the side of the bomb site, and unconsciously picked off the petals one by one.

'He loves me, He loves me not,' said David, watching her hands.

'What? Oh.' She looked at the flower that was now stripped of petals. She blushed, and quickly threw the stalk away, adding, 'Look at the lovely flowers that have grown out of nothing. But you can't believe that shops once filled these great empty holes.'

He took hold of her hand. 'Simple things make you happy, don't they?'

'Well, you know what they say about simple minds and all that.'

'I don't think that for one moment. The way you look at flowers and trees, it's almost as if you're seeing them for the first time. I noticed that at home – the way you gaze out of the windows.'

'Oh, but your garden is so lovely,' she said enthusiastically. 'And the way the seasons change! There's always something new to look at. If only cloth manufacturers could capture some of those colours.'

'See what I mean. I love that garden too. Sarah and I had some marvellous times playing there when we were children.'

'You were very lucky. All me and my brothers had was the street to play in. It must have been heaven to play on grass right outside your own door. I bet you never had many grazed knees?'

David laughed. 'Only when I went to school.'

'Did you ever play games like marbles, and knocking down ginger?'

'We played marbles, and conkers. What's knocking down ginger?'

'You bang on people's doors then run away. Sounds silly now.' She was so happy holding his hand as they strolled along. 'We had to go over the park to get our conkers, and we had to run like mad when the park-keeper came and chased us for throwing bits of wood up in trees to get the conkers down.'

He smiled and squeezed her hand. 'You're like a little ray of sunshine in my dark and miserable world. I can't tell you how pleased I am that I found you this evening.'

Polly wanted him to take her in his arms. If at that moment he'd ask her to go away with him she would have, willingly. But she also knew they were both married.

He looked at his watch. 'We'd better make our way back to the underground.'

In silence they turned and headed back. She knew at the underground David would be going one way and she the other.

'I'll see you on to your train,' he said and her heart leapt at the extra few minutes he was offering to spend with her.

They stood on the platform. Polly looked along at the people who had settled for the night. 'I've slept down here,' she said, searching for something to say.

'It must have been uncomfortable.'

'Not really. It's surprising what you can get used to . . .'

Her voice was drowned by the sound of an oncoming train. It pushed the air through the dark tunnel as it rattled to a stop.

Suddenly David took hold of her arms and kissed her full on the lips.

It was a long, hard kiss, and one to which she responded with all her heart.

Chapter 33

It was almost midnight when Polly arrived home. The house was in darkness. She silently closed the door behind her and crept up the stairs. The raids had been relatively light for months now, so they all took advantage of sleeping in their own beds. She didn't know if Sarah was home.

Polly had been happy, and her mind so full of the evening's events, that she had almost forgotten how angry she had been earlier. As she undressed and slipped into bed she felt guilty at being so annoyed with Sarah for going with Sid. After all, it was her business: she could go out with whom she pleased. Perhaps it was to buy cloth. She also felt guilty at the thought that she couldn't tell the family she had spent the evening with David.

Sleep didn't come easily. David filled her mind. Could he feel the same as she did? Was his kiss gratitude? She quickly dismissed that, as that kiss certainly wasn't brotherly. She gently touched her lips. The thrill of his kiss would keep her happy for a long while.

At breakfast the following morning Sarah announced she wouldn't be going to the factory as she was taking her mother to the synagogue. Mrs Bloom had been going to pray more frequently since the May raids, and whenever possible Sarah went with her.

'Not to worry,' said Polly, 'I'll make sure everything's in order.' She looked at her watch. 'Look at the time. I must dash.'

Sarah followed her into the hall and watched her putting on her hat. 'Was the film good?'

Polly continued pulling at her hat, and didn't meet her gaze. 'Didn't see it. I'll tell you why when I get home. Did you have a nice time last night?'

Sarah smiled wistfully. 'Yes, thank you.'

'Bye,' said Polly as she left. She was annoyed and hurt that Sarah hadn't offered to tell her all about her evening.

The morning raced on, and Polly's thoughts were full of last night, and David. Sarah really should have been in today. The parachutes were taking up more time than they had anticipated, and many evenings they had to work late. Polly even began taking work home: finishing off dresses on the machine Fred had installed a while back; doing buttonholes and the odd hem if they got too far behind with an order.

Polly was busy on her machine, but her mind was on David. Someone tapped her on the shoulder, making her jump. She swung round. 'What the hell are you playing at? I could have got my finger caught under the needle.'

'Sorry. Didn't know yer were ser engrossed.'

'What do you want here anyway? Miss Bloom's not here.'

'Ain't come ter see 'er, 'ave I?'

'I don't know.' She continued machining, and had to raise her voice to be heard. 'Did you have a good time last night?'

'Why?'

'Curious.'

'Well, yes, I did as a matter o' fact. But it ain't really none of yer business.'

'Where did you go?'

'Yer suddenly very interested in my affairs. What's yer game?'

Polly stopped machining and sat back. 'Did you take Sarah out last night?'

Sid began to laugh. 'Wot? Me take out the high and mighty Miss Bloom? Come orf it, Pol – could you honestly see 'er going out wiv the likes o' me? Wotever made yer fink that?'

Polly was stunned. 'Er, nothing, nothing.'

''Ere, she been out wiv someone and won't tell? 'Ere, she didn't say it was me, did she?'

'No, I mean, no she hasn't been out with . . . Oh, mind your own business. Anyway, what do you want?'

'Come ter see that little darling next door.'

'Who?'

'Young Rosie. She's a right little raver, I can tell yer.'

'She's married,' said Polly shortly.

So that was why Sid was always hanging around. Rosie!

'So's 'alf the girls round 'ere, but that's all right. 'Er old man's in the Navy.'

Polly suddenly thought of Yvonne. She must have had the same idea. 'You'll have to wait till Rosie's finished at one o'clock. We're a bit behind with our order, so don't go in there stopping the girls working.'

Sid sat on the edge of the table. 'OK.' He looked at his watch. 'All right if I just pop me nose round the door and tell 'er I'll see 'er in the pub when she's finished?'

'Well, yes. But don't stop them.'

He slid off the table. 'See yer later, Sis.'

Polly continued machining. Was Sid telling her the truth? On the whole she thought he probably was. But if so, who did Sarah go out with last night? She knew she would have to wait till this afternoon to find out; even then she would only know if Sarah was willing to tell.

Sarah and Mrs Bloom were in the garden when Polly arrived home. Mrs Bloom didn't cook now on a Saturday, as it was a Jewish holy day. Since the heavy bombing she had been attending her synagogue more and more, upholding her faith whenever possible. Sarah had told Polly she only went along to keep her mother happy, and felt guilty when they had a lot of work. Some Saturdays she managed to get into the factory.

'Hello, everything all right?' asked Polly.

'Fine,' said Sarah. 'I'll make a pot of tea.'

'Thanks. I'll do a bit of lunch in a minute,' said Polly, sitting in a deck chair. She closed her eyes and held her face up to the sun. 'It's a lovely day.'

'Yes, we must make the most of these few last days of summer. October will soon be here. Sarah said you didn't go to the pictures last night.'

Polly looked away. She couldn't face Mrs Bloom and tell her lies. 'No. I met a friend outside the cinema, and we went and had a drink.'

'That was nice.'

Sarah walked across the garden carrying a tray. 'What was nice?'

'Margaret was just saying she met a friend outside the cinema and they went for a drink.'

Well, that part wasn't lies, thought Polly.

'Anyone we know?' asked Sarah.

'No,' said Polly quickly, hoping her colour wouldn't rise. 'It was an old schoolfriend. Did you have a nice time last night?'

'Yes. I was telling Mother. Ted and I went out for a meal.'

'Ted?' inquired Polly, a little shocked. 'Who's Ted?'

Sarah paused. 'He's the policeman that came to the workshop earlier in the week. His real name's Edward, but he likes to be called Ted. I didn't say anything before in case it was just a one-off.'

There was a silence. Polly poured out the tea. 'And it isn't?' she asked.

'No.' Sarah smiled. 'I didn't like to say who I was going out with, as he was . . .'

'You didn't have to worry. I knew he was the one that arrested me.' She slowly stirred her tea. 'Besides, that part of my life is over now.' She looked knowingly at Sarah; they both knew Polly was only repeating what Sarah had said to her. Then Polly relaxed and laughed.

'You'll never guess who I thought it was?'

'No,' breathed Sarah, almost as if she was pleased the tension had been relieved.

'My brother Sid.'

Sarah threw back her head laughing. 'I'm sorry. I didn't mean to be rude. But your brother. Whatever made you think that?'

'Well, he'd been in just before, and I'm afraid I jumped to the wrong conclusions. I thought you were out buying cloth.'

Sarah sat forward. 'Well, I always did think he had a pretty face. But no, I'm not that gullible. So that's why I got a lecture?'

Polly nodded and sipped her tea, grateful the conversation had veered away from what she herself had done last night.

At the end of the following week, two letters arrived from David. One was to his mother, and one was for Polly.

Mrs Bloom seemed very happy reading hers, and eagerly passed every page to Sarah. Polly waited, wondering what he'd said in his letter. As they didn't make any comments, she assumed he hadn't told them about Yvonne, or that he'd been in London.

In the privacy of her room, Polly read her letter. In it he said he had written to Yvonne and asked her for a divorce. Many times he thanked her for listening to his problems, and said how he had enjoyed the evening with her. Then he began to say how much he thought of her, and how he was looking forward to Christmas when he hoped to get home. She felt herself go hot, and she panicked. What if they found themselves alone together? Could she trust herself to keep her distance? Her heart jumped. She wanted him, desperately, and she knew it was wrong. And she didn't want to deceive his family.

Four weeks had gone by and she still hadn't answered David's letter.

Mrs Bloom received another one. 'Margaret, David has asked me to remind you it's your turn to write.'

She tried to sound casual. 'Oh yes, I'll have to drop him a line. Mind you, there's not a lot to write about at the moment, not a lot has happened lately.'

'No, thank God. Anyway dear, when you get a few moments. I know he enjoys your letters.'

'Yes. Yes, when I get time.' Polly went to her room. She sat at her dressing-table, picked up her pen, and began writing. But she knew she must hide her feelings for a while longer.

Two weeks before Christmas, Polly and Sarah were coming home from work when Mrs Bloom opened the front door before they'd even arrived at the doorstep. The expression on her face told them something was wrong.

'What is it, Mother? You look as if you've seen a ghost.' Sarah quickly shut the front door behind them.

'Margaret,' whispered Mrs Bloom. 'There's another telegram for you.'

With trembling hands, Polly lifted the buff envelope.

'Would you like me to . . .?' asked Sarah.

Polly shook her head. She sat down and opened it. 'It's Billy,' she croaked, handing the paper to Sarah.

'Missing believed killed.' Sarah only read that part out loud. 'Oh Margaret, what can we say?'

She wasn't listening; her thoughts were full of Billy. With her face buried in her hands, she knew if she tried hard enough she could see his face through her tears. His baby cherub face, happy and smiling. Sobs wracked her body.

Mrs Bloom rested a hand on her shoulder. 'I'm so sorry, Margaret. What can we say?'

Polly looked up. 'He can't be dead. He's too young to die. It's not fair.'

'I'm afraid, my dear, that there's a lot in this world that isn't fair,' said Mrs Bloom.

Polly was lost for words. 'I loved Billy,' she said at last. 'He was like my dad you know, good and kind. I can't lose any more. First Mum, then Ron missing. And now Billy,' she added softly. 'There's only me and Sid left.'

'But we don't know if . . .' Sarah started to say, but Polly suddenly shouted her down.

'They wouldn't say "believed killed" if they weren't sure. He must have been blown to bits.'

Mrs Bloom took in a sharp breath. 'They could be wrong. We mustn't lose hope.'

'They only said Ron was missing, and that was months ago, and I still haven't heard if he's safe.' She picked up her handbag and stood up. 'I'm going upstairs for a little while.'

'I'll bring you up a cup of tea,' said Sarah gently.

'And I'll call you when dinner's ready,' said Mrs Bloom.

In the quiet of her room she cried long and hard for Billy. When her tears began to subside, she sat and wrote to David.

Chapter 34

It was the week before Christmas, and Polly was sitting at the table reading the letter she had received that morning from Shirley. In it she asked her to come to Bristol for the holiday. Polly mulled over the happy thought of seeing Shirley and Elizabeth again after all this time. Elizabeth was three years old now. She folded the letter when Sarah put the cocoa on the table.

Polly had been feeling pretty miserable, as a letter from David which had arrived a few days earlier had told her he couldn't get home for Christmas. That letter was in answer to hers, the one in which she had told him about Billy. She had also finally poured out her heart, and confessed that she loved him. And despite still being married to Ron, promised she would help him get over Yvonne. His reply had been warm and loving. He didn't know when he would be home, and said he would wait till they were all together before explaining to Sarah and his mother how much they cared for each other. He didn't want to write and tell them – he said that was a coward's way out. Nor did he want her to be alone with the family when they learned of the situation.

That letter had made Polly both happy and sad. Happy because now they had both revealed their innermost feelings to each other, and sad because she didn't know when she would see him again.

'Sarah,' said Polly, still holding Shirley's letter. 'I'd like to go and see Shirley over Christmas. Would it be all right if I left

359

at lunch-time on Thursday as it's Christmas Eve?'

'Why not take the day off and catch an early train?' Sarah pushed a cup of steaming cocoa towards Polly.

'Would you mind?'

'Of course not. Mind you, it's going to be a very lonely Christmas without you and David. But no, you must go. Besides, you could do with a break.'

'It's been two and a half years since I saw her. A lot of water's flowed under the bridge since then.' Polly looked wistful. 'I'm glad she still writes. I wonder if she's changed?'

'I shouldn't think so. Shirley will always be the same, happy-go-lucky Shirley. I'm pleased you've kept in touch though I know Mother will be disappointed.' Sarah put her elbows on the table and clasped her hands round her cup. 'She was upset at David not coming home, and was surprised he didn't mention what Yvonne would be doing this Christmas. Same as last year, I expect, when David couldn't get home – she'll be spending it with her own group of friends. I know she thinks we're very boring.'

'Will you be seeing Ted over Christmas?' Polly wanted to change the subject quickly. She knew David hadn't told Sarah or Mrs Bloom about him wanting to divorce Yvonne.

'Yes, we're going to a Christmas Eve dance.' She smiled. 'It's years since I've been to one of those. The last one was when Dad was alive. That was three years ago. That was when we got home and found we'd been . . .' She suddenly stopped.

'That was when you were robbed,' prompted Polly bravely.

'Yes.' She moved away from the table and walked over to the sink. 'That's all in the past now.'

'I remember that lovely dress you wore that night.'

'Yes, it was the blue crepe.'

'I bet it looked lovely. What are you going to wear at this one?'

'I don't know. I'm not even sure if people are still wearing long dresses for evening.'

'I should think so, especially on Christmas Eve. After all, you wouldn't feel dressed if you went in everyday clothes. And what about all the girls in uniform, I bet they'll be glad to put on something a little more feminine.'

'I suppose so. I'll have to sort out something in my wardrobe.'

'Don't forget, give me time if you want anything altered.'

'I don't think I've put on any weight, not with the rations we get.'

'Oh come on, Sarah, we don't do so badly,' said Polly, washing out her cocoa cup. 'I'm off to bed.'

'So am I. Don't wake Mother as you go up.'

'No. See you in the morning. And Sarah. Thanks.'

'Go on with you. After all you've been through, you deserve a holiday.'

A week later, Polly caught the early train to Bristol. As usual the station was packed with people on the move. She managed to find a seat, and settled down with a magazine.

When she arrived, she surprised herself by remembering which bus to catch. It was almost midday when she arrived at Shirley's house.

Vera's jaw dropped with astonishment when she opened the door. They hugged each other, then stood back. 'Polly, what a shock. I never thought we'd see you here. Shirley said something about you staying in London. Have the raids been bad again?'

'No,' said Polly laughing. 'I thought I'd come to see you.'

'Come on in. I've just got to give the kids and Mum their dinners. Did you want something to eat?'

'I haven't brought a ration book, but I've brought a few bits Mrs Bloom did up for me.'

'Are you staying over Christmas?'

'If I'm not in the way.'

'Course you won't be in the way.'

'I couldn't let Shirley know – it was a last-minute thing.'

Vera put her arm round Polly's shoulders. 'She'll be tickled pink to see you. Take your hat and coat off and come into the kitchen. We can talk in there.'

Polly was pleased Vera made her so welcome. Being a few years apart, they had never really had that much in common. Sarah Bloom always said that after many years the age gap shortens. Polly thought that between her and Vera, at that moment, it was true.

Polly looked round the cosy kitchen. The heat from the range was giving Elizabeth's, Judy's and Jane's cheeks a rosy glow. She swallowed the lump in her throat when she recalled the last time she was here. The twins had been sitting there on the floor where the girls were, and now Terry had gone.

Vera closed the door. 'Mum's still pretty bad,' and, as if reading Polly's thoughts, added, 'They still don't know what's wrong with her. She's in the front room – we've got her bed in there. It saves me keep running up and down the stairs, and it's company for her when the kids wander in and out. Betty, this is your Auntie Polly, she's come to stay for a few days.'

Elizabeth looked up from her colouring book. She had big blue eyes that twinkled mischievously, and a mop of dark hair. Polly could see Shirley in her smile.

'We've got a Christmas tree, d'yer wanner see it?' she lisped. 'It ain't very big.'

'Of course,' said Polly eagerly. 'You must show me later, after you've had your dinner.'

'Me and Judy's made lots o' paper chains. Grandad helped us put 'em up.'

'Did you know Father Christmas is coming to us tonight?' asked Judy.

'Yes, I do know. You two girls have certainly grown. How old are you now?'

'I'm nearly four, and Betty's three. She's only a baby,' said Judy confidently, pointing to Jane.

'Will 'e know you're 'ere?' asked Elizabeth. 'Have you been good? Vera said 'e only comes ter good children.'

'He's very clever. I'm sure he'll know I'm here. Have you been good?'

Elizabeth looked at Vera. 'Sometimes,' she whispered.

Vera put the plates on the table, and lifted Jane into her high chair. 'Right, girls, eat your dinner up. I'll make us a pot of tea.'

'She's the image of you, Vera. Is your husband OK?'

'As far as we know, but you know what it's like.'

Polly nodded. 'Where's James?'

'He's at a friend's.'

Polly crouched on the floor and began undoing her case. 'I've brought some tea and sugar, and there's a bit of butter. There's also some biscuits, a tin of corned beef, and Mrs Bloom has made us a cake. And,' she made the word sound long. 'De da!' With a great flourish she produced a tin of salmon.

'Salmon.' Vera's eyes lit up. 'We haven't seen that for years. I don't get time to stand in queues all day for those sort of luxuries. Not with the kids and Mum to look after.'

'Well, Mrs Bloom has a lot of friends, and we don't have bacon in our house, so I expect she does a bit of swapping.'

Elizabeth was leaning over the table gazing into Polly's case. 'Wot's them?' she asked, pointing at some neatly wrapped packets.

'They could be for good little girls. Do you know any?'

'Me, me!' shouted Elizabeth and Judy together, with Jane laughing and joining in the racket by banging her spoon on her plate.

'Well, you'll have to wait till Christmas, because that's when it's a magic time, and we get to open all our interesting parcels,' said Polly, closing the lid of her old battered brown suitcase.

'Don't know about that;' said Vera. 'Things are so hard to get, you just don't know what to get the kids. When I remember the Christmases we had.'

'I always think of the big trees you had at Christmas in Penn's Place.'

It was Vera's turn to look sad. 'That was a shame about your mum. Shirley said our old house has gone now.'

'Yes, there's so many changes. You wouldn't recognize half the streets now with so many houses missing. But enough of

363

this doom and gloom. How's Shirley?'

'Blooming, and you look well. Are you happy?' asked Vera.

Polly blushed. 'I was feeling a bit down, but now I'm here .
. . Yes, I am happy.'

'I was really upset to hear about our Ron after Terry, and about your Billy. He was a nice little thing. I don't suppose you've had any more news?'

'No.' Polly shook her head sadly. 'Can I go and see Mum?'

'I'll take her dinner in. Mind you, I don't know why I bother, she only eats like a bird. You wait till you see the change in her. I'll tell her you're here first. She's very weepy, more so since Terry and Ron have been missing.' She put a small amount of dinner on a plate and put the plate on a tray. 'Me and Shirl's going to a dance tonight. Dad's looking after the kids. Have you brought your glad rags? It could be good, it's at the camp Shirl's Ben's at.'

'So that's why you've got your curlers in? What's Ben like?'

Vera tugged at her turban and pushed the ends of her metal curlers out of sight. 'Well, we've got to try and dolly ourselves up a bit, ain't we? Ben's nice. I'll take this in to Mum, then I'll tell you all about him.'

Polly sat next to Elizabeth. 'Do you like Ben?'

'He brings us lots of sweets.'

'You're very lucky girls. I don't get many sweets now.'

'Ain't yer got a Ben then?' asked Judy.

Polly laughed. 'No, I haven't got a Ben.'

Vera returned. 'Mum was so pleased to hear it was you – she knew somebody had arrived. Pop in now, while she's still awake.'

Polly crept into the front room. 'Hello Mum. It's me, Polly.' She was taken aback at the sight of this frail-looking woman who was propped up on a mound of pillows, picking at her dinner.

''Allo, Polly love.' She held out a thin, bony hand. 'It's good ter see yer after all these years. Yer look very nice. How are yer?'

'I'm fine. What about you? What have you been up to?' Polly fought to hold back the tears. Was this the buxom Mrs Bell, her kind mother-in-law who always made her so welcome? The jolly Mrs Bell who made her a birthday cake just after she came out of hospital, after the fish bone had gone in her eye?

'Dunno. The doctor finks I'm suffering from tireditis. Christ, after seven kids and an old man who yer didn't know if 'e was at work or in the pub, I'm entitled to have a little rest. Blimey it's a wonder I'm still 'ere.' She lay back exhausted after her speech.

'You shouldn't tire yourself like that. I'll come in and see you a bit later on. You lie back and rest now. Is there anything you want?'

'No fanks, love. 'Ere, take this tray out for me.'

''Course.' She plumped up Mrs Bell's pillows and left.

All afternoon, Vera and Polly talked about the old days. She played with Judy and Elizabeth, helped do their tea and, after they were bathed and were ready for bed, she said she would read them a story.

'I could do with you around every day,' said Vera, after giving her mother her tea. 'Shirley should be home soon. I can't believe it's Christmas Eve. Years ago we always had the afternoon off and finished up in a pub.'

'Those days are over for a while. I'm surprised that Shirley's got Christmas Day off.'

With a child perched on each knee, Polly settled down to read. She was happy and contented. This was going to be a nice Christmas.

The front door shut with a bang.

'That could be James,' said Vera. 'No, it sounds more like our Shirley.'

The girls jumped off Polly's lap and raced out of the room yelling, 'Shirley, Shirley. Auntie Polly's 'ere.'

'What?' screamed Shirley. The kitchen door flew open and she was across the room in one bound, sweeping Polly off her feet and hugging the breath out of her. 'I don't believe it.' She covered her face with kisses. 'It's you. It's really you?'

When Polly got her breath back she laughed. 'Are you pleased to see me?'

'Pleased, pleased? I should say so.' She hugged her again. 'Are you staying over Christmas?'

'Till Sunday – that's if you'll have me, and I've got me breath back.'

Shirley threw her handbag, gas-mask and coat on a kitchen chair. She was wearing navy wool slacks and a red turtle-neck jumper under her overall. Her hair was hidden in a brightly coloured scarf that was twisted into a turban. 'What d'yer think of Betty? She's grown since you last saw her.'

'She certainly has. Me and her are great friends.' Polly held out her hand and Elizabeth grabbed hold of it.

'Shirley, Father Christmas is coming to Aunt Polly as well tonight,' said Judy.

'That's good,' said Shirley. 'Did Vera tell you we're going to a dance?'

'Yes, and that's going to give me a chance to meet this Ben I've been hearing so much about.'

Shirley went all starry-eyed. 'Oh Pol, 'e really is smashing. I can't believe 'e likes me.'

Vera laughed. 'Likes, that's the biggest understatement I've heard in months. He's soppy about her.'

'I'm so pleased for you,' said Polly.

Soon afterwards, James came in. Polly was amazed at the change in him. He was now a quiet, shy ten-year-old. His straight dark hair rested on his forehead, and dark button eyes behind his silver-rimmed glasses made him look stern as well as very intelligent. He told her how much he liked school and reading, and wanted to pass his scholarship and go to high school.

'He's the brainy one in the family,' said Vera, rubbing the top of his head. 'He likes reading to Mum. He's a good boy.'

James pushed Vera's hand away, and blushed at the compliment.

Mr Bell followed a little later, and he went through the same ritual of kissing and hugging Polly.

When they finished tea, the youngsters were put to bed, and the girls started getting ready for the dance.

'I feel like a kid again,' said Polly. 'I'm ever so excited.'

'You daft 'aporth. You can sleep that side of the bed. We'll 'ave ter share the mirror, so don't take too long putting yer face on.'

'I'm glad I'm in here with you. D'you know, I can't remember the last dance I went to.' She suddenly stopped; she did remember. It had been when she was in the NAAFI.

'What's up?'

'Nothing.' Polly sat at the dressing-table.

'You shut up quick.'

'Well, yes.' Polly didn't want to tell Shirley about those days. Life had been so strange then – like someone adrift. 'Anyway, tell me about Ben.'

''E's in the Canadian Air Force, and comes from Toronto. 'E worked in a garage before 'e went in the Air Force. 'E's tall, good-looking, with short brown 'air and lovely big brown eyes. He talks with a drawl and I love 'im.' Shirley giggled. 'I never fought I'd ever say that.'

Polly looked at her through the mirror. 'I'm so pleased for you. What does he say about Elizabeth?'

Shirley looked away. 'He likes 'er.'

'That all?'

'Pol. I ain't told 'im she's mine.'

'What? He's been here and seen her. He must know. She calls you Mum.' Polly stopped. 'No she doesn't.'

'Why doesn't she call you Mum?'

'I think it's because of Judy, they fink they're sisters. Well, I've never really looked after 'er, 'ave I? First it was Mum, now Vera. Truth ter tell is, I don't suppose the poor little cow knows who 'er mother is.'

'Or her father,' said Polly.

'She's 'appy enough though. She gits plenty of love from all

367

of us. Cheer up, don't let's be miserable, this is Christmas Eve and we're gonner 'ave a good time ternight, I promise yer.'

'Of course we are. I love the way you're wearing your hair. How do you keep it all piled up on top like that?'

Shirley took the cigarette that was dangling from her bright red lips, and placed it in the ash-tray. She bent down to look in the mirror. 'Masses of grips and plenty of spit.' She licked her fingers and ran them up her hair. 'I put a drop of sugar water on the little bits at the back ter keep 'em up, but don't tell our Vera, she'll go mad if she thinks I'm using up the rations.' She straightened up and looked back over her shoulder. 'D'yer fink it looks a bit like Betty Grable's?'

Polly laughed. 'Only a bit. Here, you've not got your legs insured for a million dollars, have you?'

Shirley lifted her skirt. 'And what's wrong with these pins?'

'Nothing. Mind you, you always did like to keep up with all the latest fashions. That's a nice dress.'

''Ere, 'ark at you – dress. We always used ter call 'em frocks.'

Again they laughed like a couple of schoolgirls.

'What d'yer fink of this utility stuff?'

'Not a lot, but we've got to put up with it. We try to make our designs a little bit different, but we have to comply with the Board of Trade regulations.'

Shirley laughed. 'I love the long words yer use now.' She picked up the lipstick-stained cigarette and drew long and hard on it, sending the smoke upwards. 'When me leg make-up's dry, could you pencil a seam in for me? I ain't got any coupons left ter get meself a new pair o' stockings. Bloody clothes rationing. Now we're earning a few bob, we still can't buy all we want. How are you doin'?'

'Not too bad. Me and Sarah manage to get hold of the odd bit of cloth now and again. It's surprising what you can make out of scraps. We're making parachutes now; it's lovely stuff, and we make smashing underwear out of the bits that get spoiled

– you can't use any material that's got holes in.'

'I should fink not. Cor, I'd like some of that. 'Ere, I bet a lot gets spoiled.'

'No, a bloke from the Ministry checks all that, and if there was too much waste we could lose the contract.' Polly smiled to herself. This year's Christmas present was going to be well received. 'Sid does something on the black market. Don't know how he gets the stuff but he's been to the factory a couple of times with a suitcase full of it.'

'Trust 'im. Mind you, we can get 'old of a bit o' gear without coupons now and again, but they don't 'arf charge over the top fer it.'

'What about your dad? He should know a few wrinkles. I'm surprised you don't pinch his coupons.'

'We don't see any of 'em. Dad's got himself a lady friend. I fink she gits some of 'is. She's the one that does the fire-watching with him. I told you about it in me letter.'

'Yes, I know.' Polly looked upset. 'Are you sure it's true. I didn't think he was like that, and what with your mum lying ill . . .'

Vera opened the bedroom door. 'Hurry up, you two. Ben will be here soon.'

'Just got to get Polly to do me seams,' said Shirley, standing on a chair.

'OK, but don't be long.'

'Keep still,' said Polly, carefully drawing a long thin line down the back of Shirley's leg with a black eyebrow pencil. 'OK, all done.'

The bedroom door opened again. A lump came to Polly's throat when she looked down on Elizabeth standing there in her long cream winceyette nightie. She was all pink and shining after her bath; her hair had a lovely sheen, and her big eyes sparkled. Polly wanted to sweep her up in her arms and crush her to her.

''E ain't been yet Shirley.'

'And 'e won't come all the while you're wandering about.

Now, back to bed with you, young lady.' Shirley playfully patted her daughter's bottom.

'Come on,' said Polly. 'I'll take you back to bed. But you must close your eyes tight and go to sleep. Father Christmas only comes when you're asleep.' Polly and Elizabeth left the room hand-in-hand.

'You look ever so nice, Auntie Polly,' said Judy.

'Well, thank you. And you two look ever so nice as well. Now jump into bed and I'll tuck you in. Don't make a noise, otherwise you'll wake Jane.' She looked in the cot at the tousle-haired little girl who was fast asleep. 'Good night – God bless,' she whispered, quietly closing the door behind her.

The doorbell rang and Shirley flew down the stairs. Polly picked up their handbags and followed her.

In the hall, Shirley was in Ben's arms. When they broke away Shirley said, 'This is my best friend, Polly.'

'Well hello, Polly.' He held out his free hand, the other still tightly gripping Shirley's trim waist. 'I've heard so much about you, I feel I know you already.'

'Me too.'

'Are you staying over Christmas?'

'Yes.'

'Come on Vera,' yelled Shirley. With Ben's help she pulled on her coat.

'Coming.' She came out of her mother's bedroom. 'Just saying goodnight to Mum. Ben, you've got three lovely young ladies to escort you tonight.'

Ben laughed. 'I can see I'm going to be the envy of the camp. But I've a feeling I'm gonner lose you two beauties before too long. Are we all ready? Right girls, grab your gas-masks, and we'll be off.'

Polly smiled. She could see why Shirley had fallen for this good-looking, smooth-talking guy, but she was a little worried. What if he found out Elizabeth was Shirley's? Would he be upset? Polly knew she would have to watch what she said and not let the cat out of the bag. After all, if it was that serious,

Shirley would tell him in her own good time.

Before Vera switched out the light in order to open the front door, Polly glanced up the stairs at two pairs of eyes looking through the banisters at them. She hastily blew them a kiss.

Chapter 35

Polly's feet were aching when she climbed out of the lorry, but she didn't care. She couldn't remember ever having enjoyed herself so much. The music had been swinging. The dances had been non-stop, and the company of so many charming young men delightful.

Shirley was still locked in Ben's arms when Vera slipped the key in the front door.

'Come on, Shirl!' she shouted. 'We're waiting to go in. It's cold out here.'

Ben jumped back into the lorry next to the driver. The lorry roared away, its tiny rear lights disappearing into the night, while Ben, leaning out of the window, blew kisses till they were out of sight.

'Watch the black-out,' said Vera, scrabbling in the dark to close the door and pulling the black curtains across before switching on the light.

'You looked like you was 'aving a good time tonight, Pol,' said Shirley, trying to keep her voice down.

'Not half. I love this modern music.' She started swinging her legs in a jitterbugging fashion.

'Shh,' said Vera.

'Sorry,' giggled Polly.

'Fancy a cup of cocoa?' asked Vera.

'Course,' said Shirley in a loud whisper as they passed Mrs Bell's door.

They sat at the large, well-scrubbed kitchen table, drinking

373

their cocoa. The warmth from the kitchen range was comforting, bringing a healthy glow to their cheeks.

Polly began to giggle again.

'What's tickled you?' asked Shirley.

'Your hair. You looked so elegant when you went out this evening; now you look like you've been dragged through a hedge backwards.'

'Thanks,' said Shirley, removing a hairgrip. She tucked the stray hairs that had fallen down back up, and secured them with the hairgrip she'd opened with her teeth. 'There, that better?'

'Much. I wonder if Father Christmas has been,' said Polly.

'Christ, I almost forgot. Shirl, where're those bits we've got the kids?'

'Under me bed. I'll pop up and get 'em.'

She returned a few minutes later carrying a brown-paper carrier bag. As she placed each item on the table, she said. 'Two picture books, and two colouring books, one each for the girls, and a fluffy duck for them and Jane, a propelling pencil for James, and a atlas.'

Polly looked at the toys. 'Is that it?'

''Fraid that's all we could get. A girl at work's mother made the ducks. It's bloody 'ard, but Ben's been great. 'E's got 'em some chocolate and a orange each.'

'They're in that cupboard,' said Vera, waving a limp hand in the direction of the cupboard. 'D'you remember we used to have oranges coming out of our ears when Dad had the fruit stall?' She sighed and picked up an orange Shirley had plonked on the table. 'Now I don't think Betty or Judy will know what it is. I'll be glad when this war's over.'

They all went silent. Polly guessed that, like her, they were thinking back on their own childhood, and past happy Christmases, and about the members of the family who weren't here to share it with them.

Shirley jumped up. 'I'll just wash these cups up, then we've got to put these bits in their pillow cases.'

'I'll see to the cups,' said Polly. 'You carry on. I've never played Father Christmas before.'

The following morning Polly opened her eyes to find her arm being shaken vigorously. The room was dark and she felt totally disorientated.

'Auntie Polly, Auntie Polly, wake up. Quick, wake up. He's been, he's been.'

'Who's been?' she croaked, squinting and gradually beginning to focus on somebody climbing in beside her, dragging a pillow case with them. Polly's mouth felt like the inside of an old boot.

'Father Christmas, silly,' said Judy, who had just walked in with her pillow case slung over her shoulder. Her mouth had the tell-tale stain of chocolate round it. She scrambled up and joined Elizabeth in the bed.

'Go away. Move over,' grunted Shirley.

'Oh come on, don't be a misery,' said Polly, sitting up. 'It's Christmas.' She began tickling Shirley.

'There's no rest for the wicked, is there?' said Shirley, struggling to stay in the bed.

'Look!' shouted Elizabeth excitedly as one by one the simple objects were taken out and proudly displayed. The orange was tossed to one side.

'What's wrong with this?' asked Polly, picking it up. 'It's got teeth marks in it.'

'Ehggg. I don't like it, it tastes rotten,' said Judy.

Polly laughed. 'You're supposed to peel it first. I'll show you how later. Now let's see what else you've got.'

With every item shoved under their noses, both Polly and Shirley registered surprise, and uttered the right oohs and aahs. Polly could have cried at the pleasure these simple things had given the children.

'We mustn't go downstairs yet till Vera says so,' said Judy.

'I want to see if he's left anyfink under the tree,' said Elizabeth.

'I'll slip my dressing-gown on and ask Vera how long we've got to wait,' said Polly.

'Polly,' said Shirley abruptly.

Polly stopped and looked over her shoulder at her friend, surprised at her alarmed tone.

'What is it?'

'We didn't know you were coming, so I'm, well . . . There's nothing . . .'

Polly leant over the bed and threw her arms round her neck. 'You daft 'aporth. You're my Christmas present. Being here with you lot is more than enough for me.' She kissed her cheek loudly. 'Right girls, let's go and find Vera.'

'She's getting Jane ready,' said Judy.

Polly turned in the doorway to see Shirley wiping her eyes on the sheet. 'Vera'll go mad when she sees all that mascara on that sheet.'

'Scram.' Polly ducked as a pillow came hurtling towards her.

Vera gave them permission to go down, but added a word of warning. 'Don't touch anything till Shirley and Grandad are there.'

'All right,' said Judy, running down the stairs.

'And hold on to the banisters,' Vera called after her.

Polly pulled back the heavy black-out curtains in the dining-room. Brilliant sunlight streamed through the window. 'Doesn't look as if you'll be playing snowballs today, girls.'

''Allo, Polly love, fancy a cuppa? I've just made one.'

'You're up, Grandad?' said Judy.

'With all the racket you two make, it's enough ter wake the dead.'

'Look, oh look!' screamed the two girls, jumping up and down. 'Look at all the presents under the tree.'

Polly smiled. This year the tree was no more than a few branches and twigs Vera had found in the garden. They were stuck in a pot she'd covered with crepe paper. The tree had some tinsel draped over it; a few baubles and stars dangled to give it the festive look. Polly had put her presents on the floor with the family's after the girls had gone to bed.

When breakfast was finished, Vera put the chicken in the oven and they all sat and opened their presents. Even Mrs Bell managed to shuffle into the dining-room.

Shirley and Vera were holding up the French knickers Polly had made for them from pieces of parachute silk. Shirley also had a matching slip.

'These are really smashing, I'll have ter keep 'em fer me honeymoon,' said Shirley.

Vera gently folded hers. 'I'll save these till Sam comes home.'

'You always was good wiv yer needle,' said Mrs Bell. 'But yer shouldn't 'ave bovered wiv gitting me anyfink.'

Polly looked hurt. 'Don't you like the bath salts?'

'Course she does, and fanks, girl, fer me beer mug,' said her father-in-law.

The two girls had a rag doll that Elsie Mann at the factory had made in her dinner-hour from some of the waste. Polly had made the clothes, and there was a stuffed rabbit for Jane. James was hardest to find something for in the hurriedly put-together presents, but the small case holding a set of compasses Sarah had given her when she told her of her problem was proving to be a great success.

After dinner, they relaxed and played with the children.

'I'll start getting the tea ready,' said Vera.

'D'you want any help?' asked Polly.

'No, you play with the kids. I'm only doing a few sandwiches.'

'I'll lay the table,' said Shirley.

'Is Ben coming round tonight?' asked Mr Bell.

'Yer. He hopes ter be 'ere be seven. Why?'

'Nothing, I'm going down the wardens' post later, so I might miss 'im.'

'Don't worry, I expect 'e's got sumfink fer yer.' Shirley turned to Polly. 'Sometimes 'e brings Dad in a little drop o' whisky.'

'Real good stuff it is an all,' said Mr Bell, licking his lips.

Vera walked in carrying the plate of sandwiches.

'I don't think I could manage any,' said Mrs Bell.

'I think you'll be able to manage one little one, Mum,' said Vera, grinning.

'Why? Wotcher put in 'em, love?'

'Salmon.'

'Salmon?' yelled Shirley and her father together.

'Salmon?' said Mrs Bell. 'Where did that come from?'

Vera laughed. 'Polly brought it with her.'

'Gawd bless yer Pol. You're a good girl,' said Mr Bell.

Polly laughed. 'Who ever thought a tin of salmon would be so popular?'

'Come on, eat 'em up,' said Vera.

Everybody dived on the sandwiches, smacking their lips and relishing every morsel, to the wonder of the children who couldn't make out what all the fuss was about.

'Tastes just like fishpaste,' said Judy.

'Heathen,' said Vera.

After tea Mr Bell went to the wardens' post, and Mrs Bell decided to go to bed.

'Ain't yer gonner wait till Ben gets 'ere?' asked Shirley. ''E should be 'ere any minute now.'

'Well, all right. I'll wait just another 'alf an 'our, then I'll be orf. It's been a long day.'

'You've done very well, Mum,' said Vera, plumping up the cushions behind her.

She lay back and closed her eyes.

The knocking on the front door woke her. 'Who's that?'

'It's probably Ben,' said Shirley, going to answer the door.

It was a few minutes before she returned. She looked flushed and her lipstick was smudged. Ben walked in behind her.

'Hi everybody. Hi kids. What did Santa bring you?'

'Lots,' said the girls, running up to him.

He bent down and put his arms round them.

'Look Ben. I got a compass, and a propelling pencil, and it's

378

got some spare leads,' said James.

Ben stood up. 'And what did you get?' he asked Shirley.

She giggled. 'Me and Vera 'ave got a smashing pair of French knickers.'

'Shirley,' said Vera embarrassed.

'Polly made 'em. I'll show you later.'

'I'm going orf now. Nice ter see yer, Ben.' Mrs Bell stood up and asked sadly, 'D'yer miss yer family at this time o' year?'

'I've only got a mom, and a married sister, and yes, I miss 'em a lot.'

'Come on, we're going to play cards, so get your money out,' said Vera, trying to ease the tension.

'I'll see to Mum,' said Shirley.

When she came back, Ben began giving the children bars of chocolate. He handed Shirley, Vera and Polly a small parcel each.

'What is it?' asked Polly.

'Open them and see.'

The gasps that came from the three girls told it all. Shirley leapt up and kissed Ben and Vera gave him a hug.

'Ben, that's very nice of you, but you shouldn't have,' said Polly.

'Why's that? Don't you like them?'

'Like them. I've never seen anything so lovely in my life.' She held the packet to her cheek. 'My first pair of nylons. I've heard all about them, but never owned any. They're so sheer I shall be frightened to wear them.'

Shirley laughed. 'Me and Vera have 'ad 'em before, but you 'ave ter be ever so careful wiv 'em.'

'I can't get them very often. By the way, honey, I've got another little pressy for you.' He took a small package from his pocket and handed it to her.

Her face flushed, and her eyes filled with tears when she opened the box. She flung her arms round his neck, and kissed his face all over.

'Hold on, hold on. I didn't expect that kind of reaction. Do you like it?'

'Like it, like it. I love it. 'Ere put it on.' She held out her left hand.

After Ben put the ring on her finger she proudly showed it to everyone, wiggling her fingers to show off the three diamonds to their best advantage.

After all the congratulations and kisses, the children were put to bed.

For the rest of the evening they laughed, played cards, and had a few drinks. Then all too soon it was time for Ben to go back to camp. Polly and Vera tidied the room and did the washing-up while Shirley was busy saying good night to him. Half an hour later she emerged looking happy and relaxed.

Later, in the quiet of their bedroom, Shirley asked, 'D'yer like 'im, Pol?'

It was dark and they were both lying on their backs; neither could sleep.

'Yes, I do. I think he's smashing. When are you going to get married?'

'Dunno. 'E's finding out about it. It's not like getting married over 'ere. I fink I 'ave ter 'ave a medical and blood tests.'

'Whatever for?'

'I dunno, it's ter do wiv their laws.'

'Can't say I'd fancy that. But still, you must think he's worth it.'

'Oh, I do. I can't wait ter go ter Canada.'

Polly propped herself up on her elbow. 'What about Elizabeth?'

'I don't know. I'll tell 'im later on. No point in upsetting the apple cart just yet. A lot can 'appen, as you well know. D'yer miss Ron? Don't yer ever fancy another bloke?'

Polly quickly lay down again. 'Shirley. I need to talk to someone.'

It was Shirley's turn to prop herself up. 'Why? What's 'appened?'

'Nothing yet. But I'm afraid it's going to.'

'Christ, don't keep me dangling. What's all this about?'

'David Bloom.'

'David Bloom?' repeated Shirley loudly. 'Why? What's 'e done?'

'Shh, keep your voice down.'

'Sorry. 'E's married to that, Yvonne somebody, the film star, ain't 'e?'

'Yes, but he's going to divorce her. He found her in bed with her producer.'

'No. So, what's that to do with you?'

'Well, I met him in London, and we went for a drink. And well, we've found we love each other.'

'What?'

'Shh.'

Polly sat up. 'I've known for a long while how I felt about him, but I didn't think he cared for me – well, not in that way.'

'It's not just on the rebound, is it? 'E's not looking for a bit on the side, is 'e?'

'No, I don't think so. Besides, it wouldn't be the likes of me, and remember I live in his mother's house.'

'Well, yeah. So what yer worried about?'

'Well, I am married to your brother.'

'Yeah, but 'e's still missing. You ain't 'eard any more from the Red Cross?'

'Only that he was in the Far East. They still only say he's missing; they won't commit themselves. He could be in a prisoner-of-war camp.'

'Wiv the Japs?'

'Yes,' whispered Polly.

'But wouldn't they know?'

'I don't know. Shirley, what am I going to do? If David does divorce Yvonne, I'd like to marry him one day.'

'Bloody 'ell.'

'But I can't leave Ron, not legally. What if he's still alive? It wouldn't be right.'

'What does 'is sister 'ave ter say about it?'

'I don't know. We haven't said anything to her yet.'

'Yer got yerself a bit of a problem there. David Bloom's a Jew, ain't 'e? 'Ere, does 'e wear one of those funny little skull-caps?'

'You mean a yamulke.'

''Ere, 'ark at you using all the right words.'

'It's surprising the words you can pick up living with them. But no. David's not practising.'

Shirley giggled. ''Ere. 'E ain't been, you know?' She nudged Polly. 'Circumcised. 'As 'e?'

Polly laughed. 'I don't know. I should think so. You are nosy.'

'Yer, but 'e's still a Jew.'

'Yes, I know. But he doesn't go to the synagogue. Only Mrs Bloom goes there. Sarah takes her, but she isn't at all orthodox.'

'She never was; most Saturdays she came in ter work. What's this boyfriend of 'er's like? Is 'e a Jew?'

'No. I told you all about him in my letter. He's a detective-sergeant or something.'

'Oh yeah. I don't suppose Yvonne is Jewish.'

'No.'

'What if they 'ad a kid?'

'Mrs Bloom once told me that in their religion the mother has the right to say what faith she wishes to bring her child up in. Not that I could ever see Yvonne with a child.'

'Yer never know.'

'Well, I don't think it would be David's.'

'Would you have liked a kid?'

'Sometimes I think I would have, but it was never to be.'

'Yer, it's a shame yer can't 'ave any.'

'Yes, but then again, perhaps it was meant to be that way after all that's happened to me.'

'What d'yer mean? Yer going ter prison?'

'That, and other things.'

'Pol. I know I said it in me letters, but I was real sorry about wearing yer brooch that day.'

'Forget it. It's all in the past now.'

'What was prison like?'

'Bearable, I suppose.'

'Don't yer 'old any grudges?'

'No.'

'Not even against Ron, or the Blooms fer putting yer in there?'

'No, not now. The Blooms have been very good to me since Mum died.' She sighed. 'I think the one thing this war has taught me is that life's too short to hold grudges.'

'Yer, I s'pose it is. Fancy a fag?'

'I'll get them.' Polly slipped out of bed and padded over to the dressing-table, bringing back the cigarettes, matches and ash-tray. They leaned against the bed-end, quietly drawing on the cigarettes. In the dark, the warm red glow at the end of their cigarettes lit up their faces.

'Shirley. If David asks me to go to bed with him – I will.'

'Well, that don't surprise me. And when d'yer fink yer'd get the chance? I couldn't see Mum and big sister wishing yer both good night, and you popping into 'is bed wiv their blessing.'

'We'd have to go to a hotel. Shirley, would it be very wrong? With Ron . . .'

Shirley sat forward. 'Look. Let's face it, Ron's very likely to be dead. I don't mean ter sound 'eartless, after all, 'e is me brother, but, well, we could all be dead next week.'

'Don't say things like that.'

'Well, it's true. If David's plane crashes, or if Hitler starts bombing agin, well anyfink could 'appen. Then what? Look Pol, grab all the 'appiness yer can. As you just said, life's too bloody short. And you've 'ad more than yer fair share of troubles, one way and another.' She stubbed her cigarette out in the ash-tray. 'This tastes like a load of old straw.'

Polly smiled. 'That was all I wanted, your blessing. David's coming home after Christmas. I'll write and tell him I'll meet him in London and we can have a dirty weekend together.' She too stubbed her cigarette out in the ash-tray, then leant over and kissed Shirley's cheek. 'Thank you.'

'Ger orf. I'm not David.'

'And I'm not Ben, so make sure you keep your hands to yourself tonight.'

Shirley laughed.

'What's so funny?'

'I was just finking, we've come a long way from Penn's Place. I'm engaged to a Canadian, and I'll be going to Canada to live, and hopefully you'll end up with David Bloom, a rich Jew. In some ways we've got a lot to thank Hitler for.'

'Yes, I suppose we have in some ways. But then me mum would still be alive, and Billy, Ron and your Terry would be safe.'

'Yeah, I suppose so.'

They both lay down and Polly pulled the clothes over her head. 'Shirley. When are you going to tell Ben about Elizabeth?'

'Dunno. I'll sleep on that. Good night.'

'Good night.' Polly had lots of thoughts to sleep on too.

Chapter 36

As soon as Polly put her key in the door, Sarah was in the hall. Her face was strained, and she looked unhappy. Polly sensed an atmosphere.

'Hello,' said Polly cheerfully. 'Did you have a nice Christmas?'

'It was quiet. Very quiet.'

Polly took off her hat and looked at Sarah through the hall mirror. 'Is there something wrong?'

'David managed to get home late on Christmas Eve.'

Polly froze. She had been unbuttoning her coat.

Sarah was still talking. 'He was able to stay till Boxing Day.'

'That must have been a nice surprise for you.' Polly's voice was high and unnatural.

'David told us about Yvonne.'

Polly continued taking her coat off. 'Wasn't she with him?' She tried to sound normal.

'No, and you know full well why not,' snapped Sarah.

Polly's head was swimming. What had he told them? Her mind was in a jumble, disjointedly moving from one random thought to another while she stood waiting for the next sentence. She had a strong desire to run away.

Mrs Bloom came out of the drawing-room. 'Oh, it's you, Margaret.' Her voice was cold and distant.

'What did David say?' she asked tentatively.

'You had better go in the warm, you're shivering. I'll make a cup of tea,' said Sarah, moving towards the kitchen.

'I'll just take my case up first.' As she mounted the stairs she felt the tears stinging her eyes. David had been here. What had he told them? Why did he have to come home when she wasn't here to give him support. She threw her case on the bed. Should she unpack? Did they know? What if they wanted her out of the house? She sat at the dressing-table. This had been such a wonderful Christmas, but now everything had changed. 'Oh David,' she said out loud. 'Why did you have to come home? Why didn't you wait till I was here?' She put her arms on the dressing-table and wept. When would she see him now?

Polly knew she had to go downstairs. Slowly she made up her face and did her hair, anything to delay meeting Sarah and her mother. Half an hour had passed, and she knew it was time to face the music.

'You took your time,' said Sarah, when Polly walked into the drawing-room.

Polly tried to avoid Mrs Bloom's gaze and sat at the far end of the sofa. She nervously balanced herself on the very edge of the red plush seat, waiting.

'Tea, Margaret?' asked Mrs Bloom in a crisp tone.

'Please,' she croaked.

'You knew about David and Yvonne, didn't you?' Sarah's voice was strong and commanding.

Polly nodded, keeping her head bent.

'You met him in London, didn't you?'

Again she only nodded, not wanting to meet their eyes.

'Why didn't you tell us, Margaret?' asked Mrs Bloom.

'It was an accident. I was outside . . .'

'He told us about that,' interrupted Sarah.

'David asked me not to say anything. He was very upset over Yvonne.'

'He also told us about your letters.'

Polly's head jolted up.

'He said he was very fond of you.' Sarah stood up and walked to the window. 'And he said that you feel the same way about him. Is that true?' She turned abruptly.

Suddenly Polly felt relieved. They knew. And, she realized, she didn't damn well care. He had told them. He had declared his feelings for her. She stood up. 'Yes, I do feel the same way. I love David. I love him very much, and if he asked me to go away with him, I would.'

'But . . .' started Mrs Bloom.

Polly was in full flow now, and nobody was going to stop her. She didn't care about the consequences, or the pain it could bring them. 'I know we are both married, but neither of us are happy, not now. I've never really loved Ron, not really loved him, not in the way I love David. And you know better than anyone how much trouble there's been between us.' She held up her hand to silence Sarah. 'I know what you're going to say. My husband is missing and he could be a prisoner-of-war. Well, I'll have to take that chance. He has been away for so long I've started to forget what he looks like.' She picked at her nails and continued quietly. 'I think I've forgiven him for what he did but the truth is I hardly ever think about him now; it's only when someone or something makes me remember.'

'What can we say, Margaret?' asked Sarah. There was sadness in her voice.

'Yvonne had been playing around for months. Did David tell you that?' Polly didn't wait for an answer, and her voice softened. 'When this war is over, and if we are all still alive, we will worry about the outcome then.' Tears were now falling unchecked as she walked across the room and opened the door.

'Where are you going?' asked Sarah.

'To pack the rest of my things. When I find somewhere to rent, I'll call back for the rest of them, if that's all right with you.'

'Sit down and stop being stupid,' said Sarah. She moved over and closed the door. 'David said this would be your reaction. I wanted to see if you really felt the same way about him as he obviously feels about you.'

Polly dropped on to the sofa. 'I was worried that . . . Well, it might have just been on the rebound. He was very fond of

Yvonne and, after all, I am out of your class.'

'Well, I think it's all wrong. Very wrong,' said Mrs Bloom, clearly agitated and embarrassed at this conversation. 'First he married against his father's wishes, and on the same day as his father died.'

Sarah and Polly looked shocked.

'How did you know that?' asked Sarah.

'Yvonne told me a while back. I phoned her after that Christmas business a couple of years ago.'

'You didn't tell me,' said Sarah.

'I didn't see any point.'

'I bet she took a great delight in telling you that little snippet.'

'That isn't the only thing.' Mrs Bloom's voice softened. 'David wasn't to know about his father.' She stood up, and once again became angry. 'He married a Gentile, now he wants to divorce her and take up with a married woman. You might as well know, young lady, I disapprove most strongly, and at this moment I feel I could disown him.'

'Mrs Bloom, he's your only son. Don't do that.' Polly looked down and fiddled with her handkerchief, twisting and screwing it into a ball. Without looking up she whispered, 'I know what it's like to be shut out of a family, and when that person's gone you spend the rest of your life regretting it.'

'You don't seem to be very worried about shutting out your husband,' Mrs Bloom said brusquely.

'I haven't shut him out. And what about him? He didn't seem that concerned about me going to prison. What am I to do?' She stood up and smacked her hands against her sides. 'Once again my life's in turmoil,' she said briskly. 'But life's too short to hang around waiting.'

'Don't be so dramatic, Margaret,' said Sarah. 'What if your husband comes back? What then?'

'I don't know,' Polly whispered, suddenly deflated. 'I don't know.'

'Would you leave David?' asked Mrs Bloom.

Polly left the room without answering.

The new year, 1943, was bringing very little respite from the air-raids. They were now having to run to the shelters during the day, as well as at night, causing many delays with the work.

And the new year was of little comfort to the Bloom household. For weeks the atmosphere was very strained, with Mrs Bloom avoiding Polly whenever she could.

Tempers were beginning to get very frayed, and Polly was unhappy. Her only real joy was David's letters. He wrote telling her how much he loved her, and how sorry he was he'd missed her at Christmas. He also told her of the scene he had had with his mother and sister when he told them about her and his decision to leave Yvonne. But he said Sarah had seemed to come round to seeing his point in the end: she never really liked Yvonne anyway.

It was on one particularly wet and miserable Saturday evening at the beginning of March that Polly and Sarah made their way to the hospital to see Fred. His son had come to the factory that morning to tell them that Fred had had a stroke.

They were both taken aback at the sight of the frail little man propped up in bed when only a few days ago he had been his usual laughing and joky self.

'How are you, Fred?' asked Sarah.

'Not ser bad.' His voice was hardly audible, and his words slurred into one another. He tried to smile. It was a funny, lop-sided smile. His right arm lay on top of the bedclothes, lifeless. All the while he nervously pinched and touched it, trying to bring it back to life.

'Will you be in hospital long?' asked Polly.

'Don't know.' He lay back and closed his eyes, exhausted.

'I think we'd better go,' said Sarah. 'We mustn't tire you out.'

He nodded slightly but didn't open his eyes.

As they moved away from his bed, a nurse touched Sarah's shoulder. 'I'm afraid Mr Baker is very ill.'

'Will he get better?' asked Polly.

'I'm afraid not.'

Sarah swallowed hard. 'Who will . . .?'

'His son will let you know.'

'Yes, yes of course,' said Sarah, trying to control her voice.

Outside the wind whipped the rain against their faces. It stung their cheeks, making their eyes water, mixing with their tears. They didn't speak as they turned up their coat collars and hurried to the bus stop.

The following Saturday his son came to the office and told them that Fred had passed away peacefully the night before.

Polly cried openly. 'I loved Fred,' she whispered. 'He taught me so much.'

'I remember when we were bombed in Mansell Street, he was a tower of strength,' said Sarah.

For the rest of the morning they were quiet with their thoughts, each one reflecting on their own special memories.

March was to prove to be a very unhappy month for Polly, for at the end of the month, she had a letter from Shirley telling her that Mrs Bell, her jolly, lovely mother-in-law, had died of cancer. She was devastated. The letter had arrived too late for her to attend the funeral.

Mrs Bloom and Sarah were very sympathetic. Once again, Polly found herself wearing a black armband.

'Sarah,' said Polly on Monday evening as they were getting ready to leave work. The factory was uncannily quiet; the machines were switched off and the girls had gone home. 'I've decided to get a flat.'

'What? Why?'

'I think you know why. Your mother has been a bit off towards me.'

'Yes, I know. But she'll get over it.'

'It's been three months now, and I hate to think I'm coming between David and your mother.'

'Don't worry about it. She's coming round to the fact that Yvonne wasn't for him.'

'But that doesn't mean to say she'll ever accept me.'

'Give her time. This sort of thing is a big shock to her generation. And you know deep down she thinks a lot of you.'

'Don't get me wrong. I know. But I feel under a strain, and I think she feels the same way. Besides, what will happen when David comes home?'

'I don't know, you'll have to cross that bridge when you come to it. Are you ready? I'll turn out the lights.'

The cold March wind was bitter. It blew round the corner, tossing dust and paper high into the air. Polly pulled her coat collar tighter round her throat. Tears from the cold mingled with tears of sadness and frustration. She had made up her mind; she was going to leave the Blooms' house.

With all the empty houses, it wasn't too difficult for Polly to find a flat. It was in the basement of a three-storey building, down a little mews off Whitechapel, and it was cheap. The large house had stood firm so far through the war, with just broken windows and a few slates missing, so she felt she had a good chance of surviving anything else that Hitler sent over.

Travelling to work would be no problem. It was within easy walking distance, and the underground was only round the corner, which meant she had somewhere to go if the raids got bad again.

It was a small flat, only a kitchen-cum-dining-room, bedroom and bathroom. After living in the Blooms' house a bathroom was one thing she looked for. There was going to be no sharing toilets for her, or sitting in a tin bath in front of the fire again – not if she could help it.

Because she had been bombed out of her flat in Weaver Street, the government gave her a grant to get furniture and floor covering. Polly was in her element tracking down and buying the few pieces of furniture she needed. Sarah had let her make the curtains at work, and she had insisted on coming round to help hang them.

'They look lovely,' said Sarah, standing back to admire their handiwork. 'But don't you miss the sunshine?' she asked, looking through the window at a brick wall.

'If you lean forward you can see all the feet walking past,' laughed Polly. 'And I'm hoping the sun will find its way through that gap. Come on, I'll put the kettle on and we'll put our feet up. We don't get a lot of time at work to talk about everyday things now. How's your mother?'

Sarah had sat herself down comfortably at the table. 'She's fine,' she replied. 'She does miss you, you know. Ted was surprised to hear you'd left.'

'Is he all right?' asked Polly, sitting next to Sarah.

'Yes.' Sarah straightened out imaginary creases from the table-cloth. 'Mother had a letter from David yesterday.'

'He told me he'd be writing.'

'He told her that as soon as he gets some leave he'll be coming to see her. He also told her that he's going to stay here with you.'

The loud piercing whistle of the kettle broke into their silence.

Polly jumped. 'I know. I wrote to him as soon as I got the key. I insisted he stayed at home when he was next on leave.' She had her back to Sarah, and was slowly stirring the tea in the pot. 'But he said he wanted to be with me.' She sat at the table again. 'Sarah, is it so wrong for us to want to be together?'

Sarah patted her hand. 'Do you know, I admire you so much.'

Polly quickly pulled her hand away. 'Me? Whatever for?'

'It doesn't matter what life has to throw at you, you always seem to come back smiling.'

'Not always.' Polly looked rueful. 'I'll pour out the tea.'

Sarah looked at her watch. 'I'll have to be going after that.' She glanced at the bare mantelpiece. 'I see Grandad's whip's in place.'

Polly smiled. 'I always feel at home when that's on a wall.'

'Looks like I'll have to get you a clock to put on that empty space.'

'I've got my alarm. Besides, you've been more than generous with all the bits you've given me.'

'We've got far too much in our house anyway. And Mother

was pleased to help make your flat a little more like home.' She finished her tea. 'Now I must go.'

'Sarah. If your mother wants to come round any time, she's very welcome.'

'Thanks, I'll tell her.'

Spring drifted into summer. July was full of blue skies and long days. Mrs Bloom hadn't been to see Polly, and she hadn't been invited back to the house. The thing Polly missed most was gazing out on to their beautiful garden. She could almost imagine the scent of the roses, the rich green of the soft, springy grass, and the tall lupins waving majestically in the slight breeze. Here she only had a brick wall outside her window, and a small concrete area with the odd blade of grass and weed fighting and struggling to live and breathe. They proudly displayed their bright green leaves and flowers when they finally pushed their way defiantly through the cracks in the paving.

It was Sunday morning and, feeling very restless, she decided to go for a walk. Her tracks led her to Petticoat Lane. It was bustling and full of life. Now that America had joined in the war, it also seemed full of Americans. There were, too, lots of girls in pretty summer dresses, some with their hair held in place with the latest fashion, colourful snoods. They hung on to their boyfriends' arms and their every word. Above the general hubbub of traders shouting their wares, the American drawl seemed to be all around her. The accent reminded her of Ben and Shirley. They were hoping to be married in August, and she was going to be Matron of Honour. Shirley wanted a white wedding. Polly smiled to herself at that thought.

''Allo, gel, wotcher doing up 'ere?'

'Hello, Reggie, how are you? We haven't seen you for ages.'

He feverishly looked about him. 'Well no. Now Sid's gorn orf I've lorst a lot of me contacts.'

'Yes, the girls at work have been a bit upset at him going off like that. He used to bring in a few things for them – black market, no doubt.'

'Shh, Pol, keep yer voice down.'

'Sorry.'

'D'yer know where 'e went to?'

'Yes, young Rosie, who works at our place, said he's gone to Liverpool.'

'Liverpool? Wot's 'e gorn up there for? It's gotter be a bird.'

'Could be, or it could be somebody's husband came home and caught him in his bed, or that our Miss Bloom is going out with a detective-sergeant.'

'Bloody 'ell.'

'Don't worry about Sid, Reggie, he'll turn up again, you wait and see. Bye, see you some time.'

'Oh yeah, bye.'

Polly walked away, smiling. That will give them something to talk about, she thought, swinging her handbag as she made her way home.

She pushed open her front door. A piece of paper had been slipped under the door and was lying on the mat.

Dear Margaret,

I'm sorry I missed you. Will call again.

Rachel Bloom.

'Damn, damn, damn,' said Polly out loud. 'Why did I have to be out?' She wondered just why Mrs Bloom had come – if it had been just a friendly visit surely Sarah would have come with her. Now she'd have to wait until tomorrow to find out.

Chapter 37

Polly was at work long before Sarah, and as soon as she walked through the door, Polly followed her into the office.

'Good morning, Margaret. Isn't it a lovely day?'

'Is it? Sorry, I mean yes, of course it is. Sarah, why did your mother come to see me yesterday? And why was she alone? And where were you?'

'Let me get my hat and coat off first. I wasn't with mother because I was out with Ted. And the reason she came over alone was because she'd had a phone call from David, and he told her he is coming home today, and . . .'

'He's coming home today? What time? Oh Sarah, what . . .?'

'Just calm down and let me finish. It is unexpected. He's got a forty-eight-hour pass and he should be here . . .' She looked at her watch. 'About lunch-time. Mother thought that as it was such a nice day she would use it as an excuse to come over and see you.'

Polly threw her arms round Sarah. 'Oh Sarah, what can I say? Your mother came to see me, and I wasn't in. Of all the rotten luck.' Polly stepped back. 'You said it's unexpected. It's not embarkation leave, is it?' she asked tentatively.

'Mother didn't say.'

'I'd better get back to work. Would you mind very much if I left early? Perhaps I could meet him. Did he say what time?'

'Calm down. He said he'd come here, so you'd better wait, just in case your paths cross. You could spend all his leave chasing each other across London.'

'Yes, you're right. And besides, his train could be delayed, then I'd be biting my nails away.'

'Go on, get out in the workshop, and try to concentrate. I've got to make a few phone calls,' Sarah called after her.

Although she tried hard to concentrate on her work, all morning Polly's eyes were on the door.

It was well past midday when David walked in. She thought she would burst when he walked up to her, touched her hand and whispered in her ear, 'Hello, my pretty little Polly Perkins.'

Her head was swimming, and she felt silly when the girls turned to look at her; her with a face the colour of beetroot. 'Come into the office,' she croaked.

'David, David,' said Sarah, rushing up and throwing her arms around his neck. 'It's so good to see you after all this time.'

In the office, Polly kept her distance. She desperately wanted to take him in her arms and kiss him, smother him with kisses, for she knew forty-eight hours was going to go much too fast. 'I'll just get my bag and cardigan. Sarah said I can go early.'

'Don't bother about coming in tomorrow, you can make up the work loss later.'

'Thanks, Sarah,' said David. 'We're coming over tonight. I phoned Mother when I was at the station, so we'll see you some time after seven.' He held the door open, and they walked through the factory and stepped out into the warm summer sunshine.

Outside, everything looked different to Polly. This morning, when she had walked to work, she had been worried as to why Mrs Bloom had been to see her. She had never thought, even in her wildest dreams, that a few hours later David would be here with her. Every bird seemed to be singing its heart out, and to her people looked happy and smiling. She slipped her arm through his. David looked down and gently patted her hand. He didn't speak, he only smiled, and Polly knew this was going to be the happiest two days of her life.

'Down here,' she said, skipping down the concrete stairs to her front door. Her hand was trembling as she fumbled to put the key in the lock and pushed open the door to her flat.

Inside, David quickly closed the door behind them and took her in his arms. His kiss was long and lingering. Polly thought she would die from ecstasy and excitement. He buried his head in her shoulder and gently kissed her ear. 'Margaret,' he whispered. 'You don't know how much I've been looking forward to being here with you.'

For once Polly was speechless. She wanted to say she loved him, worshipped him and adored him, but knew that whatever she said it would sound wrong. 'Me too,' was all she could utter.

When they finally broke away, her next comment was a bland, 'I'll get a cup of tea.'

'This is nice,' he said, wandering around the flat. He pushed open the bedroom door.

In the kitchen, Polly stood silently with a milk bottle clenched in her hand. She was so nervous. Was she doing the right thing? She knew she loved David, of that she was sure. But was she frightened of the consequences? Of Yvonne, and Mrs Bloom, and even Ron if he was still alive.

'I see you've got a double bed. Are you expecting company?' he called from the other room.

She laughed; it was a happy but slightly hysterical laugh. Am I dreaming all this? she said to herself, screwing up her eyes tightly. Is it a dream, and when I open my eyes I'll wake up? 'David,' she called, as if to get proof he was still here. 'This isn't embarkation leave, is it?' She hadn't dared ask him before.

He walked back into the kitchen. 'No. I had some leave due, and I've been doing a lot of thinking these past months. I decided I couldn't keep away from you any longer.'

Polly smiled and began pouring the tea into the cups.

He stood behind her, his arms gently folded around her, pulling her close. He had taken off his tunic and rolled up his shirt sleeves. She could feel the coolness of his bare arms against hers. He turned her, and very carefully tilted her chin.

Their lips met, and she knew she wasn't dreaming as they slowly made their way to the bedroom.

'I'm so glad you've come over to see us,' said Mrs Bloom, eagerly ushering them into the drawing-room after greeting David warmly and gently kissing Polly's cheek. 'I know you two must have a lot to talk about, and you've only got . . .'

'Mother, do sit down,' said Sarah. 'Hello David.' She kissed his cheek and hugged him. 'By the way, this is Ted. I told you all about him in my letters.'

Ted was already on his feet and held out his hand to David. 'We have met before, though it was a while ago. But Sarah is always talking about you, so I feel I know you well.'

'All good I hope.'

'Would you all like a drink?' asked Mrs Bloom.

'I'll get them, Mother,' said Sarah. 'You sit and talk to Margaret and David. Ted can help me.'

'I was sorry I was out yesterday when you called,' said Polly timidly.

'You've been round to the flat?' inquired David.

'Unfortunately I was out.'

'That's a shame. You should see it, Mother. Margaret has made it look really great. Thanks,' said David, as Sarah handed him a drink.

'Well, yes, perhaps some other time.'

'Cheers, everybody,' said David, raising his glass.

'Cheers,' came back the reply.

Polly looked into her glass. She knew this was going to be a long drawn-out evening. She felt uncomfortable being here with David in front of his mother. It put her on edge. She half smiled to herself, pleased that she'd decided to get her own flat. They couldn't have done what they did this afternoon if they had been staying here. Her smile broadened; she desperately wanted to go home and selfishly to have David to herself.

'You both look very well,' said Mrs Bloom.

David winked at Polly. Fortunately she was sitting down, as

her legs immediately turned to jelly. She loved him so much.

'I'll make a cup of cocoa,' said Polly when they returned home. Her voice was high and nervous.

'Don't let's bother with that.' David threw his cap on the chair and began unbuttoning his tunic. He took her into his arms and kissed her.

Polly was anxious. Although they had made love this afternoon, it had been quick and eager, but now, tonight, he was going to share her bed. Would he be disappointed with her after Yvonne's beautiful body? She tried to push those thoughts to the back of her mind. After all, to be alone with David was one of the reasons she had got the flat.

David was in bed when she returned from the bathroom. He was sitting up looking at her. She turned her back to him and quickly took off her dress, letting it fall unceremoniously to the ground. When she slipped the straps of her camiknickers from her shoulders, she immediately grabbed her nightie and wrestled inside it. Finally her head popped through the opening, covering her nakedness.

David laughed. 'I didn't think you were shy.'

She felt cold despite the sticky warmth of the July night. Her stomach bubbled, her palms were clammy, and she was in dread of making a fool of herself. She stood at the bottom of the bed; she felt young and inexperienced, and vulnerable. 'David,' her voice was weak, 'I love you.'

He smiled and held out his arms, which she crept into like a lost child seeking warmth and comfort.

'And I love you. Do you know, looking back, I think I did when I first saw you in Dad's factory all those years ago. Do you remember?'

With her head resting on his chest, she nodded. 'David, I'm afraid.'

'What, of me?'

'What if I . . . disappoint you.'

He put his finger to her lips to silence her. 'Don't you worry

399

about a thing. This night, my pretty little Polly Perkins, is ours,' he whispered, kissing her forehead. When his lips travelled down to her mouth, it was a warm, tender kiss, but full of passion and promise.

Her mind shut out everything; all she needed at that moment was reassurance and love, and with David here she was getting both.

Chapter 38

The week after David had gone back to camp, Polly received a letter from Shirley telling her she was married. It seemed Ben was being shipped abroad. All the legal and medical requirements were ready for their wedding in August, so they'd decided to get a Special Licence and get married right away, as Ben only had a thirty-six-hour pass. Shirley was worried about him being sent abroad.

Polly was very upset she hadn't been at her best friend's wedding. But she wrote to Shirley wishing them every happiness, and anxiously asked if Ben knew about Elizabeth.

Polly was also worried about David. The war was beginning to take a new turn with the RAF bombing Germany, and there was talk of the British invading soon. If that was so, would he be flying missions again?

Then at the end of the following week Polly had a letter from the Red Cross telling her they had been notified about a number of injured picked up by a ship which was on its way to Australia. Some men from Ron's regiment were amongst them, they informed her.

She sat and read the letter over and over again. It took a long while for it to sink in. It looked after all as if Ron could still be alive. What was she to do?

Polly had told Sarah about both pieces of news and that Wednesday Sarah came into the factory and called Polly into the office.

'They say everything comes in threes – here's a letter for you.

It came to our house. It must be from someone who doesn't know you've moved.'

Polly took the envelope Sarah held out. Her hand was trembling as she read the address. It had a foreign stamp, but she didn't know either the handwriting or where it had come from.

'Would you like a cup of tea?' asked Sarah.

'Yes, please.' Polly didn't want to open the envelope. She sensed it would be bad news.

'Margaret, is it from your husband?' Sarah asked, filling the kettle.

She shook her head. 'It's not his writing,' she said, still studying the envelope.

'Would you like me to read it for you?'

'No, no thank you.'

'It could be about your brother Billy.'

Polly looked up. 'Yes, yes, it could be.' She quickly tore the letter open and sat down heavily on the chair.

'Margaret, are you all right?'

'Yes,' she whispered.

The loud whistling of the kettle suddenly filled the room with its noise, waking Polly from her dreamlike state. 'It's from a hospital in Australia.' She looked up at Sarah. 'It's about Ron. A nurse found my address in his pocket. It seems he's very ill and can't write yet, but he has started talking, and he's improving all the time.' She turned over the page. 'He's told her all about me. And he's got a photo of me.'

'Was he in a prisoner-of-war camp?'

'She doesn't say. This was posted weeks ago, in June.'

'Margaret. What difference will this make between you and David?'

Polly looked up. Tears were running down her face. 'I don't know Sarah. I really don't know.'

'Is Ron on his way home?'

'She doesn't say anything like that. I'll have to answer it.'

'Of course you must. Do you want to go home?'

She shook her head. 'What good will that do?'

'Give you time to think.'

'I don't want to think.' Polly took a handkerchief and a powder compact from her handbag. She blew her nose, then repaired her make-up. She stood up and, smoothing down her skirt, said, 'I'm going to finish those dresses; we mustn't get too far behind with that order.'

'Drink your tea first.'

'I'll take it out to the work-room with me.' Polly picked up the cup and left the office.

In the quiet of her flat, Polly tried many times to write to David, and to Ron. The nib of her pen was splayed out through being constantly pressed down hard on the paper, and pieces of paper were strewn over the floor. She screwed the lid back on the bottle of ink and decided to try again tomorrow.

In bed she tossed and turned. What was she to do? Her husband was alive, but she loved David. Her words were coming back to her over and over again.

'I know we're both married, but neither of us are happy. I've never really loved Ron, not like I love David.'

She could see Mrs Bloom asking, 'What if your husband comes back?'

'I don't know,' she said out loud. 'I don't know. What if Ron was injured? With only one leg or arm. She couldn't turn her back on him, not now, even after what he'd done to her.

Polly cried herself to sleep. It was a fitful sleep, full of dreams. Every time she held David in her arms, and he was about to kiss her, somehow he slipped away and his place was taken by a grinning Ron.

When dawn finally lightened her room, she crawled wearily out of bed and looked in the mirror. 'Margaret Bell, you look a mess,' she said to her reflection. 'Now, you've got to pull yourself together and sit down and write to Ron and David straightaway. You must tell David, and you must find out more about Ron.' Without dressing first, she did just that.

Two weeks later there was another letter from Ron's nurse.

'She seems very keen to get in touch with you,' said Sarah, handing Polly the letter.

'It'll take weeks for him to get my letter,' she said, tearing at the envelope and quickly scanning the pages. She looked up at Sarah. 'It seems he still can't write, but he's improving all the time. He's now sitting up and talking, and . . .' Polly began reading out loud. 'We both have a lot in common as I came from the Walworth Road, so it's good to have a cockney to talk to.'

'Does she say why he can't write?'

'No.' Polly folded the letter and put it in her handbag. 'I have asked her a lot of questions, so perhaps the next one will give me a few more answers.'

'What did David have to say about this?'

'He told me to wait before I tell Ron about us. He didn't see any point in worrying him if he's ill.'

'Very wise. Now back to work.'

The weeks slowly slipped by. Shirley had written and was pleased to hear Ron was alive. She still hadn't told Polly if Ben knew Elizabeth was hers.

She lay on her back looking up at the ceiling. It was Sunday, so she had no reason to get up early. Her thoughts were flitting from one thing to another. Last Friday the war had been raging for four years. Four years, and although things appeared to be going well abroad, and the raids had almost ceased, there didn't seem to be any end in sight. Such a lot had happened in those four years. To her, Ron, Billy, David and Shirley. She wondered when Shirley would go to Canada? She would miss her – and Elizabeth. I'll go down to Bristol to see them at Christmas, she decided.

Polly sat up to reach over to get a cigarette, and suddenly felt peculiar. She jumped out of bed and rushed to the bathroom, where she was sick.

She sat on the end of the bath and held her head in her hands. 'I can't be,' she wailed out loud. 'Ron always said it was my fault we couldn't have children.' But deep down she knew this was the reason she had missed last month.

All day she worried and wondered what she could do. She knew she wanted this baby – David's baby – more than anything else, but who could she tell? Would David be pleased? How would she manage? What would Sarah say? What about her job? And what would Mrs Bloom say? The more she thought about it, the more problems she created for herself.

The next morning she was sick again, and her worst fears were confirmed. When she looked in the mirror before leaving for work, she knew Sarah would ask her what was wrong, as she looked so dreadful.

'Christ Polly, yer look like yer've 'ad a night on the tiles,' called Elsie Mann when she walked in.

'I'm all right. I think I must have eaten something that's upset me.'

'You don't look so good, Margaret. Would you like to go home?' asked Sarah.

'No, I'll be all right.' Polly sat at her machine and began working.

Six o'clock came and Sarah called her into the office. 'I've been wanting to talk to you all day, but you've been so busy finishing off those new dresses, I didn't like to stop you. Margaret, Ted and I are going to get married.'

Polly stared at her.

'Well, aren't you pleased for us?'

'Oh, Sarah, of course I am.' She held her close and kissed her cheek. 'Congratulations. What does your mother have to say about it?'

'She's happy for us. She likes Ted.'

'But he's not Jewish.'

'No, but she has accepted that. A lot of her old ideas and values have changed. She's even coming round to the fact that David is divorcing Yvonne.'

Polly turned her head as tears began to trickle slowly down her cheeks.

'Margaret? What is it?' Sarah's tone was full of concern. 'I thought you would be pleased for us? Oh, I'm sorry, I forgot, you're not feeling very well. Would you like me to walk home with you?'

Polly shook her head. 'I am happy for you and Ted, very happy.' She sat on the chair and cried.

Sarah looked bewildered. 'What is it?'

Polly looked up. Her mascara had run down her face, and when she wiped her tears with the back of her hand it streaked across her cheek. 'I'm sorry, Sarah, I must be feeling sorry for myself.' She blew her nose and wiped her face. 'Now, come on, tell me all about this wedding,' she said, pulling herself together. 'When's it to be?'

'Well, we're not sure yet, we have a lot to discuss. We want you to come over for the day next Sunday so we can sort out some of the arrangements.'

'What d'you mean?' asked Polly apprehensively.

'We'll wait till Sunday. Now, you get on home, take a couple of aspirins, and get a good night's sleep. I need you in here bright and cheerful tomorrow. Pick up your handbag, and I'll turn out the lights.'

It'll take more than a couple of aspirins to take away my problem, Polly thought.

Outside they went their separate ways. 'Margaret,' called Sarah over her shoulder before disappearing round the corner. 'If anything's worrying you, you will let me know, won't you?'

'Course,' replied Polly, trying to sound light-hearted.

All the way home she thought about Sarah. She was pleased for her. They made a lovely couple. She wondered when they would get married. And where were they going to live? Ted had his own house out Richmond way. Sarah had told her it was quite large and right on the river. He lived with his father who was an invalid. Polly couldn't see him leaving him on his own. Would Sarah live there? If so, what about Mrs Bloom? She wouldn't leave her house. Would she want David to live with her? And would David want to marry her if she were free? Once

406

again tears welled up inside her. But she wasn't free, she reminded herself. Ron was still her husband.

For the rest of the week it seemed Sarah and Polly didn't have five minutes alone together. They were both working very hard: the new dresses had to go to the shops, and the government wanted them to make more parachutes. Most evenings the girls on the shop floor worked a couple of extra hours to help out. Not that they minded, as they were being well paid.

Every morning before she left home, Polly was sick. It had now become part of her day, and she was beginning to accept it. Many times Polly had tried to write and tell David about the baby, but every time something stopped her. She did her best to keep her letters as loving as before, but she knew they weren't the same.

On Sunday morning she put on one of her prettiest dresses, and her white straw hat and gloves. With her handbag tucked under her arm, and gas-mask and cardigan over her shoulders, she made her way to the Blooms'. She had taken special care over her make-up in order to hide her dark, sunken eyes.

When Mrs Bloom opened the door, Polly knew by her gestures that she was genuinely pleased to see her.

'Come into the garden. It is such a lovely day it's almost wicked not to make the most of it.'

Sarah and Ted were sitting on the striped canvas deck chairs at the far end of the lawn. They were both leaning forward, engrossed in deep conversation.

'Sarah, Margaret's here,' called Mrs Bloom. She turned to Polly. 'I'll put the kettle on, I'm sure you could do with a cup of tea?'

'Yes, yes please.' Polly strolled across the lawn. Once again she was in this lovely garden. The grass was springy, just as she remembered, but the smell of Mrs Bloom's favourite flowers – roses – was to her in her state nauseating. Her stomach heaved. She stopped and took long, deep breaths. The birds, high in the trees, were chattering ceaselessly. Ted looked up and was quickly on his feet, walking towards her.

'Hello Margaret, how are you?'

She took his outstretched hand. 'I'm fine,' she lied. 'And you?'

'In the pink. Come and sit down.' He led the way to the chairs grouped round a table that was set in the middle of the lawn.

'You look very pretty this morning,' said Sarah. 'But you still look a little off colour.'

'I'm fine.' She sat in the chair and removed her hat, fluffing her blonde hair up at the back, trying to appear nonchalant. 'Now, I want to hear all your plans for this wedding.'

'Well, we want to get married in about six months. We haven't set a date yet, but we hope it'll be in the spring.' Sarah took Ted's hand.

Polly breathed in sharply, quickly adding up the months. How far gone would she be then?

Ted and Sarah looked at her. 'What's wrong?' asked Sarah.

'Nothing, oh nothing. Where are you going to live?'

Sarah glanced at Ted before answering. 'We have a small problem. We want to live in Ted's house, but, well, Mother is against that. She wants us to live here.' She lowered her voice. 'Mother's coming now, so we'll be able to explain things better.'

Mrs Bloom put the tray on the table. 'Well, Margaret, what do you think of these two then?'

'I think it's lovely. When are you getting your ring?'

'I've already got it. It's being made larger. I've got fat fingers.' Sarah wiggled her fingers.

'You very nearly didn't have any fingers at all a while back,' said Polly, looking away from the cake that Mrs Bloom was cutting.

'Cake, Margaret?'

'No, thank you. I had a big breakfast.'

'Well,' said Sarah, with a glance at her mother. 'Back to what we were saying. If we go and live in Ted's house, Mother wants David to come back here when he comes out of the Air Force.'

'What does David have to say about that?' asked Polly.

'We haven't asked him yet. Also, Mother wants you to come back here to live, now.'

'I can't do that,' Polly cried.

'Why not?' asked Mrs Bloom.

'Well, what if David doesn't want me to? I mean, I can't just assume he'd want me here with him. And what about Ron?'

'We have discussed that,' said Sarah hastily.

Polly stood up. 'Oh, have you?'

'Now sit down and listen.'

Polly obeyed Sarah, and she continued. 'You know we are all very fond of you, and as a partner in Bloom's Fashions I'm going to give you more of a free hand. This war won't last forever, and when the cloth situation gets better I intend to expand. That will mean you being in charge of another factory.' Sarah slowly stirred her tea. 'I don't know what will happen between you and Ron, but I do know David wants to marry you one day. He has told me so in his letters. Margaret, are you listening to me?'

Polly was trying hard to listen. To take charge of a factory. David wants to marry her. She was trying hard to take it all in, but a rushing sound echoing inside her head shut out all other noise and she fell to the ground.

'Margaret. Margaret.' A distant voice was coming to her; gradually it got louder. 'I think she's coming round. Margaret.' She recognized Sarah's voice.

Slowly she sat up. 'What happened?'

'You fainted.' Sarah was leaning over her holding a wet flannel against her forehead. 'I think you should see a doctor. You haven't been well all week.'

With Ted's help, Polly struggled to her feet. 'I'm all right. I've had a bit of an upset tummy, that's all.' She looked at Sarah. 'Would you mind if I went home?'

'You must stay till you feel better. Besides, what about lunch?' said Mrs Bloom.

'I'd rather not, if you don't mind.' She gathered up her handbag and hat.

'I don't think you should go home on your own,' said Ted. 'Let me take you.'

'Oh no, I couldn't put you out.'

'I insist. If you wait till after lunch, then both Sarah and I will take you.'

'Well, all right then.'

'Good,' said Mrs Bloom. 'That's settled. Sarah, I think we could have lunch out here as it is such a nice day.'

'I'll help you, Mother.'

'Mrs Bloom.' Sarah and her mother both stopped clearing the table at Polly's tone. 'I have something to tell you.'

Sarah said quickly, 'I'm sure it can wait till later. Let's have lunch first.'

Polly looked at her and, out of sight of the others, Sarah screwed up her face and quickly shook her head. Polly blushed. *She knows, she knows.* The words screamed inside her head. 'Yes, of course,' she said quickly. 'It's not that important anyway.'

Chapter 39

As Sarah walked through the factory on Monday morning she called Polly into the office.

'Sit down, Margaret. I didn't want to say anything yesterday in front of Ted and Mother, but I think you have something to tell me.'

'You know, don't you?' said Polly quietly.

'Well, I'm just guessing, but I think I've got it right.'

Polly nodded.

'Does David know?'

Polly jerked her head up. 'No, and I want him to hear it from me, and when I'm ready.'

'I wouldn't dream of telling him. Margaret, what are you going to do?'

'I don't know. I really don't know.'

'Have you been to see a doctor?'

'No. I want this baby, Sarah. I really do, and I love David.'

'What about your husband?'

'I don't know.'

'You must tell David.'

'I can't, not yet.' Polly stood up. She couldn't tell Sarah her fears. What if she lost it, or David didn't want children?

The telephone's shrill bell interrupted them.

'I'll talk to you later,' said Polly, glad of the excuse to leave the office.

For the rest of the day they were busy, and that evening Sarah walked home with Polly.

'Take your coat off, I'll make a cup of tea,' Polly said as they got inside.

'I mustn't stay long. You two have certainly got things moving quickly. But congratulations!'

Polly smiled but still looked doubtful. 'I don't think your mother will approve of this,' she said, patting her stomach.

'No. And I can't see her giving her blessing to you and David living together, not under her roof, not now, not when she finds out your husband is alive.'

'You mean she doesn't know about Ron?'

'I was very selfish. I thought it would be easier for me to leave home if you and David were living there and I didn't tell her because, once you were back home, I reckoned well, that things might change.'

'I wondered why she didn't say anything yesterday. Sarah you are very devious, and now I've spoilt your plans.'

'I'm afraid so. Still, six months is a long way off, and a lot can happen between now and then.'

Over the next three months, many letters were exchanged between Ron's nurse, Sally, and Polly. She learnt that he had been fighting in the jungle where a gun had blown up, and injured him. At first Ron had been suffering from loss of memory. He had also been quite badly burned, and had lost two fingers from his right hand.

Polly felt guilty when she looked down at her swelling stomach. Only Sarah knew, although Elsie Mann said she thought Polly was looking well, and gave her a knowing look. Once or twice she caught some of the younger girls sniggering behind their hands when she walked through the workshop.

The baby was due around the beginning of April, and she still hadn't told David. She had tried to keep her letters loving and light-hearted. He had been unable to get leave, and was trying to arrange to be home after Christmas. He said one of his fellow officers wanted to be home for Christmas, so he stepped down this year. Polly had decided to wait and tell him face to face;

that way she would see his reaction.

She also had many letters from Shirley. She hoped to be one of the first war brides to go to Canada. Polly had told her about the baby and she was thrilled. Polly smiled at Shirley's letter: she simply didn't worry about anything or anyone.

It had been a cold and miserable start to December, and Polly's basement flat was damp. She was thinking of moving to somewhere better, but worried about how she would manage. How could she pay her rent if David didn't want her and the baby? She hated the thought of being so vulnerable for she knew she would have to give up work when the baby was born since she had no one to look after it. Ever since she'd left school she'd been able to work and earn money but now, with the baby, she wouldn't be able to. She felt so exposed.

One Saturday lunch-time, after the girls had left the factory, Sarah said, 'Let's have a cup of tea before we leave. I've got the kettle on.'

Polly moved some papers from off a chair.

'Margaret, I can't keep putting Mother off, she wants to see you. And she asked what you were doing for Christmas.'

Polly straightened up and put her hands in the small of her back. 'I can't let her see me like this.'

'You must tell her soon, and what about David?'

Polly sat on the chair and took the cup of tea Sarah offered. 'I'm going to see Shirley this Christmas, and David hopes to be home at the beginning of the year. I shall wait till then to tell him. Then I'll be able to see in his face what he really thinks, and if . . .' her voice drifted off miserably.

'What do you mean? You're thinking of going off on your own, are you? You're not going to break away from the family?'

'You can't really call me family.'

'Well I think of you as a sister now, after all these years, and what we've been through together. Besides, you can't deprive me of my niece or nephew, now can you?' Sarah laughed.

'But what if David doesn't want to be a father?'

'Well, it's a bit late now. He presumably played some part

413

in it too! But honestly, I think he'll be pleased.'

. 'Do you really think so? You see, we've never discussed the possibility of children – I never thought I could have any.' Sarah took Polly's empty cup and Polly paused, anxiously. 'I would hate David to think I've deceived him.'

'Don't be silly. He wouldn't think that.'

'I don't know. What if he doesn't want anything to do with . . .'

A shaft of light swept across the workshop floor as the factory door was opened. They both looked up.

'I wonder who that is creeping around at this time of day?' said Sarah, going to the door of the office. 'What are you doing here?' she called.

. Polly froze as a woman's clear voice said, 'Hello, I thought I might have missed you.' It was a voice which Polly knew very well. She quickly sat down.

'Hello, Margaret. I'm glad I caught you here. I know I shouldn't do this sort of thing on the Sabbath, but I was hoping to . . .'

'Hello, Mrs Bloom. How are you?'

She didn't answer. The expression on her face was one of shock as she stared at Polly.

'I'm surprised you came over here.' Sarah was trying to pay no attention to the obvious.

'Is this why you haven't been to see us?' asked Mrs Bloom, completely ignoring her daughter, her eyes riveted on Polly.

Polly nodded.

'Sarah, Sarah.' Her voice rose. 'You knew about this?' She pointed to Polly.

Sarah laughed. 'Well, Margaret can't very well disguise it, now can she?'

'You knew. And by the sound of it, you approve. Why didn't you tell me? And why hasn't David told me?' Mrs Bloom's face flushed with anger.

'Sit down, Mother, and we'll explain.'

'This doesn't need a great deal of explaining.' She waved

her arm at Polly. 'And what have you got to say for yourself, young lady? And what about your husband?'

'Mother, one thing at a time.'

'Oh, I suppose you are going to defend her again.'

'What do you mean, again?' asked Polly angrily.

'The last time you brought trouble to our house, Sarah stuck up for you.'

Polly sank back in her chair. Would she have to spend the rest of her life trying to live down her past? Would Mrs Bloom ever really forget that awful brooch affair?

'Mother. That was very unfair,' said Sarah furiously. 'And remember it takes two to make a baby, and the father is your son.'

'You don't have to explain the facts of life to me.' Mrs Bloom tossed her head in the air. 'And why hasn't my son had the decency to tell me about this?'

'He doesn't know,' whispered Polly.

'What? Why doesn't he know? Is it his?'

Polly looked astounded. 'What do you think I am?'

'Calm down, Margaret. Mother, that was unkind. Now listen, Margaret hasn't told David because she's waiting to see him. She doesn't think it's a matter to write about.'

'It's going to come as a bit of a shock when he does see her. Have you ever discussed the possibility of having children with him?'

'I didn't think I could have any, so the question never arose.'

'I see, and what if he doesn't want anything to do with it?'

'That's what I shall ask him, and I'll be able to see the truth in his face,' she said, forcing herself to be calm.

'Oh, I see.'

'I'll be going home now. I'll see you on Monday, Sarah. Goodbye, Mrs Bloom, and don't think too badly of me and David.' Polly tried to walk out of the office with dignity. If she was like this over the baby, what was she going to say when she found out Ron was alive? Panic rose up in her again and the cold biting wind brought tears to her eyes, so she could cry openly without anyone being any the wiser.

When she arrived home there was a letter from Shirley. She was coming to Polly's for Christmas. She said she had to come to London to sort out some business about going to Canada, and decided to make it over Christmas and bring Elizabeth to see her Auntie Polly. Polly was disappointed at not going to Bristol, and knew it wouldn't be so exciting in her tiny flat, without all the Bells.

Shirley was arriving in London on Christmas Eve, and Polly was at the station to meet them. After all the hugs and kisses amongst the usual chaos at the station, they made their way on the underground to Whitechapel.

'Look at you,' said Shirley. 'Got quite a bump there.' She gently patted Polly's stomach.

'I can't hide it any more. Hold my hand, Elizabeth,' said Polly.

The little girl grabbed Polly's hand. She looked terrified. She was frightened of the trains that roared out through the blackness at the end of the platform, and hid her head in Polly's skirt. She wouldn't put her foot on the escalator because it wouldn't keep still long enough for her to jump on.

'Come on, you daft thing,' said Shirley.

'I don't like it,' she whined. 'Can't we go on a bus?'

When they arrived at the flat, Shirley had a good look round. 'It's bloody cold in 'ere. Is this the best you could find?'

'I like it. It's cheap and it's got a bathroom and it's near work. What do you think of the paper chains, Elizabeth? I made them especially for you.'

'They're all right. Where am I sleeping?'

'You and Mummy are in . . .'

'She ain't me mum,' interrupted Elizabeth.

Polly looked at Shirley, and hesitated, trying to find the right words. 'You two can sleep in my bed,' she said finally.

'Where are you going?' asked Shirley.

'I can sleep in the kitchen. I've got a camp bed. After all, it's only for a couple of nights.'

All evening there was a strange atmosphere. It wasn't like before, almost as if something had died. After Elizabeth had gone to bed and was asleep, the mood changed, but only slightly.

'Bit different ter last Christmas Eve. We 'ad a good time at that dance, didn't we?'

Polly sighed. 'Yes. Things have changed so quickly. You're getting ready to go to Canada, and I've got a bun in the oven.'

'Yeah, who'd a' thought that? Have you told David yet?'

Polly shook her head. 'And have you told Ben that Elizabeth's yours?'

It was Shirley's turn to shake her head.

'Why not? How are you going to explain her when you take her to Canada?'

'I'm not taking 'er.'

Polly sat back in stunned silence. '*What?*' she said, drawing out the word very slowly.

Shirley lit a cigarette. 'Want one?' She offered Polly the packet. Polly shook her head. 'Please yerself.' She put the packet and matches on the floor beside her chair, then sat back and inhaled long and hard on the cigarette. She nervously tapped the end into the ash-tray. 'That's one of the reasons I'm up 'ere.'

'Why? What are you going to do?'

Shirley leaned forward. 'You see, if I've got a kid I can't go to the top of the list. If I'm at the top of the list, I stand a good chance of being on the first boat to Canada. So as far as I'm concerned, I ain't got one.'

Polly looked shocked. 'Shirley, that's awful. What are you going to do with her?'

'Well, I ain't really 'ad a lot to do with 'er, now 'ave I? I was 'oping Vera would 'ave 'er, but she's turned funny about it. So, I thought, you'll be giving up work soon, and instead of looking after one, yer could look after two.'

'Shirley, you can't be serious?'

'I ain't never been so serious in me life before.'

'I will hardly be able to afford to look after myself, let alone two children.'

'Don't worry, I'll send yer some money, and I expect the Blooms will cough up when yours is 'ere.' She stubbed her cigarette out in the ash-tray. 'That's more than can be said for 'er father. By the way, where is the bold Sid these days?'

'Nobody knows. Up North somewhere. I haven't seen him for ages. Shirley, what if David wants to marry me?'

'But yer can't. What about Ron?'

'What if he just wants to live with me? I can't say to him, Oh, by the way, I've got my sister-in-law's child to bring up as well.'

'That could be a problem, but I'm sure you'd get over it,' she said nonchalantly.

Polly sat back in her chair and put her hand over her eyes. 'I don't believe this is happening,' she said out loud.

'Polly if you don't 'ave 'er, I'm gonner 'ave 'er adopted.'

'What?' Polly sat forward. 'You can't mean that?'

'I do. You know me, I always was a selfish cow. Well, I ain't letting this one slip away. Me and Ben are married, and as far as 'e's concerned it's just me and 'im, for now.'

'I'll make a cup of cocoa,' said Polly. 'You had better get Elizabeth's things ready to put in her pillow case.'

'Bit different to last year,' said Shirley, taking some parcels from her case. 'And we 'ad a bit more room. If you're gonner look after that baby, well, you've gotter get out of 'ere. This damp will kill it.'

'Here's a few bits and pieces I've managed to get hold of,' said Polly, pushing some more parcels towards Shirley and trying to control her anger.

That night on her camp bed she couldn't sleep, she was so uncomfortable and unhappy. Poor Elizabeth. What was she to do? The little girl had never known a real mother or father. Polly's thoughts went to her own father. How he would have loved Elizabeth, his first grandchild – and her own baby. But both were conceived out of wedlock. Would David want her baby? It would be such a shock for him. Could they live together as a family? Why, she wondered miserably, does life have to have so many problems?

Christmas Day was quiet, so very different from last year, and, as far as Polly was concerned, very miserable. She was glad when it was all over.

'What train are you catching tomorrow?' asked Polly as she filled the hot-water bottles.

'Didn't I tell yer? We ain't going termorrow, I've got me business ter see to. Don't worry, I've got our ration books.'

Polly sank in the chair and clutched her bottle to her chest. She didn't dare ask Shirley how long she was staying.

When Polly walked into the office, Sarah was already working.

'Did you have a nice Christmas?' asked Sarah. Without waiting for an answer she went on, 'Ours was very quiet, not like yours. I've heard you and Shirley together . . .' She stopped. 'Margaret, what is it? Are you feeling all right?'

Polly flopped in the chair. 'I've got another problem.'

'Everything all right? You know, I mean with the baby?'

Polly nodded. She was pleased at Sarah's genuine concern. 'No. It's Shirley.' Polly felt she couldn't keep all these things to herself any longer, so she sat and told all. When she finished, Sarah stood up.

'What are you going to do?' she asked.

'I don't know, I really don't know.'

'Don't you think it's about time you involved David? He does have some rights, you know.'

'I honestly don't know, Sarah. So many things seem to be happening to me all at once.'

'Would you like me to write to him?'

'No. He should be home soon, then perhaps everything will be fine.' She smiled. It was a weak, half-hearted smile, and at the back of her mind was the thought that it could never be that easy.

When Polly got home from work that evening, Shirley had cooked their meal.

419

·· 'This is nice,' said Polly, pulling her chair closer to the table. 'And what have you two been doing with yourselves today?'

'We've been ter see Tower Bridge. It goes up and down,' said Elizabeth excitedly.

'Did you manage to get everything done?'

'No,' said Shirley. 'They ain't open till later on in the week. But I tell yer what I 'ave done.' She sat back with a satisfied look on her face. 'I've found you another place ter live.'

'What?' Polly dropped her knife and fork, which landed with a clatter on her plate. 'What are you talking about?'

'Well, you can't stay 'ere, not with a baby and Betty, and what if David wants ter live with yer? Yer gotter 'ave more room than this.'

'I don't believe this. Shirley, what have you done?'

'I told yer, I've found you a 'ouse.'

'A house? Where?'

'Penn's Place.'

Polly's face went the colour of chalk. 'Where?' she whispered.

'Penn's Place.'

'What were you doing there?'

'I took Betty ter see our old 'ouse.'

'It ain't there any more, Polly,' said Elizabeth.

'No, I know, love. Most of the road was bombed. So what are you talking about, Shirley?'

'Our end was bombed right enough. That's all been cleared away now, but up the other end's all right. And do you remember that posh 'ouse right down the bottom? Not the arches end, the sunny end. Number 90.'

'Yes, what about it?'

'Well, it's empty, so I went and found out it's for rent. We went and 'ad a butcher's, didn't we love?'

Elizabeth nodded.

'As it's the last one along that row,' continued Shirley enthusiastically, 'it's got a side entrance, so the coalmen don't 'ave ter traipse down the passage dropping coal all over the place.'

'My mum used to go mad when she saw coal dust all up the passage and stairs,' said Polly wistfully.

'Yer, well now 'e can go round the back and dump it in the coal bin.'

Polly looked alarmed. 'Shirley. What have you done?'

'I ain't done nufink. We just 'ad a look, and I told the landlord we'd come over on Saturday and let 'im know. It's really nice, Pol, you'll love it, and it's got a bathroom. It seems those posh people 'ad it put in.'

Polly stared at her in disbelief. She couldn't take it all in. 'I can't go back there to live.'

'Why not?'

'Don't be so damned heartless.'

'Look, Pol, it's a nice 'ouse with a nice little back yard, and the sun shines up that end. It'll be good for you and the baby, and there's plenty of room for all of you.'

'What? What about . . .?' Polly didn't go on, for it sounded as if her friend had come to stay for a while.

'You'll like it, Pol.'

'I can't move, Shirley, not yet. What if David comes home unexpectedly? He won't know where to find me.'

'Course 'e will. Miss Bloom will tell 'im.'

'And what if the Red Cross sends me letters about Billy?'

'You ain't 'eard any more about 'im, 'ave you?'

'No, unfortunately. But what about Ron's letters?'

'You said yer landlady upstairs was a nice old dear, so I reckon she'll always post 'em on to yer.'

'I suppose so, but what about the rent? How much is it?'

'Wait till yer sees it 'fore yer makes up yer mind?'

'I've still got to get to work.'

'Yer, but not for much longer.'

Polly knew she had to find somewhere better to live, and Shirley was steadily pushing every obstacle out of her way.

Chapter 40

On Saturday afternoon, after they had collected the key from the landlord, Polly, Shirley and Elizabeth went to Penn's Place. Polly stood at the top of the road as all the memories of that dreadful day when she had last been here came flooding back. As they got nearer Number 15, she could almost hear again the sound of frantic digging, then men shouting for everyone to be quiet, and the smell of dust and acrid smoke clogging her nostrils. That fear, the fear that took her breath away when they brought her mother out of the hole in the ground was still with her. A lump came to her throat when she looked at the gaping hole between the houses. Now it was a flattened piece of land, a piece of land that was once her home. Why did Shirley want her to move back here? Polly shuddered.

'Cold?' asked Shirley.

'No, I think someone just walked over my grave,' she whispered.

Elizabeth was tugging at her hand. 'Is this where you lived, Polly?'

Polly nodded, trying to stem the tears.

'Come on,' said Shirley walking on. 'It's too bloody cold to stand about out 'ere.'

They crossed the road and walked down to Number 90.

'I don't know if I could live here again,' said Polly.

'What 'appened is all in the past. Just you wait till yer see inside 'ere. I think yer'll soon change yer mind.' Shirley put the key in the lock and pushed open the front door.

Polly was surprised at the bright, clean house. Excited, Elizabeth began running from room to room, and then clattered up the stairs. 'Come up 'ere, Shirl, there's a nice bed in 'ere. And look, it's got a better bathroom than you, Polly.'

'Why has so much furniture been left?' asked Polly, pushing open the door to the front room. 'What happened to the people who lived here?'

'It seems they've gorn orf somewhere, and the landlord don't want the furniture. 'E said 'e could sell it, but it ain't worth the bovver, so 'e's left it for the next tenant.'

'You must have had a long talk with him.'

'Yer, well, I spun 'im a bit of a line about both of us being war widders, and you with a baby on the way that yer old man will never see. I think 'e felt sorry for us.'

'You'll never change,' said Polly over her shoulder as she went upstairs.

'Well, that's as may be,' said Shirley as they wandered from room to room. 'I'll be able ter get some dockets for furniture and curtains from the government, as I used ter live in Number 13. That's been bombed, so I'm entitled.'

Polly stood and stared at her. 'You coming up here to live? To live with me?'

'Yer. You see me and Dad 'ave 'ad this big row about 'im and the fire-watching woman.' She walked over to the window. 'It's got a nice little yard down there. We'll be able to put our bit o' washing on the line.'

Polly walked over to her and pulled her arm. 'Shirley, what about Vera?'

Shirley looked round for Elizabeth. When she saw she had gone downstairs, she said, 'She's got Judy and James, as well as 'er Jane ter look after now Mum's died, and Dad's buggered off with that woman, and she said she don't want Betty as well. We 'ad a big fight, and that's when I thought of you.'

'Thanks.'

'I'm gonner stay up 'ere till I get a boat, so I'll be able ter look after yer and 'elp out with the rent. I get a good allowance from the Canadian government. Do you know, I bet my wife's allotment is twice as much as yours.'

'I wouldn't be at all surprised. I think you had this all worked out. What if I want to go and live with David? Or at Mrs Bloom's?'

'Come off it. You said she didn't want to know. Besides, I hope to be long gone before David gets out of the RAF. By the way, what's 'e gonner do with 'imself when 'e gets out?'

'He'd like to fly commercially. He thinks there could be quite a future in that, and he loves flying.'

'That sounds good. Let's 'ope we all live long enough to 'ave our dreams come true. Now, what about this 'ouse?'

Polly could see all the arguments were stacked against her. She had to be honest, it would be lovely to have Shirley stay. They used to admire this house years ago. It was somehow different from all the others in Penn's Place. It was bright and clean-looking; just the sort of house she could be happy in. 'All right, you win,' she said at last.

Shirley threw her arms round Polly. 'I knew you'd say that, once you saw it. Come on, let's go and see the landlord and let 'im know.'

It was New Year's Eve, and Polly and Shirley had sat up to watch 1944 come in.

'What's your new year resolution?' Polly asked Shirley.

'Ain't got one, what about you?'

'To sleep in my own bed tonight, and every night till we move.'

'I was going to say it's my turn on the camp bed. Still, next week we'll both be in proper beds, and I'll be living in our new 'ouse, and not just going over there ter clean it.'

'Yes.' Polly smiled. 'I'm glad I kept the flat on till David comes home next weekend. He's got a whole seven days.' She hugged herself, full of anxiety and excitement. 'I can't wait to see him.'

'You going to the station?'

'No, since he's going to be here some time on Saturday I'm having the morning off. Sarah reckons I should be at home when David first sees me. I've got the week off as well.'

'I should think so, with all the extra hours you put in.'

'Yes, but don't forget I am a sort of partner.'

'Yeah, but do you 'ave any say?'

'Some, especially where the dresses are concerned.'

'Yeah, but do yer get any extra money?'

'Not really, some of it has to go back into the business. We're keeping all the money in the bank ready for after the war so we can expand.'

'Well, you're expanding right enough. What about that?' laughed Shirley, pointing at Polly's stomach. 'Will yer still go to work?'

'I'd like to be a business woman and a mother. But I'll cross that bridge when I come to it.'

'Would Sarah give you any of the money if you left the firm?'

'I don't know. Shirley, I'm scared stiff. Perhaps I should have said something to David in my letters. This is going to come as an awful shock.'

'It's too late now. Why didn't you tell 'im?'

'To be truthful, I didn't think I would be able to carry, and I thought if I lost the baby, well, then all explanations would have been unnecessary.' She didn't tell Shirley how she'd worried that David would think she'd trapped him.

'That sounds a bit daft to me.'

'Thinking about it now, it sounds daft to me. Come on, let's get to bed.'

Elizabeth was sleeping soundly when Polly crept in beside her. She looked at her for a few moments before settling down. Polly's head was full of thoughts. This time next week she could be sharing her bed with David, or, if he walked out on her, she could be alone. Elizabeth sighed, turning over to throw her arm across Polly; it was warm and comforting.

* * *

The morning dragged as Polly waited impatiently for David. She knew he was coming from Scotland on last night's sleeper. Shirley and Elizabeth had gone to Penn's Place on Friday night, so Polly had time to clean her flat in readiness for David.

All morning she had tried to look up at the road above her basement window at the many feet passing by. Looking for those familiar black shoes to turn and come down her steps. The waiting seemed to go on and on. All sorts of fears took their turn to make themselves known. What if he couldn't get leave? There was no way he could let her know. What if he was ill? Perhaps the train had been delayed. She made herself another cup of tea and settled down to read the newspaper again.

It was well into the afternoon when the sound of someone banging on the front door woke her. The newspaper had slipped down and was draped over her feet. For a moment she was disorientated.

Polly was nervous, her mouth went dry and she felt her face flush as she stood up. What would she say to him? She should have told him, warned him. He'd be shocked. Would there be an argument? Slowly she turned the latch and opened the door.

'I thought you were out,' said David, standing there with his hold-all at his feet. He stepped over it, took her in his arms, and kissed her. She threw her arms round his neck. Tears ran down her face, making his kisses taste salty.

When they broke away he picked up his hold-all and closed the door behind them.

'Now, young lady, why didn't you tell me about this?' He patted her stomach.

'You know? How did . . .? How did you find . . .? Who told . . .?' Polly was spluttering. Then all the months of worry and wondering surfaced. She slumped into the chair and cried.

'What is it? What's wrong?' David dropped to his knees and pulled her close to him.

She brought her head up. His face was full of concern. 'I'm sorry, I should have told you.'

427

'Yes, you should have told me. Oh, Margaret, did you think I would run away?'

She nodded.

He lifted her chin, and as she looked into his dark brown eyes they were almost twinkling with joy. This was what she had been waiting to see. This look convinced her he loved her and wanted the baby. She took his face in her hands and covered it with kisses. Her tears and laughter were all mixed together.

'David, I do love you so very much.'

'And I love you. Now, my darling, put the kettle on, you've got a lot of explaining to do.'

As she filled the kettle she asked over her shoulder, 'Who told you?'

'Mother.'

Polly froze. 'When did she tell you?'

'I phoned at Christmas.' He stood behind her and put his arms around her. 'I can't believe I'm going to be a dad.'

'Do you mind? Are you happy about it?'

'I'm thrilled now.' He buried his head in her neck, then turned her and gently kissed her.

She pushed him away. 'Did your mother tell you how annoyed she was at me trying to keep it from you?'

'Yes.'

'Well?'

'The kettle's boiling.'

'David, you're being so, so . . .'

'Make the tea while I get out of this uniform. My slacks still here?' he called from the bedroom.

'In the wardrobe.'

'I see Shirley has left some of her belongings. Is she coming back to London?'

'She hasn't left.' Polly put the tea-pot on the table. 'David, we have got so much to talk about.'

'It's a good thing I've got seven days then.' He sat beside her, took hold of her hand, and kissed it.

'Were you shocked when you found out?'

'Yes, I must admit that it did come as a bit of a shock. I suppose I've never thought about having children.'

Polly sat at the table. 'Do you like children?'

'I don't know – haven't ever thought of myself as a father before. I've never had a lot to do with them, but I must say the idea is growing on me, rather nicely.'

Polly laughed and patted her stomach. 'It's growing on me too.' She paused. 'You know I never thought I could have any, so at first, it came as a bit of a shock to me as well.' She touched his hand. 'Were you very angry with me when you found out?'

'Yes. At the time I was.'

'So was your mother.'

'Yes, I know. When I calmed down, I guessed you must have a good reason for not telling me, so I phoned Sarah.'

'She didn't tell me.'

'I told her not to.'

'It seems that neither of us have been very honest with each other.'

'Sarah told me your reason for keeping it to yourself, that you didn't want to force me into anything, that you weren't even sure you'd be able to carry it. I was very proud of you. She also said how brave you've been, bearing all your problems alone, first with Ron, and then Mother. I thought how lucky my son's going to be, to have such a wonderful, loving mother – not forgetting, of course, his good-looking father.'

Polly laughed and ruffled his hair. 'What if it's not a boy?'

'Then, my dear, we shall just have to try again, and the next time, my darling, I shall want to be the first to know about it.'

'I promise I shall never keep anything from you again. David, what about Ron and Yvonne?'

His face took on a serious expression. 'Yes, we do have a problem there. Not with Yvonne, she's more than willing about the divorce. It's Ron I'm worried about.'

'Yes.'

'Is he going to be sent home?'

'I don't know. Sally, his nurse, who does all the writing, hasn't mentioned it.'

'Margaret, when this war is over, and I come out of the RAF, will you live with me? Even when Ron comes back?'

'Yes. But the bargain is that till then you have got to live with me.'

'I'll make you a generous allowance.'

She paused. 'I'm moving.'

'Where to? I know Sarah wants you to go back home, but . . .'

'I know. Are you pleased she's marrying Ted?'

'Yes, he seems a straight enough guy, despite being a police-man. Where are you moving to?'

Polly took a deep breath. 'Shirley hasn't gone back to Bristol. She's staying here.'

'Here in this flat?'

'Not now, I'm coming to that, and I have another problem to face, but we can talk about that one later. I told you Shirley was married. Well, she's waiting for a boat to Canada, so she has brought Elizabeth to London till she goes. It seems she had a big row at home after her mother died.'

'I know the feeling,' he said sadly. 'I remember how miser-able I felt when I found out Dad had died, and I took Yvonne home for the first time.'

She patted his hand and kissed his cheek. 'Well, that's all over. You've got me to put up with now. Anyway, Shirley has found us a house; she says this flat is too damp to bring a baby up in.'

'She has a lot of sense. That was one of the first things I was going to sort out this week. It's not the right place to bring up a baby. Where are you moving to?'

'Penn's Place.'

'Penn's Place? Where's that?'

'It's where we used to live.'

'Is that where your mother . . . That was a bit insensitive of the girl.'

'That's what I thought. But it's a very nice house, with a small garden, and the rent is reasonable.'

'You should have found something better. I'll take care of the rent.'

'David, I didn't know whether you would still want me, and I had to think of being on my own and bringing up our . . .'

He leaned over, kissed her, and then whispered, 'I promise you I'll never leave you.'

'Shirley is going to stay with me, and help me with the baby and Elizabeth, till she goes that is.'

'Well, that's good. Margaret, I think Mother's very sorry, and I think she's worried that you'll shut her out. After all, this is going to be her first grandchild.'

'I don't want to shut her out. I know she was angry, and in anger we all say things we don't mean, but I really love your mother. We've had a lot of ups and downs together, but after all, she will be our baby's only grandparent, and I know how important it was for me to have a grandad.'

'Good, that's all I wanted to hear. Would you be very cross with me if I told you we were going over there tomorrow?'

'No, in fact I'd be very pleased; then on Monday we can go to Penn's Place and you can meet Shirley and Elizabeth.'

'After all your letters about them, I feel I know them already. I still think it's funny that the child doesn't call her "Mother".'

'Well, as I said, there were so many women in the house, and so many little uns, they didn't know who belonged to who. And don't you go calling Shirley her mum.'

He saluted. 'No, Ma'am. Now, when's our baby due?'

'End of March some time, so the doctor said. We've got to think of some names, and if you're a good boy I'll let you feel it kick.'

He placed his hand on her stomach. 'But I don't intend to be a good boy at all during this next seven days. Is that all right?' he asked anxiously.

'According to the book, yes.'

* * *

On Tuesday morning, Polly was very cross when Shirley brought Elizabeth to the flat and asked Polly if they would mind having Elizabeth for the day while she sorted out some of her affairs.

'Why didn't you say something yesterday when we saw you? We're supposed to be going to Mrs Bloom's this morning?' said Polly tersely.

'I'll be back before you get 'ome,' said Shirley, following Polly into the kitchen. 'So it won't put you out that much. 'Sides it'll give David a chance ter get ter know 'er better. Mind you, they got on all right yesterday, didn't they?'

'Shh, keep your voice down.' Polly looked apprehensively at the bathroom door. 'I haven't mentioned it yet.'

'Well, I fink yer should.'

'I don't want to spoil our week.'

David came out of the bathroom. 'Hello Shirley. I thought I heard voices out here. Hello Elizabeth.' He ruffled the top of her dark hair. 'And how are you today?'

Elizabeth hid her head. 'I'm all right thank you, Uncle David.'

'Made a snowman yet?'

Elizabeth shook her head. 'Shirley won't come out in the yard with me.'

'Shame on you. And what can we do for you this brisk morning, Shirley?'

'I've got to go and sort out a few things, and I was wondering if you'd mind looking after young Miss 'ere.'

'We'd love to, wouldn't we?' He turned to Polly.

'We are supposed to be going over to your mother's for lunch,' she said hastily.

'That's all right, we can take Elizabeth. Then we can make a snowman in my old garden like my sister and I used to. Would you like that?'

Elizabeth jumped up and down. 'Yes please, yes please.'

'I should be back before you get 'ome. I've still got me key.

Thanks, David. See yer both later.' With that Shirley left.

'You didn't have to do that,' said Polly.

'No I know, but she is such a nice little thing, and I know you think the world of her.'

When it was the end of the day and they were getting ready for bed, Polly was sitting at her dressing-table brushing her hair. She looked through the mirror at David propped up in bed. 'You enjoyed yourself today, didn't you?'

He smiled. 'She's a good little girl. I was thinking, while I was playing with Elizabeth, about our son, and me making a snowman for him.'

'You like her, don't you?'

'Yes.'

She turned and faced him, the hairbrush still in her hand. 'I've got something to ask you.'

'Is it serious?'

She nodded, and sat on the bed. 'It's about Elizabeth.'

All too soon, David's leave was over. To Polly the last seven days had been wonderful, full of love and laughter. She couldn't remember ever being so happy. She longed for the war to end so they could be together for always. Many times they visited Mrs Bloom, who gave Polly trinkets for her new house, to make it homely she said, and any rift was quickly healed, with Mrs Bloom making it clear that, now they had Penn's Place, they didn't need to feel obliged to live with her. For that Polly was grateful.

She and David had discussed at great length whether to tell Mrs Bloom about Ron. After weighing up the pros and cons, and much against Polly's conscience, they decided to wait.

'Let's get one hurdle over at a time; it's better to wait until after the baby's born – I've only got seven days and I don't see the point of creating too many problems at this stage. Besides, anything could happen before Ron comes home.'

That had been before he knew about Elizabeth.

Now Polly stood at the door of her little flat for the last time. She had been happy here: extremely happy, when she thought of the nights with David.

'You ready yet?' called Shirley. 'This taxi ain't gonner stay 'ere forever.'

'Coming.' She closed the front door and climbed into the taxi next to Elizabeth. 'This is a luxury.'

'Well, I'm not carting this lot on a bus.'

Polly put her hand in her coat pocket and her fingers tightened on the letter she had received that morning from Sally, which in all the confusion she hadn't had time to read.

At the end of the day, when Elizabeth was asleep and they had settled in front of the fire, Shirley said, 'I reckon your David's a bit of all right. Look at all the nice thing's 'e's bought.'

Polly smiled and nodded. 'Mmmm, I think so too.'

'I still can't believe 'e's accepted Betty, just like that.'

'Don't you believe it was just like that. We sat for hours talking about it.'

'Yeah. 'E told me.'

'Well, I was worried about it, but when I told him she could be adopted if I didn't have her he nearly went mad. He couldn't believe anyone would want to give their baby away. You certainly dropped in his estimation.'

'Yeah I know, but when I explained about me and Ben, and me wanting ter start a new life, 'e came round in the end.'

Polly grinned at her friend. She was incorrigible. 'Shirley, you could charm anyone round to your way of thinking. David did agree that Elizabeth would be good company for our one, and she and David got on so well together.'

'Yeah, it was good ter see 'em playing. 'E was just like a big kid 'imself at times.'

'You should have seen them over at his house. Mrs Bloom and Sarah are very fond of Elizabeth.'

'Do they know yet?'

'No, let them get over one shock at a time.'

'Not like David, poor bloke. 'E comes home on leave to find 'e's got one kid on the way and 'e's about to adopt another.'

'I told you all along that he's very special.'

'You're very lucky, Pol. Still, it's about time 'im up there looked after yer.' She raised her eyes to the ceiling.

Polly too looked up, but it was Grandad's whip curled up above the fireplace that held her gaze. 'I never thought that would be back in Penn's Place.' A lump came to her throat. 'I've just remembered: I had a letter from Sally this morning and I haven't had a chance to read it. It's in my coat pocket.' Polly went into the hall and returned a few minutes later.

'I'll make the cocoa while yer reading it. I'll tell yer what, it's good ter 'ave a bit of room to move about in.'

'Yes, that flat was rather small, but then it was only intended for me in the beginning. I didn't expect half the . . .' Her voice trailed off as she read the letter.

Shirley raced out of the kitchenette into the dining-room. 'What is it?' What's wrong?'

'This is from Ron. Look. He's learnt to type.' She thrust the letter under Shirley's nose.

''E ain't very good at it.'

'Give him a chance. He's only got two fingers on his right hand. He says here he's feeling a lot better and he's been out and about with Sally. He says she's been wonderful and she's making a new man of him.'

''Bout time somebody did. Sounds like she's taken quite a shine to 'im. I'll get yer cocoa.'

Winter gave way to spring and before long March had come to a close. Polly lay on top of the bed. All day she'd had back-ache, and she was trying to rest. As it was Sunday, Mrs Bloom and Sarah had been over on one of their fortnightly visits, and Mrs Bloom had been fussing round her. When they left they gave Shirley strict instructions to phone them the minute anything happened, as they in turn had strict instructions to phone David.

435

'Shirley said do you want anyfing, I mean *thing*?' Elizabeth giggled and put her hand to her mouth.

'Come and sit on here with me.' Polly patted the bed. 'Do you like Sarah and Mrs Bloom?'

'Yes, they always bring me nice –' she hesitated, 'things.'

Polly laughed, and remembered Sarah teaching her to speak properly. Now they were having a go with Elizabeth.

'Grandma Bloom.'

'Grandma Bloom?' exclaimed Polly. 'You mustn't let her hear you say that.'

Elizabeth's face fell in disappointment. 'Why not?'

'Well . . .'

'She said I could. When I said I didn't have a grandma, she cuddled me and said, "Will I do?" Why can't I have her as my very own grandma, Pol?'

Polly threw her arms round her and hugged her. 'Of course you can.' She kissed her upturned face. 'Tell Shirley I think we might be going to the hospital soon.' She winced as the strongest contraction yet took her breath.

'Is it the baby? Are we going to get you a baby?'

'I think so. What shall I get, a boy or a girl?'

'I'd like a boy, I think. But I don't really mind, I like all babies. I'll tell Shirley.'

On Monday 3 April, 1944, Thomas David William yelled his way into the world.

Mrs Bloom, Sarah and Shirley formed a steady stream of visitors.

'I left a message for David as soon as Shirley phoned,' said Sarah. 'They only allow two round a bed, so I'll go and let Shirley come in.'

'And someone has to sit outside with Elizabeth,' said Mrs Bloom. 'It's a pity she can't see the new baby, she's full of it. It seems she asked you for a boy.'

'I try to please. David wanted a boy. I hope you didn't mind me naming him after my father?' She looked down at the mop of black hair that was soft and curly like David's. However the little wrinkled face, peering out from beneath the beautiful shawl Sarah had given her, reminded her of a wizened old man.

'Not at all, and it's nice you've added your young brother's name. You haven't heard any more about him, or your husband?'

Polly blushed. 'I think after all this time I must accept that Billy's dead.' She sniffed and looked around for her handkerchief.

'Here, take this one,' said Mrs Bloom, looking embarrassed. 'I'm sorry, I shouldn't upset you. Margaret. I don't know if you are aware of our . . .'

'I think I know what you are going to say,' quickly interrupted Polly, pleased at the chance to change the subject. 'And David and I discussed this at great length. I know I have the right to choose his religion, and I have decided that he is going to take yours, so if you could arrange that for me . . .'

Mrs Bloom kissed Polly's cheek. 'Thank you. Thank you so much.' She hurriedly left the room.

'What have you been saying to Mother? She's sitting out there crying, and little Elizabeth is trying to comfort her.' It was Sarah who had come back in.

'I've told her I want Thomas to be brought up in the Jewish faith.'

'Well, no wonder.' Sarah pulled back the shawl. 'I'm pleased you didn't wait too long before you made your entrance, young man. Now you'll be able to come to my wedding.'

'I'm glad you and Ted are waiting till May.'

'I had to, who else could I trust to make my dress?' Sarah gently held the baby's tiny hand. 'My nephew really is lovely. Oh look, he smiled at me.'

Polly didn't have the heart to tell her it was probably just wind.

'Margaret, have you thought any more about moving back with Mother?'

'When David was home we did talk about it, and he said he

437

would leave it up to me. When I get out of hospital I'll come over and we'll discuss it.' Polly nervously picked at the blanket. 'You see, Sarah, it won't be as easy as that.'

'Why not? If you're worried about Elizabeth, David has told us all about that.'

Polly was taken aback. 'When did he tell you?'

'It was after Mother had written telling him about Elizabeth being upset at not having a grandma, and Mother asked her if she would do?'

'Yes, I know,' interrupted Polly. 'But she's only just told me. They must have talked about that weeks ago.'

'Well, it seems David then told Mother about your plans to adopt her. So you see, you need have no worries over that. She's a delightful little girl – Mother's fallen in love with her.'

'But Sarah, what about Ron? She won't want me living with her son when she finds out he's still alive.'

'I think she now realizes that everybody's life is being turned upside down through this war, that you and David have got to grab happiness whilst you can. She'll realize you'll sort something out with Ron if and when he turns up. And, remember I shall be leaving home, she'll be all by herself in that big house and she won't want to do without her grandchild. We all have a small selfish streak in us and Mother's no different. Look how she's taken to Elizabeth without question! I'm sure she won't be able to resist Thomas, you wait and see. And, whatever happens, she's very fond of you.'

Shirley came bouncing into the ward carrying a bunch of flowers. 'Sorry I'm late, I've been ter see the sister.'

'Everything all right?' asked Polly, still smiling at Sarah's words.

'Yes. She said 'e's a healthy little boy.' Shirley plonked the flowers on the bed. 'By the way, I've got a letter for you. It's from Ron.'

The smile left Polly's face and, without opening it, she placed the letter on the bed. 'I suppose I'll have to tell him one day.'

'How is he?' asked Sarah.

'He seems to be getting on fine. His typing has improved, and he seems to like Australia.'

'I must go. I'll see you tomorrow,' said Sarah, handing the baby to Shirley and making a graceful exit.

'Yes, yes, all right,' said Polly.

'Open yer letter then,' said Shirley impatiently.

Slowly Polly opened the envelope. Suddenly a smile spread across her face. 'Shirley, you are never going to believe this. Ron wants to stay in Australia. He says he and Sally would like to get a farm when the war's over.' Her laughter was loud and hysterical, making her son jump. He whimpered.

'Shh,' said Shirley, hugging the baby before handing him back to Polly.

'Sorry, my love,' said Polly, kissing his forehead.

Shirley was now reading Ron's letter. 'I don't believe this. Ron on a farm. 'E don't know one end of a cow from the other.'

The bell rang for all visitors to leave.

'I'll put Tommy in 'is cot,' said Shirley taking Polly's new baby and gently tucking him in. She looked up. 'What yer crying for?'

Polly wiped her eyes on Mrs Bloom's handkerchief. 'Read what he's put at the bottom.' She handed the last page to Shirley.

'Well I'll be buggered.' She sank in the chair and read out loud. "P.S. Sally thinks I should tell you that I don't think I'll be coming back to Blighty. I'm sorry for all the grief I've caused you. Me and another bloke done the Blooms that night. We'd had a bit too much to drink, and well we got talking, and you know the rest. But I was only the look-out Pol, and I only got that brooch. I still love you a bit, but I love Sally and Australia a lot more. Sorry about that. Take care. Love Ron.'"

'I don't suppose you'll ever seem 'im again.'

Polly smiled. 'It doesn't matter now, just as long as he's happy as well.'

'It certainly sounds like it. This Sally's certainly made a new man out of 'im.' She stood up. 'See yer tomorrow Pol.'

A nurse walked down the ward. 'Mrs Bell, I have a telegram for you.'

'Thank you.' She knew who had sent it. The message was simple.

'Thank you, my clever Polly Perkins. See you soon in Penn's Place. Love, David.'

Now you can buy any of these other bestselling books by **Dee Williams** from your bookshop or *direct from her publisher.*

FREE P&P AND UK DELIVERY
(Overseas and Ireland £3.50 per book)

Forgive and Forget	£5.99
Sorrows and Smiles	£5.99
Katie's Kitchen	£5.99
Maggie's Market	£5.99
Ellie of Elmleigh Square	£5.99
Sally of Sefton Grove	£5.99
Hannah of Hope Street	£5.99
Annie of Albert Mews	£6.99
Polly of Penns Place	£5.99
Carrie of Culver Road	£6.99

TO ORDER SIMPLY CALL THIS NUMBER

01235 400 414

or e-mail orders@bookpoint.co.uk

Prices and availability subject to change without notice.